THE LUCKY ONE

BARBARA DEVLIN

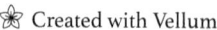 Created with Vellum

This book is dedicated to my amazing Lady Knights. Because behind every successful writer is a group of maniacal women readers bent on world domination, and I do love them for that.

PROLOGUE

The Ascendants
England
The Year of Our Lord 1315

"Waste not your breath, brothers, as I have no need of your advice. And I am remarkably skilled in the sensuous arts." Straightening the collar of his tunic, Morgan smirked. "Unlike the three of you, I harbor no fear of the weaker sex, given my prurient pedagogy. No doubt my bride will count herself most fortunate in the hands of a past master, and I foresee no trouble pleasing her, between the sheets."

The married friends, including the newlywed Morgan, gathered in their favorite dank tavern to toast the day's nuptials, and Arucard fretted for the cocky young knight. Regardless of the combined wealth of experience in spousal affairs, which Arucard, Demetrius, and Aristide sought to impart, with the best of intentions, the most junior member of the Brethren of the Coast refused to heed their sage counsel.

"Have you spoken with her?" With a huff of impatience, Aristide cast a wary glance at Arucard. "As it was only yesterday, when you apprised me that you had shared no conversation with your new mate."

"Which does not bode well for nurturing affection." Arucard stiffened his spine. "Trust me, you will need that."

"And the loss of her maidenhead can be a very traumatic, not to mention dangerous, escapade for you, both." Demetrius elbowed Aristide in the ribs. "Just ask our brother, hither."

"Very funny." Aristide frowned. "I admit I had a rough start, but I found my way in the matrimonial bed, soon enough. Need I remind you of the recent birth of my son? And my Dion and I endeavor to produce another, every morning and night."

"Ah, it is good to be a husband." Demetrius snickered, as he and Aristide clinked their mugs. "And my Lily increases, with our second offspring, as we speak."

"As does Isolde." With a surge of pride, and sweet memories of his naughty maneuvers in the attainment of that much-cherished goal, Arucard waggled his brows. "And the begetting is half the fun, when you expend the effort to do it right."

"Which is wherefore you must not squander your concern on my behalf." Morgan smoothed his hair and preened. "As I have never failed to rouse my whores."

In the process of downing half of his last bit of ale, Arucard choked violently. "Are you out of your mind?"

"What?" The boastful gadling cast an arrogant smile. "One woman's body is the same as the next, and I shall play my Hawisia's anatomy as a finely tuned instrument, just wait and see."

Aristide blanched. "Yes, but you have no—"

"Then we wish you merry, and we should not delay you." Arucard raised his tankard in toast, and, with his foot, beneath the table he kicked Aristide in the shin. "To Morgan and Hawisia. May your wedding be every bit as blessed as the union I enjoy with Isolde, as Demetrius favors with Athelyna, and as Aristide delights with Dionysia."

"I will drink to that." The shameless scamp winked and drained his mug. "And now I bid you good rest, as I shall require all my strength for the night to come."

As his fellow Nautionnier Knight exited the tavern, Arucard chuckled. "Poor bastard."

"Wherefore did you not apprise him of the obvious?" Demetrius frowned. "You comprehend the significance of his statement, do you not? He confuses wives with doxies."

"Indeed, I understand, and I leave it to him to discover the difference." Arucard grinned. "As he is sporting for a much deserved, long overdue comeuppance, who am I to deny his mate such joy?"

"In that I will not argue, but what of the misfortunate, unsuspecting lady?" Aristide grimaced. "Are we not honor-bound to save her?"

"Think about it, brothers." Arucard inclined his head. "Given what we know of the female temperament, particularly in regard to the portentous loss of maidenhood, and Morgan's misplaced confidence, whose skull do you believe in greater peril—his or his bride's?"

For a few seconds, Demetrius and Aristide pondered the situation. At last, they met Arucard's stare and burst into unrestrained mirth.

"God's bones, but I will grant ye that." Aristide rubbed the back of his neck. "Yet I would not wish such misery on the worst enemy of my acquaintance. But Morgan can never claim we did not try to intervene, in a sincere desire to save his bumptious hide. Now I can only hope he survives, as I am left to wonder to what lengths he will resort, in his quest to capture her prize."

"Can you not imagine it? My sweet Isolde damn near scared me to death with her cry of the banshee, when I did naught more than remove my belt." Slapping a thigh, Arucard collapsed in uncontrollable jollity. "The soul of patience, I attempted to allay her concerns, and she came at me with my old halberd. I intended to spend the dark hours in the solar, with one eye open, for fear she might finish the deed, but she relented. And I would argue she alarmed me more than I alarmed her."

"You think that bad?" Demetrius arched a brow. "Lily barricaded the door to our chambers. When I tried to climb through the window, she bit my fingers. We did not consummate our vows for two months."

"*Two months*?" Arucard whistled in monotone. "And I thought it took us forever."

"Oh? Do tell." Demetrius rubbed his chin. "How long was it for you?"

"Three weeks." Arucard scowled, as he recalled the vicious suffering that denoted that time. "The most painful, gut-wrenching, frustrating, and exhaustive twenty-one days of my existence."

"Ah, but I would presume the end of the delay more than compensated for your hardship." Averting his gaze, Aristide sighed. "My Dion is a seraph."

"And what of you, brother?" Arucard asked Aristide. "We know of your rocky start, aside from your bloody injuries."

"Do not remind me." Aristide winced. "After the assault, and retracing my steps, given my egregious exercise in monumental stupidity, when I apprised my wife that I had been forced to the altar, it took this mountain stag a month to stir her waters. But she was well worth the wait, as Dion holds my heart."

The men shared sly smiles in companionable silence.

Arucard peered over his shoulder and then gazed at the husbands. "My money is on Hawisia."

Demetrius groaned. "Mine, too."

"Well I am not so foolish to side with Morgan, as I know better." Aristide snorted. "So whither does that leave me, as we cannot all favor the mare in this race?"

"Perchance we should adapt our contest to the unique situation." Arucard calculated the possibilities. "How long do you suppose the gadling will last, at her hands, in light of his haphazard and downright dangerous temerity?"

"I would say in the time it takes to drink two more tankards of ale." Demetrius propped an elbow on the table. "But no more, as I would satisfy my wife, when I return to her. She is quite the demanding little thing, but I am not complaining."

"I do not concur, given the boy's questionable talents." Aristide narrowed his stare. "Morgan possesses knowledge with which none of us were endowed, when faced with the same terrifying circumstances, so I believe he has the advantage. I give him three tankards, before he rejoins us."

"And what of you?" Demetrius gave Arucard a gentle nudge. "Have you another guess?"

"Indeed, I do." As Arucard examined the contents of his mug, he pondered Morgan's pomposity and wondered how Isolde would have responded, had Arucard employed such stratagem. "Brothers, I stake my claim on the minutes it takes me to consume my current beverage."

In unison, Demetrius and Aristide blinked.

"No."

"You must be joking."

"But I am quite earnest." Laughing, Arucard flagged a passing bar wench and signaled for another round. "We will need four tankards, please."

"You order Morgan's drink?" Aristide slumped against the table. "How can you be so certain of the outcome and that you will prevail?"

Demetrius scratched his forehead. "What have you not told us?"

"Naught have I withheld." Arucard shrugged. "But I know Morgan, as do you. In light of his misplaced confidence, and what we know of our respective wives, how do you suppose Hawisia will respond to his bawdy machinations and impudent inclinations?"

For a pregnant moment, his fellow knights sat, stockstill. Then, in concert, Demetrius and Aristide collapsed in convulsive hilarity.

"So what is the winner's boon?" Wiping a tear from his eye, Demetrius sniffed. "Two groats?"

"A pound?" Aristide inquired.

"How about the losers pay the night's debt?" Arucard assessed the minute amount of ale in his mug and realized he may have overstated his deduction. "After all, I am as much—"

"No." Aristide chucked Demetrius on the shoulder. "Look, brother."

"Sad sack of ignorance." Demetrius emptied his tankard and tossed a few coins into the mug. "I do not believe it."

Then Aristide pulled a decent sum from his money pouch and added to the collection. Before Arucard could react to their retorts of surprise, and their generous offering, Morgan reappeared. Plopping to the bench, the newlywed groom grunted, glanced at the collective of drinks, and claimed a flagon.

"Are you all right, brother?" Arucard queried, in a low voice.

"Wherefore do you ask?" Morgan scowled.

"Your nose bleeds."

CHAPTER ONE

The Descendants
Portsea Island, England
March, 1814

The diminutive, hooded thief, bearing a rucksack over his shoulder, skulked along the waist, hesitated for a scarce second, and then scampered below decks and into the cargo hold. Following in the scoundrel's wake, Dalton Randolph hugged the shadows and grinned, as the unknown gadling lifted the lid on a barrel and retrieved several potatoes.

After a French ship had landed one too many direct hits to the *Siren's* boards, Dalton had anchored off Portsea Island for an emergency field refitting. Once the leaks had been sealed, he had permitted the greater portion of his crew to indulge in a bit of local entertainment, while he remained aboard ship.

As a Nautionnier Knight of the Brethren of the Coast, a daring band of experienced sea captains descended of the

Templars, the warriors of the Crusades, he savored the quiet hours, with nothing but the wind thrumming in the rat lines and the waves lapping at the hull. And even at the age of one and thirty, stargazing reigned supreme as a particular favored hobby, so he often doused the stern lanterns and studied the night sky, which is why the three bandits had not noted his presence, or the first mate, when they scampered over the larboard rail.

Given the interloper's small frame, Dalton guessed the criminal could not have been more than a lad. As the *Siren's* stores contained plenty of supplies, and hunger persisted during times of war, he abided the bit of mischief, in the spirit of generosity.

The plunderer bent to pilfer a tin of tea, and his breeches stretched taut over his backside. To Dalton's amazement, he realized the villain was a woman, as he would know the telltale shapely, feminine derriere from a distance of fifty paces. Judging from the silhouette, the mystery lady had been blessed with a prime figure, which he ached to know on a more intimate level.

"You know, there are easier ways to earn a bit of coin and food, my dear." He emerged from his hiding place. "Take off your hood, and let me gaze upon the rest of you. If I like what I see, we may broker a deal."

The infinitely interesting prey shrieked and cringed. Then she edged toward the companion ladder, but he beat her to it.

"Come now, dove. There is no need to fear me, as we might strike a bargain, which benefits us, both." Now he noted her ample bosom, as his soon-to-be bunkmate faced him. Fascinated, he longed to assess her complexion, as he splayed wide his arms. "And if you apply yourself, in earnest, and please me, I shall bestow upon you a handsome reward, and you need never burgle passing ships, again, as it is dangerous business."

When he moved in her direction, she emitted the softest whimper and retreated. Clutching the bag to her chest, she skittered to the left and sheltered behind a few crates of vegetables. His quarry was fast, but Dalton was faster. As he closed the distance between them, she leaped atop a heap of sacks containing rice and dried beans.

The thrill of the chase burned in his loins and piqued the pirate in his pants, which had suffered serious neglect, in recent months. Given the importuning antics of his latest paramour, the well-used Lady Moreton, whose harbor had seen more action than Deptford, he sported for a new conquest, and it appeared she had found him, to his credit.

In the soft lamplight, he discovered the purest blue eyes he had ever glimpsed, peeking from the mask, and a lush mouth with lips as red as a pomegranate, and he had to have her. But the captivating swindler remained mute and refused to cooperate, as she evaded his spontaneous lunge. While his grand maneuver granted him nothing more than a close inspection of the wood grain on the deck, she availed herself of the opportunity to sprint to the companion ladder, and he shot to his feet and pursued what he vowed would be his future courtesan.

At the waist, she collided with one of her cohorts, just as shouts of alarm signaled the first mate and the cook, who wielded a large frying pan, chased the third conspirator.

"Come back here, you rascal." Mr. Shaw bounded onto the deck, with a pistol aimed at the tallest of the boarders. "You there, hold hard."

"As you were, Mr. Shaw." Dalton stayed the first mate.

"There is no need for violence, given the lady and I have just entered negotiations. What say you, pretty britches? I shall let your friends go free, if you agree to spend the night with me."

For a few seconds, the odd trio shuffled their feet and exchanged wary glances. Then the two heartier thieves drew the woman to the rear and shook their heads.

"More's the pity." Dalton chuckled. "As you leave me no option but to summon the watch and have you arrested."

The female flinched, and he could smell her fear. Together, the clumsy band of vagabonds inched closer to the rail. When the woman peered over the side, he guessed her intent.

"Steady, love. Do not attempt something you might later regret, as we are all friends, here." With palms upraised in implied surrender, Dalton glanced at the first mate. "Mr. Shaw, lower the weapon."

The first mate vented a snort of disgust. "But, sir—"

"Lower the bloody weapon. That is an order." Dalton took two tentative steps forward. "Easy, love. Remain calm, as I will not hurt you."

Just then, one of the bandits untied and kicked over an empty rain barrel, which had been lashed to the side, and sent it tumbling in Dalton's direction. In a panic, the first mate discharged the pistol, and the female screamed.

"Stand down, Mr. Shaw." Dalton cursed under his breath, as two of the thieves jumped the railing. After unleashing a second barrel, the last of the criminals escaped.

"Hell and the Reaper." The cook blanched and scratched his chin. "I presumed you were joking, but they had a woman in their midst."

"Sorry, Cap'n." The first mate tucked the firearm in his waistband. "Had I known of the lady, I would not have fired."

"No worries, as their theft consisted of nothing more than food from our stores, and I do not believe you hit anyone." Standing a-larboard, Dalton smiled, as the brazen crooks eluded capture via a small rowboat. Then a scrap of red caught his attention. The velvet pouch, which he bent to retrieve, had protected a valuable artifact, but now it sat empty. "Did our uninvited guests invade my cabin?"

"Aye, sir." Mr. Shaw nodded. "That is when I roused the villains."

In that instant, Dalton frowned. "Then the nameless scoundrels are not harmless, and their cause is not so noble, as I had thought, given they have taken something invaluable to my family, so we shall meet again."

"But how will we find them, sir?" The cook hugged his cast-iron skillet. "As they have disappeared around the bend."

"Fret not, old friend." Dalton lowered his chin and flipped his familiar coin, which landed, however apropos, on tails. "They do not call me the lucky one, for nothing."

THE BEAUTIFUL SPRING morning dawned with nary a hint of the wicked tempest that had struck Portsea Island two days ago. Stretching her arms, Daphne Harcourt gazed out the window, which boasted a spectacular view of the Channel, and reminisced of the carefree existence of her youth, when she often ran through the grassy meadow that flanked Courtenay Hall. But that time had long since passed, which had been emphasized by recent harrowing events, the dark nature of which she had yet to untangle, so she drank the last of her tea and pushed from the dining room table.

In the main corridor of her childhood home, which doubled as the governor's official residence, as was her father's post, she paused before the oval mirror and checked her appearance. At the age of three and twenty, she was, for all intents and purposes, a spinster. A bluestocking. On the shelf. Oh, there were endless names to describe the seemingly hopeless despair of maidenhood to which she had resigned herself, in the wake of unforeseen incidents that had left her scrambling to maintain her family and property, with no possibility of a future of her own or the fantasies she had coveted.

With a sigh of lament for the misspent dreams of her early years, she adjourned to papa's study, settled in the leather chair behind his desk, and opened the account ledger. After twice calculating the sum of the month's expenditures, she collapsed in the seat and vented a plaintive cry. Growing ever more desperate with each successive week, she could discern no escape from her perilous predicament, despite many sleepless nights in search of a solution.

"Excuse me, Miss Daphne." Hicks, the butler, cleared his throat. "There is a gentleman just arrived to see your father."

"Oh?" Sifting through the various logs, she located the appointment book, flipped to the current date, and frowned. "There is no scheduled meeting."

"Shall I make your excuses?" the servant inquired, with an expression of sympathy.

"No." She stood and smoothed the skirt of her pale

yellow morning dress. "To turn away our caller would rouse unwanted suspicion. Show him in, at once."

"Very good, ma'am." Hicks dipped his chin.

With a quick assessment of the surroundings, she nodded at no one and strolled to the window, which overlooked the rose garden. How many afternoons she had enjoyed, tending the plants her mother had pruned with love and care.

"Miss Daphne, allow me to present Sir Dalton Randolph." With very proper airs, which she found rather amusing, given his usual affable mannerisms, Hicks made the introductions. "Sir Dalton, this is Miss Daphne Harcourt, Governor Harcourt's eldest child."

It was then she spared a glance at her visitor—and almost fainted.

At well over six feet tall, the imposing figure of a man would have intimidated her under any circumstance. With sun-kissed brown hair, amber eyes that harked a comparison with papa's brandy, chiseled cheekbones, and a patrician nose, his masculine aura bespoke raw power mingled with sinful beauty. And when he smiled, gooseflesh covered her from top to toe.

Wearing an evergreen coat, a tan waistcoat, a crisp white cravat, fawn-colored breeches, and polished hessians, the tailored noble's garb had done little to temper the enormity of his frame or dispel the danger he exuded. Even in the dim light from his cargo hold, and later, above deck, she had thought him quite stunning, as he had chased her. But looming as the specter of doom in her midst, he well nigh took her breath away, for more reasons than one.

"Sir Dalton—"

"Oh, let us dispense with the formalities." With brazen immodesty, he surveyed her, and she swallowed hard. "It is just Dalton.   And may I be so bold as to address you informally?"

"Of course." With a casual wave, she dismissed Hicks and then extended her hand. "What can I do for you, Dalton?"

"You may begin by telling me why I have never had the pleasure of your charming company in the *ton's* ballrooms." Then he grasped her fingers, bent, and pressed his lips to her bare knuckles, lingering a tad too long by her estimation, and she shuddered. Although she had uttered a silent prayer he had not noted her reaction to his otherwise innocuous kiss, his arched brow and devilish grin belied her hope. "Are you unwell, my dear?"

"Why do you ask?" Panic wreaked havoc on her senses, when she attempted to withdraw, and he held firm. She had heard of his sort, the kind of superficial seducer that was more than happy to avail himself of her attributes but had no interest in her heart, and she girded herself with that knowledge. "And I have never journeyed to London."

"How exceedingly cruel, as you deny us one of England's brightest flowers." The rake had the audacity to wink. "And now might I have a word with Governor Harcourt?"

"You pay me a great compliment." Still, he would not relinquish her hand. "And I am sorry to disappoint you, but my father is not in residence."

"What time do you expect him?" Dalton drew imaginary circles in her palm.

"He is away." She inhaled a shaky breath.

"When will he return?" His voice poured over her, like honey on a hot scone.

Clinging to her wits by a thread, Daphne struggled to relax. "I cannot say."

"Where has he gone?" Why could she not tear herself from his clutch?

"He is on the mainland." Because she had not wanted to incite any alarm, she acquiesced.

"You are curiously vague." He shifted his weight.

"And I might charge you are quite intrusive." She shuffled her feet.

"I beg your pardon, my dear." He pressed her palm to the crook of his arm. "And who has the Crown appointed to serve in Governor Harcourt's stead?"

She blinked. "I do not follow."

"No doubt your father notified the King of the temporary absence, as required by his station?" Bereft of compunction and any semblance of polite conduct, he gazed upon her as if he knew how she looked in her chemise, and she cursed the burn of a blush. "As someone of singular authority must supervise the territory and safeguard the governor's fascinating daughter."

"Portsea is a small community. We are, in every respect, an extended family." Goodness, the dimpled man was lethal, and she ignored his last statement. How many bloody questions would he ask, as she had to get rid of him? "And I often assume my father's duties, sir. Daresay he saw no reason to concern the King."

"Given we are at war, and the advantageous location, Portsea Island is of vital importance to the Crown's military interests." Dalton led her to a Hepplewhite chair, and then he occupied the mate. "Never would His Majesty abandon the superior landscape to a mere wisp of a girl."

"You insult me, sir." Daphne folded her arms and found safe harbor in his effrontery. "I would have you know I have had no need of a governess for some four years."

"*Four* years?" He whistled in monotone. "You are a regular Hester Stanhope."

"And now you make sport of me." It was too late, when she realized she had taken his bait, and she averted her stare. "Let me assure you, Sir Dalton, that I am quite capable of managing the daily functions of my father's office, as I have often helped him, with his tutelage, encouragement, and blessing. So how may I serve you?"

"What a provocative proposal, and I vow to weigh your offer with due consideration." He chuckled, a rich throaty rumble that had her curling her toes in her slippers. "But, for now, I wonder if the governor has mentioned a rogue band of vagabonds stealing from docked ships, in the area?"

"Why—yes." Daphne almost swallowed her tongue. "But they are, to my knowledge, harmless, as they seek nothing more than food. Would you raise such a ruckus over a few missing potatoes?"

"How remarkable that you seize upon some of the precise missing items, as I said nothing of what the thieves pinched from my stores." Dalton caught her in a steely glare. "Can you explain your extraordinary powers of divination, my dear?"

"Actually, my father has apprised me of the situation and the complaints." So enthralled by his bold behavior, she almost betrayed the truth. "But no one has pursued charges, as their loss was minimal, and hunger thrives in these difficult times. Do you lack a measure of compassion for those less fortunate than yourself?"

"I take issue with your characterization, as these particular criminals are not so virtuous as you have been led to believe. Indeed, they stole a priceless family heirloom from my cabin, and I will not cease my hunt for the villains, until the item is surrendered to my custody." In that instant, the curious agitator stood and rested hands on hips. "Do you condone such theft? Is lawlessness the standard in these parts?"

"No, of course not." The implications of his words struck her as a bucket of icy water, and she shivered. "But— are you absolutely certain of your accusation? Perhaps you lost the item."

"The invaluable bauble had rested on my desk." At that moment, her mesmerizing guest produced a red velvet purse and held it for her inspection. "It was a lady's brooch fashioned of solid gold, etched with a lotus and bearing a large oval sapphire and four rubies, and it was contained in this pouch, which the scoundrel dropped as he fled my ship. Given to my ancestors, for services rendered to the Crown, in the fourteenth century, it is more than a piece of jewelry. It is an irreplaceable part of our history, and I will not stop until the artifact is recovered and the unknown miscreants are captured, brought to justice, and punished."

"Sir Dalton, you are angry, and I understand your ire." Daphne prayed for calm, as her mind raced in search of a response to placate her new nemesis. Then she would confront the source responsible for the significant complication, reclaim the article, and somehow restore the precious gem to its rightful owner, without discovery. "But there is no reason to overreact, when I might intervene on your behalf, with favorable results. If you would allow me to make some discreet inquiries, I am positive I can retrieve your expensive keepsake."

"You pose a compelling, if not altogether satisfactory, proposition, Miss Daphne." Then Dalton lowered his chin, and she gulped. "What have you to persuade me not to notify the Crown of your father's dereliction of duty and to accept your approach to our conundrum?"

"I do not comprehend your meaning, sir." She would have taken issue with his unflattering and unfair assault on her father's character, but she could ill afford to insult the unwelcome interloper. Lost in her musings, she started, as he drew her from the chair and escorted her to the window. Her first instinct was to run in the opposite direction. "What would you have of me?"

"You are blessed with the bluest eyes I have ever seen." For a long while, he simply met her gaze, and the air sizzled with a foreign intensity she tried but failed to identify. But all of a sudden, he cupped her jaw in his hand, turned her left and then right, and his expression sobered. "Have dinner with me."

It took her several seconds to realize he had spoken, and even longer to discern his overture, which left her wondering at his motives. "You, sir, are without doubt the most presumptuous man of my acquaintance."

"And without doubt, I shall take that as a compliment." Now he trailed his thumb to her lower lip, and some strange but alluring sensation unfurled within her, fanning comforting heat, spreading slowly, suffusing her muscles from the pit of her belly to her limbs. "And what a tempting mouth you possess. Really, it is a masterpiece, and what I would do with it, were you mine."

"Upon my word, but you are too bold." Myriad recriminations and rebukes formed in her brain. Yet, to her chagrin, Daphne burst into nervous laughter. "Oh, Sir Dalton, I wager you are a favorite among society ladies, but I am too wise to dice with you. So what do you require for your cooperation?"

"You know my terms." Then he inclined his head. "Did you know that when the sun catches your blonde hair, you look quite angelic, as though you wear a halo?"

"I can assure you, Sir Dalton, I am no angel." She couldn't help but snicker at his absurd statement. "So you wish me to dine with you? Simple enough—"

"Unchaperoned." He grinned, and his dimples all but beckoned her to accept his request.

"Are you planning to make advances?" She bit her tongue against further spontaneous conjecture.

"No."

"Oh."

"You sound disappointed." He chortled.

"Well it would have been nice, not to mention flattering, if you had exhibited the tiniest bit of interest." Her spirits flagged. "Then again, I am not sure I would have recognized it, if you had."

"Is there no local dandy to pay call on a lovely woman, such as yourself?" To her delight, though she could not explain why his action thrilled her, he trailed a finger along the curve of her cheek. "And who says I am not interested?"

"Now you compliment me, but I am not fooled by your feigned blandishments." She gazed at the horizon. "My cousin has expressed a desire to wed, but it is only because he seeks my father's office and presumes I present the shortest path to that goal."

"That does not speak well for the swains of Portsea Island." Again, he scrutinized her, and she bore the weight of his attention as a sumptuous down counterpane. "Then it is safe to assume you remain unspoken for and are, therefore, unattached?"

"Yes." Not entirely true, but she could pretend, if only for a few days.

"Then I insist you accept my invitation." In play, he tapped the tip of her nose. "And I will brook no refusal."

"Has any woman ever refused you anything?" Despite

her earlier apprehension, she would give an untold bounty to know him better, to revel in the comfort and security of an estimable specimen of means and persist as his lady. Had she ever savored such stability and happiness more, in her lifetime? Then again, such men often eschewed monogamous relationships, as had her father, in regard to her mother, and Daphne would settle for nothing less.

"Not that I can recall." The rake rocked on his heels, and in that simple gesture she discovered his lure. The boyish innocence coupled with the confidence of an elder proved a potent appeal, as he evaded her usual stalwart defenses.

"Then who am I to buck the popular trend?" They strolled to the door, and to her chagrin, she rued his departure, as he provided fortuitous distraction.

"Wonderful." Now he steered her into the hall. "Since I have taken a suite at the inn, I shall book a private dining room for tomorrow night, at seven."

"I look forward to it, Sir Dalton." They paused in the foyer. "And what is the attire?"

"Formal, of course." In the grand entry, he again brought her knuckles to his lips, but then he surprised her, when he flipped her hand and pressed a kiss to the inner side of her wrist. "Until next we meet, I would have you think of me with fondness."

Daphne's knees buckled. "I shall endeavor to fulfill your expectations and would bid you the same, of me."

"No worries, angel." He released her. "As scarcely a second will pass that you do not occupy my thoughts."

His declaration, which she suspected was more facetious than serious, touched her more than she was willing to admit, to herself or anyone else. "My, what an elegant coach."

"I summoned my traveling equipage from London,

when I estimated the extent of the damage to the *Siren*." A liveried footman leaped to open the door. With one last glance over his shoulder, Dalton saluted and said, "I shall send my rig to collect you, tomorrow."

"And I will be ready." With a light heart, she curtseyed and ran into the house. Giggling, she hugged herself. Then she jolted to reality, when it dawned on her that Dalton posed the greatest threat to her secrets and, thereby, her family. In a flash, Daphne glared at the landing and marched up the grand staircase. On the second floor, she veered left, navigated the passageway, and charged into the third room. "All right. Which one of you stole the brooch?"

"What brooch?" Robert, her nineteen-year-old brother, dropped a model ship to the floor and jumped to his feet. "I gave you my rucksack, and you know I took only some ham, cheese, and bread."

Huddled on the carpet, Richard, the youngest, at ten and seven, lingered in uncharacteristic quiet. When he refused to meet her gaze, Daphne's spirits plunged to heretofore-unimagined depths. Until that moment, until that very instant, she had clung to some scrap of hope that Dalton's accusation had been unfounded, and her brother's were innocent.

"Richard, where is the brooch?" She knelt at his side and took his hand in hers. "Please, you must give it to me. Whatever your reasons for taking it, the owner visited me, just now. It is a precious family heirloom. If I do not restore the item, posthaste, he will notify the King of father's absence, and I cannot allow that."

"But I thought we could sell it, to buy more food. And the captain had very fine things, so I thought he could spare it." Richard lifted his chin and cast a watery stare. "I am always hungry."

"What a stupid thing to do, and now we could all be exposed." Robert folded his arms and huffed in unmasked disgust. "You should be spanked—"

"I know, darling." With a sharp wave, she silenced Robert, given she could withstand anything but Richard's tears, and she framed his cheeks to offer a modicum of comfort, as his intentions were honorable. "But we cannot save our family based on the misery and misfortune of another, and the brooch is not ours to barter. I promise, come what may, I will find a way to fill our pantry. Now, bring me the bauble."

"What are you going to do with it?" Richard frowned. "If we are in trouble, then I am to blame, and I should face the consequences."

"Worry not, little one." When her youngest sibling jumped up and ran to his armoire, she stood. From one of his coat pockets, he produced the expensive piece of jewelry. "I will take care of it."

"How?" With a furrowed brow, Robert appeared skeptical. "If you give it back, they will know we stole it."

"Then I shall figure out a course of action to return it, with none the wiser." In truth, Daphne had no idea how she would accomplish that feat, but she would not burden her brothers with that none too little snag. "I will see you at dinner."

"What are we having?" Richard inquired, with a grimace. "Can we eat some of the ham and cheese, as I have had my fill of toast?"

"Yes, sweetheart." Turning the ancient trinket in her palm, which fit Dalton's description to the letter, she pondered the possibilities. "If we forgo lunch, or consume only mutton broth, we may indulge ourselves, tonight. And I have a bit of good news. I sold the furniture from the last guestroom, so I will purchase some chickens, which should provide eggs, on a regular basis."

"What of father's monthly stipend?" Robert shifted his weight. "Have you already spent it?"

"I used it to pay down some of the debt." Yet it was nowhere near enough, and April could prove the most arduous challenge, to date. "Next I will broker a trade with Mr. Barker, for my cedar chest, as it should fetch a decent sum."

"But grandmother left that to you, when she died." Richard sniffed. "Are we to barter everything?"

"And have you considered my suggestion of securing a commission in the Army?" Raking his fingers through his hair, a nervous habit he had exhibited almost from infancy, Robert paced. "As I could earn steady pay and send home every penny, for you and Richard."

"No, and I will not, as I refuse to risk your life to save mine." And if she grew desperate, she could always cede the fight and marry their cousin. "I cannot, in good conscience, allow you to make such a sacrifice."

"Would you rather we were condemned to the work-houses and you to debtor's prison?" Her oldest brother halted and smacked a fist to a palm. "Do you find that solution preferable, because I protest. And you may be the first-born, but I am the man in this household."

"Robert, I have never loved you more than I do now." Daphne splayed wide her arms and flicked her fingers. Together, the three huddled. "But it will not come to that, I swear."

"Well I will not permit you to wed cousin Harold." Robert scowled, even as he hugged her. "That is a fate worse than death."

"Thank you." Perched on tiptoes, because Robert was

much taller than her, she kissed her staunch protector's cheek. "We will survive this difficult time, brothers. And we will be far stronger for having endured, integrity intact. Somehow, some way, we will persist—I must believe that. And if all else fails, there is always the odd chance that a grand knight in shining armor shall ride to our rescue."

CHAPTER TWO

*H*ow long had it been since a young woman had captured his interest with such uncontrollable ferocity? Given his potent response to the inimitable Miss Harcourt, and a night spent drifting amid a haze of lusty dreams, involving the singular blonde's luscious body and judicious use of his tongue, it had been too long. In the oval mirror that hung on the wall, Dalton checked his appearance, straightened his cravat, and consulted his timepiece. Behind him, in the private dining room, a waiter lit the candles on the table and adjusted the silverware placement.

"Will that be all, sir?" the servant inquired.

"Yes, thank you." Dalton buttoned his coat and pondered what he had learned of the Harcourts, just that morning. "We shall serve ourselves."

"Very good, sir." He bowed, opened the door, and almost trounced the guest of honor. "I beg your pardon, miss."

"No, it is my fault." The governor's daughter blushed. "I should have knocked."

"Come in, Miss Daphne." The thrill of the hunt burned

in his loins, as his prey, and she was his prey, though she knew it not, unbuttoned her pelisse, revealing a satin gown of deep burgundy. "Your timing is perfect. And may I take your wrap?"

"Yes, thank you." With a shy smile, she shrugged from the garment. "Something smells delicious."

"Are you hungry?" As he deposited the coat over the back of a daybed, he noted the outdated style and the threadbare edges of the cuffs. Upon closer inspection, he noticed her frock represented not the current fashion, and it looked a tad small, which emphasized her thin frame and piqued his already over-stimulated curiosity, where the woman was concerned. According to several townsfolk, the missing governor had amassed quite a bit of debt with various vendors, which might explain her humble clothes. "May I pour you some wine?"

"I am famished, and, yes, please do so." When she neared the fantasy he had created just for her, her mouth fell agape, and she caressed a rosebud. "Are you celebrating something of importance, of which you neglected to apprise me?"

"Why do you ask?" Given most ladies rewarded his efforts with a kiss, which often led to more enticing scenarios, her surprise had him wondering if he had miscalculated. "And is our first dinner date not something to mark with a suitable ceremony?"

"Our first?" She blinked. "You wish to see me again, before this evening has commenced?"

"Of many, I hope." He could not help but chuckle at her expression of utter astonishment. During Dalton's brief investigation of her history, the locals imparted one exceptional statement with frequency. With an unblemished reputation, and a well-established penchant for benevolent enterprises, Daphne Harcourt manifested the backbone of the family and, indeed, her father's office. No matter the situation, she could always be counted on to provide assistance, which was why most citizens sought her advice over the governor's. It was that fact, alone, that had swayed him and set his course of action in an altogether different direction. "And why would I not favor your company? Do you think yourself unattractive?"

"I am unsure how to answer your query." Daphne shrugged, and he realized, in that instant, she spoke the truth. Had he thought her fascinating? In light of her incredible beauty, which grew in epic proportions when contrasted by her staunch modesty, the woman was an enigma and far more arresting than any polished courtesan or uninspiring debutante. "And I have never studied myself in such detail, nor could I ever be considered an impartial critic, so I should refrain from a pointless self-assessment."

"Spoken like a formidable paragon and an angel of mercy." He held her chair, and she sat. "I might think you too good to be true."

"But I told you yesterday that I am no angel." She draped her lap with her napkin.

"That is not what the widow Cartwright says, or Mr. Holmes, who sang your praises for the better part of an hour." After situating a covered dish before her, he lifted the lid. Then he claimed his plate and assumed his place. "They are grateful for the ham, cheese, potatoes, and bread."

"Are you making a survey of me?" Fear invested her blue eyes, her face paled, and he cursed himself for frightening her, as that was not his aim. "It is no crime to feed those who cannot fend for themselves."

"In that, we are in agreement, as yours was an admirable

gesture, my dear." And he had no doubt the food she shared constituted a portion of the pilfered contents from his stores. What he could not reconcile was the theft of the brooch by one of her brothers, whose existence he uncovered from the innkeeper. "I commend your sense of compassion and would make a contribution to your charity, if you tell me what you require."

"Do you mean that?" With a tear-filled gaze and guileless desperation, Daphne humbled him, and he suspected she could be counted among the starving members of her community. "You would assist my cause?"

"Yes." As Dalton cut his steak, he monitored her progress, and he needed no further proof of her condition, as she devoured her meal, while humming her appreciation of the fare. "If you would accompany me to the market, tomorrow afternoon, we might fill your pantry."

"Oh, thank you. Thank you. I will compose a list, when I return home." Then she stared at the carrots he had not consumed. "Are you going to eat those?"

"No." He shook his head.

"May I?" For the umpteenth time, she stunned him, as most young women ate less than that essential to sustain a bird, when in the company of gentlemen, but she dined with unabashed gusto. Then and there, he vowed Daphne would never again suffer an empty belly.

"Be my guest." He scooted his plate toward the center of the table. "But I would caution you to save room for the final course, as I selected a delicious assortment from the bakery."

"You did?" A host of emotions invested her countenance, as she bounced with unmasked joy, and Dalton found her alluring beyond words. "I can't remember the last time I partook of dessert."

"I shall remember that, for future reference." When he retrieved a platter of sweets and displayed the tempting variety, her eyes grew wide with unconcealed excitement, and a strange sensation filled his chest. "Have I made you happy?"

"Will you think me a simpleton if I admit as much?" How he adored her bashful grin.

"Not at all." As he served her a generous sampling, he leaned near. "As I find you inexpressibly captivating."

The poor thing choked violently on her wine, and he recalled his agenda for the night.

"Let me assure you that I am quite boring, sir." With recovered grace and ease, she dabbed the corners of her mouth. "There is little excitement in Portsea, and I daresay our provincial society would disappoint one acquainted with the cosmopolitan ballrooms of the *ton*."

"Present company excepted." It was past due to initiate the interrogation. "So tell me of your younger brothers, and are they in residence?"

Stopping mid-chew, she swallowed hard. "How did you learn of my brothers?"

"As I said, from your neighbors." He poured two brandies and passed her a glass of liquid courage. "Although they hold a rather vacillating opinion of—how did the butcher put it, oh, yes, 'the two devil-spawn rapscallions.'"

"I resent that mischaracterization, as Robert and Richard are nothing more than young boys, struggling to find their identity." With high dudgeon, she folded her arms. "Despite the brevity of our association, I am sure you engaged in your fair share of harmless mischief, at their age. And they are accused of everything, even when they are innocent."

"And a great deal of not so harmless mayhem, most of

which I blamed on my elder sibling, Dirk, so you have me there." In order to impress upon her the gravity of the theft of the brooch, Dalton had brought the accompanying journal, which he hoped would foster sympathy for his plight. "I thought you might enjoy reading a bit of lore, regarding my missing family heirloom, as it possesses mystical powers and a vaunted past."

"I beg your pardon." She snapped to attention. "Mystical powers?"

"Indeed." He nodded and handed her the leather-bound diary. "Read the opening inscription."

"All right." Daphne flipped to the first page. "The parchment has yellowed, with age, and the ink has faded. 'Ye lady what dons this brooch of ethereal sight, shall enjoy unfettered dreams of her one true knight.' How remarkable."

"The entries describe what the brooch revealed to my ancestors, over the years." While she perused the old tome, he availed himself of the opportunity to make an unfettered examination of her profile, which he found inexpressibly striking. "The most recent notation records a relationship between two people very near and dear to my heart."

"Oh?" Ignoring the fact that he had moved his chair to sit beside her, she turned to the last item. "You know Lady Amanda Gascoigne-Lake?"

"She has persisted as Lady Amanda Douglas these twenty-eight years, and she and Admiral Douglas have two daughters, both wed and equally content." He pointed to the conditions for inheritance of the unique piece of jewelry. "As Lady Amanda's sister has no daughters, she intended to pass the brooch to Lady Cara, and that was my task, after I rendezvoused with George, Lady Olivia's son, off the coast of Belgium."

"And is she still happy with her match?" A hint of sadness marred her delicate features. "As feelings change, over time, and some men seek satisfaction elsewhere."

"What a curious thing to say." He frowned. "Let me alleviate any concerns, in that respect, as I am happy to report the Admiral and his lady remain very much in love."

"So some vows do last forever." It was a statement, not a question. For a while, Daphne bowed her head and sat in silence. When she lifted her chin and met his gaze, he caught his breath. "You will have your brooch, Sir Dalton. I would stake my life on it."

GASPING FOR AIR, Daphne shot upright in bed. It took her a few seconds to realize she resided in her bedchamber, safe and sound, after a glorious dinner, which resembled something more akin to the realm of fantasy, with Sir Dalton, the previous evening. Then she peered at the brooch that she had pinned to her cotton nightgown.

No, she had no right to make use of the curious artifact, as it was not hers to covet. Yet the lore, so carefully detailed by her dashing companion, had struck a chord and fostered hope, as she had scarcely known in recent weeks, so she had employed it in a last ditch effort to identify a solution to her current problem.

True to the cryptic proclamation, she had experienced a very intense, rather odd dream of which she could make no sense. Ensconced in a warm, comforting glow, the heat of which had suffused her from top to toe, a single image played in her brain, again and again, of a unique gold coin tossing about, as though suspended. There had been no hint or suggestion of the owner of what appeared to be an ancient Roman monetary piece, given the writing and the female profile etched on one side. But what she could neither comprehend nor explain was the opposite end.

Although her mother had died when Daphne was ten and nine, never had they engaged in any discussion of marital relations, so what little knowledge she possessed had been gleaned from observing farm animals. The particular act, a crude and bawdy depiction, involved a man and a woman and reminded her of two cats that were quite fond of each other. Just revisiting the reverie brought the burn of a blush to her cheeks.

After wrenching aside the blankets, she dropped her legs over the edge of the mattress and stood. Stretching long, she yawned and then smiled, as she gazed at the crystal vase filled with two-dozen red roses, which Dalton had insisted she accept, as a personal gift. While polite decorum frowned upon such exchanges of familiarity, given their brief acquaintance, she could not resist the temptation he presented. And that was why she also had permitted her host to request the waiter pack the remaining dinner and dessert portions, so her brothers might enjoy the fare.

At the windows overlooking the rose garden, she drew back the threadbare drapes and basked in the shimmering sunlight. As she assessed her private quarters, which remained bedecked in girlish pink hues, because her family lacked the funds to redecorate, and had seen far better days, Daphne fixed her attention on the cedar chest that had belonged to her grandmother. Like Dalton's brooch, the old trunk was a treasured heirloom. But times were desperate, and despite the enthralling sea captain's generous overture, she may still be forced to sell her beloved keepsake to save her family.

For the moment, she could relax, so she strolled to the

armoire and fanned through a selection of modest, worn day dresses that had been altered on two separate occasions to accommodate her changing body. As was the case with everything else, she had no money to replace her outdated wardrobe. Never before had she spared much thought for her attire, but Dalton sported only the best fashions, so she wished to make a good impression on her escort. In short, she wanted to look pretty for him—as she had for no one else. A knock at the door intruded on her deliberation.

"Come." She drew forth a pale blue sprig muslin gown with a lace collar and frowned, when she noted the tattered cuffs.

"Good morning, Miss Daphne." Mrs. Jones, the housekeeper, strolled into the room. "The boys inhaled the steak and eggs, as did Hicks, but I saved you a portion. Shall I help you prepare for your appointment?"

"Yes, please, as I wish to dazzle Sir Dalton." Daphne sat at her vanity. "And did you eat your share of the feast?"

"Of course." Mrs. Jones smiled. "The filet was delicious, and it was kind of you to think of us, though I am not surprised, as you have possessed a generous nature since you were born. But Hicks thought you might go to your grave before accepting charity from a stranger."

"As much as I regret it, our circumstances are desperate, so I will not allow pride to condemn this household and our most vulnerable neighbors to hunger." Coiffed and garbed as close to perfection as she could muster, she stood and smoothed her skirts. "Now, I should breakfast prior to our newfound benefactor's arrival."

En route to the dining room, she scrutinized her childhood home and rued its clean but shabby décor, ragged carpets, peeling paint, chipped plaster, and faded wall coverings. In well-established tradition, the Harcourt men had governed Portsea Island for more than a hundred years, and the residence, built in the seventeenth century in the Baroque style and handed down through several generations, had marked their success, for visitors far and wide. Because her father had long nursed a penchant for expensive brandy, imported cigars, gambling, and bad luck, the once splendorous Courtenay Hall had foundered, in a slow and painful demise. Yet she vowed to restore the house and its property to its former glory.

At the table, she savored the weak tea, which she had stolen from Dalton's ship. While she preferred a stronger brew, she could enjoy the simple drink, which had become an indulgence, for several weeks, if she used less leaves in the pot. And although she was quite famished, nerves had rendered her belly unstable, and Daphne could not clean her plate, to her dismay.

"I beg your pardon, Miss Daphne." Hicks loomed in the doorway. "Sir Dalton Randolph is just arrived and awaits your presence, in the foyer."

"Oh, dear." She jumped from her chair, gulped the last of her tea, wiped her mouth on a napkin, and ran into the hall. Just as she rounded the corner, she slowed her pace and rolled her shoulders. But when she caught sight of the handsome sea captain, her heart raced. Searching for something witty to say, her mind blanked, and she opted for the obvious. "Hello."

"And how are you this fine morning, Miss Daphne?" Sporting a navy coat, a chocolate brown waistcoat, a fine lawn shirt, a snowy cravat, with a diamond twinkling at center, and buckskin breeches, which disappeared into polished top boots, again her dashing escort rendered her a pauper by comparison. Yet his dimpled smile and precise bow disarmed her. "I trust you slept well, after I brought you home?"

"I did, indeed." She lied, as she half curtseyed. Even as she donned her pelisse, she thought of the intriguing gold coin, with its salacious image, tossing in the air. After collecting her reticule, she met her companion's gaze. "I have composed a list of necessary items, which should sustain our most vulnerable citizens, until I can identify a long-term solution."

"You mean—until your father returns." He held open the heavy portal, and she crossed the threshold. "And when will that be?"

"I know not, as the governor does not see fit to apprise me of all his business." Oh, she had walked right into that one. "But I expect him, any day now."

"Why do I not believe you?" He snickered, as he handed her into his equipage. "As I am beginning to think Governor Harcourt persists only as a myth."

"I beg your pardon?" Sinking into the squabs, she cautioned herself not to take offense to his jab, as righteous indignation was a luxury she could ill afford, and she could not risk alienating her newfound benefactor. "I am sure my father—"

"Please, do not insult me with further excuses, recriminations, and denials, as one so lovely should never spin falsehoods." The devilish charmer had the audacity to wink. "The truth is your father has not been in residence for an estimated two to three weeks, given his last recorded appearance, according to the locals. Is there a family difficulty, which you would not divulge to the general public, but you could entrust to my confidence? Perhaps I can be of assistance."

"Did we not travel this road, last night?" The passing

landscape provided fortuitous distraction, and the coach bobbled along the lane. Beyond the verge, frothy waves crashed into the craggy shoreline, and she followed the winding, arbitrary path of a gull, which seemed to symbolize her life's uncertainty. "And I answered your query."

"Not to my satisfaction." Despite the suspect content of their discussion, his playful tone belied the seriousness of the exchange. And then he grasped the edge of his bench, leaned forward, and arched a brow. "Do you know that when you are stressed, you have a slight tic over your left eye?"

"Posh." She sniffed and stared out the window, as they entered the village. "You hardly know me."

"People can share space and time, for years, and remain nothing more than casual acquaintances, while others can read each other, as a favorite book, in a matter of minutes." The scamp chuckled. "And from the moment we met, sweet lady, I figured us for the latter."

"Did you?" Daphne snapped to attention, just as the coach halted. "You assume too much, Sir—"

"It is Dalton. Just Dalton." He exited the rig and then turned to hand her to the sidewalk. "So we are to begin with the butcher?"

"Yes, as I would have select cuts delivered, posthaste." She entered the meat market.

"I shall be with you shortly." Old Mr. Wilkes glanced at her and smiled. "Miss Daphne, what a pleasure it is to see you. Have you come to settle your father's account?"

Standing stock-still, she could have swallowed her tongue, even as Dalton stumbled into her. It had never occurred to her that the meager payments she had made would not suffice or forestall embarrassing queries. What could she do to avoid further shame at future stops, as her father owed money to just about every merchant in Portsea?

"What is the amount of the debt?" Dalton inquired.

"Fifteen pounds, sir." The butcher narrowed his stare. "And who might you be?"

"Sir Dalton Randolph, of London." Her antagonist dipped his chin. "And you may add the sum to our order, as we are here to purchase items for Miss Daphne's community pantry."

"Oh?" Mr. Wilkes all but leaped for joy. "Well that is—"

"—Completely out of the question." Leashing her temper, she counted to five and sighed. "While I appreciate your most munificent gesture, it breaches untold social dictates, as we are not family, and you are not my...that is to say, we are not...what I mean is we have no understanding and neither do we intend to enter such arrangement."

"How do you know my aspirations?" With a flirty grin, the tempting sea captain rocked on his heels. "Do you presume to know my mind and possible aims?"

For a scarce second, Daphne blinked and stuttered, as she pondered his proposal, if she could call it that. He could not have known it, but Dalton manifested the answer to her prayers, in more ways than one. In a low voice, she posited, "Are you asking me to marry you?"

In a flash, his expression sobered. "Uh—no."

"Well, of course not." And so her fledgling hopes deflated as quickly as they had bloomed. "I was joking, Sir Dalton."

"Ah, we are back to titles, so I think not." He frowned. "Forgive me, dear lady, if I misled you. But, to be candid, if I may, I am not husband material."

"Now you sell yourself short, Sir Dalton." She folded her arms and inclined her head, as she was not the only one suppressing secrets, which rendered him infinitely more interesting. "And I wonder at your reasons for concealing your true nature. What have you to hide?"

"Do you speculate in regard to my character to deflect attention from yourself?" he stated, with a snort.

"You answer a question with a question, which piques my suspicion." At last, she found her footing. "I believe you are a better man than you admit."

"On the contrary, I hold much in common with the care-free wind, or a playful breeze, never landing too long in any one spot." Dalton clucked his tongue and waggled his brows. "In fact, some might call me a rake, as my tastes are as variable as the weather."

"An imposter is more like it." Oh, despite his best attempts, he could not fool her. "Or do you prefer charlatan, as that may better describe your pretend predilections?"

"Easy, love." He shuffled near, and she refused to retreat, but gooseflesh covered her arms. "You claim intimate knowledge of my character, given our brief association."

"And were you not the one who boasted the same of me?" She looked him in the eyes, daring him to profess otherwise. "Is it so surprising that I possess the ability to—how did you put it? Ah, yes, 'to read you as a favorite book.'"

"*Touché*, my dear." With a huff, he ushered her to the counter. "Give the butcher your list, and do not argue with me, else I shall end this outing, this instant."

And so commenced the duel.

INHALING THE SEA AIR, and tossing his ever-present lucky coin, which often calmed his agitated state, Dalton shifted in the saddle of his black stallion and gazed at the surrounding Portsea landscape. Uncharacteristic restlessness permeated every pore, as he had promised himself he would not seek the incomparable but unnerving Miss Harcourt's company for a sennight. To his chagrin, his heretofore-vaunted self-discipline had endured a mere two days, as he steered for Courtenay Hall. And although he would deny it should anyone ask, he had survived that long only because he had been distracted by preparations for the *Siren's* move to Portsmouth, for additional repairs.

To his complete and utter befuddlement, the backwater governor's daughter had seen through his well-composed rogue façade and seized upon and struck the chink in his armor, when he had fooled untold cosmopolitans for years. Then again, polite society had been all too ready to believe the worst of him, had even expanded upon his rumored rakish romps, so he had expended little effort to maintain the ruse.

Of course, he had not bothered to correct the mistaken assumptions, given his ribald reputation afforded a few benefits, and the ladies often competed for his favors, when they ignored his titled but tedious elder brother. How would the *ton* have reacted, had they discovered Dalton was, in fact, a mirror copy of the stodgy Dirk?

Just as he had pocketed his talisman, he spied the source of his uneasy reflection, with her head bowed, wearing her tattered pelisse, a démodé bonnet, and carrying a basket, as she walked in the lane. Without warning, a ripple of awareness coursed his spine and pooled in his gut, as she worked on him in ways he could neither explain nor evade. "Good afternoon, Miss Daphne."

"Sir Dalton." Peering at him, she favored him with a brilliant smile, and he sucked in a breath. "This is a treat, as

I had thought, perhaps, you had departed our humble isle. And what is your destination, if I might inquire?"

"Why, to see you, my dear." Salacious skills honed in the embraces of some of London's most notorious courtesans and widows charged the fore, but he reminded himself that he required her cooperation, if he had any hope of recovering the brooch. "And what, may I ask, is your port of call?"

"Oh, I must check on Mrs. Oldman, as the twins are teething, and she gets little sleep. And Mr. Tolly had a cold last week, so I should make sure he is on the mend and deliver the chicken soup Mrs. Jones prepared." She counted on her fingers. "Then I need to convey a parcel of ham, cheese, and bread to the widow Cartwright."

"And you intend to do so, on foot?" Dalton stretched upright. "Where is your coach? Or why do you not take a horse?"

"It is a lovely day, and I am rather fond of long walks." She set her chin firm, as if to convince him of her claim, yet he suspected otherwise. "And I might have missed you, had I done as you suggest."

"And now you flatter me, in an effort to spike my guns." In that instant, he dismounted. When he charged Miss Daphne, she retreated, but he caught her about the waist. "Hold tight to your basket, sweet lady."

"What are you doing?" Shock invested her charming features, as she stammered and sputtered, when he lifted her to the saddle. "Sir Dalton, I protest."

"My mother raised a gentleman, and I could not leave you to roam the countryside, alone, as it is not done. Now, scoot forward." After she had done as he bade, he lunged and perched behind her. "Hand me the reins, love."

"This is not a good idea." When she shifted, her soft bottom teased his crotch, and his loins erupted in flames.

"And please do not call me that, as it makes you sound disingenuous."

"On the contrary, it is an excellent idea." Even as he uttered the words, he doubted his sanity, as the old one-eyed marauder came to life. "And you object to a term of endearment?"

"Not all terms—just that one." She wiggled, and he gritted his teeth. "As I know you love me not."

"Would you care to explain yourself, as you could not think me serious?" Perhaps it would have been better to walk alongside his horse, as his current position challenged the limits of his self-control and his breeches. "Sit still, before you send us both toppling to the ground."

"Do not rip at me, as I never asked for a ride." She fixed her stare on the road. "And my father called my mother by such pet names, yet his expressions were insincere."

"So my actions evoke unpleasant memories." Without thinking, he pulled her close and whispered in her ear, "My apologies, as I never meant to upset you."

"Turn left, please." Gooseflesh covered her arms. "Continue straight until we reach the pond. Then veer right."

"Are you chilled?" He studied the elegant curve of her neck and her fleshy earlobe, which manifested a wicked enticement. Then a gentle breeze carried a subtle lilac scent from her blonde locks to his nose, and he bit back a groan. In search of diversion, he shrugged from his coat, one arm at a time, and draped it over her. "Better?"

"Yes." She stiffened her spine. "Although my shawl sufficed for a stroll, which I would much prefer, if only you would put me down."

"That is not going to happen." He followed her directions and steered his stallion to the west. "So, have you had any luck tracking my pilfered heirloom?"

"Some." A subtle flinch belied her calm demeanor and all but highlighted her internal unrest. "I wager you will celebrate the return of the brooch, soon."

"Oh?" Bloody hell. Prying secrets from her was like peeling a turtle. "Do you know the perpetrators of the dastardly deed, as you sound very certain?"

"I told you before, Portsea is a small community. Everyone knows everyone, here." She hugged her basket to her chest. "And the guilty party meant no harm."

"Do you not reference the thief?" A violent shudder rocked her frame and declared he had scored a direct hit. If he had any doubts to the identity of the bandit, her response had erased them. One of her brother's had stolen the trinket. "Perhaps you are familiar with the villain? Do you intend to protect the scoundrel?"

"He is no scoundrel—and I know not his identity. I spoke in the general sense." She shifted to meet Dalton's stare. "Hunger is rampant, and our townspeople have been forced into desperate circumstances, with most of our able-bodied men at war. But I pled your cause, and the individual will surrender the item in question."

"So you know the criminal, and you are acquainted." It was a statement, not a query. "And you have seen the brooch?"

"Yes—no." Daphne bowed her head. "That is to say, I know of him, of his existence, and I do not doubt his word. What happened is out of character and will not occur again."

"And what of justice?" At her offhand rejoinder, he tamped his temper; else he might frighten the artless girl into silence. "What of the rule of law? I would have the villain arrested."

"You will have your precious keepsake." She swallowed

hard. "Is that not enough?"

"So it would seem, for now." He counted to three. "And what news of your father?"

"I have had none." She sighed. "Draw rein, here."

"Where?" Aside from a rudimentary shack in which he would not stable his horse, as it appeared on the verge of collapse, there remained only an open field. "Are we to walk the rest of the way, to the house?"

"Quiet, Sir Dalton." She handed him the basket, after he disembarked. "This is their home, and they might hear you."

"You can't be serious." He lowered her from the saddle, even as he scrutinized the dilapidated structure. "Are you telling me someone lives here?"

"Yes." She snatched the basket from his grasp. "And I would thank you not to make disparaging comments about our neighbors or their unfortunate accommodations. Not everyone can afford a Mayfair mansion, and if you cannot hold your tongue, then you may wait outside."

Duly chastised, Dalton followed the beautiful governor's daughter on her charitable sojourn, and his respect for her grew by leaps and bounds with each passing hour. At one stop, she washed dishes and swept floors, while he chopped firewood. At another destination, she cleaned and bandaged a wound, as he cleared refuse. But what struck him was Daphne's genuine care and concern for those she considered her responsibility.

No petition seemed too unreasonable, to her. Whatever the townsfolk asked of her, the charming young woman either fulfilled their request or promised to do so, as soon as possible. And the citizens adored the incomparable Miss Harcourt. By the time he steered his mount for Courtenay Hall, with the source of his quandary nestled between his thighs and humming a flirty little ditty, he knew not what to do next.

"It was awfully kind of you to indulge the widow Cartwright's boys." She grinned, as he handed her to the graveled drive. "And I am so sorry little Amy Oldman puked on your beautiful coat, but you were a good sport."

"No worries, as my young niece has done the same thing, on occasions too numerous to count." Without thought or consideration of the consequences, he toyed with a wayward curl and then caressed the crest of her ear. "And I quite enjoyed our day, Miss Daphne."

"As did I." At her brilliant smile, his breath hitched in his chest. "Must confess I have never found my chores so entertaining, as I did in your company. Never would I have guessed you were so handy with an axe, though I feared you might sacrifice a few fingers while you toiled, as you cannot be accustomed to hard labor."

"Very funny." In play, he tapped the tip of her nose. "I would have you know that commanding a ship is no easy task, and I am often required to soil my hands."

"Is that so?" He found her answering giggle far more intoxicating than the most skilled doxy, as he realized, in that instant, he wanted Daphne Harcourt. "Then I suppose you are not interested in joining my family for dinner, tomorrow night, in appreciation of your efforts."

"Now I would not say that." For some unfathomable exercise in foolishness, Dalton bent his head and claimed a quick but lethal buss. Again, to his indefinable confusion, the earth beneath his feet rocked, the world tilted on end, and molten fire scorched a path from his lips to his crotch. When she emitted a soft gasp of surprise, he retreated a step. "I beg your pardon, Miss Daphne, as such behavior is unforgivable."

"Oh, please, do not apologize." With an expression of pure wonder, she touched a finger to her mouth, and the apples of her cheeks flushed a charming rose hue. "I would take it as the height of insult were you to mark my first kiss with an exclamation of regret."

"Your *first* kiss?" For the second time in as many minutes, shock invested his frame. "Do you mean you have never indulged in a bit of harmless love play with the local dandies?"

"I have not." She frowned and thrust her adorable chin. "What do you take me for, Sir Dalton? Let me assure you, I am no woman of loose morals."

"And I never implied such, but—what about when you were a young girl?" Incredulity rattled him to his toes. "Did you not explore any newfound physical urges with someone of similar age?"

"What physical urges?" She blinked, and he reminded himself the governor's daughter was but a backwater lass, reared on an island, no less. "I know nothing of the sort."

"You must have been curious." Stunned by the revelation, and the newfound temptation she manifested, he sputtered and stammered. Then he surmised she joked. "Pull my other leg."

"Pull your leg? Are you mad?" She scoffed and backed beyond reach. "I will do no such thing."

"Relax, as it is a harmless old adage, my dear." Dalton splayed his palms. "It was not my intent to alarm you, but you have addled my brain, given your unexpected, rare, and altogether arresting naïveté."

"Are you complimenting or insulting me, sir?" She gulped. "As I am unsure."

"Believe me, I pay you the ultimate compliment, loveliest Daphne." Never in his life had he possessed carnal knowledge of a virgin, as his tastes leaned toward more experienced territory, but he wrestled with a sudden urge to explore Miss Harcourt's uncharted harbor. "And it would be my honor to dine with you."

"Then we shall welcome you at six, tomorrow evening." She sketched a half-curtsey and then, to his befuddlement and delight, leaped forward, pressed her lips to his with a resounding smack, squealed, and ran into the house. Never had such an innocuous overture impacted him with such fervor, as the cannon in his crotch primed for battle. His ears pealed, like the bells in a Wren steeple, and telltale warmth pervaded his chest. For several seconds, he just stood there, grinning as a giddy schoolboy, for no particular reason. When his stallion whinnied, Dalton jumped into the saddle and steered for the lane.

A side path, which led behind the estate, caught his attention, and Dalton veered to the right, even as he retrieved his lucky coin from his waistcoat pocket and flipped the talisman into the air, as was his way. He kept the horse to a simple trot along the verge and ventured forth, scanning either side of the trail. Soon a rundown barn loomed, and he neared with care, on alert for any possible witnesses. After circling the structure, he dismounted.

What struck him as odd was the fact that no stable hand had appeared. In fact, the outbuilding seemed all but abandoned. Inside, each stall sat empty, devoid of even a scrap of hay. There remained not a single tackle, saddle, or coach, and only one phaeton, dust-covered and marred by a broken spring, parked in the main area.

As he stepped into the sunlight, he gazed at the sky and frowned. "Miss Daphne, your situation is more dire than I had thought."

CHAPTER THREE

alpable silence filled her ears, excepting the repetitive beat of her heart, more deafening than the most ominous clap of thunder or piercing scream. A black chasm encompassed the world, absent any sign of life, save the riveting gold coin, which glowed as a beacon of what she knew not, yet it inspired no fear or trepidation, as it tossed in the air.

Gasping for breath, Daphne lurched upright in her bed, in what had become an all too common occurrence, after napping with the brooch affixed to her dress. As always, the dream gave no hint or clue to the owner of the curious object, other than the respective lore that indicated the item belonged to her one true knight. But how could she solve the mystery? Should she enact impromptu interrogations? Was she to rifle through the pockets of the entire local population of townsmen?

Of course, deep down inside, where she was always honest with herself, she had to admit that only a single prospective suitor had captured her attention, in defiance of the artifact's predictive nature. Although she would deny it, should anyone ask, she had grown fond of the dashing Sir

Dalton Randolph, as never had she met anyone of his stature, and he stirred something within her, something magical, which she could neither identify nor explain.

"Oh, you are awake." Mrs. Jones carried an outdated gown to the foot of the bed. "I mended the sleeves and let out the hem, as much as possible, Miss Daphne."

"What time is it?" Sitting, she stretched her arms over her head and yawned. "It seems as though I slept an eternity."

"You needed the rest, given the amount of work you have assumed." The housekeeper, more a second mother than a servant, smoothed the skirt of her latest alteration. "And it is just after six."

"*What*?" Panic broke the calm, as she scrambled to the floor. "How could you let me linger so long? I want to look my best for our guest, and he will be here in less than an hour."

"That sea captain is a fine, sturdy one." Mrs. Jones chuckled. "They did not make them like that when I was your age."

"Sir Dalton is one-of-a-kind." If she were smart, Daphne would have concentrated her efforts on locating her true knight, but she could not resist the handsome gentleman from London and could only hope she found her fated suitor half so appealing. So she sat at her vanity, picked up her brush, and arranged her hair in her most flattering style. Gazing at her reflection in the mirror, she frowned, as a particular wayward curl refused to cooperate. "And he has been so generous with his time and money, to the benefit of our community, which is why I issued the invitation."

"Then we should endeavor to present him with a most pleasant evening, as well as an elegant escort, in grateful appreciation of his admirable altruism." The housekeeper stood behind Daphne and assumed command of her coiffure. "Lord, but you look more and more like your mother, every day, and she would be so proud."

"Do you really think so?" Daphne sighed, as she pondered how different their situation would have been, had her mother survived the nasty fever she had contracted, while caring for some of Portsea's most unfortunate citizens. "Dear mama, how I miss her."

"There, now." Mrs. Jones yielded the silver-backed brush, folded her arms, and assessed her work. "I don't expect the most expensive stylist could have done better."

"You are a miracle worker." With a quick glance from side to side, Daphne stood. "Oh, if only I could purchase a new dress."

"Why will you not wear some of Mrs. Harcourt's things? We could take them in much easier than altering your old clothes." The housekeeper cupped Daphne's chin. "She would want you to make use of them."

"I know, as yours is a logical suggestion." At the mere prospect, tears welled, and she gulped, as Mrs. Jones loosened the laces of Daphne's morning dress, which slipped to the floor. "But I can't bring myself to do it."

"Then what about the shoes, given yours pinch your toes?" Mrs. Jones frowned. "Do not even try to convince me you are comfortable."

"Everyone must sacrifice something, and my feet pale in comparison with what others have surrendered." With a wiggle of her hips, Daphne shimmied into the unflattering and immature gown. "And mama's slippers are too big— Oh, you removed the ruffles."

"Well, I had to open the seams, so it struck me as an obvious revision." The housekeeper adjusted the collar and grinned. "No one would guess it is but a girl's frock."

"That has to be the sweetest lie you have ever told, old friend." The powder blue satin, with the conservative neckline and passé bodice, screamed youth and innocence. On normal occasions, Daphne bothered not with such shallow concerns, but for the first time in her life, she rued the deficiencies of her wardrobe and struggled with shame. "All right, enough primping. Let us go downstairs and subvert whatever mischief my brothers entertain."

"You should watch Robert, as he does not approve of your alliance with Sir Dalton." Mrs. Jones opened the door, and they strolled into the hall. "And Richard follows his elder brother's example."

"Yes, he does, much to my chagrin. And we cannot risk insulting Captain Randolph, given all he has done for us." She noted the shine on the newel post. "Did you polish the bannister?"

"Hicks did, this afternoon, while I beat the rugs." Mrs. Jones adjusted a stunning arrangement of fresh flowers, which brightened the foyer. "And these arrived only an hour ago. The accompanying card is addressed to you."

"I am sure it is nothing." Daphne ripped the envelope and withdrew a note.

My Dear Miss Harcourt,

Please accept this meager offering to your incomparable beauty, in thanks for the dinner invitation, which I await with baited breath. Until this evening, think of me with fondness, as I shall think of you.

Your most humble servant,
Dalton Randolph

"I wager I was correct in my assumption, regarding the sender?" Mrs. Jones giggled. "As you blush."

"Indeed, they are from Sir Dalton." Daphne's knees buckled, and her fingers shook, as she read and reread the missive. A strange sensation blossomed in the pit of her belly, and a giddy euphoria invested her consciousness, as hope filled her chest. "Mrs. Jones, do you think a worldly man of the sea could ever love a simple backwater girl, blessed with no connections or fortune?"

"I do not see why not." The housekeeper arched a brow. "This is eighteen fourteen, not the Middle Ages."

"But London society lives by its own rules, and it is notorious for its rejection of outsiders that do not conform to its sensibilities." Yet Daphne could not quell the fantasies coloring her vision, no matter how unrealistic. "And Sir Dalton is a knight of the Crown, though I know not in what capacity."

"You care for him." With an expression of utter shock, Mrs. Jones pressed a clenched fist to her breast, and her mouth fell agape. "I had thought you tolerated him, but you have developed a sincere attachment to the captain."

"Yes, I have, but I know not what to do about it." And she had no experience with matters of the heart, beyond the books she had read, thus her current situation prevented her from mingling an illusory fictional existence with a harsh reality. "But since he anchored at Portsea, when I am with Sir Dalton, I feel safe, as though nothing could hurt me, and I dream of that which I never thought possible—a husband, a family, and a comfortable home absent financial worries and the stress of my responsibilities. Am I being silly, Mrs. Jones? Is it wrong to want such things? Am I selfish?"

"Merciful heavens, no." The portly housekeeper wrapped an arm about Daphne's shoulders. "You are the sweetest young woman I have ever had the pleasure of serving, and I will do so, until I die. And Sir Dalton is most fortunate, if he has earned your regard."

"Sir Dalton's coach is just arrived, Miss Daphne." Hicks adjusted his collar, tugged on his sleeves, and straightened his coat. "And everything is in order, per your instructions."

"Wonderful. Open the door, so we might welcome our esteemed guest." She assumed her station in the entryway and noted the empty positions to her immediate right. "Where are my brothers?"

"I am not sure, Miss Daphne." With a mighty frown, Hicks shook his head and twisted the latch. "They have disappeared."

"What do you mean?" With her shoulders rolled back, she lifted her chin and stiffened her spine. "Are they or are they not in residence?"

"I have no idea, Miss Daphne." Hicks set wide the oak panel and stood at attention, just as the graceful equipage slowed to a halt. "When I entered their chambers, Richard and Robert were gone."

"How dare they insult Sir Dalton, after all he has done for us? I shall have words with them, tonight." As the oh-so-dashing sea captain descended the coach, she mustered a smile, although she lamented her appearance, in light of his unrivaled attire. "Mrs. Jones, could you please serve refreshments—"

"I have taken the liberty of arranging a bottle of wine, some cheese, and bread in the back parlor," Hicks said, in a low voice. "Sir Dalton, may I take your coat and gloves?"

"Thank you, Hicks." And then she met her unwitting champion's gaze, which softened whenever he met her stare. "Good evening, Sir Dalton."

"Miss Daphne." As usual, he studied her from top to toe, before taking her hand in his to place a chaste kiss on her knuckles. "I swear you grow more beautiful with each passing day."

"How is it you always know what to say to give me shivers?" Realizing, too late, what she had just declared aloud, she winced and bit her tongue. Had she not always spoken her mind? Yet never had she considered it a curse—until now. "I had not intended to share that bit of information."

"Somehow I guessed that." The incorrigible sailor chuckled and winked. "But let us explore your unutterably charming revelation, perhaps, in your drawing room, as we await dinner?"

"Actually, I had thought we might adjourn to the back parlor, as it is more cozy." And Courtenay Hall no longer included a serviceable drawing room, but she would divulge that regrettable fact over her dead body. So she endeavored to persevere, as she accepted his proffered escort. "Shall we?"

"I see you received my flowers." Sir Dalton arched a brow. "Do they please you, Miss Daphne?"

"You know they do, and thank you." Although Hicks and Mrs. Jones kept the wood paneling and trim polished to a high shine, Daphne wished her refined visitor would not notice the once vivid but now faded and outdated Chintz-style woodblock wallpaper or the tattered Oriental hall rugs. But she had moved the best furnishings that remained in the home to the back parlor, and Daphne and Mrs. Jones had taken the newest drapes and carpets from a long unused guestroom to complete a renovation, of sorts. As they entered the relaxed chamber, she ushered Sir Dalton to the *chaise*. "May I pour you a glass of wine?"

"Only if you join me." After resituating some pillows, he sat. "And what news have you of the brooch?"

"I wondered if you had considered an alternate conclusion to the quest for the missing jewelry." With a courage-bolstering gulp of wine, she perched on the edge of a chair. "Are you certain you did not misplace the pin? Could it not be lost in your cabin?"

"I have made a thorough inspection of my quarters, and the heirloom is gone." He narrowed his stare. "And you gave me the impression you knew the location of the arti-fact, as well as the identity of the thief. Are you changing your story, my dear?"

"I beg your pardon? I have made polite inquiries, and I may or may not know the location of the missing item, but your threat to summon the authorities could complicate matters. And if I am to—" It was then she discovered Sir Dalton's dimpled grin. "You deliberately baited me."

"I did." He snickered.

"But, why?" Inwardly cursing herself, she sought distraction in a bit of cheese.

"Because I enjoy our verbal fencing, Miss Daphne." Leaning forward, he rested elbows to knees. "And your cheeks manifest a tantalizing shade of red. Perhaps now you will tell me about those shivers I give you?"

"I suppose it is too much to hope you might overlook my less than graceful admission." She smoothed her skirt and attempted to ignore his devilish expression. "A gentleman would, no doubt, pretend he had not heard the spontaneous and clumsy confession."

"Not a chance, as I have never claimed to possess such noble characteristics." He laughed when she frowned. "And I shall never forget your disarming disclosure, as I will carry it to the grave and beyond. So let us not avoid the topic foremost on my mind."

"I apologize for my brothers' absence." She adjusted her sleeve, and her thoughts raced to ascertain an escape. "But they are young and spirited, so I am sure you can relate and forgive any unintended slight."

"Oh, I understand more than you realize, and I do not think their slight is unintended, but I find it more amusing than insulting." Dalton shifted his weight. "Now about your shivers—"

"Can we please change the subject?" Once again, quivering in a heady pool of frustration mixed with temptation, Daphne stood and paced before the window. "Diverted by your arrival, I inadvertently made known my unusual affliction, which I had sought to keep secret."

"But you must know that I am not the sort of man with whom you can share such an enthralling detail and possibly expect me to disregard the obvious implications?" His throaty voice enveloped her, as honey on a hot scone. "So I influence you as no other? Has no one else thus affected you?"

"No." Wringing her fingers, she turned to discover herself toe-to-toe with the source of her internal unrest, and she shrieked. But when he set his hands to her waist and pulled her close, she swallowed hard. "Sir Dalton, what are you doing?"

"I thought it evident." He bent his head. "I am going to kiss you."

The prospect defied the limits of sagacity, and Daphne pondered a hasty retreat, yet she held her position. For several seconds, she savored the warmth of his amber gaze, as he had captured her. When he caressed her bottom lip with his thumb, she shuddered.

"Now that is what I was waiting for, and you did not disappoint me." Then he covered her mouth with his, her knees buckled, and he groaned and hugged her close.

Again and again, he sashayed his flesh to hers, in a

sumptuous massage unlike any she had ever known. Her heart pounded in her chest, fire simmered in her veins, an unfamiliar tension tugged at her belly, and she all but melted against his stalwart frame. Licking and suckling, in a playful but tantalizing frolic, his flirty actions bespoke something she could not quite fathom, until she gasped, and he plunged his tongue between her parted teeth, to forge a new and enticing bond, illicit but enthralling. Then, to her shock, dismay, and silent regret, he set her at arm's length.

"Did I do something wrong?" To her infinite embarrassment, she trembled violently.

"No, sweetheart." He drew a handkerchief from his coat pocket and daubed his brow. "Trust me, you did everything right and more than I ever expected."

"Then why did you stop?" She inhaled a shaky breath.

"Because you test my heretofore-vaunted self control, and I am no longer certain of myself." Dalton stepped back, affording additional distance, which she rued. "While I am more than willing to assume the blame for my lack of fortitude, I assert that you also are at fault, as you are dangerous, Miss Daphne Harcourt."

THE DINING TABLE boasted a tattered lace cloth, a hole in his napkin had been mended, and a chip in the china pattern marred his soup bowl. The faded red wallpaper puckered and peeled in random places, and the chandeliers were missing crystal adornments. Never before would Dalton have bothered with such tedium, but he spared no opportunity to glean information about the Harcourts. The less than glamorous service conveyed more evidence of the dire financial straits he suspected had led to the theft of the brooch. But what had happened to the governor?

"I beg your pardon, Miss Daphne." Hicks bowed, and Dalton marked the devoted manservant as the family's chief protector. "But I have located Mister Robert and Mister Richard."

The two lads, one wearing a hat, which Hicks promptly snatched, glared at Dalton, and he just managed to stifle a snort of laughter. Then Hicks shoved the scamps forward. The tallest sibling stared Dalton in the eye, almost daring him to blink. The youngest shuffled his feet, scowled, and pressed his chin to his chest.

"Good evening." Much to his surprise, he had been given the place of honor, at the head, and he stood to welcome the late arrivals. "I am Sir Dalton Randolph. Pleased to make your acquaintance, at last."

"Sir Dalton, these are my brothers, Robert and Richard." With an impressive glower, Daphne rested dainty hands on luscious hips. "And I am certain they regret not being here to welcome you to our home, they are very sorry for their ill-mannered behavior, and they humbly ask your forgiveness. Is that not so?"

"Yes," the gadlings grumbled their response, in unison.

"Then take your seats." With a huff, Daphne returned to her chair.

Just as Dalton had settled himself, he discovered a frog in his lap. "Miss Harcourt, might I trouble you for the salt cellar?"

"Of course." With his lady diverted, Dalton passed the reptile to Robert, who jutted his lower lip, sagged his shoulders, and sighed.

When she passed the silver dish, the uninvited guest

jumped atop the table, and its owner leaped forward, knocking over his glass. "Edwin, come back here."

"Richard, how many times have I told you not to bring your pets to dinner?" Daphne dropped her fork and folded her arms, just as Hicks collected the unique interloper. "I shall speak to you, tonight."

"But Robert made me do it."

"I did not, you little tattletale."

"Why should I take the blame, when it was your idea?"

"Poor bantling."

"*Enough*." Daphne drew a deep breath and cast Dalton a woeful expression. "I am so sorry."

"No apologies necessary, my dear." He winked, in an attempt to allay her concerns. "I pulled similar pranks at their age, and theirs is nothing more than harmless fun."

"Please, do not encourage them." She rolled her eyes. "I have enough trouble managing the boys, when Papa is away."

"I am a man, not a boy." Robert pressed a clenched fist to his chest. "And no one manages me."

"And if you persist in ruining our lovely meal, you may retire to your private apartment with an empty belly." The expression Daphne sported reminded Dalton of his mother. Just when it appeared Richard might protest, she cast her younger brother a lethal stare, which quieted the lad. "Very well. Hicks, you may serve the main entrée."

A tense silence punctuated the dinner comprised of the simple fare of baked ham, boiled potatoes, sliced bread, and gooseberry cheese, from which he constructed a sandwich, save the vegetable. And all the while, he grasped at every conceivable excuse to explore the grand but battered home. The answer to his quandary, when it came to him, seemed so obvious.

"Miss Daphne, I was thinking of your desire to assess the Portsea citizenry, and I may have an elementary solution." He cleared his throat. "And I should be too delighted to assist you, if you are amenable to my plan."

"Oh? That is very kind of you, Sir Dalton." The object of his interest turned to face him. "And I am intrigued."

"Given the hospitality your island community has shown my men, during our unanticipated field refitting, I should like to express my appreciation by holding a country dance. That would give you the opportunity to meet with the townspeople, and we could provide a substantial meal to those who refuse to accept your charity." To avoid rousing suspicion, he had to induce her to follow his lead. "Of course, I know not of any venue that would suit, as the inn has no room large enough to accommodate us. Perhaps it was not a good idea."

"On the contrary, it is a marvelous notion. And Courtenay Hall has a grand ballroom, although it has been vacant for some years." She pushed from the table and stood. "If you would care to join me, I will show you the space."

"If it is not an imposition." A double-door entry on the side wall, which he had not noticed until he followed in her wake, opened to reveal a cavernous chamber. Grasping a candelabrum, he scanned the vicinity and was stunned to discover another gem concealed amid the timeworn structure. "Miss Daphne, this is magnificent."

As was the case with the residence, the ballroom boasted the signature Rococo décor, albeit in much better condition, including mezzo-frescoes reminiscent of Tiepolo, vivid pastorals, and gilt-bronze floor to ceiling mirrors framed with abstract and asymmetrical stuccowork unlike any he had ever seen. But the *pièce de résistance* was a ceiling mural composed of an impromptu outdoor celebration. In the majestic, colorful scene, the gentry frolicked amid the woods, and couples hid amid the trees, engaging in passionate trysts, while chubby cupids flew overhead, firing arrows into a blue sky. For some reason he could not explain, he smiled as he studied the images.

"We held spectacular parties here, before my mother died." With sadness investing her delicate features, Daphne gazed into the darkness and sniffed. "She permitted me to stay up past my bedtime, when I was but ten and six, and I drank my first champagne at one of our galas. Mama always promised me that, some day, I would dance in the arms of my beloved in this ballroom. To know it will never happen just breaks my heart."

"Why so sorrowful, love?" Her despair struck a blow, and Dalton ached to comfort her. "You are young, and it is—"

"Sir Dalton, I asked you not to address me as such, unless you meant it." She thrust her chin, in a now-familiar affectation he found quite endearing, and how he admired her spirit. "It is strange how we covet whimsical dreams and aspirations, far and away beyond the point of madness. Yet we cling to our fantasies, praying for a miracle, which might save us from the cold hard reality of our circumstances."

"Daphne, will you not share your burden?" As he neared the same precipice, the solution to her confounding riddle, he approached with care. "You have my word, as a gentleman, I would do whatever you require. I could write the King and ask to be appointed interim governor, until your father returns."

"Why would you do that, Sir Dalton?" Robert asked. "What do you hope to gain? And what are your intentions, regarding my sister?"

"I believe you misconstrue my motives, lad. So I am prepared to look past the slight." Caught with his hand in the cherry compote, Dalton could only feign innocence. "Given your sister's altruistic proclivities, and your father's unexplained absence, my cause is just, and my aim is true. I wish to maintain order in Portsea, provide protection for your family, and recover the brooch."

"If you contact the King, you could sabotage my sister's efforts to locate your precious heirloom, as you are a stranger in these parts." Dalton had grossly underestimated the elder brother, and Robert evoked comparisons with Dirk. "What would you do then, *Londoner*?"

"I understand." The scamp's tone defined the referenced city as an epithet, but Dalton refused to take the bait. It was then he discovered himself the subject of Daphne's scrutiny. "I could forgo a letter to the Crown, if you permit me the use of your home for the impromptu festivity."

"What have you to offer us, in exchange for our cooperation?" Stiffening his spine, Robert folded his arms. "And who is going to pay for the food, drink, and servants, to tend the guests of your party?"

"You do not presume that I would invite myself into your home and charge you with the costs." Myriad possibilities flooded his brain, but he reminded himself he needed nothing more than the chance to search Courtenay Hall. "I shall cover the expenses, hire additional personnel from the inn, and I can rent the ballroom, if you would but name a price."

"That is not necessary, Sir Dalton." Daphne stood beside her brother, and thus the lines of allegiance were drawn. "You may have the ballroom, *gratis*, in fair trade for your discretion, regarding my father's unplanned leave."

"Perfect." Dalton smiled. "Then we have an agreement."

A SENNIGHT LATER, Daphne skimmed the contents of her armoire and bemoaned the state of her wardrobe, as she did so wish to look pretty for a certain knight. For the past week, she had spent most of her time in the company of Dalton Randolph, preparing for the impromptu gala, and he had spared no expense.

The grand ballroom boasted new Chippendale chairs and matching tables, along with sumptuous velvet drapes. As he had gifted the items to her family, in exchange for the use of Courtenay Hall, she considered the boon a blessing, as she would sell the lot once Dalton had departed Portsea Island. At the thought, tears welled.

"Stop it, Daphne. You could never win his heart." The party started in three hours, and she had not made a final selection from her girlish dresses.

"Miss Daphne, a package just arrived for you." Mrs. Jones strolled into the bedchamber carrying a large parcel, which she placed on the *chaise*. "And here is the accompanying card."

"Thank you." She recognized the bold script with the emphatic flourish beneath her written name and ripped into the envelope. "Oh, what has he done now?"

My Dear Miss Daphne,

It has long been my desire to see you garbed as befits your inimitable beauty. As you have so graciously agreed to act as my hostess, I would reward your gesture with a humble token of appreciation intended to bring a smile to your lovely face.

Your most devoted servant,
Dalton

In utter shock, she dropped the missive, tore the brown paper, lifted the lid, and gasped. The sapphire creation, made of some lush material she could not identify, featured puffed sleeves, a fitted bodice, and a conical skirt. But the signature detail was a diaphanous cream overlay, heavily embroidered with fanciful swirls and embellished with tiny seed pearls, which bedecked the bodice and trimmed the bottom edge of the skirt.

"Mrs. Jones, have you ever seen anything so exquisite?" When Daphne drew the spectacular gown from the bed of cotton, she discovered a pair of matching slippers. "How could he have managed this? And what if they do not fit?"

"I might have helped Sir Dalton with measurements." The housekeeper glanced at the ceiling and clucked her tongue. "He is a persuasive rogue."

"You didn't." Studying her reflection in the long mirror, Daphne held the superb garment, the finest she had ever owned, to her chin and smiled. "Mrs. Jones, I am so happy I could cry."

"Well, do not do that, as you will make your eyes puffy." Mrs. Jones sniffed. "Now let me style your hair, as we require an elegant coiffure to compliment your attire."

In a flash, Daphne plopped into the seat before her vanity and all but shivered with nervous excitement. Mrs. Jones fussed and fretted, as she tarried, arranging Daphne's blonde tresses into loose curls, which framed her face, and a single thick lock traced the curve of her neck and rested at her throat.

"What would I do without you, Mrs. Jones?" Daphne stood and untied her robe. "Now, will you help me into Sir Dalton's magnanimous gift?"

"Of course." With great care, the housekeeper draped

the gown over Daphne's head and shoulders. "Give me a shimmy, my girl."

"The way I did as a child?" Daphne giggled and wiggled her hips, and the skirt dropped into place, with a whispery shush. "Oh, Mrs. Jones. I feel so regal, like a princess."

"Hold still, while I tie your laces." A familiar chorus of grunts and groans signaled the battle had commenced, as Mrs. Jones pulled Daphne left and then right, in an awkward tug of war. "Exhale, Miss Daphne."

"This is so unfair." She hugged the corner of her four-poster. "I wager men have never suffered such degradation in the name of fashion."

"All right." The housekeeper retreated. "Turn around and let me have a look at you."

"What do you think?" Daphne rotated. "Will Sir Dalton be pleased?"

"Perhaps." Narrowing her stare, Mrs. Jones frowned. "Wait right here."

Alone, Daphne stepped into the new slippers, walked to the center of her chamber, extended her arms, and whirled. An imaginary world, straight from a fairy story, material-ized, with brilliant pastorals, azure skies, and mischievous cherubs, as she hummed a little ditty and squealed with delight. When the door opened, she skidded to a halt.

"Did you find what you sought, Mrs. Jones?" Daphne inquired with a hastily mustered air of ennui.

"Yes." The housekeeper loosened the ties of a velvet bag. "I think these will suit the color of your dress."

"Mama's pearls." In a flash, visions from the past composed a staccato of precious moments. Sewing tutori-als, history lessons, lute practice, stillroom organization, and charitable visitation. Her mother had always indulged Daphne's insouciant dreams of independence and then taught her another recipe or household management skill. "Dare I wear them?"

"Mrs. Harcourt always intended you to have them." Mrs. Jones secured the necklace in place, as Daphne donned the matching earrings. "And there is no better time than the present."

"But she had saved them for my wedding day." She trailed her fingers over the delicate orbs. Standing before the long mirror, Daphne did not recognize the woman in the reflection. "Do you think Sir Dalton will find me satisfactory?"

"Oh, I say." Mrs. Jones snorted. "If he can summon a coherent comment, upon spying you, I will eat my old purple bonnet."

CHAPTER FOUR

The sun rested below the yardarm, and Dalton stowed his lucky coin and checked his pocket watch, as the coach halted before Courtenay Hall. As usual, he was punctual. After a quick assessment of his black formalwear, which he had summoned, along with his valet, from London, he descended to the graveled drive and then skipped up the front stairs.

"Good evening, Sir Dalton." Hicks bowed. "Miss Daphne awaits your presence in the ballroom, as we will use the separate side entrance for the guests. If you will follow me, I will take you to her."

"Excellent." For some odd reason he could not fathom, his palms dampened, and his pulse raced. He wondered if Daphne favored the garment he had sent or if he had insulted her with his well-intentioned gift. When he passed through the double doors and spied his lady, he clenched his gut, sucked in a breath, and an invisible but nonetheless potent lightning bolt seared him, on the spot.

"Sir Dalton, how handsome you look." The source of his strange affliction cast him a shimmering smile, and she bestowed upon him a radiant countenance. "And I cannot thank you enough for the beautiful gown."

In that instant, she rotated for his inspection, and the one-eyed marauder below his belly button woke with a vengeance. Numerous polite compliments and even more not-so-nice propositions echoed in his brain, as he fought to maintain composure.

"There, now." The housekeeper, Mrs. Jones, grinned, as she elbowed Daphne. "What did I tell you?"

"It appears your old bonnet is safe." Daphne giggled, but he could make no sense of her statement. "Will you join me, in the receiving line, Sir Dalton?"

"Yes." He shuffled his feet, tugged on his cravat, and cleared his throat. "I-I am fine."

"I beg your pardon?" The stunning Miss Harcourt blinked, as she could not possibly comprehend what she had done to him, and he dared not apprise her. "Are you all right?"

"Where are your brothers?" Until he could marshal his wits and leash the beast, he sought safe harbor in an innocuous subject. "Should we not assume our positions?"

"Yes, as I believe we have our first arrivals." Daphne peered over his shoulder. "Robert, Richard, take your places, and no grumbling."

"We will be but a moment, as I require a word with your brothers." The scamps attempted to evade him, but Dalton splayed his arms. "Gentlemen, this evening is important to your sister, and I will not allow you to spoil it. Robert, if you upset her, in any way, I will box your ears. And Richard, whatever wiggles in your coat pocket had better remain there else I will make you swallow it. Are we clear?"

"Yes, sir," the gadlings replied in concert.

"Wait a minute." Dalton adjusted Richard's neck cloth. "Who taught you to tie a cravat?"

"I did." With a mighty scowl, Robert folded his arms. "And I think it looks fine."

"Well that explains it." Never had he dealt with such unruly delinquents. Dalton gave his attention to the elder sibling and a butchered mathematical. "Yours is not much of an improvement on his."

"What do you care?" As he reworked the yard-length of linen, Dalton met Robert's harsh stare. "And what are your intentions, in regard to Daphne?"

"This is neither the time nor the locale to discuss such matters, and button your coat." And Dalton had no idea how to answer the question, as he had not pondered his fledgling feelings for the governor's daughter. "You will do. Now march, and smile for your sister."

After a lengthy tour of duty at the entrance, welcoming what he presumed was the entire Portsea population, the orchestra, if he could call it that, as it was comprised of an awkward assemblage of resident musicians—again a generous description, struck the signature, if less than graceful, notes of a waltz. And given their brief rehearsal, he could only hope they maintained a consistent rhythm. As prearranged, he claimed his hostess for the evening, to commence the gala.

"Shall we show your neighbors how it is done?" Just the simple practice of anchoring his arm about her waist had Dalton pondering how any man had resisted Daphne, as she manifested a potent combination of innocence mixed with unassuming strength, which could drive a sane man mad as a March hare from an overwhelming desire to possess her.

"I do so wish to make a good impression." With a

glowing expression, she rested her palm on his shoulder, and they clasped hands. "But I am nervous, as I have never danced with anyone but my father."

"Then you may rely on me, as I am an expert." For a scarce second, he doubted her inexperience. Then again, Miss Daphne had spent her entire life, thus far, on an island. "Stay close, my dear."

In that instant, Dalton steered the impeccable backwater lady in what he hoped was the most refined ride of her existence. Around and around, they twirled in each other's embrace, moving as one entity, until he could no longer discern where he ended and she began. Soon they slipped the bonds of the mortal coil and whirled beyond the crowded confines of the palatial ballroom, soaring ever higher. Swathed in an imaginary indigo blanket filled with twinkling stars, and aware of nothing save the constant beat of his heart, he luxuriated in her ocean blue gaze.

And then a pebble struck him in the cheek.

Gritting his teeth, he glanced to his left and discovered her brother Richard, standing at the edge of the dance floor, grinning as he tucked a slingshot into his coat.

"Is something wrong?" Daphne traced circles on the back of his neck. "Did I trounce your toes?"

"No." For several seconds, he studied her plump and rosy lips. "Promise me something."

"Anything, Sir Dalton." All manner of naughty requests echoed in his ears, given her generous offer.

"While I understand you must entertain your guests, I would have you save your waltzes for me, alone." The simple request would raise many eyebrows in London, but they swayed not within the *ton*'s confines, so he would make his own rules. "Will you do that, for me?"

"It would be my honor, Sir Dalton. As nothing would

please me more." Her charming confession, bereft of arti-
fice, warmed him to his toes. "And I have a surprise for
you."

"Then we are of similar disposition, because I have news
to impart." The orchestra segued into another waltz, and he
veered to the right, to evade a prospective interloper, as he
refused to relinquish his bounty. "I am to depart for
Portsmouth."

"What?" Her smile faded, and her chin quivered.
"When?"

"Tomorrow, I am afraid." That afternoon, he had
pondered her reaction to his revelation, and she had not
disappointed him. "I received my orders this morning, and I
am to remove the *Siren* to the naval docks, for additional
repairs."

"So soon?" She bit her bottom lip. "When shall I see
you again, or do you depart for London, thereafter?"

"Once I secure my ship, I plan to return to your fair isle,
but I may be recalled to Greenwich, without warning." And
now he had to divulge the harsh truth and pray she would
not sever all ties with him. "Daphne, given my service to the
Crown, I cannot, in good conscience, abandon Portsea into
your hands, as we are at war, and the situation is dangerous.
In light of the raid on the *Siren*, however unexceptionable, I
must notify the King of your father's absence, and I am
honor-bound to report the theft of the brooch to the
constable."

"But what if you located it?" An underlying flinch
betrayed her discomfit. "Why can you not leave us as you
found us? I would consider it a personal favor."

"Because my allegiance is to His Majesty." How he hated
to discompose her. "But you must not misconstrue my

action as an attack on you and your family, as I seek to protect you."

"By usurping my father's position?" With a half-sob, she squeezed his fingers. "I beg you, do not place us in peril, as you know not the whole situation."

"Would you care to share the circumstances with me?" Just then, he realized the music had ended, and he escorted her to the long dining table, where Mrs. Jones had arranged the refreshments, which Dalton had purchased for the event. "I would very much like to help—"

"Miss Daphne, we are ready." The widow Cartwright clutched his arm. "And Sir Dalton, we have a special seat, just for you."

"By all means, lead the way, Mrs. Cartwright." As Daphne disappeared into the throng, Dalton weaved between the revelers, until the crowd parted, just in front of the orchestra, where a chair had been situated. "I gather this is for me?"

"Indeed, Sir Dalton." The grey-haired widow chuckled. "Miss Daphne has practiced for days, in order to serenade you."

As she settled before the assemblage of musicians, Daphne hugged a lute. For a few seconds, she plucked the strings, and then she glanced at the guests.

"My dear friends of Portsea, I cannot thank you, enough, for your hard work in preparation for our impromptu ball. But I would like to dedicate my performance to the person responsible for this wonderful fête, as it has been far too long since Courtenay Hall hosted a party." And then she fixed her gaze on him. "Sir Dalton Randolph, tonight, I play and sing for you."

What followed her elementary proclamation was the most precious experience of his life. As his lady strummed an exquisite melody, with the expertise of a professional, and intoned the lyrics of love, as a nightingale, in what he suspected was a local folk ballad, he dreamed of her naked, sitting at the foot of his bed, in a private production. He pictured her in the ballroom at Randolph House, entertaining his family and friends. At last, he envisioned her in the drawing room of his Mayfair home, diverting their visitors, while he stood as a proud husband.

That singular thought brought him alert, in a flash.

Perched upright, he focused on Miss Daphne and tried to convince himself she was not so spectacular, as he had believed. He had created her. He had idealized her. He had turned her into a damsel in distress and posited himself as her knight rescuer, in some frivolous romantic notion he neither coveted nor possessed the ability to fulfill, and he cursed himself a fool.

The night's mission charged the fore, and he rolled his shoulders. When Daphne ceased her spontaneous rendering, he stood and clapped, and the gathered citizens lauded her talents with boisterous hoots and hollers. The orchestra screeched the initial hints of a quadrille, and the butcher claimed Daphne as his partner, which provided Dalton the perfect opportunity to instigate his search of the house.

In mere minutes, he spied Hicks poised at the side entry, Mrs. Jones refilled a platter with slices of boiled chicken, Robert groused as the innkeeper's daughter dragged him into the mix, and Richard had scrambled beneath a table and taken aim at another unsuspecting partygoer. So Dalton retreated, slow and steady, to avoid rousing suspicion, until he backed into the main hall.

With nary a witness about, he strode to the drawing room, tossing his familiar lucky coin to ease the tension investing his frame, flung open the doors, and was shocked to discover—nothing. To his inexplicable confusion, the chamber sat empty, bereft of a single stick of furniture or a rug. So he reversed course, scanned the immediate vicinity, and skipped up the grand staircase. On the landing, he snatched a taper from a candelabrum and reconnoitered the second floor, which exhibited decrepit conditions similar to the ground level.

After a quick inspection of the master suites, which appeared to have been vacant for a length of time and further stimulated his curiosity, he learned most apartments mirrored the drawing room's condition. Only three other quarters sported accouterments indicative of the occupant, and Daphne's accommodation rendered him bewildered, as it seemed more accustomed to a young girl of eight or nine, given the profuse pink décor, not a woman of three and twenty.

In haste, he returned to the foyer and traveled the side hall, which led to the study. Ensconced in the man's domain, he rifled through the large oak desk and uncovered an appointment book. Based on the information therein, he discerned the governor had not held a meeting, of any sort, in more than a couple of months. Just as Dalton had opened an account ledger, voices snared his attention. After replacing the items, he closed the drawer and sheltered behind the thick velvet drapery, just as the door creaked.

"Mr. Allen, why have you come here, tonight, of all nights?" In a high-pitched tone, Daphne heralded her distress. "I thought we had an agreement."

"Seeing as how you have the money to throw this big festivity, I figured you could spare me a few extra pounds this month." The blackguard snickered, and Dalton eased back the heavy fabric to catch a glimpse of his lady's tormentor. "And just look at your fancy garb and baubles. Perhaps you have played me false."

"I have done no such thing," she exclaimed. "It is common knowledge Sir Dalton Randolph, of London, funded the gala. The dress was a gift, and the pearls were my mother's."

"No doubt a rich man's whore can afford all manner of luxuries, and he will not miss a few trinkets." The oily bastard sneered. "Or should I apprise the good citizens of Portsea of the governor's debts and true character?"

"How dare you, as I am no man's whore." She thrust her chin, in her usual frank bravado, but Dalton could smell her fear. "And I gave you half my father's stipend at the first of the month, as arranged. If it interests you, I will sell the gown and give you the proceeds."

"And the jewels." The villain approached Daphne, and Dalton almost revealed his presence, but he summoned patience, knowing he could intervene on her behalf, if necessary. "Which I will take—now."

"Get away from my sister." The impetuous Robert charged the field. "If you touch her, I will raise the alarm, and all of Portsea will answer the call."

"And maybe I will tell them of your beloved sire's gambling habit." The sullen Mr. Allen flexed his fists. "I own the governor's markers, and I must be paid, else I will shame your family and foreclose on Courtenay Hall."

"Wait." After a pregnant pause, Daphne sighed and removed the necklace and earrings. "Here, you may take them as additional payment toward the final sum."

"Daphne, no." Robert came to a halt at her side. "We have sacrificed enough to this mongrel."

"But we must settle papa's financial obligations." She leveled a stony gaze on the enemy, and Dalton vowed to aid her, however he could. Had he thought her strong? She was formidable. "Until such time, we will surrender what we must. However, Mr. Allen, if you disparage my father's name, in any way, in violation of our terms, I will consider the matter closed and report your nefarious enterprises to the constable. Do we understand each other?"

"My lady." The scoundrel sketched a mock bow and exited the study.

"What are you doing, Daphne?" Robert raked a hand through his hair and paced. "Why will you not sell Courtenay Hall, and let us leave this place and start anew, somewhere else?"

"Because this is our home, our legacy." With her palms pressed to the blotter, she leaned over the desk. "Mama is buried on this land, along with our ancestors. Would you abandon all that we are, out of convenience?"

"Yet we risk losing everything, if we stay the course." The lad faced his sister. "What of Sir Dalton? Perhaps we could appeal to him—"

"No." She shook her head, and Dalton could only speculate in regard to her refusal. "He departs Portsea, tomorrow. And I would not drag him into this mess."

"But he might help us." The elder brother stiffened his spine. "He seems very fond of you, and I know you are fond of him."

"It does not signify." Daphne glanced toward the window, and Dalton feared, for an instant, she spied him. "Go back to the party, and I shall follow, soon after."

Without a word of protest, Robert abided her request. Alone, as far as she knew, his lady walked to the window, where he hid. Had she glanced to her right, she would have discovered him, but she gave her attention to the world beyond the glass. Then she broke.

"How much more must I withstand?" As she wept, she stared toward the heavens. "Papa, what have you done to us?"

As he observed her anguish, a cold and dull ache pervaded his chest. Each successive mournful sob struck a vicious blow to his heart and mind, and he longed to hold her, to comfort her, to reassure her. And just when he could tolerate no more, she wiped her eyes, turned on a heel, and strolled from the room.

Shaken to his core, he had no idea what to make of recent developments. Yet a few things were certain. Daphne attempted to conceal her father's gambling problem and cover his markers with a local ruffian. Courtenay Hall was in a state of utter disrepair, and her family, entrenched in poverty, bordered on starvation. But one question remained unanswered. Where was Governor Harcourt?

Moving swift and sure, Dalton made for the door and set the oak panel ajar. The hall was empty, so he slipped into the passageway and headed straight for the ballroom. Just as he rejoined the gala, a commotion at the side entry lured the crowd, so no one noticed his abrupt reappearance, and a rush of whispers echoed in the cavernous chamber. Then the revelers parted to reveal a familiar face, and he smiled and nodded a greeting.

Hicks stood tall and proud, and his chest expanded, as he inhaled. "Citizens of Portsea Island, it is my honor to announce his lordship, Dirk Randolph, Viscount Wainsbrough."

THE MOON CAST a silvery glow on the water, which sparkled as a sea of diamonds, as Daphne pushed the small rowboat from the shore. Trepidation danced a jig down her spine, as never had she ventured beyond the coastline on her own, but she had to return the brooch before Dalton moved the *Siren* to Portsmouth, and she refused to implicate her brothers, so she swallowed her apprehension.

She had thought to present the family jewel to its owner, after the celebration, but the arrival of his brother, a viscount, no less, had forestalled her plans. It was past due to face facts. Regardless of her hopes and dreams, she had to accept that Sir Dalton, a member of the peerage, was far above her station and not an option. For the past month, she had lived a fantasy, conjuring various happily-ever-after scenarios, involving the amber-eyed Londoner.

As she rowed toward the majestic ship, which listed gently to and fro with the tide, she scanned the deck for any sign of a watch. Although the dashing naval captain had explained the majority of the tars had journeyed via stage to Greenwich, a skeleton crew would sail the vessel to the navy docks.

To her good fortune, the *Siren's* jollyboats bobbed in a queue just off the mainsail hull. After securing her modest rowboat, she grasped the ship's line and shimmied to the larboard rail. When she gained the deck, she trembled violently, though she knew not why. Hugging herself, she glanced left and then right and discerned no one lurked about the waist.

For a few minutes, Daphne reconsidered her strategy. Perhaps she should have listened to Robert and confessed everything to Sir Dalton. But his unequivocal intent to apprise the constable of the theft had destroyed her fledgling trust in the gorgeous sea captain. She would grieve his departure, but now was not the time for tears, so she would cry tomorrow.

The dark stern companionway encompassed her in palpable fear, as she tiptoed into the bowels of the impressive *Siren*. The vacant galley had her breathing a sigh of relief, so she continued into the commissioned officer quarters. In the wardroom, she toyed with the brooch, tucked safe and secure in the pocket of her breeches, as she sidled toward the captain's cabin.

At the large portal, she placed her hand on the knob, which was cool against her damp palm, and then she paused. Sir Dalton had assured her he would remain at the inn, with his brother, so what had she to worry?

As she inched into the masculine domain, a hint of cigar smoke mixed with a spicy fragrance she could not quite identify. The large chamber, illuminated by the pale blue glow from moonlight filtering through the stern windows, boasted lush furnishings unlike anything she had expected.

A massive desk occupied the premier position along the back wall, and an equally impressive bunk sported the softest sheets, a mountain of fluffy pillows, and a sapphire damask counterpane. A small side room revealed a washstand and a wardrobe, and she stopped to caress a fine lawn shirt.

"Oh, Dalton." To her frustration, tears beckoned. "How I wish the brooch had revealed something—anything of you, as my one true knight. Alas, it is not to be, so I must bid you farewell, yet I would never let go of you, were it my choice."

Wrenching herself to reality, Daphne returned to the desk, given that was where Richard had stolen the artifact. But how should she stage the item, so Dalton would find it before notifying the constable? When she opened the top drawer, she discovered a unique gold seal, fashioned in a wind-star design, engraved with the Latin phrase *Nulli Secundus*, and featuring a grand jewel at the center. Next she located a leather-bound log, and she flipped through the pages, smiling as she recognized his dramatic script. Maps and charts had been tossed inside the compartment, in a haphazard fashion, so she considered it the logical place to restore the heirloom.

"Perfect." With a final assessment of the precious gem, she sighed and placed the antique between stacks of papers. "There. He should have no trouble locating it."

Then she strolled to the bed, picked up a cushion, and buried her face in it. Dalton's scent filled her senses, as she closed her eyes and envisioned him, as he had danced with her. Little by little, she shed the whimsical aspirations that had sustained her since his arrival, as trees drop their leaves in autumn, until nothing remained, except loneliness and defeatism.

As a cold chill nestled in her chest, she resituated the pillow, turned on a heel—and shrieked in horror.

"Well, now." A surly tar rested hands on hips, as he kicked the door shut behind him. "What 'ave we here?"

"I am here to see Captain Randolph." Myriad excuses rendered her dizzy, as she sought a valid defense. "But I seem to have missed him."

"Cap'n has taken a room in town, missy." The stodgy sailor pulled a length of rope from his pocket. "And even without your mask, you look like one of those vagabonds who stole from us, when we first dropped anchor. They had a woman with them. Where are your partners in crime?"

"Wait." In that instant, she recognized the man as the gun-toting mariner, and she seized on the details from the ill-fated invasion. "You are mistaken, Mr. Shaw. I am a friend of Sir Dalton's, and I was to meet him."

"You are not Cap'n's usual fare, and I would know, as I have served him in some capacity for more than ten years." He narrowed his stare. "And how do you know my name?"

"Because I am telling you the truth." She splayed her hands. "I am sorry if I startled you. Perhaps I misunderstood Sir Dalton, and I should contact him at the inn."

"You are going nowhere." Mr. Shaw neared, and she sprinted to the desk. "Come now, dove. Do not make me chase you."

"Keep your distance, sir." When he lunged across the blotter, strewing various items, she leaped beyond reach and sheltered behind a small dining table. An eerie sensation of *déjà vu* shivered over her flesh, and she shuffled free, just as he toppled a chair. "Please, let me go, and I will say nothing."

"Not a chance, as Cap'n bade me guard the *Siren* with my life." Mr. Shaw swerved and blocked her path. "You are my prisoner."

"No." Daphne gulped and ran in the opposite direction. As he pursued her, she knocked over another chair, and Mr. Shaw tripped and fell to the floor. And that was her chance to flee, so she made for the exit, threw open the oak panel, and struck another sailor square in the chest.

"Not so fast, lovey." The cook dropped his now familiar cast-iron skillet and caught her in a bear hug. "What are you doing on the boards, Mr. Shaw?"

"The chit is a fast one." From behind, Mr. Shaw grabbed her wrists. "Hold her, while I bind her for Cap'n."

"I beg you, this is wrong." She squirmed and kicked the cook in the shins. "Unhand me, you brute."

"*Ouch.* And you look like such a nice lady." When she

screamed, he winced. "Hurry up, Mr. Shaw. Before she takes out something important, tie her ankles, too. And use one of Cap'n's cravats to gag her, as I will not listen to her screeching until dawn."

It was then she realized her grave error in judgment. Never should she have ventured to Dalton's ship. Trussed as a Christmas goose, and dying of shame, Daphne wept when the men threw her atop the bunk. But the worst was yet to come, and she struggled against her tethers, as Mr. Shaw laughed.

"That will teach you a lesson, nasty thief." Mr. Shaw snickered and then addressed the cook. "Send Tommy to fetch Cap'n at first light."

CHAPTER FIVE

a s was their custom since they were in shortcoats, and before his elder brother married Rebecca, Dalton and Dirk broke their fast before dawn and set off for an early morning ride. Competitive even in adulthood, they charged along the beach, racing, laughing, and jumping dunes. When the sun peeked over the horizon, Dalton drew reign and pondered his parting words to Miss Daphne.

"The governor's daughter is quite beautiful." Well that comment had come sooner than anticipated. Dirk chucked Dalton's shoulder. "Admit it, you are fond of her."

"What do you know of anything?" He peered at Dirk, who smirked. Dalton rolled his eyes. "Oh, all right. While your ability to read my thoughts remains the bane of my existence, I must confess she is altogether fascinating. And you never told me what brought you to Portsea."

"Can you not guess? I will give you one word." Dirk arched a brow. "Rebecca."

"What—why?" Dalton huffed a breath and shifted in his saddle. "She is not my mother, I am not a child, and I have no need of a nursemaid."

"She was concerned, and you know how my wife worries." Dirk shrugged. "And she is pregnant, so her emotions are on alert for the slightest sign of trouble. You remember what happened when she carried Angeline, so I was reluctant to leave her, but she insisted I check on you."

"Have the nightmares returned?" Dalton glanced at his sibling and frowned. "You do not have to answer that question."

"It began just after we found out she increases with what she insists is my heir. She wakes in the middle of the night, screaming in terror. Dr. Handley supposes her condition stimulates vivid recollections of her imprisonment, as she lost our first child, in captivity." Dirk lowered his chin and shook his head. "If I could kill Varringdale again, I would do so, if only to give her peace."

"I am so sorry, brother. As this should be a happy occasion." At one time, Rebecca served the Counterintelligence Corps as the spy, *L'araignee*, the spider. Dirk met her, when he was tasked with her safe passage to England, after her partner in espionage was murdered. After a surprise attack rendered Dirk wounded and incapacitated, Rebecca led their assailants on a merry chase, before she was apprehended, tortured, and left for dead. "But to be honest, I still suffer the odd hideous dream of Varringdale's sadistic chamber of horrors and how we located her."

"So do I." Dirk rubbed the back of his neck. "Yet I would have no other, as I love my Becca, to distraction. But I suspect she hides something from me, some hellish detail of her ordeal she does not want me to know."

"To what purpose?" Dalton considered the possibility and shuddered, as what he knew of her misery was bad enough. "What could she hope to achieve?"

"Who can say, for certain, how the female mind works?"

Dirk scratched his temple. "But I think she withholds information in the misguided but well-meaning attempt to spare
me additional distress, regarding her trauma. In short, she
does not wish to cause me pain, yet I believe her refusal to
reveal the full extent of her experience festers as an open
wound and fosters renewed torment."

"Have you talked to her about it?" He swallowed hard,
as he remembered discovering Rebecca's torn and bloody
riding habit. "She may confess everything, if you confront
her."

"Would you treat my wife thus, given your knowledge of
what she endured?" Dirk cast a menacing expression. "She
will tell me when she is ready. Until then, I will indulge her
every desire, as I owe her my life, and I am nothing without
her."

"My apologies, brother." Dalton gazed at the clouds, as
he had on the cliff that terrible day. "Dr. Handley
confirmed, based on her injuries, the beating and the starvation. And we found her chained to a pike, on the shore,
almost drowned. That she may have survived even worse—
I cannot fathom it. I do not want to fathom it."

"Neither do I." A gull keened in the distance, and Dirk
pointed at the bird. For a long while, they simply sat in
companionable silence. "I have never shared with you what
flashed before me, what ravaged my innards, as I stood on
the precipice, overlooking the ocean, having just realized
Rebecca was, for all intents and purposes, dead. In those
few excruciating minutes, I thought my world at an end, as I
could see no future without her in it. The loss, the inde-
scribable agony was more than I could bear. When I
crawled to the edge of the escarpment, I had planned to—"

"No." He wanted to cover his ears against the harsh

truth his sibling, the lone person Dalton had always admired and emulated, had imparted. "You are the strongest and best man of my acquaintance, and you will never convince me otherwise."

"You mistake my aim in apprising you of these events, little brother." Dirk sighed and then smiled. "I want you to understand that nothing compares to what I enjoy with my bride and our daughter. What I found with Rebecca—there are no words to adequately relate what we have, but I can only pray you find a woman of such estimable qualities, so you may know how it feels to exist as something more than yourself, to prevail as partners, as lovers, and as friends. I want that sort of deep, abiding devotion for you."

"Me, too." Dalton compressed his lips and pictured Daphne. "And it will happen."

"When you least expect it." Dirk chuckled. "And you will wonder what you ever did without her. Now, shall we journey to the inn, as you must move the *Siren* to Portsmouth, and I should like to depart for London, as I am anxious to return home."

"Of course, brother." Dalton heeled the flanks of his stallion.

"And what are your intentions, in regard to Miss Harcourt?" Dirk averted his gaze. "As you could have assigned the requisite duties to your first mate, so I gather you wish to remain here for other reasons."

"As I informed you during breakfast, she is in trouble." And her predicament had kept him awake most of the night. "And I must discern the governor's whereabouts. Given the Treaty of Fontainebleau, Napoleon's exile to Elba, and our recent orders to stand down, I thought I could be of assistance."

"You could leave such business for the constable to investigate." Dirk's accompanying grin belied his seriousness, as they galloped down the lane. "There is no need to take personal involvement in their private matters."

"As I have nothing better to do, I disagree." And he would never hear the end of it. Braced for all manner of ribbing, he had not long to wait.

"I am sure you do, but can you explain your rationale?" Dirk inquired, with a snort. "As I am sure you are not the only one capable of aiding the damsel in distress, though you may be the most bumptious."

"No." Dalton groaned. "But if I think of a reason, you will be the first to know it."

Dirk burst into laughter, just as they reigned in and stopped before the inn.

"Cap'n, I have urgent news from Mr. Shaw." Tommy, the carpenter's mate, made his obedience. "He asks you to return to the *Siren*, at once, sir. We caught a thief."

MAD AS A HORNET'S NEST, Dalton boarded his ship, with his brother in tow. Problem was he knew not who had angered him more, Daphne or Mr. Shaw. While he had his suspicions, regarding Miss Harcourt's second assault on the *Siren*, he could not begin to comprehend the first mate's decision to imprison her as a common criminal.

"Cap'n." Mr. Shaw saluted. "She is locked in your cabin, sir. And she is bound and gagged."

"What?" Dalton halted in his tracks, as seething ire poured through his veins. Without warning, he lunged and grabbed fistfuls of the first mate's shirt. "I ought to keelhaul—"

"Easy, brother." Dirk intervened and separated Dalton from Mr. Shaw. "Let us check on the lady, and then you may kill your first mate."

"Right." After flinging aside Mr. Shaw, Dalton charged down the companionway toward his quarters. Guarding the door, a young tar glanced at Dalton, jerked, saluted, turned the key, set the oak panel wide, and retreated a safe distance.

He had expected a hailstorm of curses intermingled with feminine sobs of lament. Instead, the room was quiet. Lying in his bunk, a sight that should have summoned bawdy innuendos and salacious images, Daphne slept on her side, but he could muster nothing more than gut-wrenching remorse, as he assessed her condition.

As he perched at the edge of the makeshift bed, he discovered her tear-stained cheeks, but it was the bloody, raw skin on her wrists and ankles that left him gritting his teeth, especially when he noted she wore the slippers he had gifted her, after Mrs. Jones apprised him that all of Daphne's shoes were too small.

"Fetch some fresh water and bandages." Dalton pressed a clenched fist to his mouth. "And have cook prepare a pot of tea—she prefers the Indian blend, and a light repast."

"Aye, sir." Mr. Shaw all but ran from the chamber.

"You should wake her, before you release her." Dirk produced a knife, which he gave to Dalton. "Else you risk frightening her."

"I would prefer to untie the gag, first." Dalton grasped the knot and attempted to loosen the linen.

With a violent flinch, Daphne came awake. Wide-eyed and shivering, she bucked as an unbroken horse and mumbled incoherently. How his heart ached, when he spied the sheer terror in her gaze. As Dalton tried to hold her still, she wriggled and kicked.

"Easy, love." He splayed his palms. "I am not going to hurt you. I only want to cut your bonds, and then we will talk."

When he approached, she recoiled, and he paused. After he displayed the blade for her inspection, she nodded once. Dalton reached behind her head and severed the cravat. He had anticipated a sharp rebuke delivered in her customary haughty tone, but she just whimpered, as he removed the ropes. Then he drew her into his lap and held her, as she wept and trembled without restraint.

Mr. Shaw reappeared, bearing a tray with an ewer of water, a towel, and some rolled cotton. "Shall I tend her, Cap'n?"

"No." At that instant, Daphne sobbed and clung to Dalton. "I will care for her."

"Beg your pardon, sir." The first mate situated the tray on the bunk and shuffled his feet. "I had no idea—"

"Get out." Dalton snatched a cloth, wet it, and pressed it to Daphne's wrists, and she winced. "I know it burns, but I need to clean your wounds."

"Let me help." Dirk knelt and treated her ankles. "Have you any salve, else the bandages will stick to her flesh?"

"Top right drawer of my desk." At last, he could bear no more of her torment, so he tipped her chin and covered her lips with his. It was a kiss meant to comfort, not to arouse, and he licked and suckled her tender flesh until she relaxed in his arms and ceased shuddering. When he lifted his head, Dalton found himself the subject of intense scrutiny, as Dirk stood there, mouth agape and brows cocked in surprise. "Not a word, brother."

"I shall be as quiet as the grave." But Dirk's smile declared what he had not stated, as he rubbed the balm to her injuries. "For now."

"Better?" He caressed her cheek and then smeared ointment on her wrists, which he swaddled. "Are you hungry, love?"

"Yes." When she rested her head to his chest, he lifted her in his arms and carried her to the table. With his foot, he pulled out a chair and then sat, again cradling her in his embrace. After pouring a cup of tea, he held it for her. "Here, sweetheart. Take a sip."

"Oh." She tensed and brought her shaking fingers to her chin. "My jaw is sore."

"Go slow." And with that, Dalton proceeded to feed her bites of fruit, scrambled eggs, and toast, suffering her groans of discomfit as vicious marks on his conscience. All the while, he fought to ignore Dirk's ever-present perusal. "I am so sorry, Daphne. Never did it occur to me that my men could be such bloody idiots."

"But it is my fault." She scooted from his hold and walked to the stern windows. "I should not have come here."

"Why did you raid my ship a second time?" To calm his frayed nerves and ease the tension investing his shoulders, Dalton toyed with his lucky coin, which he pulled from his pocket and tossed into the air. "You knew I remained at the inn."

"I wanted to return the missing brooch, which I tucked in the center drawer, between your maps and charts." With her arms wrapped about herself, she emitted something between a sob and a sigh. "I had hoped you would not notify the constable."

"You lost Lady Amanda's family heirloom?" Dirk inquired with an air of incredulity, as he located the priceless heirloom. "I would not want to be in your boots when you tell the admiral."

"He did not lose it." Daphne peered at Dirk. "My younger brother Richard stole it, so we might sell it to purchase food, as we are starving."

"Daphne, I know of your financial difficulties, as there is talk in the town, but I have no idea how you arrived at such dire straits." At long last, Dalton hoped to learn the truth of her situation, as he stood. "Where is your father?"

"Papa is—" Slowly, she rotated to look at him. Stockstill, Daphne clutched her throat, her face paled, and she swayed. Then she launched herself at Dalton, and he almost toppled to the floor. Hugging him at the waist, she squeezed hard. Before he could respond, she wrenched free and snatched his talisman from his grasp. "This is yours?"

"Aye, but it is hardly fit for a young lady of character." When she studied the crude sexual depiction, appropriately engraved on the tail end, he shifted his weight and prayed Dirk would forgo a witty rejoinder. To Dalton's relief, his brother pretended an interest in the timbers. "You should not view such things."

"What is it?" She traced the jagged edge with her fingertip. "Never have I seen anything of its nature."

"I should think not, as it is a Roman brothel token." Most women would have been shocked by the purposive nature of the piece, but Daphne seemed intrigued, and he could make no sense of her fascination. "Wealthy men purchased them to exchange for the particular service depicted thereon."

"Where did you get it?" She flipped the gold coinage in her palm. "Is it rather commonplace?"

"I found it on the banks of the Thames, during a particularly dry summer, when I was but a lad." Dalton thought her an enigma, but her behavior well nigh stupefied him. "And it is very rare, as I have never seen its equal."

"I should have known." She sniffed and then laughed, shaking her head. "I should have doubted you not, but I was afraid."

"I wager I am partly to blame for that." He glanced at Dirk, who simply shrugged. "Will you trust me, now? I give you my word, as a gentleman, I only wish to help you."

"Well, of course, you do." How she glowed when she gazed at him. "And I should have given you a chance, as even my brother Robert suggested I rely on you."

"Then you will confide in me?" Dalton stepped in her direction. "You will disclose your secrets?"

"Yes." She nodded once and mirrored his moves. "My parents tolerated each other, but their marriage was plagued by friction, much of which resulted from my father's predilection for drinking, gambling, and loose women. We bore the toll of his questionable conduct, but none more so than my mother."

"My dear, I am more sorry than I can say." He inched closer. "And I admire your courage, in the face of such adversity. So what happened to the governor? Has he run from his responsibilities, given your circumstances are grave?"

"The situation is grim, as once mama died, papa indulged his iniquitous proclivities to excess." When he flicked his fingers, she strolled into his waiting embrace, without hesitation. "I managed, as best I could, but my father amassed a mountain of debt, and he owes substantial markers to a local reprobate. In desperation, I bartered precious personal effects for added income, but I could not keep pace with papa's arrears. I sold most of the furnishings from Courtenay Hall and released a large portion of our staff, to pare down our expenses, which is why I never received you in the drawing room, as it is empty."

"I gathered as much." Lamenting the difficulties she had endured, Dalton speared his fingers through her hair and gave her a gentle nudge. "In light of what you have just revealed, you truly are my brave little thing."

"I do not feel so brave," she replied, in a small voice. "Because I am scared."

"Darling Daphne, at last, I understand the extent of your burden." In truth, his heart bled for her. "But you need not fret, as I am not going anywhere until the governor returns, and we settle his affairs to my satisfaction."

"But that is not possible." She burrowed to his chest.

"Why?" Dalton glanced at Dirk, who frowned. "Has he abandoned his family?"

"No." She shifted to meet his stare, and a tear trailed her cheek. "My father is dead."

WHAT A RELIEF it had been to share her troubles, as well as her grief. As the viscount's posh traveling coach slowed to a halt before Courtenay Hall, Daphne glanced at Dirk, who winked just then. In that moment, she decided she liked him, despite their brief acquaintance. Sitting beside her, and holding her hand, Dalton remained quiet, and what she would have given to know his thoughts.

For a scarce second, she had considered apprising him of the brooch's revelation, but how would he have responded? Inside, she danced a jig, and it was all she could do not to bounce in the squabs. For good or ill, Sir Dalton Randolph of London was Daphne's one true knight, according to the curious bauble's associative lore. And while she had never put much faith in what she had previously deemed superstitious endeavors, she pinned her future on the artifact's mystical powers.

When a footman opened the door, Dirk exited, followed by Dalton. Then her gallant savior turned to lift her to the graveled drive. Hicks appeared at the front entry, and soon Robert and Richard sprinted to the fore.

"Where have you been?" Robert grabbed her by the shoulders, shook her twice, and then hugged her. "God, Daphne. I thought the worst."

"What did you do to my sister?" At her left, Richard kicked Dalton in the shin. "If you hurt her, I will kill you."

"Easy, pup." Dirk yanked Richard by the shirt collar. "We are not your enemies."

"Undisciplined gadabout." With a wicked grimace, Dalton massaged his offended appendage. "I ought to heat your posterior." To Dirk, Dalton said, "You have no idea of the amount of trouble these two are capable of causing."

"Oh, no." Dirk glanced at the sky. "I would have no idea."

Richard waved a clenched fist. "You try it and—"

"Boys, please." She wagged a finger in warning. "Richard, behave yourself."

"Miss Daphne, you gave us such a fright." Mrs. Jones wiped a stray tear. "What happened to you?"

"Let us gather in the back parlor, and I will explain everything." To the housekeeper, Daphne smiled and said, "Will you prepare tea and refreshments for our guests, while I change clothes?"

"Of course." Mrs. Jones curtseyed and ushered everyone down the hall. "Gentlemen, please follow me."

In the foyer, Dalton lingered and caught her about the waist. "Are you all right, sweet Daphne?"

"I assure you, I am fine." When he bent his head, she

lifted her chin, met him halfway, and kissed him, as she gazed into his amber eyes. "And even better, now."

"There's a girl." He claimed another quick buss. "You are an extraordinary woman, Miss Harcourt. More so than I had realized."

"Thank you, Sir Dalton." She leaped and smacked her lips to his, before sprinting upstairs, and he chuckled in her wake.

In her private apartment, she kicked off her slippers, wiggled out of the breeches, and doffed her lawn shirt. At her armoire, she opted for the same pale yellow morning dress she had worn the day she met her one true knight. At her vanity, she loosened her topknot and brushed her thick locks, as she wanted to be pretty for her dashing protector.

"Miss Daphne, let me help you." Mrs. Jones rushed into the chamber. "Your young man just told us a hair-raising tale. What on earth possessed you to undertake such an adventure on your own?"

"You know, very well, I had to return the brooch." She adjusted the bandage on her wrist. "And I could not, in good conscience, involve my brothers."

"But you could have enlightened me or Hicks." Mrs. Jones scoffed. "What if you had an accident, fell out of the boat, and were swept to sea?"

"You could have done nothing to prevent it, and your concern is unwarranted." Daphne revisited Dalton's tender care, when he found her in his bunk. "As the oldest in this family, it was my responsibility to restore the antique to its rightful owner."

"And now it is done." Mrs. Jones pinned an unruly curl into place. "So why are Sir Dalton and the viscount here? What do they want with you?"

"I am not entirely sure." Daphne assessed her appearance. "Let us join them and find out."

Retracing her steps, she turned right in the foyer and strolled down the hall. When she entered the morning room, Dalton and Dirk stood. In silence, she strolled to the tea trolley, poured a cup of the steaming brew, and claimed a seat on the *chaise*.

"Your brother tells me he wishes to enlist, and his is a noble cause." The viscount rubbed his chin. "Given his age, it would be to his credit to purchase a commission, without delay."

"How, when we have no money?" Daphne glared at Robert, as he had just compounded her shame. "It is all I can manage to keep food on our table."

"But your plan is entirely unrealistic." Robert slapped his thighs and stood. "We cannot conceal our plight for another two years, and even if we could, there is no guarantee the King would appoint me governor. Plus, Harold desires the position, as well as your hand in marriage."

"That I will not accept." To her relief, Dalton moved to sit beside her, as she needed his strength. "You deserve a man who cares for you, not for the office."

"But Harold is a Harcourt." She pondered the possibility, as she counted her cousin a friend. "And Harcourts have presided over Portsea Island for centuries, yet I had hoped you would follow in father's footsteps."

"While I loathe disappointing you, I must admit I covet other aims, Daphne." Robert folded his arms. "I wish to join the military, and I have made no secret of that desire."

"Your brother is right." The viscount compressed his lips. "While I admire your dedication to duty, the King must be apprised of your father's demise."

"Is there not some other way?" She wrung her fingers.

"And what of Courtenay Hall? This is our home, and we have nowhere to go."

"Excuse me, Miss Daphne." Hicks cleared his throat. "But Mister Harold Harcourt is just arrived. Shall I show him to the study?"

"No." Dalton took her hand in his and squeezed. "Bring him in, as he may help us resolve some of our quandary."

"Very good, Sir Dalton." Hicks dipped his chin.

"Oh, no." She tensed, as that was the last thing she needed. "What is he doing here?"

"I sent my man for him, as your relation may settle part of your problem, and we have no time to waste." Dalton massaged her knuckles with his thumb, and she relaxed, to a degree. "Worry not, as I promised I would not abandon you."

"All right." Swallowing her trepidation, she reminded herself he was her one true knight. Then she leaned close and whispered, "But I am still afraid."

"Forgive my informal attire, Viscount Wainsbrough." Harold loomed in the entrance and bowed. "I was inspecting a bridge on the south end of my property and only just received your summons. Thought it best to ride straight here, as you said it was urgent."

Dirk and Dalton stood to exchange pleasantries.

"That was very kind of you." Dirk glanced at Mrs. Jones and nodded. "May we offer you a spot of tea?"

"No, thank you." Harold hitched his breeches and eased to the sofa. "Must confess I am rather curious, as your vague note conveyed little information, but I suppose it safe to presume it has something to do with Governor Harcourt's whereabouts."

"Father is dead." Robert draped an arm about Richard's shoulders, and her youngest brother stared at the floor. "I found him in the rose garden, face down, over a month ago. We had thought him merely unconscious from too much drink, which was not uncommon. But he had an empty bottle of laudanum in his clutch, so we suspect he abused the substance to his own end."

"Bloody hell." Harold snapped to attention and met her gaze. "Daphne, why did you not tell me?"

At seven and twenty, and the eldest of four, Harold had always been a cherished and reliable friend. With bright blue eyes, sandy brown hair, and a sturdy frame, he was the catch of Portsea Island. What girl had not fancied herself his bride? In short, none but one, as Daphne had never considered her cousin anything more than a lifelong chum.

"I did not wish to burden you, Harold." The expectant shame threatened to overwhelm her. "And I could not risk your reputation, should our situation erupt in scandal."

"But we are family." Resting elbows to knees, Harold leaned forward. "And our parents presume we shall wed, so you have should have known you could rely on me."

"Harold, any woman would count herself fortunate to have you as her husband." She swallowed hard.

"But not you." Her cousin smiled. "May I ask why you refuse my suit?"

"Because you love Ellen, the butcher's daughter, and everyone knows it." For the second time that day, she spilt one of her closest guarded secrets, and it was such a relief. "I could not, in good conscience, allow you to sacrifice yourself for my benefit."

"Given we speak candidly, you should know the townsfolk are aware of your father's less than virtuous habits, as well as your role in governing Portsea." With a sigh, Harold shook his head. "You have assumed responsibilities that were not yours to carry, and your character does not hinge on your father's, God rest him. Know that whatever you decide, I will support you. And if you require my pledge, I will marry you, Daphne. Although my heart belongs to another, we would get on well, you and I. Never would I treat you as your father dishonored your mother."

"She will not call upon you to meet that obligation," her true knight declared in an acerbic tone. Was it her imagination, or had Harold annoyed Dalton, somehow? "But I would have my brother write the King and ask to have you appointed interim governor, if that is amenable to you."

"Sir Dalton, nothing would please me more." Harold shifted his weight. "But what of Courtenay Hall and the governor's debts?"

"You know about that?" In that moment, her heart fractured.

"Dear Daphne, you know, very well, that Portsea is a small community." Harold cast an expression of pure sympathy. "The more apt question is who is not aware of your financial difficulties."

"Oh, no." Despite her hard work, her family name had been ruined. "Then all is lost, and we are paupers, in every respect."

"No, darling." Dalton gave her a gentle nudge. "All is not lost."

"Have you any claim to Courtenay Hall?" Dirk inquired. "Or do the standard rules of primogeniture and entail apply to the estate?"

"No, sir. While Courtenay Hall has persisted as Portsea's seat of governance, there are no entailments, to my knowledge, in regard to the inheritance." With a nod to Robert, Harold rubbed his chin. "The property, and its accrued arrears, passes to the oldest son."

"So we need only contrive a plausible explanation for

Governor Harcourt's extended absence and announce his demise." The viscount stood and paced. Then he halted and peered at Dalton. "Damian's ancestral pile is not too far. We could circulate rumors of the governor's visit to Penhurst, along with a mysterious illness. After a suitable period, Harold could post news of the death."

"Who is Damian?" As Daphne pondered their machinations, fear knotted her belly. "And can we trust him?"

"The Duke of Weston." Dirk ticked off an imaginary list on his fingers. "To us, he is a brother, and I would trust him with my life."

"A duke?" Harold's brows almost reached his hairline. "Oh, I say. Daphne, do not argue."

"Dirk, I would ask a favor." Dalton tugged at his cravat, and she wondered at his purpose. "While I know you wish to return home, I would prefer you remain here, for an additional two days. In that time, I shall remove the *Siren* to the naval yard at Portsmouth and transfer supervision of the repairs to my first mate. If you could pen a missive to His Majesty, supporting Harold's promotion to the office, dispatch young Robert in my coach to the War Office, with a commission sponsorship, and review Courtenay Hall's accounts, I shall rejoin you, whereupon we will journey to the city, with Miss Harcourt."

"What?" Daphne leaped to her feet. "Why must I leave my home? And what of Richard?"

"Richard will stay here, with Hicks and Mrs. Jones to guard him." Dalton caught her in his sights, and his unmasked determination gave her a shiver. "And you need a husband—a simple, dull, uninspired fellow with an ocean of patience and deep pockets. There is no better place to find such a creature than the marriage mart, which does a brisk business in the ballrooms of the *ton*, as the Season is in full swing."

And just like that, Daphne Harcourt, backwater girl, pondered an impending trip to that magical, mythical place known as London.

CHAPTER SIX

A smattering of buildings declared they neared the heart of the British Empire, and Daphne kept her nose pressed to the glass, as she fidgeted with excitement. Soon the landscape yielded to clusters of structures, until the crowded streets of the city consumed the view beyond the windows. And while he found her delight infectious, all Dalton could wonder was what had possessed him to bring the delectable provincial to London.

"I shall drop you at your bachelor lodgings." Dirk adjusted the lace trim of his sleeve. "And then Miss Harcourt and I will continue to Randolph House."

"But Daphne is staying with me." Yes, he knew it was wrong, but Dalton could not bear to let her out of his sight. "I promised Robert I would care for her, so she is my charge."

"That is out of the question." His stuffy elder brother gave Dalton *the look*, which conveyed a wealth of recriminations and reproaches he knew too well. "You cannot quarter an un-chaperoned, unwed woman of character. It is not done. And I doubt her sibling intended you to share your residence with her."

"But these circumstances are unusual, and I shall hire a lady's maid." Numerous justifications danced in his brain, but the simple fact was he wanted Daphne at his side. "As she has no acquaintances in town, what objection could you have?"

"Do you want the long or the short list?" Dirk arched a brow. "You know better, brother."

"Have I a say in the matter?" the source of his discomfort inquired.

"No." What was he doing? Why could he not leave her at Dirk's doorstep, so Rebecca might find Daphne a husband? Were he smart, he would abandon her to his sister's care and resume his rakish endeavors. "And there will be no more discussion."

As the coach slowed to a halt before Dalton's Mayfair residence, Dirk mouthed, *Bad form*.

Anxious to avoid an upbraiding, he had not waited for the footman to open the door. Instead, Dalton jumped to the sidewalk and turned to assist Daphne. After a quick check of the vicinity, he ushered her up the entrance stairs and into the foyer.

"Have Miss Harcourt's trunk conveyed to the red room," Dalton instructed his butler. "And have cook prepare an early dinner, as we are hungry."

"Yes, sir." Merton bowed and then rushed to fulfill the requests.

"What is the red room?" The picture of innocence, Daphne blinked. "And are you certain I should reside here, with you?"

"Right now, I am certain of nothing." At a loss to explain his behavior, Dalton grabbed her hand, dragged her down the side hall, and hauled her into his study. After he poured two balloons of liquid courage, he offered her a glass, which he clinked with his. "Here is to your health."

"And the same to you." Then she sipped the amber intoxicant and choked violently.

"Are you all right?" He patted her back. "Are you ill?"

"No." She cleared her throat. "I have partaken little brandy, so I am unaccustomed to it. It is quite different from wine, and it burns."

And there it was—her naïveté on full display, which he could not ignore. In search of relief, he downed the contents of his snifter, snatched hers, emptied it in a single gulp, snared her by the wrist, and retraced his steps. In the foyer, he veered right and led her upstairs. At the landing, he steered left and strolled into what he had hastily designated her chamber.

To his surprise, she wriggled free, so he released her, and she moved to the center of the opulent apartment. Garbed in a lavender frock, which he had purchased from a boutique in Portsmouth, she looked out of place in her accommodation, which sported a bold crimson décor, adequate to its primary use. Circling slowly, she studied her surroundings, and the stark contrast between her innocence and the immorality that had occurred in the bed, which loomed as a lascivious backdrop, struck him between the eyes.

The previous November, during a rare instance of sheer depravity, after an evening of heavy drinking, he had done something terrible, something appalling. He had engaged in conduct that would shame his mother, embarrass his brother, and scandalize his entire family, were it known throughout society. Worse, it could cost him Daphne. It had not been a proud moment.

"Sir Dalton, I hope you do not think me ungrateful, but I would prefer to consider the viscount's generous offer." When she peered at the four-poster, she gulped and then frowned. "As I do not wish to inconvenience you, and you seem unprepared for guests."

"Perhaps you are right." He speared his fingers through his hair. "I can summon—"

A commotion downstairs gave him pause. Dalton stomped to the landing, with Daphne in his wake, just as Rebecca stormed into the foyer.

"Where is she?" Dirk's wife inquired of Merton. "What has he done with her?"

"I beg your pardon, your ladyship." The butler bowed. "To whom do you refer?"

"Who is that woman?" With a half-smothered shriek, Daphne yanked hard on his coat sleeve. "And what is she to you?"

"There you are." At that second, Rebecca came alert. As she ascended the stairs, on a wave of high dudgeon that bespoke trouble, she cast an expression of molten ire. "You ought to be horsewhipped."

Had he thought the circumstances grim? It had just gone from bad to worse. There was no escape, so he sought to spike the former spy's guns, as he tugged on his cravat.

"Miss Daphne Harcourt, may I present my sister-in-law, Lady Rebecca, Viscountess Wainsbrough." Then he braced for the assault. "Becca, this is Daphne."

"How are you, poor dear?" Rebecca embraced the governor's daughter. "Dirk told me of your misfortune, and I am so sorry for your loss." And then she caught Dalton in her sights. "How can you possibly think it acceptable to board an unmarried woman of character in your bachelor lodgings?"

"Do not claim I did not warn you." Dirk chuckled, as he neared. To Rebecca, he said, "Shall I have Miss Harcourt's things conveyed to our coach?"

"Please, do so, as she will reside at Randolph House for the duration of her London stay, and I shall brook no refusal." With an arm draped about Daphne's shoulders, Rebecca returned to the foyer. "I have all sorts of events planned, and tomorrow you will meet our extended family, at a special dinner I shall arrange, to welcome you to the city."

"I hope you have not gone to too much trouble, on my account." Daphne glanced over her shoulder, with a countenance of utter helplessness. "And it is wonderful to make your acquaintance."

"What did I tell you?" Dirk arched a brow, as he elbowed Dalton. "My wife has a habit of deciding, for herself, what is or is not appropriate, and you would be wise not to challenge her, as she is bloody formidable when she sets her mind to something. Now help me fetch the lady's belongings."

"Could you not have forestalled her intrusion, as this is a private matter?" Dalton clutched the handle at one end of the trunk, while his brother perched at the opposite side, and together they hoisted the old chest. Yet, even as they exited what Dalton had come to deem a garish dwelling, he knew Rebecca was right. "What am I to do, brother? As I am at sea, and nothing makes sense."

"You find yourself in a quandary, when it comes to the impeccable Miss Harcourt?" Dirk smiled, as they descended the stairs. "She muddles your thoughts?"

"Daphne muddles everything." Outside, Dalton relinquished his burden to the liveried footman. "How can such a sweet little thing disrupt my entire life?"

To his dismay, Dirk merely stared at Dalton and smirked.

"Oh, no." Dalton shuddered. "Do not even attempt to suggest I am smitten with Miss Daphne. She is not my type. She is too pure. I am a rake. We do not suit. I am not in love."

Dirk burst into laughter. "Brother, I do not envy you, as you are in for the ride of your existence."

"What do you mean?" He followed his elder sibling and waited until Dirk occupied the seat beside his bride.

"You will learn soon enough." Dirk claimed Becca's hand and brought it to his lips. "Are we ready, darling?"

"Indeed, my love." She giggled, until she noticed Dalton attempting to enter the spacious equipage. "And where do you think you are going?"

"Uh, I had thought to join you, at Randolph House." In light of the frigidity of her stare, he halted in his tracks. "Given I maintain a—perhaps I should remain here."

"I should say so." Rebecca humphed. "Ridiculous fool."

"You know I rather fancy your feisty side, sweetheart." Dirk kissed his wife's forehead. "What say we retire to my study, upon our arrival home, and after you settle our guest?"

"My lord, I shall be too delighted to indulge you." Rebecca narrowed her stare, as Dalton retreated to the side-walk. "And we will see you tomorrow, for dinner, Dalton. Be prompt, as I cannot abide tardiness."

"Yes, ma'am." He nodded.

"Drive on," Dirk stated.

Alone at his doorstep, Dalton sighed and wondered what had just happened.

THE LONDON RESIDENCE of the Viscount and Viscountess Wainsbrough boasted red brick with Portland stone trim and stood at almost twice the size of Courtenay Hall. The interior featured rich mahogany, leather wall inserts, and burgundy accouterments. In contrast to Dalton's bachelor lodgings, with its less than elegant décor, Randolph House presented a classic but sophisticated abode Daphne found somewhat intimidating in its grandeur.

The previous evening, after unpacking her meager belongings, she had dined in the sitting room of her opulent bedchamber and retired early. The soul of gentility, Rebecca had recommended a good sleep, as they would venture into the shopping district, today. And then they were supposed to have lunch with the Brethren women, but that meant nothing to Daphne.

Gowned in the simple but stunning dress of sprig muslin, which Rebecca had sent with her lady's maid just after breakfast, Daphne located the butler in the foyer.

"May I be of assistance, Miss Daphne?" Hughes bowed.

"Lady Rebecca summoned me." Reminiscent of Hicks, the very proper manservant smiled, and Daphne liked him in an instant. "Do you know where I might find her?"

"Her ladyship is in the morning room, with his lordship." Hughes stood tall. "If you will follow me, I shall show you the way."

"Oh, that is not necessary." She peered about the chasmal foyer. "If you would point me in the right direction, I will announce myself."

"Down the hall to the left." Hughes inclined his head. "It is the last door on the right."

"Thank you." With a half-curtsey, she grinned and then sought her host and hostess. As she neared the end of the well-appointed passage, she heard voices and discovered the oak panel ajar. Inside, seated on a sofa, the viscount hugged the viscountess, who nestled in his lap.

"You were superb, last night, sweetheart." Dirk growled and nipped his wife's nose.

"Only last night?" Rebecca pouted. "As I exercised you quite thoroughly this morning, too."

"Now that was inspiring, beyond words." He tipped Rebecca's chin and engaged her in a shockingly intimate kiss, which brought the burn of a blush to Daphne's cheeks.

Averting her stare, she retreated a step. But fascination brought her to the portal, and she could not stop herself from studying the heated clinch, as never had her father and mother exchanged such depth of affection.

"I love you, darling." Dirk rested his forehead to Rebecca's. "And I missed you terribly."

"Well I abhor sharing our bed with nothing more than a cold pillow, as I much prefer your warm body at my side." The viscountess trailed her tongue along his bottom lip. "And I love you, too, with all my heart. But I apologize for disturbing your slumber, after your long road trip."

"You could never disturb me, my lady." He caressed Rebecca's cheek. "I just wish we could identify the source of your nightmares, that we might curtail them, as I cannot bear your torment. It hurts me to see you suffer."

"Yet I do so favor your special brand of medicine, which never fails to soothe my distress." Rebecca wound her arms about his neck. "And I would not have you fret for me."

When Dirk drew Rebecca close for another remarkable kiss, Daphne stepped back, cleared her throat, grasped the knob, and knocked before peeking around the edge of the door. "Hello. Am I interrupting anything?"

The couple stood in the center of the stylish but cozy

room, as Daphne entered, and Dirk adjusted his coat and winked at his wife. "Morning, Miss Daphne."

"How are you, my dear?" Rebecca came forward. "Are you settled and comfortably situated? Is there anything you require, as I would have you lack for nothing?"

"On the contrary, everything is wonderful." How the smitten couple riveted Daphne, as they enjoyed what she had never believed possible, and she coveted hope for her future. "You had mentioned a visit to Bond St. When should we depart?"

"Posthaste." The viscountess scrutinized Daphne's appearance. "And you look marvelous."

"Thank you." Daphne envied Rebecca's air of poise and grace. "I appreciate the use of your wardrobe."

"So you venture out?" Dirk inquired of his wife, as he caught her by the waist.

"Yes." Rebecca smoothed a lock of hair from his face. "Our charge requires new clothes suitable for the marriage mart and Almack's. And that reminds me, will you secure the necessary vouchers?"

"Please, do not bankrupt the viscountcy." He grimaced. "And you know I detest knee breeches."

"But you will make the sacrifice, for me, else I must tour the hallowed hall, on my own." Then Rebecca laughed. "And your brother has given Miss Daphne *carte blanche*, so he finances her trousseau."

"Permit my ravishing bride to wander the *ton*'s ballrooms sans escort?" Dirk snickered. "Not by a long chalk. And Dalton assumes responsibility for the bills? By all means, spend at will, darling. And when can I expect you in residence?"

"How magnanimous is my husband with another man's

wallet?" Rebecca cooed. "And I shall return home, at two, for my nap, should anyone wish to join me."

"Until then, take care." Despite Daphne's presence, Dirk again kissed his wife. "And you know, very well, I will guard your rest."

"Then I shall away and formulate something to inspire you, once again." With that, Rebecca set her sights on Daphne. "Come, my dear. As we have much to accomplish and little time prior to lunch with my sisters."

"But I do not wish to be a burden." With Rebecca as taskmaster, Daphne charged the foyer. "And how many sisters do you have?"

"There are five, in all." The viscountess glanced at the butler. "Hughes, is the coach ready?"

"Yes, your ladyship." The manservant bowed and then rushed to the fore, with pelisses in his grasp.

"Oh." Rebecca snapped her fingers. "Is there any peach jam pudding leftover from last night's supper?"

"Yes, your ladyship." Hughes smiled. "I had cook prepare an extra large dish, in the event you preferred an additional portion."

"How perceptive, as I craved it constantly when I carried Angeline. What would I do without you?" Rebecca grinned, and the butler blushed. "I expect to return promptly at two, and I should like to wash away the road dust, soon thereafter. Will you have a bath waiting, along with the dessert, in his lordship's sitting room?"

"Of course, my lady." Hicks opened the door and then stood at attention.

As they stepped into the sunlight, Daphne shielded her eyes, and myriad questions swirled in her brain. Dizzy, she swayed, but Rebecca provided unshakeable support and stability.

"Are you unwell?" the viscountess queried. "Should we postpone our errands?"

"No." Daphne wiped her brow and then accepted the footman's assistance. Settling into the squabs, she rolled her shoulders. "So much has happened in the past few days, and I find it a bit overwhelming."

In that moment, in that fragment of space, at that very second of her existence, Daphne, at last, allowed herself to ponder Dalton's proclamation. Given what she knew of the brooch, of its lore and predictive nature, how should she respond to his demand that she find a husband, when he offered not for the position?

"Then we shall fortify your defenses, Miss Harcourt." Rebecca brushed her skirts. "As you will need all your strength, plus a few weapons you have yet to employ, for the forthcoming battle, in order to snare your prey."

"I beg your pardon?" Confused, Daphne blinked, as the equipage lurched. "What do you mean? What battle? And who is my prey?"

"Come now, my husband shared the whole of your dilemma, in detail, as he tells me everything, and I am so sorry for your hardship. Yet that is behind you, as you are to be family." Rebecca tugged on her gloves and adjusted her sleeves. "Be that as it may, the skirmish to net a spouse is unlike any you have ever encountered, as it is an unparalleled struggle, because the male sex is stubborn to the point of stupidity, on occasion. But you should know that when Dalton described your prospective candidate as 'a simple, dull, uninspired fellow with an ocean of patience and deep pockets,' he referenced himself."

∾

SIDEWALKS FILLED to capacity with fashionable ladies and gentlemen, rushing in varied directions, as the merchant district presented a beehive of activity and all manner of temptations.   And everyone who was anyone stopped to address Lady Rebecca, which Daphne found quite intimidating, given Dirk's wife never failed to make introductions, and the unveiled scrutiny was almost more than a provincial could bear.   After quick but productive visits to the milliners, the hosiers, and the glovers, whereupon the viscountess organized the purchases as a general outfitting the troops, Rebecca rushed Daphne to the coach.

"Hurry, my dear." Rebecca bounced to her seat. "We are late, and I am famished, but that was such fun.   Now I understand Beth's predilection when I first arrived, as it is rather exciting to outfit you for war.   Dirk's mother and I shopped to excess, before my first season, and you and I shall maintain the tradition. And what do you think of the sheer confection I procured?"

"The burgundy?" Daphne could not suppress a giggle, when she pictured the garment, as it amounted to almost nothing. "It is beautiful, but will you not be chilled, given its transparency, and you bought nothing to wear beneath it?"

"Oh, no." Rebecca lowered her chin and arched a brow. "The robe is done in my husband's favorite shade, and it should light his fire, so I shall be quite warm. And I intend to model it for him, donning naught but a smile, when we return to Randolph House, this afternoon."

"How wonderful." To her chagrin, her cheeks burned with embarrassment.

"Does such talk make you uncomfortable, as there is nothing wrong in pleasing one's spouse?" The viscountess narrowed her stare. "Have I made you nervous? You realize you may confide in me, and I do so wish you would call me Becca."

"Thank you." Daphne inhaled a deep, calming breath, as she needed a friend, just then. "Everything seems so confusing, and my life spirals beyond my control, offering no time to adapt to my new circumstances. But nothing discomposed me more than what I witnessed this morning, when I happened upon you and the viscount. You were kissing, and you looked so natural."

"But it is perfectly logical for a husband and a wife to kiss." Shock invested Rebecca's features, as she pressed a hand to her chest. "You must know Dirk and I love each other, and I will not settle for less than such a match, for you. What about your parents? Surely they expressed affection in comparable displays?"

"Theirs was not a happy union." The pain of the past revisited her, and she fought tears. "My father did not uphold his vows, and my mother suffered, in silence, as a result of his infidelity. May I confess that is my greatest fear —that I might endure a similar fate?"

"Over my dead body." Rebecca compressed her lips and then reached for Daphne's hand. "You will have the dream. I swear on my life and that of my unborn babe."

The equipage came to an abrupt halt before the London residence of the Marquess and Marchioness of Raynesford, cutting short the conversation, and Daphne's jaw dropped, as the footman handed her to the drive. "Goodness, but it is a magnificent structure. Are none of your friends untitled paupers?"

"You will accustom yourself to it, in no time." Rebecca chuckled and glanced at the butler, as they doffed their pelisses. "Hello, Banks. This is Miss Daphne Harcourt. Are the other ladies present?"

"Yes, your ladyship. Allow me the pleasure of announcing your arrival." As customary, he bowed and then ushered them to a double door entry. "The Viscountess Wainsbrough and Miss Daphne Harcourt."

Chatting and laughing, an array of dazzling ladies suddenly grew hushed, and Daphne found herself the center of attention.

"Here she is, Dalton's prospective bride." A heavily pregnant and boisterous woman, with raven locks, blue eyes, and a huge grin, grabbed Daphne's wrists. "I am Sabrina, Countess of Woverton, but you must call me Brie, like the cheese. And loafing on the *chaise*, because she has yet to learn how to manage her swollen belly, is my elder sibling Cara, Marchioness of Raynesford."

"Welcome to my home." Cara waved a greeting. "May I address you as Daphne? And you must ignore my little sister's forthright demeanor, as that is her way, and she has yet to outgrow it."

"Of course." Daphne nodded, as she knew not what to make of the contrasting relations. "You may call me whatever you wish."

"Now what did I say that she does not already know, as we all understand why she is here?" Sabrina clucked her tongue. "And why temper the truth and lead her to believe we are something we are not?"

"Some things never change." Cara rolled her eyes. "I hope you do not mind the casual atmosphere, but I had thought we could take our lunch in here, as my joyous bundle impedes my approach to the dining room table."

"Hello, my dear. I am Lady Alexandra Collingwood, but it is Alex to family, and we never stand on formality, in private." The charming, polished noble drew Daphne to an overstuffed chair. "On the sofa is Caroline, Countess of

Lockwood, beside her is Lady Elaine Prescott, and at the other end is Lady Celia Devane, a friend of Sabrina's."

"I am honored to make your acquaintance." That was putting it mildly, as Daphne shuffled her feet. "And I gather Sir Dalton would claim otherwise, despite your assertion."

"That is because he is a man." Caroline smirked. "And they are always the last to know what is good for them. But I suspect he is not what he would have us believe, given the time I spent with him, aboard the *Siren*, and he is ripe for courtship. But the road to happiness can be paved with heartache, so you should gird yourself for the fight."

One by one, the wives, characters all, shared their tales of marital bliss hard won, with the single ladies. Some had endured incredible misery and humiliation, in the quest to win their mates. Caroline had been mistaken for a courtesan and kidnapped by her future husband, Rebecca had thrown herself in the path of a murderous traitor to save Dirk, Sabrina had enacted a painful personal renovation, of sorts, to claim Everett, Cara had seduced Lance, and Alex had thrown caution and societal precepts to the wind and chased her captain to Plymouth.

"I am humbled by your confidence and your courage." Wringing her fingers, and plagued by doubt, Daphne sighed, as the polished female collective served to emphasized her shortcomings. "Yet you must know I have no fortune or connections."

"But you are Dalton's choice, so it matters not," Caroline asserted. "Do you not want him?"

"Given your candor, I must confess I am enamored of him." Yet Daphne was a realist. Whereas in Portsea, she was the matriarch of the county, in London she was nothing. "But he wishes me to marry another and has stated as much, in no uncertain terms."

"Oh, I do not know about that." Rebecca poured a cup of tea from the trolley. "My brother-in-law recovered the pilfered brooch, refused to call the authorities after you twice raided his ship, purchased food for Courtenay Hall's stores, and gave Daphne *carte blanche* to acquire a new wardrobe."

"He didn't." Cara shoved a pillow behind her and grimaced. "Excuse me, but my babe grows restless. Now then, under normal circumstances, I would be inclined to covet misgivings in regard to the constancy of Dalton's admiration, as he has labored to construct a dubious reputation, but nothing parts a man from his money faster than engaged affections."

"Excepting Dirk." Rebecca giggled. "But his mother warned me, from the outset, so I knew what I was getting in the bargain."

"Is he no longer gifting paperweights?" Sabrina snickered. "My Everett still brings me daisies, by the armful, on a weekly basis."

"Oh, I receive them, with regularity, along with roses," the viscountess replied with a ghost of a smile. "But I would argue Dirk relishes grousing about the purchases as much as he delights in my thanks."

"As does Trevor." Caroline swiped a sugary scone from a plate of sweets. "He procures knickknacks faster than I can place them."

"And Lance has resumed his childhood habit of obtaining wooden figurines to add to my collection." Cara averted her misty gaze. "How I love him."

"Men are such funny creatures." Alex glanced at Daphne. "By his own admission, Jason neglected me during our courtship, but he never forgets me, now. In fact, every time he docks in Deptford, he brings a surprise, of some sort, and poetry, written in his own hand."

"That reminds me. Why have you never read us one of his original offerings, as we are the souls of discretion?" Elaine inquired. "No offense, but I struggle to imagine Jason composing prose of adoration and romance."

"Well therein lies the quandary, as the captain of my heart does not employ the usual refined language you might expect." Then Alex vented a half-smothered snort. "Suffice it to say his ribald work is not for mixed company, but the sole focus of his bawdy efforts entails various descriptions of my body, his unorthodox utilization of his tongue, and his effuse appreciation of our...connubial activities. However, I am continually impressed with his resourcefulness, as I never knew so many words rhyme with breasts."

In concert, the ladies collapsed in a fit of hilarity.

"Poetry, paperweights, knickknacks, figurines, and daisies? Oh, what a sweet treasure." Celia rested elbows to knees and cupped her chin. "That sounds nothing like my father. Then again, my parents have an arranged marriage, and I narrowly escaped the same fate."

"Lance threatened to contract my nuptials." A delicate Elaine peered at Daphne and frowned. "But I told him I would run away, as did Caroline, if that happened."

"Worry not, dear friend." Cara balanced a plate, piled with small sandwiches, atop her prominent protuberance. "Because I declared my abandonment of his bed, should that occur."

"So there will be no more talk of arranged marriages in this household." A veritable mountain of a man, with hair as black as a crow's feather, chiseled features, and emerald eyes strolled into the room, and Daphne would have wagered all the women of Portsea would have swooned at his toes, at first glance, as he was gorgeous. "Good afternoon, ladies. And how does my glowing mother-to-be fare?"

"Give me a kiss, and I shall answer your question." Cara bit her lip. "And welcome Miss Daphne to our coterie."

"Now that is a command I dare not refuse." Without hesitation, Cara's husband bent and set his mouth to hers.

To her dismay, Daphne grew warm, as she could not stop herself from gawking at the charming pair. As was the case with Rebecca and Dirk, Cara and Lance expressed mutual admiration with unimpaired aplomb, as though they knew no other way, yet Daphne found such unrestrained passion a foreign concept. When Sabrina whistled in monotone, the tension broke, and the twosome came up for air.

"How do you feel?" Lance rubbed his nose to Cara's. "Are you all right?"

"I am perfect." Cara patted his cheek. "So you may stop fussing over me."

"Not a chance, love. Ah, yes." He pulled a silver bell from his coat pocket. "You forgot this at your vanity. How can you signal me, if you do not keep it with you?"

"Lance, you are being silly." Cara huffed. "Dr. Handley assured us there will be plenty of time to summon him, so you must relax."

"Darling, I will not risk your life or that of my heir, so you will indulge me." With that, he kissed her hard and fast. "Now I shall adjourn to my study, and you will ring for me, if you need me. And welcome, Miss Daphne."

"Yes, sir." Cara sketched a mock salute. Just as Lance neared the threshold, the marchioness jiggled the bell, and he whipped about, in a flash. "My lord, I need you, without fail."

With a wide grin, the marquess lifted his chin and winked, and then he exited the chamber.

"Are they always like that?" Daphne asked Rebecca, as the fervent exchanges would befuddle any well-bred backwater girl.

"Has no one told you?" Sabrina shoved almost half a sandwich in her mouth. "Brethren marry for love."

"And who, precisely, are the Brethren?" Daphne had heard Dalton and Dirk make the same reference, when they thought her unaware, and the curious moniker intrigued her. "Or is it some great secret?"

Alex glanced at Rebecca, who gazed at Cara, who peered at Caroline, who, in turn, stared at Sabrina.

"It is what we call our somewhat odd extended family." Elaine chuckled, as she leaned back on the sofa. "As children, we fancied ourselves great warriors for the Crown, and the fantasy lives in each of us, even today."

"Sabrina told me you played pirate games, when you were young." Celia daubed the corners of her lips with a napkin. "Do you imagine the next generation will follow suit?"

"Oh, I hope so." Caroline splayed her fingers over her belly. "As I would have them know the same fellowship with which we have been blessed."

"Are you increasing, as well?" Daphne asked.

"Although I am just beginning to show, Trevor and I eagerly anticipate our third babe, as my husband desires a large family," Caroline explained. "His upbringing was not so whimsical."

"And this is my second, and Everett is thrilled, as he shared Trevor's difficulties, and they are lifelong chums." Sabrina scooted to the edge of her seat. "And we want the same happy matches for you, Elaine, and Celia."

"Indeed." Alex inched forward and clasped Sabrina's hand. "And I vow on my third offspring to see you merrily wed."

Soon, the ladies mirrored the simple gesture, forming a circle of sisterhood that brought Daphne to the brink of tears. "But how should we proceed, as Dalton does not cooperate?"

"With the exception of my remarkable spouse, most men never do." Rebecca furrowed her brow. "But if Dalton wishes you to consider other candidates, you may have to do just that, for appearances. And I know the perfect foil for the younger Randolph."

"Sisters, it sounds as if we intend to embark upon another matchmaking campaign." Alex fidgeted. "And I gave Jason my word I would never enact such contentious business again, after Lance and Cara's affair. If we do this, I must tell him, else he warned I would not sit comfortably for a sennight if I ever broke my promise."

"But I do not want to cause trouble." Daphne reflected on the possibility of success, which seemed fleeting, given Alex's declaration. "If I cannot win Dalton on merit, I will not take him by trickery."

"How do you define trickery?" Sabrina stretched her slippered feet. "When Dalton may need nothing more than a bit of enticement, as did my Everett."

"Yet I would rather not involve Trevor." Caroline studied the floor. "As I am not sure he would approve."

"That is all the more reason to enlist their aid." Rebecca nodded once. "In fact, Alex is a genius, as we would do well to make use of our happily wedded husbands, which would enable us to engage in a two-pronged assault, such as no bachelor has ever confronted."

"And that is a good thing?" Daphne shuddered, as she pondered the prospects.

"Of course." Cara's eyes grew wide. "And what male, sane or otherwise, could resist such temptation?"

"Then it is settled." Rebecca squeezed Daphne's fingers. "Tonight, you shall meet the whole of our family, and you will wear the green gown as an opening salvo. And tomorrow, we recruit our men to bring Dalton to his knees—I mean, to the altar."

CHAPTER SEVEN

"$\mathcal{N}$ ot bad, for a provincial." Dirk elbowed Dalton in the ribs. "Instead of staring at her, from across the drawing room, why not talk to her?"

Dalton had been asking himself the same question since his arrival at Randolph House for the family dinner, and he had yet to form a sensible response. While Blake and Damian buzzed about the backwater girl turned sultry seraph, outfitted in emerald silk, which highlighted her creamy complexion and transformed her already piercing blue eyes into something altogether ethereal, Dalton had remained rooted to the floor. But he worried not, as the dynamic ducal duo were confirmed bachelors.

"When I asked your wife to prepare Daphne for the *ton's* ballrooms, I never said anything about remaking her into an enchanting seductress." He raked his fingers through his hair. "Look at her. She is Venus, Aphrodite, and a virginal handmaiden, all rolled into one. What was Rebecca thinking?"

"You catch more flies with honey, dear brother."

Rebecca tittered, as she twirled and then leaned into Dirk. "Do you like my new dress, as it is your favorite color?"

"You know, very well, I do." Dirk kissed her forehead. "And I shall enjoy it, even more, tonight, when I take it off you."

Confused, because the singular shade was their sire's preference, Dalton scratched his temple. "But burgundy was—"

"—My choice, from birth." Dirk shot Dalton a warning glance. "And is that Lucien, in the hall?"

"Oh, he is here." Becca inclined her head and gazed a Dalton, and for some odd reason he could not decipher, he shuddered. "Do you believe Miss Daphne would prefer a titled groom, as Lucien must marry, and I think her an ideal candidate?"

"No, I do not agree." The mere image of Daphne wedded to the randy Wentworth was enough to give Dalton collywobbles. "They do not suit."

"And what, pray tell, is your objection to my sibling?" Becca thrust her chin, and Dalton knew he was in trouble. "He just made post."

"Daphne would have to move to the Peak District," he replied, with conviction.

"And what is wrong with Derbyshire?" Rebecca rested hands on hips. "As it is the place of my birth."

"Miss Harcourt prefers Portsea Island." Tugging on his cravat, Dalton shifted his weight. "And I meant no offense."

"Darling, go welcome your brother." Dirk trailed a finger along her jawline and then pressed his lips to hers. "And I shall endeavor to express my appreciation of your stunning attire, in our private apartment, after our guests depart."

"Oh, I do so look forward to it, my lusty lord." With one last scowl at Dalton, Rebecca turned and waved at Lucien.

"Why have you not told her the truth, that burgundy was father's signature hue?" he inquired, after Becca had moved beyond earshot. "And you have never developed such partiality."

"Dalton, you know that, and I know that, but my bride remains blissfully ignorant, even after almost three years of marriage, and I would not disabuse her of the notion for anything in the world." Dirk arched a brow and snickered. "You see she came home from her shopping trip, with a sheer confection that left nothing to the imagination, which she bought because it was done in what she believes is my preferred shade, and proceeded to enact an erotic dance, among other things, wearing naught but said garment, for my benefit. And, *oh*, did I benefit. Now, do you honestly think I give a damn about the color?"

"I see your point." In an instant, Dalton conjured visions of Daphne, in similar circumstances. "But you cannot allow Becca to betroth poor Daphne to Lord Calvert, as he is a notorious rake."

"Then you should offer for her," Dirk stated, as if imparting news of the weather.

"What?" Dalton snapped to attention. "Why would I do that?"

"Because you care for her." Dirk folded his arms, in the annoying manner Dalton knew too well. "Don't even attempt to deny it."

"I admit I hold her in high esteem." In truth, she was glorious, and he was an unworthy reprobate of the worst sort. "Plus her carriage is first rate."

"And I said the same thing about my Becca." Dirk chuckled. "Yet it is no secret she claimed my heart the second she set foot aboard the *Gawain*. So I would give you a bit of unsolicited advice intended to spare you the extended suffering I inflicted upon myself."

"Let me guess, you wish me to kneel before her and propose, this instant." Not a bad idea, given Rebecca had just introduced Daphne to Lucien, and Dalton seethed in silence. "Let us say, for the sake of curiosity, I am amenable to your sage counsel—and do not dare ask why. But what if I imparted certain disreputable information, which revealed aspects of my character, or lack thereof, and rendered me unsuitable? And regardless how hard I labored for the remains of my days, I could never deserve Daphne."

"In light of our connections and fortune, you deem yourself beneath the governor's daughter?" With a countenance of astonishment, Dirk narrowed his stare. "What have you done?"

The world shifted in a blur, and Dalton transported to the past, to a different time and place. Bodies bumped and ground, mingling perspiration to a cacophony of grunts and groans, as a trio of lust-driven beings conceded to base instincts. Fueled by heady intoxicants and a desire to partake of unknown debauchery, the likes of which could have rivaled the licentious acts of the Marquis de Sade, Dalton had surrendered to a heretofore-foreign animalistic urge.

Disgust wrenched him to the present, and he studied the angelic ingénue. "If I relayed that information, you would never speak to me again."

"Wait a minute, brother." Glancing left and then right, Dirk checked his tone and stiffened his spine. "Are we talking about an adulterous tryst or something far more profligate?"

"The worst libertine conceivable." How could he have

surrendered control, to that extent? "And there is more than one witness."

"What—who?" Dirk came alert, just as the butler announced dinner. "Belay my queries, as we will discuss the situation tomorrow evening, at White's. Until then, say nothing."

"Aye." It had to be done. He had to confess his nefarious deeds and face the consequences, because his actions could embroil the family in scandal, and no one would escape the repercussions.

It was with that revelation swirling in his brain that Dalton entered the dining room and discovered his place beside Daphne, and he girded himself for the challenge, as he ached to kiss her. For the umpteenth time, he wondered whatever possessed him to bring her to London.

The epitome of innocence smiled. "How are you, Dalton?"

Condemned to hellfire and brimstone for the atrocity he had committed. "Fine, Daphne. And how are you? Are you enjoying your stay with my brother and sister-in-law?"

"Yes." Gushing with enthusiasm, she glowed, as she all but bounced in her chair, and it touched him that he had brought such unabashed joy to her face. "I am afraid Becca took you at your word, when you generously offered to finance my new wardrobe, and I have a pair of slippers for each day of the week. But it is too much, and you must allow me to repay you, somehow, for all the beautiful clothes."

"My dear Daphne, your captivating expression is sufficient repayment." Without hesitation, he claimed her hand, brought it to his lips, and just suppressed a groan of delight when she shivered. "And that I count a priceless boon."

"You are a bold one, Sir Dalton. But I like that about

you." She stuck her tongue in her cheek. "And I wonder if I might pose a personal question?"

"Of course." Something inside him braced, as he revisited the salacious scene in the red room. Then it dawned on him that she could not possibly know of his shame. "Ask away."

"Have you a favorite color?" she inquired, as she leaned forward, with unshakeable eagerness.

"I do, indeed." He opened his mouth and then closed it, as he guessed at her motives. Given the conversation with Dirk, and Rebecca's seduction-driven selections, a host of tempting scenarios featuring the sumptuous virgin composed an irresistible visual tapestry of desire. "But I would have thought it obvious."

"I do not understand." For a few seconds, she fumbled with her napkin. And then she flinched. "The sapphire gown you gave me in Portsea—that is your preference?"

"Correct." He weaved his fingers through hers and squeezed. "So my gesture was quite selfish."

"Nonsense." She scoffed, as a servant filled Daphne's glass with wine. "You are the most generous man of my acquaintance. So Thursday night, at the Richmond's gala, I shall wear the dress just for you, my gallant knight. And I will save all my waltzes for you."

"Then I shall endeavor to deserve the honor." But he reminded himself they were no longer in Portsea. "However, I cannot, in good conscience, permit you to enact an egregious breach of decorum, should we indulge in anything beyond a single dance. To do so would make an unintended declaration that could harm your prospects with aspiring suitors."

"Oh." Crestfallen, she sighed. "And that would displease you?"

"Yes." No, as he would sooner lock her away from potential beaus and keep her for himself, but he was unprepared for the commitment she required. "But I should content myself with whatever privilege you bestow upon me."

When Dirk cleared his throat, Dalton glanced up and discovered his extended family focused on his exchange with Daphne. He shifted in his chair, just as Blake waggled his brows and Damian whispered something to his partner in nefarious enterprises.

"My apologies, if we have held up the meal." Dalton could only pray for mercy. "And the roasted chicken looks delicious."

"But it appears you prefer your poultry a little on the tender side." Damian elbowed Blake in the ribs, and the two chuckled.

"Damian, behave yourself." Alex wagged a finger. "Just wait until it is your turn."

"His turn for what?" Daphne asked Dalton.

"Ignore them," Caroline replied. "They will get theirs."

"And why are you so quiet?" Blake queried Trevor. "Is this not your favorite sport? I believe you and Everett claim to be past masters in the sentimental realm."

"Now how did I get in the middle of your affairs?" Everett passed the apple loaf to Sabrina. "Darling, you are my witness. I was just sitting here, minding my own business."

"Poor bantling." Sabrina favored Everett with an exaggerated pout. "Shall I soothe your ruffled feathers, when we get home?"

"Do not upset my wife, Blake." Trevor leaned to the side and claimed a quick kiss from Caroline. "Else I will box your ears, and you are already a frightful sight."

"The widow Grainer did not think so, last night." Blake winked.

"I knew it." Damian pounded a fist to the table. "Kleinfeld owes me, as I wagered ten pounds you would best Lord Sheldon."

A collective of feminine gasps brought the puerile celebration to a halt.

"Blake, while this is an informal family gathering, I would appreciate it if you would refrain from discussing such intimate topics at the table." Rebecca handed Daphne a bowl of potatoes. "Now, let us eat, as I spent hours composing the menu."

"Are they always like this?" Daphne said in a hushed tone.

"Worse." Dalton chanced a glimpse of the duly chastised rakes. Blake drew a finger across his throat, Damian smirked, and Dalton had never been more afraid in his life.

GOWNED IN PALE GREEN, Daphne stood tall and gazed at her reflection in the long mirror. With her hair swept in a cascade of curls, as arranged by Rebecca's personal lady's maid, Daphne cut the perfect picture of feminine deportment and respectability. Then she yawned.

Dinner the previous evening had left her in a state of confusion, as Dalton had whispered sweet compliments at the table and then abandoned her. He had spared not a word or a glance for the remainder of the night, and she knew not what to make of his peculiar behavior, so she had slept little.

"I beg your pardon, Miss Daphne." Hughes bowed. "I

knocked, but you did not answer, and her ladyship requests your presence in the back parlor, at once."

"Oh, I am sorry." Suppressing a chill of unease, she marched forth, per her ally's plan. "I shall go to her, posthaste."

In the hall, she admired the rich mahogany trim and lush burgundy carpets of Randolph House. The grand home boasted an understated refinement, which bespoke power and privilege without the garish décor that often accompanied such opulence. Had she the funds, she would mimic the sparse but sufficient ornamentation in a much-needed renovation of Courtenay Hall.

A footman opened the door, as she approached the back parlor, and she dipped her chin, in acknowledgement, as she had limited experience with such formalities. In the chamber, the full compliment of Brethren husbands stood.

"Good afternoon, Miss Daphne. My wife has explained some of your predicament with us, and we understand your concerns, but I am at a loss as to how I can help." Just as Rebecca had said he would, Dirk vacated his chair and stepped to the side. "Will you not take my seat?"

"Thank you." As Daphne settled her skirts, she bit her tongue against laughter, because her primary conspirator launched the prearranged plot.

"Darling, come here." Rebecca rose from the sofa. "There is no reason we cannot share my spot."

"What?" The viscount acquiesced, as Becca ushered him to her place. "You cannot mean to—"

"Posh, as we are all family here." Before he could protest, the viscountess eased to his lap. "There. Is that not better?"

"Well, of course." An endearing flush spread from Dirk's neck to his cheeks. "But we have—"

The remaining wives assumed similar positions with their respective spouses, and the room grew as quiet as a tomb. Wrestling with apprehension and a dark sense of foreboding, Daphne clasped her hands to portray a modicum of confidence.

"Sabrina, just what are you about?" Everett shuffled her in his grasp. "My countess wants something—do not try to deny it."

"Now why do you say that?" Brie wrapped an arm about his shoulders and hugged him. "I just love you, that is all."

"I know you too well, my saucy Sabrina." Everett narrowed his stare. "Have you overspent your allowance?"

"Well I like that." Sabrina pouted and humphed. "Can a wife not express adoration of her beloved mate without reservation?"

"Gentlemen, why do I suspect we have just been ambushed?" Jason arched a brow.

In an instant, Daphne grew unseasonably hot, and she feared she might swoon, as the men seemed on the verge of discovering the ploy. Just as she considered entering the fray, Rebecca winked, and Daphne rallied patience and reclined.

"I believe you are correct, brother." Lance grimaced, and he drew a heavily pregnant Cara closer. "Sugar kisses, you cannot fool me."

"We need your assistance." Cara snuggled up to Lance. "Is that so wrong?"

"To what purpose?" the marquess inquired.

"Miss Daphne requires your aid." Rebecca pressed her lips to Dirk's forehead. "And I know my chivalrous knight would never refuse a virtuous cause or a damsel in distress."

"Oh, no." Dirk cast an expression of horror. "Rebecca, I am no matchmaker."

"Alex, I told you never again to meddle in other people's affairs." Jason wagged a finger. "If you were not with child, I would put you over my knee and heat your posterior for the mere suggestion."

"Do not rip at her, as she is the reason we confide in you." Sabrina folded her arms. "Else we would charge the field without you."

"I knew it." Everett rolled his eyes. To Brie, he said, "I will not involve myself in such shenanigans. Furthermore, I forbid you from inserting yourself into Dalton's private liaisons."

"I concur." Trevor groaned, as he caught Caroline in a lethal glare, and Daphne squirmed. "And if I discover otherwise, you will not sit comfortably for a sennight."

"But you conspired with Everett to induce me to betray Sabrina's location, when she thought Everett sought a divorce, and she journeyed to our beach cottage." Caroline bowed her head. "How is that different?"

"I had thought we were never going to mention that scene, outside our home." Trevor shot a quick glance at Everett. "And she has us there."

"So you are practiced in such sappy endeavors?" Lance queried, with a snort of laughter. "Do you negotiate contracts, too?"

"Oh, shut up." Everett cupped Brie's chin. "Darling, I love you. But I am no machinating mama, and I will go to my grave before I allow you to subject me to such humiliation."

"But Dalton is our brother, and Daphne is to be our sister, so there is no nobler goal." Sabrina wound her arms about her husband's neck. "And I love you, too, my shameless lord."

"Captain of my heart, I will obey whatever you

command, as I promised I would never to lie to you. But I beg you, do not refuse Daphne's plea, as it would persist as a painful stain on my conscience, and I only want them to be as happy as we are, my cherished seaman." With a tear-filled gaze, Alex asked, in a small voice, "Are you not happy, Jason?"

"Oh, I say." Lance winced. "If you can dig yourself out of that one, without landing in the proverbial doghouse, you shall have earned my everlasting esteem and gratitude."

Tension hung in the air, as the men and the women squared off as two opponents on the battlefield, and neither side blinked. Daphne feared the fairer sex might flinch, as the husbands would not yield. But Rebecca assured Daphne the wives knew their spouses, and the ladies would win the day, if they worked together to achieve their objective. So she uttered a silent prayer and stayed the course, as she longed to claim Dalton's heart. And just when Daphne thought she could withstand no more, and she prepared to concede the fight, Caroline emitted a soft sob. Then Sabrina whimpered, and Alex, Cara, and Rebecca followed suit.

"Bloody hell."

"Oh, no. Not that."

"Sweet Alex."

Sugar kisses."

"Darling Becca, please, do not cry."

"Belay the blasted tears, and I will assist you." Jason pulled a handkerchief from his coat pocket and dried Alex's cheeks. "While I loathe participating in your scheme, regardless of your benevolent aim, I am fascinated by your pledge to 'do whatever I command.' So I will make you a bargain, my blushing bride."

"A bargain?" Alex bit her lip and blinked. "But a

gentleman would accommodate us for the good of the cause."

"Perhaps." The blonde giant, who intimidated Daphne far and away beyond anyone she had ever known, as he looked more than a little dangerous, scrutinized his wife, and he seemed quite preoccupied with her bosom. "Yet you know I am no gentleman, so let us dispense with the niceties, shall we? For each day you require my cooperation, I shall claim a boon, in payment, the tenure of which ceases when the happy couple weds."

"And what would you have of me?" Alex peered over her shoulder and shrugged. "You already have my dowry."

"The money is deposited for our babes, and there it will remain. But you know my favorite coin, where you are concerned." Jason cast her a lazy smile. "And as for your daily remittance, that, my devoted wife, shall depend on my mood. Yet our awkward concordat, of sorts, shall serve both our purposes, as I submit there is no better way to highlight the benefits of marriage for a prospective groom, as even I had not foreseen the unrivaled advantages of matrimony, in that respect. So, do we or do we not have an arrangement?"

"I agree," Alex responded without hesitation.

"You know, you truly are smarter than you look." Everett snickered. "And I prefer those terms. What say you, my most unlikely lady?"

"Done." Brie dipped her chin.

Before Trevor could broach the question, Caroline pinned him with her stare and said, "I accept."

"I suppose you have no objections?" Lance studied Cara's huge belly. "Excepting your current condition?"

"None, whatsoever, my hero." Cara giggled. "We may delay your reimbursements, until I have given birth and healed, as our pact may enable us to conceive a second child."

Daphne could have danced a jig, as everything had fallen into place. Then she realized a lone individual had not entered the collective, and she gazed at Dirk and Rebecca. Would Dalton's elder brother upend Daphne's plan? Had he deemed her unsuitable?

"You are awfully quiet, Dirk." Rebecca nudged him. "Have you any complaints regarding our accord?"

"No, darling." Yet something appeared amiss, as Dirk trailed a finger along Becca's nose. Was it Daphne's imagination, or did he seem melancholy? "As ever, I am at your service, and I demand no remuneration."

"You are so wonderful, and I shall express my appreciation of your efforts, every day, regardless." Rebecca slid from his lap. "Now then, we need you to emphasize the joys of wedded bliss, whenever Dalton is present."

"Tell him how you wake, every morning, thrilled to be married." Sabrina toyed with Everett's cravat. "Explain that you could not envision your future without your wife."

"In other words, you want us to be ourselves, as I am nothing without my rebellious countess." Everett, the epitome of a suave rake, excepting his unmasked love of his mate, wound a lock of Brie's hair about a finger and gave her a gentle tug. "And I wonder if I might persuade you to come home with me, now, and forgo Rebecca's luncheon?"

"Scandalous, my naughty lord." Sabrina's half-baked attempt at reproach had not fooled Daphne. "But I am hungry, and so is the babe that grows inside me. Would you neglect us?"

"Oh, I will feed you, sweetheart. With my own hands, I shall indulge you." At that instant, Everett scooted to the edge of his seat and then stood, with Sabrina ensconced in his arms. "Besides, I am eager to collect my reward."

"As am I." Clutching Alex, Jason mirrored Everett's stance. "Come away with me, love."

"But you have done nothing to merit an exchange." Alex squealed, as Jason nuzzled her neck and growled. "Captain of my heart, you are insatiable."

"Always, where my gorgeous wife is concerned." Jason followed Everett into the hall, with Caroline, Trevor, Cara, Lance, Rebecca, Dirk, and Daphne in the rear. "And like Woverton, I shall guard your health and welfare, with my life. But I submit that, as my participation in your plot begins immediately, then so, too, must my recompense."

In the foyer, Hughes set wide the oak panels and then conveyed the appropriate coats and pelisses to their respective owners. Outside, liveried footmen scattered to provide assistance, as Trevor ushered Caroline into their rig. Lance lifted Cara into their sumptuous equipage and waved, as they departed. Everett hugged Sabrina in his lap, as he eased to the squabs, which left a single couple preparing to decamp the unusual assembly.

"To the park, and make the rotation, until I order otherwise." Jason directed the driver and then waggled his brows. "Up you go, sweetheart. And draw the shades."

Alex obeyed his command but cast Daphne and Rebecca a mischievous grin and sketched a mock salute before lowering the last blind, when Jason slammed shut the door. Just as the driver was about to flick the reins, the coach pitched and rolled, a feminine shriek pierced the calm, and Rebecca laughed.

"Oh, dear." Daphne jumped. "Will she be all right?"

"No worries." Rebecca elbowed Daphne. "Alex knows well her husband's appetite, and she imparted prior to our meeting that she wore something provocative beneath her gown, to inspire him for such an occasion. And I believe he will satisfy her."

AS DALTON STROLLED into White's, he shuddered for some odd reason he could not comprehend, which had become an annoying and frequent occurrence, since meeting Daphne. Amid the leather wall coverings, the plush high back chairs, the various décor that bespoke masculine domination, the glasses filled with expensive brandy, and the pungent aroma of cigar smoke, the powerful male elites of London society shared ribald tales of their latest conquests, boasted of their familial connections and fortune, and detailed their most recent financial or military achievements. In short, the elegant establishment had been built for liars.

How ironic it was that he had arrived at the prearranged time to confess his sins, seek absolution, and discuss the prospect of marrying Daphne. In a private room, his brothers had gathered, and a lone vacant seat beckoned, when he made his presence known.

"And there he is, the source of so much intrigue." Shaking his head, Blake compressed his lips. "What have you done now?"

"I would like to know how you could possibly best your last escapade." Damian narrowed his stare and frowned. "When you were found half-naked, and I reference the lower half, and three sheets to the wind, wandering the Heath near the Highgate ladies' bathing pond, with no inkling of how you came to be there."

"At least, that was your story." Lance rolled his eyes and

snorted in unveiled skepticism. "Though I suspect other-wise, as I have heard tales of a certain young widow's licen-tious proclivities with a respectable viscount's drunken sibling."

"Please tell me you are too wise to involve yourself beyond a simple one-night tryst with Lady Moreton." Everett peered at Trevor and whistled in monotone. "That rum doxy almost cost me my chance with Sabrina."

"She has wrecked more marriages than du Barry." Leaning forward, Trevor planted forearms to thighs. "It is my understanding she is no longer welcome in several of the *ton*'s good homes."

"During our courtship, my Alex nearly took off my head, when I did nothing more than ask Lady Moreton to dance, at the Northcote's ball." Jason winced. "Henceforth, I endeavor to avoid even a haphazard glance at that sparrow-mouthed wench."

"And yet you embroiled yourself in her corrupt arti-fices." It was a statement, not a question, which Dirk declared with unimpaired equanimity, and Dalton ached to protest, but he could not. "I much preferred your immature antics, like the night you hid beneath the bed in my bach-elor lodgings, while I docked in Lady Spencer's harbor."

"I never knew you stirred her waters." Blake raised his crystal balloon in toast. "I am impressed."

"It is not a topic for discussion, in deference to my wife." Crossing his legs, Dirk gazed at the floor. "And I would not insult Rebecca by spreading carnal canards, which occurred before we met, as nothing signifies prior to my nuptials. So, why are we here?"

The center of attention, Dalton had benefitted from the spontaneous chatter, as it had allowed him the opportunity to gather his thoughts. But the awful truth was there existed no possible evasion, and he had to warn his family of the dangers of his making.

"Do you recall our successful supply runs just before the Battle of St. Pierre, last December?" Dalton inquired.

"When you took that French frigate a prize?" Damian reclined and sighed. "How could we forget, as you crowed for a sennight?"

That comment gave Dalton pause, as he had not realized he had exhibited such appalling manners. Cursed with uncharacteristic embarrassment, he wondered if he had a right to wed Daphne.

"As I was saying, we had much to celebrate, when we returned to England, and I admit I indulged in more than my fair share of liquid gratification." How he dreaded imparting the salient points of his err in judgment. "In the ensuing festivities, I ventured to Lady Darrow's, where I joined forces with Lady Moreton and Lord Sheldon."

"You did what?" Trevor choked on his brandy. "Are you out of your mind? That bastard has been trying to bring down our family ever since Caroline snubbed him."

"You drank too much." Dirk bared his teeth. "It is always the same with you. Do you take responsibility for nothing? Will you not be satisfied until you destroy our good name?"

"I deserve that and more, because I have not apprised you of the worst of it." With a deep breath, he braced himself. "You see Sheldon possessed a foreign substance, of some sort, which he indicated would increase arousal and pleasure, and he gave Lady Moreton and I a portion, which we consumed in our drinks. The concoction left me at sixes and sevens, and I scarcely know how we came to be at my bachelor lodgings. In my residence, we engaged in an *ménage à trois*. To my everlasting shame, I took Lady Moreton, hard and fast, and docked in every orifice the bawdy widow possesses, even as Sheldon used her."

And so it was done.

Tension weighed heavy, as each man avoided his gaze, and Dalton had never felt more alone in his life. While he had disappointed himself, he had injured his familial alliances, and that truly hurt. Never before had he regretted his juvenile pursuits, because he had born the repercussions, exclusively.

"What is the matter with you?" Dirk scoffed, just as Dalton had anticipated. "You were loved, you were tended as befits a prince, and you have been given every advantage. Is this how you thank mama and honor our father's memory? And if you care nothing for our parents, what of my wife, my daughter, and my unborn child? What have they done to you, that you would embroil them in such a nasty scandal, because you know, very well, Sheldon will out you, and we will all suffer the consequences."

"I am sorry, brother." Slumped forward, Dalton rested elbows to knees and cupped his chin in his hands. "I know not why I do the things I do." But that was a lie.

"I believe I have the answer to the mystery." After signaling for a refill, Everett stretched his legs and shifted in his seat. "You have persisted in the shadow of a titled sibling."

And in that moment, Trevor's childhood chum reduced Dalton's never-ending agony to a single pedestrian sentence.

"Oh, come now—"

"Bear with me, Dirk. As I know something of the situation, given my history." Everett pointed for emphasis. "Although your sire may have loved you with equal enthusiasm, the population, as a whole, treats second sons with open disdain, and no one knows the hardship like one who survived it."

"You seek to excuse his antics?" Dirk asked, with unmistakable disgust. "You would acquit him of his offense?"

"No, not excuse or acquit." When the waiter brought a fresh glass, Everett gazed into the amber liquid and furrowed his brow. "My intent is to help you apprehend his difficulties, which have plagued his existence from birth, given he wears his deficiency as a mark on his forehead, and people do not see him but for you. In your absence, Dalton functions as a non-entity. He would do better as a manservant, as society would at least deem him necessary, in some respects. So Dalton resorts to capricious capers and wild stunts, which increased in intensity, as he grew older, if only to force the *ton* to acknowledge his presence."

"Gentlemen, I fear I am going to vomit." Wiping his eyes, Dalton inhaled and exhaled, as the room seemed to spin out of control, and excruciating memories flashed a brief but concise inventory of his youth, adolescence, and adulthood. All of a sudden, the Brethren—save Dirk and Everett, retreated, scooting their chairs beyond the danger.

"Easy, brother. It will pass." Dirk patted Dalton on the back. "Is Everett correct? Is this how you have felt, all these years?"

"Yes." Somehow, Dalton had expected great relief, having his long-held secret recognized. Instead, a new form of torment weighed heavy on his heart and mind.

"Like you, I spent countless hours devising ways to garner attention, as I was so often overlooked, in favor of Charles. I studied hard, excelled at university, expended extra effort in service to the Crown, amassed a personal fortune Croesus would envy, and yet my lack of rank defined my worth." Everett compressed his lips. "And I hate myself for admitting it, but I'd wager you know my ignominy."

"Aye." In a flash, Dalton met Everett's stare. "And the torture."

"But I have always protected Dalton." Dirk smacked a fist to a palm. "And I have never mistreated him."

"You do not have to, because society does it for you. Did you know that prior to Charles's demise, the only women who ever approached me were those seeking either a night of passion or access to the heir—with a lone exception." With a ghost of a smile, Everett chuckled. "Sabrina is my salvation. My most unlikely lady wanted me, however she could get me. And I am so grateful for her, as I would be a lonely, miserable, and jaded earl, without my wife and son. So I understand Dalton's motivations and would not judge him. He made a mistake, albeit in spectacular fashion. Who among us is perfect?"

"Yet you ultimately gained the title." And Dalton envied Everett, though he would never declare it. "Your suffering has ended."

"You might think so, but you are wrong." Everett scooted to the edge of his seat and reclined against the armrest. "That particular noose brings with it a whole host of new problems I had never foreseen. And in some ways, I remain invisible, as no one is interested in forming an acquaintance with Lord Everett Markham. Rather, they wish to know the earl of Woverton. Likewise, the title has brought my countess unwanted overtures Sabrina Markham never would have confronted. Do you recall the contretemps with Lord Belford, last fall, during the Little Season?"

"When Sabrina trounced the rake's foot and broke his big toe, during a waltz at the Richmond's gala?" Trevor guffawed. "Smarmy bastard got his comeuppance."

"Is my bride not magnificent?" Everett slapped his thigh. "Gifted her a parure of sapphires and diamonds, as I was so proud of her for that, and how I love my Brie."

"No, no, no." Wrinkling his nose, Blake rose from his chair. "While I sympathize with Dalton, regarding his travails, I draw the line at such sappy emotional expressions. This conversation has turned too maudlin for my tastes, and I would take my leave."

"I concur." Standing, Damian winced. "While there will, no doubt, come a day when we require your assistance in such mawkish endeavors, now is not the time. Until then, you may find me plowing the fields."

"But I would caution you to remember something." Blake met Dalton's stare. "Not many second sons have two dukes, at the ready, to do his bidding. And you are a better man than you realize, even if you are a bit droopy about the ears. This business with the Moreton wench and Sheldon will pass, and you will not ride the storm on your own, as we are with you, come what may. And therein lies the beauty of societal dictates, because no one can ignore us."

"Thank you, brothers." Dalton dipped his chin, and the ducal duo departed.

"So what do you intend where the charming Miss Harcourt is concerned?" Lance queried. "Have you composed a proposal?"

"Now there is where I require your expertise, as Dirk has assured me courtship is a far cry from seduction." And in that moment, Dalton made his decision. "But I will marry her, if she will have me."

"Really?" Everett blinked. "How marvelous for you. Then I suppose you should—"

"Heed our counsel." Trevor elbowed Everett. "As we are past masters in the game of hearts. For example, while courtesans favor monetary expressions of interest, wives savor romance. Trust me, you do not want to disillusion the poor girl."

"So I should wait?" But now that Dalton's course was set, he was anxious to secure Daphne's hand. "For how long would you suggest?"

"A fortnight, at least." Scratching his cheek, Jason glanced at Lance, who nodded. "That should permit us—I mean, you to gain sufficient ground."

"Oh, I say, Collingwood is correct." Everett cleared his throat. "Got ahead of myself, you know. Now, you must schedule regular deliveries from the hothouse. Is she partial to a particular bloom?"

"And what of chocolates?" Lance winked. "Cara loves truffles, and she conveys her gratitude with profuse enthusiasm. And do not forget monogrammed handkerchiefs. My sugar kisses treasures them."

For some strange reason, Dirk scowled. "Brothers—"

"Are we or are we not offering wise guidance, as not every man is fortunate enough to have his bride-to-be seduce him?" Trevor snorted. "And do not forget useless knickknacks. Does she stockpile a particular dust collector, such as paperweights?"

"Very funny." Dirk folded his arms. "And I would have you know Rebecca adores her paperweights."

"My friends, I owe you a debt I can never repay, as I could never manage without your sage advice." For the first time in a long time, Dalton hoped. "Else I would kneel before Daphne, at the next opportunity, pledge my troth, and bungle it. How can I ever thank you?"

"To quote my darling Alex, stuff and nonsense." Jason grinned. "As your future happiness is our just reward, and we shall satisfy ourselves with that."

CHAPTER EIGHT

*T*he roses arrived just after noon, the beautiful box of lace-edged monogrammed handkerchiefs appeared around two, and a liveried messenger delivered the tin of delicious chocolates at three. Sitting in her chamber at Randolph House, surrounded by her treasure, Daphne read and reread the accompanying cards, stark but resplendent in their simplicity. The sender, alone, would have sparked excitement, but it was the singular salutation with which he had signed each missive that captured her attention and rendered her lightheaded with dizzying euphoria.

> *Love,*
> *Dalton*

Were there two more glorious words in the entire world? Hugging herself, she bubbled over with nervous laughter, and gooseflesh covered her from top to toe, so she scarcely heard the knock at the door.

"Come." Daphne stood and smoothed the skirts of her lavender gown, as her gracious hostess entered the room.

"Are you ready for the Promenade?" Bedecked in her signature shade of burgundy, which she declared Dirk's favorite, Rebecca beamed with inexpressible joy. "My dear, you look so sophisticated in your new finery. And Dalton is downstairs."

"Dirk told me Dalton has always avoided the spectacle, like the plague." A shiver of delight traipsed her spine, as Daphne pondered the abrupt about face of her extraordinary suitor. "Oh, Becca, is it too soon to covet hope? Am I counting my eggs before they are in the pudding? Do you believe Dalton intends to propose?"

"I think our men did their part, as they gathered last night, at White's." The glamorous viscountess lifted her chin and narrowed her stare. "And I shall thank my husband, into the wee hours, for his unfailing support of our cause."

"May I ask a personal question?" Daphne accepted Becca's haphazard escort.

"Of course." Rebecca nodded once. "What do you wish to know?"

"Were you always so confident, in matters involving... that is to say...what I wonder is...where did you gain such information regarding the connubial bed?" Daphne's cheeks burned with embarrassment, and she cursed the ever-increasing blushes. "I would never dream of impinging upon our fledgling friendship, but I am curious, and you seem so comfortable discussing what I had thought a taboo topic. You, along with the Brethren wives, make marital relations sound so natural and, to my amazement, enjoyable."

"Well, indeed, marital relations constitute an integral

and indispensable aspect of wedded bliss." Rebecca halted on the landing, and Daphne almost tripped. "My dear, what happens between a husband and a wife is quite natural and enjoyable, especially when they are in love, as are Dirk and I. And as for my knowledge, some I learned in service to His Majesty, but I acquired most of my experience in my devoted Dirk's ardent embrace and gentle tutelage."

"Might you be willing to share some of your instruction with me?" Daphne inhaled a shaky breath. "As I must confess the prospect of my honeymoon terrifies me."

"Then we shall do something about that, at another luncheon with our sisters." Rebecca drew Daphne downstairs. "And now I deliver you to your endearing companion, and Dirk and I will chaperone."

"Ah, here are our ladies." Dirk came forward and claimed Rebecca. "Darling, you wear another splendid creation in my favorite color."

"Hello, Dalton." Daphne had prepared a short speech to convey—something. But when her true knight grasped her gloved hand, twirled her once, and then brought her knuckles to his lips, every single coherent thought fled her.

"Hello, Daphne." The devilishly handsome man had the nerve to wink. Garbed in an evergreen coat, with a tan waistcoat, which highlighted his crisp cravat, black wool breeches, and polished Hessians, Dalton would have made many a fair Portsea maiden swoon. "Shall we depart?"

After gathering pelisses and coats, the foursome journeyed by coach to the park, where a huge crowd made the rotations. Near a tall hedge, the odd extended family waited. As they approached the well-matched couples, it dawned on Daphne that if she married Dalton, that would be her life. She would subsist in a magical world of fashionable ladies and powerful men, confined by a tangle of unwritten and unspoken rules, and spend her days in a never-ending repetition of tea parties, galas, and requisite outings. Taken care of by a gentleman of considerable fortune, she would want for nothing. Yet she longed for the backwater and her charities.

"You are awfully quiet." Dalton settled her securely at his side, as they strolled, with the married compliment in their wake. "Did my offerings to your incomparable beauty not please you?"

"Oh, no. I mean—yes." Daphne clamped shut her mouth and counted to three. "What I intended to say is I love everything. The roses, the handkerchiefs, and the chocolates are wonderful, and I thank you. But why did you send them?"

"I thought it obvious." He favored her with a shy smile, and how she adored him. "I am courting you."

"What?" Her ears rang, her heart skipped a beat, and she stumbled.

"Are you all right?" Dalton slowed his pace. "Daphne, look at me. You are as white as a sheet."

"Sorry." She peered over her shoulder and discovered their legion of chaperones attempting to appear invested in conversation, as everyone avoided glancing in her direction. "But you gave me no warning, and given your behavior, which has confounded me, I fretted you marked me for another, because you stated as much."

He opened and then closed his mouth, as he shuffled his feet.

"Dalton. Daphne." Lady Elaine waved, with Lady Celia, Lady Amanda, and Admiral Douglas, in tow. "We hoped we would see you."

"Why did you not come with Lance and Cara?" Daphne discovered Dalton had retreated to speak with Dirk, and although her prospective suitor whispered, he gestured wildly and shifted his weight. Had she offended him? "And hello, Celia."

"Oh, we will never attract a beau with our brothers about, as they are veritable terrors." Elaine rolled her eyes. "So the admiral and Amanda act as minders."

"Miss Daphne." Exuding strength and dominance in his regimentals, Admiral Douglas bowed. "How do you find the city?"

"A bit overwhelming, sir." Addled by Dalton's declaration, Daphne rallied her wits and seized the moment. "Lady Amanda, I wonder if I might call on you about an urgent matter?"

"Certainly, Miss Daphne." Wearing a navy coat festooned with insignia identical to that of her husband's uniform, the matriarch of the family inclined her head and studied Daphne. "How very mysterious. What about Tuesday, next, at four? You can join me for afternoon tea."

"I would like that very much." And perhaps Lady Amanda could ease some of Daphne's qualms. "And I am in desperate need of counsel, so I will be prompt."

"My Amanda, shall we continue our walk?" The admiral pointed with discretion. "Elaine has located Sir Ross, and she is anxious to greet him."

"Should we allow it?" Lady Amanda frowned. "Lance does not want us to encourage her, as he does not consider Sir Ross a viable swain."

"Do you honestly believe we can stop her, if she is so fixed?" the admiral asked, with a chuckle. "Our younger generation is a stubborn sort."

"Hmm." Lady Amanda sidled close to her husband. "As were we, my dashing sailor, despite my father's conditions, so I sympathize with her predicament. Regardless of potential resistance, you know Elaine must follow her heart."

"Then let us do our duty, as I would not have her compromised into a union." The admiral tipped his hat. "Miss Daphne, we bid you *adieu*."

Just then, Dirk shoved Dalton forward and hissed. "Now get in there."

An endearing red hue spread from his collar to his face, and Daphne tried but failed to stifle a giggle. "Is anything amiss?"

"What was that all about?" Dalton inquired, ignoring her question.

"Apparently, Elaine fancies someone named Sir Ross." Given the openness of his family, Daphne saw no reason to temper her words. But as she settled her hand in the crook of his arm, she checked her enthusiasm when his muscles tensed beneath her palm. "Is there a problem with her choice?"

"There could be, but I wager Lance will fight that battle, should it become necessary." Dalton acknowledged a passing gentleman. "Now, let us turn our attention back to the discourse we began before we were interrupted."

"But I prefer to remain on focus." Daphne lowered her voice, as they merged into the crush. "Why would Lance object to Sir Ross?"

"Right now, I do not want to talk about Sir Ross and Elaine." Dalton steered her to the left, along a pebbled path. "My dearest Daphne, I apologize for my insolent manner, and I would never take you for granted, so I would make my plans clear and avoid any confusion. Consider this my formal proclamation of courtship. I propose we make the rounds, for a fortnight, and then we announce our engagement, if you are amenable. My mother and brother would arrange for a ceremony and a license, so we could take our vows in the first week of June, just prior to Parliament's summer recess and the end of the Season."

"Wait a minute." As Daphne and Dalton halted in a small garden surrounded by tall hedges, the Brethren compliment stood guard at the entrance. When Dalton took her hands in his, and brought her to face him, she squared her shoulders. "Am I to understand you wish to marry me? Because I asked you that in Portsea, and you indicated otherwise."

"Can I plead momentary insanity, kindest and loveliest Daphne?" How could anyone refuse his dimpled grin? "What say you, darling? Will you have me?"

"I know not how to answer, as you quite take my breath away." Bolstered by memories of a difficult childhood, due to her father's infidelities and her mother's disappointments, she would not be cajoled into making the most important commitment of her life. "Do you love me?"

"I beg your pardon?" Was it her imagination, or had he paled?

"I believe I spoke plainly, sir." Daphne pulled free and folded her arms. "Are your affections engaged?"

"I think so." He shifted his weight. "I would not insult you and claim certainty, as these are frightfully unfamiliar waters for me."

"You are serious." It was a statement, not a question, and everything seemed to twist and turn within her.

"Never more so," her knight replied, without hesitation.

"Oh." She paused and prepared for the onslaught of excitement, euphoria, or elation, yet a cold emptiness pervaded her senses, and she sighed. "As many nights as I have dreamed of this very scenario, I had thought I would feel different."

"Are you rejecting me?" He appeared so deflated, as his smile faltered.

"I know not what to do." She squeezed her fingers. "What of Courtenay Hall, and I must shield my brothers."

"No worries, as I dispatched a solicitor to reconcile your father's accounts and pay the taxes on the estate, the day we arrived in London," Dalton explained. "Robert is commissioned as an *aide de camp* for General Beresford, as he wanted, and Richard remains in Portsea, under the supervision of Hicks and your cousin Harold."

"What?" Daphne's knees buckled, and she would have fallen to the ground if Dalton hadn't caught her. "You discharged papa's debts?"

"You seem surprised." He held her upright, and she leaned against him, drawing strength from his unfailing support. "Darling Daphne, I told you I would take care of everything."

"Just like that." She emitted something between a sob and a snort of laughter, as the weight of the world abated. "And what of papa?"

"As per Dirk's request, Damian has circulated a rumor of the governor's impromptu visit to Penhurst and his sudden illness, which a physician fears may be contagious." Dalton cupped her cheek. "The story is you enjoy our protection until your father can join you, in the city, but we both know that will never happen. We need only play our parts, and everything will be fine."

"And why would we not wait for papa, to celebrate our wedding?" Myriad possibilities raced in her mind. "Would our hasty nuptials not raise the alarm?"

"So you accept my proposal?" He lifted her chin, bringing her gaze to his. "You will marry me?"

"I don't see how I can refuse, given the obligations you

have assumed, on my behalf." Daphne gulped as the reality of her circumstances beckoned. "According to law, as you have purchased papa's markers, you own me."

"Bloody hell." He grimaced. "It sounds rather nefarious, when you put it that way."

"I am sorry." The world pitched and rolled beneath her feet, and she closed her eyes. "I need to sit."

"There is a bench over here." Her erstwhile reluctant suitor navigated to a stone pew.

"For years, I have endured the stress of papa's destructive behavior, with no solution in sight." Despite her best efforts, tears of relief flowed as a rushing river, which she daubed with one of the handkerchiefs he had given her. "When you showed up at my doorstep, detailing the brooch's theft, and I discovered Richard had taken it, I feared we had at last met our doom. Instead, you are my salvation, and I am so grateful for you."

"I do not want your gratitude, Daphne." Dalton glanced left and right and then swooped to claim a quick kiss. "While I will not lie to you and claim an undying affection you know, very well, I do not harbor, that does not mean I will never grow to love you. But do not let that diminish the monumental significance of what I do feel for you, which is something altogether mystifying, as I only know I cannot begin to contemplate my future without you in it. When I envision my life, it is with you at my side. When at sea, your image will haunt my slumber, and I ache at the mere thought of being separated from you. When next I dock in London or Portsea, yours is the face for which I will search, and when we are apart, I shall count the hours until we are reunited. Were it within my power, I would employ all manner of romantic overtures to woo you, but I prefer to speak plainly, and I would not deceive you."

"That is more than my mother ever had with my father, so I think it a fine place to start." After a few calming breaths, she stretched upright and noted the green grass, the buds on the verge of flowering, the puffs of white contrasting with an azure sky, and the cheery singsong of birds. How had she missed such beauty when she entered the park, and when had she ever indulged such simple luxuries? "I accept your proposal and pledge to do credit to your good name."

To her confusion, his expression sobered. "On that note, there is something I must tell you—"

"Oh, no." Filled with hope for the first time in a long time, Daphne stood and dragged him with her. "No confessions today, as I would stroll, and let everyone know I am yours, and you are mine."

AFTER CHECKING HIS BLACK FORMALWEAR, Dalton peered at Daphne and winked. Standing just behind Rebecca and Dirk, he waited as the manservant announced the viscount and viscountess of Wainsbrough. Then he stepped forward with his lady, stunning in the blue gown he had purchased for the impromptu ball in Portsea, and braced himself.

"Sir Dalton Randolph and Miss Daphne Harcourt," the Richmond's butler announced.

"And so it is done, my dear. Welcome to the *ton*." As Dalton had expected, a murmur built, slow at first, and a sea of confident debutantes and emboldened rakes came alert, as a new entrant into society graced their company. Inside, he cursed himself for encouraging her to wear the sapphire confection, as he had selected it, in part, due to the low neckline.

"Do you think they will like me?" She blinked.

"Oh, yes." The men, in particular, would fancy the angelic blonde, as she possessed just the right combination of innocence mixed with an underlying sensuality. To shield his bride-to-be, he remained fixed in Dirk's wake, with the delectable Daphne anchored at his side, and resolved to guard her for the entire affair. When he spied Lady Moreton fast approaching, he spared the trouble-maker nary a glance, as he had ended their brief but damning liaison the previous evening, at his bachelor lodging.

At the usual back corner, the Brethren gathered, and he sighed in relief, when he ushered Daphne to the safety of the group. As Dirk had promised to enlist Rebecca's aid in protecting Daphne, it had not surprised Dalton when the wives encircled the backwater girl.

"Have you told her?" Dirk inquired in a whisper.

"Not yet." But he would rectify that omission at the first opportunity. "She wanted nothing to spoil the occasion of our prearranged engagement, and I could not bring myself to disappoint her."

"Our brothers have vowed to provide additional protec-tion, but I would not delay." Dirk glanced toward the terrace doors. "The sharks lurk in our midst."

"We shall have to remain vigilant, until I explain the situation to Daphne and win her forgiveness." Just as Dalton had feared, Lady Moreton and Lord Sheldon had their heads together in conversation, and a chill of dread pervaded Dalton's chest. "Did you apprise Rebecca of my lapse in judgment?"

"Indeed." Dirk gazed at his wife, and as always his expression softened. "I keep nothing from my viscountess, and you would do well to follow my example, as spouses have an uncanny ability of winkling secrets out of husbands."

"But Rebecca was a spy." Dalton folded his arms. "She should excel at winkling."

"Then what is Sabrina's excuse?" Everett elbowed Dalton. "As you would presume my most unlikely lady had chaired the Counterintelligence Corps, given her capacity for inducing spontaneous confessions."

"And I would swear my sweet Caroline reads minds." Trevor winced. "It is bloody frightening, and I dare not attempt to conceal anything from her."

"So Sabrina and Caroline know, too?" That was all he needed to compound his problems. "Could you not have kept it from them?"

"Not if I wish to remain welcome in my wife's bed." Everett wrinkled his nose. "Given we share an apartment and a single four-poster, that might prove tricky, otherwise."

"You could always sleep on the sofa in your study." Trevor snickered. "Though it is a back breaker."

"And you would know." Everett chuckled. "Considering how many nights you spent on my poor substitute for the proverbial doghouse, during the early days of your marriage."

"Are we not witty?" With a mighty scowl, Trevor stared at Dalton. "Heed my counsel, and tell Daphne what happened, with all due haste, as you do not want her to find out from someone else."

"Believe me, I am trying, but I would not do so in the middle of a crowded ballroom." The signature notes of the opening waltz had him searching for Daphne. "But at this instant I have a dance to claim with my lady."

So Dalton mustered a smile, as he drew Daphne from

her newfound allies, ignored Rebecca's countenance of reproach, and led his bride-to-be to the throng of couples.

"Oh, Dalton. Never have I attended anything so grand as the Richmond's gala." With his arm settled about her waist, and their fingers twined, she beamed inexpressible joy, and a strange sensation welled within him, warming his insides and quelling his unrest. "The fashions are spectacular, the jewels are extraordinary, the hothouse roses are magnificent, and the tapestries are awe-inspiring. I can't help but wonder if I belong here, as I have no fortune or connections."

"Of course, you belong here." It bothered him that she deemed herself unworthy, when she possessed more integrity in her little finger than the collective of revelers. "And I would ask a favor, if I may."

"Your wish is my command, sir." She squealed with delight, as he whirled her in rhythm with the music. "As you have made me so happy."

"I like the sound of that." He found her enthusiasm contagious, as the dark thoughts infesting his consciousness yielded to her euphoria, and the waltz worked on him in way he had never experienced. "But I would request a private audience, tomorrow morning, as I have an urgent matter I must explain before we venture to another party."

"Is something wrong?" Her bright light dimmed, and he cursed himself for ruining her celebration. "Have I embarrassed you? If you have reappraised the situation and wish to rescind your offer, I will understand."

"Would you surrender me so easily, angel?" The second he voiced the query he hated himself for asking it.

"Never." The subtle flinch of her fingers betrayed her internal unrest. "But neither would I hold you to our bargain, if you choose to end it, as I care too much for you to force you into a marriage you no longer covet."

"You care for me?" She could not know it, but she had just caught the attention of every inch of him—and a few wicked ones, in particular. "I mean, your affections are engaged?"

"Yes." Her eyes flared. "And I—"

"Excuse me." Lord Sheldon smirked. "But I believe this quadrille is mine."

Everything within him railed, as he refused to cede the gently reared virgin to the wolf of London. But how could he avoid causing a scene and shaming Daphne?

"There must be some mistake, as this is my dance." Damian bowed and extended a hand. "Now be a good lad and shove off, Sheldon."

"Your Grace." The blackguard gritted his teeth and disappeared amid the crush.

With Daphne safe from harm, Dalton turned and discovered Lady Moreton. Without a word of acknowledgement, he dipped his chin and returned to the Brethren's customary meeting place, only to find Everett struggling to keep a visibly distressed Sabrina upright.

"Dalton, fetch our coach, as I fear my wife is in labor." Everett waved at Blake, who lent assistance. "Hurry, man."

Winding his way through the mass of attendees, he located the butler. "Summon the Earl of Woverton's rig, at once. And send a messenger to Dr. Handley, with due haste, as it is an emergency."

"Yes, sir." The manservant bowed and rushed to relay the orders.

"I told you we should have stayed home, as did Lance and Cara." Everett walked Sabrina to the entrance. "When you carry our next child, I shall confine you to Beaumaris, as I will not risk your life or that of our babe for a silly ball."

"But I only wanted to—*oh*." Wincing, Sabrina bit her lip and hugged her belly. "Everett, I am afraid, as it is too early."

"Hold on to me, darling." Despite the public venue, Everett kissed her forehead, stared at Dalton, and frowned. "I will let nothing hurt you or our second born."

"Where is mama?" Sabrina moaned and then shrieked, as a puddle of fluid pooled at her feet. "Oh, no. My water just broke."

"Bloody hell." Everett waved with frantic intensity, as the coach arrived, and footmen scurried to assist Everett and Sabrina. "Dalton, locate the admiral and Lady Amanda, and tell them what happened."

"I will find them." In the main hall, Dalton glanced straight ahead and then right. The admiral preferred to linger among the old guard, and Lady Amanda never left his side, so he veered toward the salon. As the venerable leader of the Brethren traded war stories with retired Royal Navy men, Sabrina's mother perched at the end of a sofa, sharing conversation with the wives.

When she spied Dalton, her smile morphed into a frown, and she stood. "Mark, I think something is wrong."

"What is it?" the admiral asked, as they huddled near the front wall.

"Sabrina is in labor, and Everett has taken her home," Dalton said, in a low voice.

"But she is not due for another few weeks." Lady Amanda clutched her husband's arm. "Hurry, Mark. We must go to her."

"I will relay the information to the others." Then Dalton sprinted into the ballroom. In mere minutes, he related the pertinent details to Blake, Damian, Elaine, and Celia. When Dirk and Rebecca exited the dance floor, Dalton signaled his brother and sister-in-law and explained the events. "Where is Daphne?"

"She is with Elaine and Celia," Rebecca replied, as she scanned the vicinity.

"No, she is not." A dark sense of foreboding shrouded him in palpable anxiety. "I found Elaine and Celia, and Daphne was not with them."

"I will check the dining room, as she may be at the buffet." To Dirk, Rebecca said, "Darling, will you look in the back parlor, as she may have ventured in there."

"Then I will search the terrace." Dalton glimpsed the open doors. "And we will meet in the foyer."

As he navigated the ocean of couples, he shrugged off the panic pulsing within his muscles and told himself he was overreacting. Daphne was curious, and she had probably enacted an impromptu exploration of the Richmond's home. When he stepped to the flagged surface, and the cool night air penetrated his clothes, he shivered. Following a graveled path, hushed voices brought him to the side garden, and he halted in his tracks.

Bathed in the silvery glow of a full moon, an obscene congregate, of sorts, framed his future wife at either side. Whispering in her ears, Lady Moreton and Lord Sheldon stood as two foul bookends, and Daphne sobbed when she spotted Dalton. Tears glistened as they streamed her cheeks, her expression manifested unspoken horror, and her gaze struck him as a vicious punch between the eyes.

"*Enough.*" Daphne wrenched free and raised a clenched fist. "I would thank you never again to intrude upon my hospitality, as I may be moved to violence."

And then she ran in the opposite direction.

CHAPTER NINE

ive days later, Daphne huddled on the landing at Randolph House and fought cursed tears. Repulsed by her own weak spirit, she dried her face on her sleeve and vowed not to cry again. Of course, she would break that oath, as she had done little else after the Richmond's ball. Given what Lady Moreton and Lord Sheldon had disclosed of Daphne's erstwhile true knight, she loomed at a painful impasse, and she prayed her appointment would provide some comfort and much needed insight.

"I am sorry, Sir Dalton." Hughes clasped his hands behind his back. "Miss Daphne bade me convey her regrets, as she remains unwell and unavailable."

"Thank you, Hughes." Dirk chucked Dalton's shoulder. "Worry not, brother. She will come around, as she is a sensible girl, but she needs time. Why not join me in the study for a brandy?"

"But I need to explain what happened." Dalton appeared bedraggled, as if he had not slept since last Thursday. "Sheldon drugged me, and I ended my affair with Lady

Moreton. They hurt Daphne on purpose, because of me, and I must make amends, as I cannot lose her."

Dalton's spontaneous and unintended confession captured her attention, as he had just altered her perspective, though he knew it not. Mollified, to an extent, she gazed at the ceiling and sighed, as she hated being at odds with her savior. Covering her mouth with her hand, she hugged the wall and almost screamed when Rebecca tapped Daphne on the shoulder.

"Down the back stairs, now." The viscountess led the way. "I had the coach brought to the mews, so you might avoid Dalton until you are ready to receive him."

"Becca, do you think ill of me?" Daphne bumped into her hostess, when Rebecca came to an abrupt halt. "Am I wrong to seek some understanding of Dalton's actions, before granting him an audience?"

"No." At the terrace doors, Rebecca retrieved Daphne's pelisse from a chair and draped the coat about Daphne's shoulders. "When Dirk related Dalton's discreditable behavior, my first desire was to string the younger Randolph from the highest yardarm, as I could not stomach his stupidity."

"But now you feel otherwise." Desperate for the minutest measure of solace, Daphne grasped Becca's hands. "Tell me I am wrong. Tell me I am making too much of nothing. Tell me to believe in him, and I will do so."

"My dear, calm yourself." Rebecca squeezed Daphne's fingers. "Come. Let us get you in the rig, so you might find peace and make your decision, as the choice must be yours, freely made. And I can't advise you in this matter, as I have no right to judge Dalton, because I am hardly an impartial critic without sin."

"So you have an opinion?" Together, they walked through the garden. "I would love to hear it."

"After you have reached your conclusion, I will explain an intimate part of my past, which has direct bearing on your situation with Dalton." Rebecca unlatched and opened a gate. "But not until you reconcile things with him, as I would not influence your position."

"I understand." In the rear courtyard, a footman handed Daphne to the coach. "Thank you, Becca."

The former spy winked, retreated a step, and shouted, "Drive on."

As she reclined in the squabs, Daphne examined the ermine trim of her lavender pelisse, the matching day dress, and her crisp white gloves, all purchased with Dalton's funds. Whenever she pondered the fact that his money had supplied every stitch of clothing on her body, she shivered. She owed him so much, yet she could not ignore the salacious deeds Lady Moreton and Lord Sheldon had described in embarrassing detail.

When she had accepted Dalton's less than romantic proposal, the happy bargain had not included an ill-mannered former mistress and a handsome but cunning reprobate bent on spreading ill will. But the simple fact remained that she cared for Dalton, and she had faith in him, though he tested her conviction to new lengths. And while she had withdrawn from society, as she had to gather her wits, and she refused to cry in public, what hurt her most was the prospect of never winning Dalton's heart. But how could she compete, given his carnal predilections?

Just then, the coach halted before a resplendent brick mansion, which boasted a double-door entrance and the number 24 etched in the masonry. As she ascended the stairs, a very proper butler set wide the oak panels and then bowed.

"Miss Daphne, I presume?" The manservant smiled.

"Yes." She nodded, stepped into the foyer, and doffed her outerwear. "I have a prior engagement with Lady Amanda."

"Her ladyship awaits your presence in the drawing room." The butler lifted his chin. "If you will follow me, please."

The elegant chamber sported distemper wall coverings trimmed in mahogany, velvet drapes, a damask sofa and matching *chaise*, and two Hepplewhite chairs, bathed in rich navy blue. A fire burned in the hearth, which abated the unseasonably cool May afternoon. Seated amid the majesty, the graceful hostess, with hair black as a crow's feather, regal features, and crystal blue eyes, smiled.

"Miss Daphne is just arrived, your ladyship." The manservant bowed.

"Thank you, Hamilton. That will be all." Lady Amanda stood and approached, with arms outstretched. "Daphne, how wonderful to see you. And how are you, my poor dear? I have heard some of your travails, when Rebecca visited Sabrina and my new granddaughter, yesterday."

"How is Sabrina?" At Lady Amanda's urging, Daphne eased to the sofa. "And what of Phoebe? Rebecca tells me the baby is beautiful, and Everett is thrilled."

"Daresay I have never seen a prouder papa, and I have no doubt my son-in-law will spoil her, as Everett dotes on her, already." Lady Amanda giggled. "But I would have it no other way. And Dr. Handley assures us Phoebe and her mother is in fine fettle. Yet you did not journey here to trade pleasantries about the latest addition to our family, and I must confess I am intrigued. How might I be of service?"

"I know not where to begin." Daphne accepted a cup of tea and resituated herself, as Lady Amanda perched to the right. "So much has happened in so little time, and I am at a loss to keep pace."

"Perhaps you might start with the obvious question." Lady Amanda inclined her head. "What has this to do with me?"

"Well, in truth, nothing directly." Daphne gazed at the plush carpet and frowned. "I had hoped we could discuss the brooch and its predictive nature."

"The brooch?" With an owlish expression, Lady Amanda dropped a napkin to her lap. "Ah, yes. Dalton relayed the events surrounding your initial meeting and the temporary absence of my family heirloom."

"I apologize for that." Awash in shame, she slumped forward. "My youngest brother, Richard, took it from Dalton's ship, so we could sell it for food."

"A noble endeavor." Then Lady Amanda's countenance sobered. "You wore it."

"I beg your pardon?" Daphne bit her tongue.

"Do not try to deny it." The admiral's wife scooted close. "What did it show you?"

Myriad repudiations flitted through her brain, as Daphne had not planned to reveal such intimate revelations. Then again, she had read Lady Amanda's most private thoughts, so it was only fair to share. "A gold coin, tossing about in the air."

"Upon my word." Marked by a demeanor of utter shock, Lady Amanda gasped. "Dalton is your one true knight."

"Do you believe so?"

"I do not doubt it for an instant."

"How can you be sure?"

"Because I know, firsthand, the power of the artifact."

Lady Amanda averted her stare. "Although it has been years, I made use of it, after my sister loaned it to me, while my beloved Mark was at sea. Do you know what it imparted?"

"Yes, as Dalton allowed me to peruse the journal." With trembling fingers, Daphne returned the cup and saucer to the tray. "I hope you are not offended when I say I found your entry quite romantic, but it was your certainty, regarding the lore, which brought me here. And I must know, do you accept the visions as irrefutable fact?"

"I do," Lady Amanda responded with unshakeable conviction. Then she extended a hand. "Do you see the band I referenced?"

"'*Ego dilecto meo et dilectus meus mihi.*'" Daphne twisted the simple gold ring. "It is lovely, but what does it mean?"

"I am my beloved's, and my beloved is mine." A tad misty-eyed, and with a ghost of a smile, Lady Amanda sighed. "Mark gifted it just prior to casting off, after my father denied my dashing sailor's initial request to wed me, and never have I removed it, since. During our separation, which reigns as the most painful period of my life, as we were so in love, Olivia insisted I consult the brooch, in an effort to ascertain whether or not Mark was my one true knight."

"But you dreamed of a captain's insignia." Daphne recalled the tender archive. "Did you ever vacillate?"

"Never." The striking noblewoman lifted her chin. "As I had pledged my troth to my Mark, or I vowed I would die a spinster. When he surprised me at my father's birthday celebration, gorgeous in his new regimentals, I was ecstatic."

"So you think I should marry Dalton." Daphne grasped at the slightest bit of optimism. "As the brooch must be correct."

"I would not go that far, as you must decide, for yourself, what you want for your future, because it is an irrevocable commitment, once it is sworn at the altar." For a while, Lady Amanda simply studied Daphne, and she shifted beneath the scrutiny. "But I would wager you know in your heart what you desire."

"I love Dalton." And so she declared her deepest secret, and it had not destroyed her, as she had feared it would. Instead, Daphne could not help but laugh, as the misery from the past five days seemed to evaporate, in a flash. "I love him, I do. I did so wish the coin was his, before I discovered it belonged to Dalton."

"Then Dalton is your match, in every way. He is your one true knight." Then Lady Amanda furrowed her brow and sank against the cushions. "I apologize, but I have been unwell, of late."

"Oh, no." Daphne provided assistance, as she collected Lady Amanda's cup and brought it to her. "You should have cancelled our appointment, as I would have understood."

"It hardly signifies." She sipped her tea. "I have no idea what is wrong with me, as I am always tired, I often suffer dizzy spells, and my belly has been downright temperamental, especially in the morning."

"It sounds as if you are pregnant." Daphne chuckled.

"Oh, my goodness." Peering left and then right, Lady Amanda's mouth fell agape. Then she grabbed Daphne's arm. "That had not occurred to me, until this very moment."

"But—is it possible?" Given Lady Amanda's advanced age, Daphne presumed the suggestion ridiculous.

"It is most definitely possible, yet I should summon Dr. Handley, tomorrow." The noblewoman surrendered to a strange fit of mirth. "But it has been so long. Wait until I tell Mark."

A knock at the door silenced the spontaneous celebration.

"Come." The oak panel creaked, a bouquet of red roses appeared, as if from nowhere, and Lady Amanda pressed a finger to her lips. "Who is it?"

"Who do you think?" Sporting a charming pout, the admiral, a veritable mountain of a man and quite handsome, peered into the room. When he spotted Daphne, he started. "I say, thought you were alone, my Amanda."

"I do so love it when you call me that, after all these years, my glorious Lieutenant Douglas." Lady Amanda flicked her fingers, and her husband presented the spray of hothouse blossoms. Instead of accepting the elegant offering, she tugged her husband's coat sleeve. "I want a kiss."

"But you have company, darling." Daphne swallowed a gurgle of laughter, as the admiral blushed.

"Miss Daphne is not company, she is to be family, and so the usual rules do not apply." Lady Amanda yanked the admiral's wrist. "A kiss—now."

Planting a palm on the back of the sofa, at either side of his wife, the admiral bent and set his mouth to Lady Amanda's. In deference to the devoted couple, Daphne pretended to find the ceiling infinitely fascinating.

"Are you feeling better, my Amanda?" the admiral inquired. "You looked a bit peaked this morning, and I am worried about you."

"I am much improved, as you are home." As she spoke, Lady Amanda's voice grew almost husky, and Daphne fidgeted. "And I wonder if you might do something for me?"

"Anything, sweetheart." The admiral rubbed his nose to

his wife's, and Daphne envied their ardent relationship. "As I am yours to command."

"I like the sound of that." Lady Amanda cooed. "If you would forgo your ritual visit to White's, in favor of an early dinner in our sitting room, and have Ellie put the blooms in a vase atop our bedside table, I would thank you properly for the roses."

"That is an offer I dare not refuse." The admiral stood upright and straightened his coat. "I shall leave you ladies to your tea."

"And I should go." Daphne folded her napkin.

"But you have not explained your hesitancy, where Dalton is concerned, and I would not permit you to leave, when you remain perplexed." Lady Amanda swiped a square of shortbread from a plate. "If you are familiar with the brooch's mystical powers, what frightens you?"

"Two guests at the Richmond's ball conveyed a dastardly deed I could never repeat, aloud." Just recalling the licentious disclosure made Daphne shudder in disgust. "But it involved Dalton."

"Could you whisper it to me?" Lady Amanda leaned near, and Daphne cupped her ear and recited the nefarious affair. "Upon my word. If Beth finds out, Dalton may not live to regret it."

"Who is Beth?" she asked. "And what has she to do with Dalton?"

"The dowager viscountess of Wainsbrough and Dalton's mother." Lady Amanda snorted. "And she is a force with which to be reckoned, but you should fear not, as she will love you."

"You do not seem scandalized by my report." Daphne smoothed her skirts. "How would you have felt, had you heard a similar account of the admiral?"

"Well, if it had occurred after we met, we never would have married." She folded her arms. "But I have no doubts where my husband's fidelity is concerned, as he keeps me busy, in that department. However, prior to our acquaintance, I know he was no saint, as he made that clear. Yet I would not judge him, as society holds men to a different standard, in that respect. Had Mark remained chaste, his peers would have deemed him less a man. But women are presented with a contrary set of edicts, which, if violated, can result in their ruin."

"I am not sure I follow you." Daphne rubbed the back of her neck.

"My dear, we live in a patriarchal society, where the right of primogeniture grants men exclusive reins of power and privilege, with one important exception." She tapped her cheek. "While women are prohibited from inheriting titles, property, or fortunes, and the law classifies us as chattel, from birth to death, we are charged with the preservation of our chastity and, thereby, our reputation. In short, we are defined by our abstinence, whereas men are encouraged, even praised, in their naughty indulgences. Your only advantage is to marry someone who respects you, who views you as his equal—who loves you. Though I do not condone his rakish antics, the scandal with Dalton will run its course, and the *ton* will forgive and forget, because of his sex. I suspect he cares for you. The question is how much weight will you give something that happened before Dalton knew of your existence?"

"I understand." And everything fell into place. Leaping to her feet, Daphne knew exactly what she would do, and she needed to depart, as she would not delay. "How can I ever thank you?"

"Make the most of every moment you have with him, as

time flies, and it is never enough." Together, they walked into the foyer. "Hamilton, send for Miss Daphne's coach."

"Yes, my lady." The butler stepped onto the landing and signaled the driver.

"I wish you a pleasant evening, Lady Amanda." Daphne shrugged into her pelisse and then tugged on her gloves. "And I will maintain your confidence, until you make the announcement, but I am so thrilled for you and the admiral."

"You are a good omen, and I knew I could rely on you, which I must do, as I would share my glad tidings with Mark, exclusively, as our own treasured secret." Lady Amanda hugged Daphne. "And if it makes you feel better, I believe you made the right decision."

"Thank you, again." With a squeal of delight, Daphne jumped into the rig and hollered, "To Randolph House, and hurry."

≈

"DESOLATION, THY NAME IS DALTON." Draped across a high back leather chair, with one leg dangling over an armrest, he swirled the amber liquid in his brandy balloon, downed the contents in a single gulp, and huffed a breath. "Everything has gone to the deuce. What am I to do, brother?"

"You know, for the first time in your life, I believe you are truly contrite." Dirk swiped the decanter before Dalton could pour a refill. "And you have enough problems, without getting foxed, in the process."

"Ever since we were in shortcoats, you have always reacted the same whenever you have unfortunate news to impart. So what is your big revelation, which requires an intoxicating overture?" As if the situation could get any worse. Dalton set his empty glass on a side table. "Out with it. What have you heard?"

"Word has spread of your *ménage à trois*." Dirk stared at the flames in the hearth. "When I stopped by Howell's to collect Rebecca's order of chamomile tea, as she could not wait for their standard delivery, I overhead a rather fatuous conversation, which devolved to gossip of your liaison with Lord Sheldon and an, as yet, unnamed woman."

"Bloody hell." He shot to his feet and paced, a habit he never indulged. "Well that is that. I have lost her. There is no way Daphne will ever forgive me."

"Do you think her so fickle?" With her hand resting on the doorknob, Rebecca loomed in the entry. "Then you know Daphne not at all, as she is a vast deal stronger than you apprehend, and you would be wise not to underestimate her."

"You support me?" Dalton stiffened his spine, as he had anticipated a lethal reproach from his sister-in-law. "You would champion my cause?"

"Yes." Rebecca nodded once, as Dirk stood. "Because I know how it feels to carry past encumbrances into a relationship and enjoy an unconditional pardon from the one you love."

"But yours were born of service to the Crown, while mine are of my own making." She could have knocked him over with a feather. "Why should you advocate my suit?"

"Do you recall our discussion, en route to the church, on my wedding day?" With a regal air, Becca glided across the room, into her husband's waiting arms. Hugging Dirk about the waist, she rested her head to his chest. "You may not have realized it, at the time, but you betrayed your true nature, and you have never fooled me, since. While you might portray yourself as the black sheep of our family, and you have done your best to fulfill that role, you are, in actuality, just like your elder brother. So I know what occurred with Daphne has wounded you."

"What?" Dirk withdrew, ever so slightly, to look his wife in the eyes. "You can't mean that. Dalton and I are as night and day."

"That is what he wants you to believe, and he has done an excellent job of supporting that assumption." Rebecca snickered. "But I know otherwise."

Tugging on his cravat, Dalton shuffled his feet and shifted his weight, as Rebecca's abrupt character assessment had, for all intents and purposes, just stripped him bare, and he knew not how to rebut her assertion. For years, his reputation had functioned as invisible armor, shielding him against the cutting remarks and cruel treatment of the *ton*.

"I would argue you have read too much into a brief interaction." Relying on an old habit, he drew his lucky coin from his pocket and flipped his familiar talisman, as he mustered unimpaired aplomb. "And I am like the wind, carefree and ever changing direction."

"Just what did you two talk about, prior to our nuptials?" Dirk kissed the top of her head. "And why have you not mentioned it before?"

"Because it did not signify until now." She drew Dirk close and suckled his bottom lip. "And I will tell you the whole of it, tonight, in our bed."

"And then you will distract me." Dirk arched a brow.

"Yes." She spread her fingers over Dirk's chest. "But for now we should turn our thoughts to dinner, as the meal is ready, and I would have Dalton join us."

"But what of Daphne, as she is your guest?" Dalton asked. "I would not upset her. Well, anymore than I have already."

"She has taken her evening meals in her chambers, since your contretemps, so you would disturb no one." Clutching Dirk's elbow, Rebecca flicked her fingers, and Dalton positioned himself at her left. "And you would not want to disappointment me, given I had Hughes situate your place setting at the end of the table, in our informal family seating."

"Rebecca, you could charm candy from a babe." Ignoring the despondency seeping into his veins, Dalton managed a smile for his hostess, as they navigated the hall.

"Brother, you have no idea." Dirk chuckled.

"Is that a complaint?" Rebecca inquired.

"Never." Dirk growled. "As I am rather partial to your brand of persuasion."

In the foyer, Hughes stood at the entry.

"Expecting company?" Dalton glanced beyond the open doors and came to an abrupt halt.

"Oh, dear." Rebecca gasped.

As Daphne crossed the threshold, she pulled off her gloves and passed them to Hughes. It was then she spied Dalton. For a scarce second, she simply stared at him. Then she mouthed his name and charged.

"Daphne." With arms splayed, Dalton caught her and lifted her from her feet. "My angel, how I have missed you."

"I am sorry." She kissed him hard and fast. "I am so sorry. At the first test of faith, I wavered. Can you ever forgive me?"

"Darling, I am to blame, as I should have told you of my past." Now Dalton claimed her mouth, as he ached to taste her.

"Er, Dalton." Dirk cleared his throat. "Perhaps you should move your reunion to the drawing room, and we shall await you in the dining room."

It was all he could do to carry his lady across the foyer and into the chamber, away from prying eyes. As he kicked the oak panel shut, he paused to savor her tender flesh, and dank desolation yielded to desire. At long last, they came up for air, and he rested his forehead to hers.

"I owe you the apology, love." He could not help but squeeze her. "But in my defense, I tried to tell you of my shame, that evening in the park, when I proposed, but you would not hear it. I would have you know my character, if you intend to wed me."

"It is of no importance, in the grand scheme, because you knew not of Daphne Harcourt, when it occurred." She framed is face. "And I know your character, sir. As we have spent the better part of the last two months together, I know you quite well. You could have left us, in Portsea. You could have walked away, but you stayed. You gave me your protection, shielded my brothers, when you could have turned them over to the authorities, stocked my community pantry, and financed a ball, so I could feed the more stubborn Portsea citizens. If that is not noble, then tell me what constitutes such attribute?"

"Do not be fooled, as I am not a good man, Daphne." He rubbed his nose to hers. "But you make me want to change. I want to be good for you."

"You need alter nothing, because you are my gallant savior." She caressed his cheek with her thumb. "You are my one true knight."

"No." He shook his head. "I am—"

"Listen to me." When she met his stare, he caught his breath, as the strength of her conviction shone bright as the sun. "I wore the brooch."

"What brooch?" And then it dawned on him that she

referenced the family heirloom. "Sweetheart, that is nothing but lore."

"No, it is not." As if to emphasize her point, she favored him with a potent kiss, parting her lips to tickle his tongue with hers.

Everything inside him tensed, as he poised to take her in the most elemental fashion, right there beneath his brother's roof. Some invisible but powerful force stayed the beast within, so he held tight to the reins of lust, as she was his lady, and Dalton resolved to respect her virtue. When he returned home, he would take a cold bath and put four fingers and a thumb to excellent use, as the cannon in his crotch had loaded for battle.

"Daphne, you know not what danger you court." Gritting his teeth, he summoned unimpassioned thoughts, but nothing provided serviceable results. At last, he set her feet on the floor and retreated behind the sofa. "And I have made other mistakes, which I would catalogue for you."

"Promise you will honor our vows, and your commitment, and I will believe you." She moved in his direction. "Because you are my match. I napped with the artifact pinned to my dress, prior to returning the antique to you. I was desperate for a solution to my family's troubles, and the brooch offered the possibility of an answer, so I availed myself of the bauble. Do you know what it showed me?"

"What did you see, love?" He had not the courage to trample her confidence, so he indulged her. "Of what did you dream?"

"A gold coin, with a rather questionable image on one side, tossing in the air." With a half-smothered sob, she pressed her clasped hands to her chest. "I knew not the owner of the curious item, as the visions gave me no other clue. But I wanted it to be you. I prayed it was you."

For several minutes, he searched his memory, and various confusing moments fell into place. Then he snapped his fingers. "That is why you flung yourself at me, aboard the *Siren*, after you were caught in my cabin, when I had thought you might flee?"

"Yes." And he suspected she would have repeated the maneuver, had he not taken refuge near the *chaise*, as she stalked him. "It was the first time you wielded the token in my presence, and I was shocked and elated, at once. So you see, we are fated to be together. Our destinies are intertwined, and nothing you say will convince me otherwise. If you will have me, I will be your wife."

"I do not deserve you, but, heaven help me, I want you." When he gave her his back, she almost knocked him down, as she hugged him tight from behind. "Daphne, the road ahead will be difficult, as the rumor is out, and I am marked by scandal."

"What care I for scandal, when I have you?" She sniffed. "And I would just as soon go home, as I find London society lacking."

"But I cannot abandon my responsibilities, so our only option is to weather the storm." How he regretted tainting her with his disreputable activities. "We must make the rounds, accept the invitations issued, and endure the scrutiny. Trust me, everyone will watch us. And Lord Sheldon and Lady Moreton will haunt our every move, seeking to tear us apart, as our happiness is their misery."

"Then why not just marry me, now?" she asked in a small voice.

"Because I would court you properly, as rushed nuptials would yield additional unfavorable gossip, which would cast a cloud over you, and that I will not tolerate." He turned in her embrace, but another scenario brought him to the overstuffed chair. How often he had walked in on his brother and Rebecca, sharing a single seat, and Dirk insisted such positioning was without equal for heartfelt discussions. So Dalton situated himself and then slapped his thighs in invitation. "Come here, love."

At first, Daphne blinked. Then she stepped about his knees, descended to his lap, and rested against his chest. "Are you afraid?"

"Yes." He held her close, cupped her head, and sighed. The urge to protect her, almost violent in intensity, invested his frame. "Never before have I suffered weakness, as I cared not for my safety. But my enemies may strike me by hurting you, and the prospect terrifies me. There are those who will ridicule us, those who will shun us, and we must bear it."

"Stuff and nonsense." She nuzzled him. "I believe in you, and as long as I am your lady, they cannot injure me."

"If you would agree, I would ask you to ignore spurious rumors, and heed nothing that is not confirmed by me, as I vow to hide nothing from you." Yet he knew not what more to reveal, as he scarcely knew himself.

"My gallant Dalton, you have my solemn pledge." Her certitude rendered him renewed confidence.

"So we will stay the course." He tipped her chin, bringing her gaze to his. "We will fight."

"My one true knight, we will borrow from Shakespeare, plot our attack, and give society an exchange such as it has never seen." Daphne smiled. "And if that foul woman comes near me again, I shall cry, 'havoc,' and let slip the dogs of war."

CHAPTER TEN

"*W*ell I heard Dalton Randolph woos the backwater girl, because no one in London would have him." An anonymous disparager chortled. "After all, he is a second son."

"But he possesses a vast fortune and excellent connections." Another unknown belittler snickered. "I could put up with quite a bit of mischief for such benefits, given he is easy on the eyes, but my father requires I marry a titled gentleman."

"Ladies of quality do not tolerate such devilment, regardless of money or familial ties." A third detractor scoffed. "But he would be fun for a night of naughty recreation, if you take my meaning."

The three hens broke into a fit of cackles, and Daphne clutched her beau's hand and squeezed his fingers, in a show of support. Dirk frowned and compressed his lips, while Rebecca craned her neck, as the foursome enjoyed tea and sweetmeats at Pâtisserie François, a quaint establishment where the notables converged to see and be seen. Were they in Portsea, she would have taken the detractors to task over their rude comments, but so-called polite society, which were anything but polite, played by its own rules.

A sennight had passed since the initial disclosure of Dalton's discreditable act, along with Lord Sheldon's part in the debauchery, and the *ton* was rife with speculation regarding the woman's identity. Some had suggested Daphne completed the titillating triumvirate, but as she had just arrived in the city that spring, the rumor had not gone far.

"I am sorry, Daphne." Dalton leaned near and imparted in a low voice, "If you would prefer to leave, I can have your selections packaged."

"Nonsense." After choosing a tempting lime-blossom madeleine, Daphne winked at her man, as nothing could spoil her afternoon with Dalton. "I am a proud provincial, and those self-professed *ladies* are nothing to me, so what care I for their good opinion?"

"Be that as it may, I shall remove their names from the guest list, for our fall gala." Acting as chief-chaperone-in-charge, Rebecca folded her arms and humphed. "If they can be rude, then so, too, can I."

"Darling, I love it when you are ruthless." Dirk whispered in her ear, and Becca giggled. "What say you, sweetheart?"

"My randy lord, great minds think alike." Rebecca fed her husband a small bite of shortbread. "And I shall don the new burgundy, again, just for you."

"Promise me something." Resolved to persevere, Daphne admired the viscount and viscountess, as they flirted without restraint or shame.

"Anything, angel." Dalton scooted his chair closer. "What would you have of me?"

"Once we are wed, you will adore me, in public, as Dirk

does Rebecca, and as the admiral does Lady Amanda." Now that Daphne had made her decision, she would accept nothing less than her fantasy, and she wanted everything. And as she had delved into charitable work on Portsea Island, and management of the governorship in papa's absence, she dove into courtship with her gallant knight, embracing all manner of social outings, musicales, and balls. Most of all, she desired a match based on affection. "Since I was a little girl, I have dreamed of being cherished, and I would never complain or grow tired of it."

"My dear Miss Daphne, I would not even have to try to fulfill that request." Now he favored her with his dimpled grin, and she could not help but laugh. "In fact, I may spoil you, as I cannot wait to make you mine."

"But I am not asking you to buy me things, because you have done so much for me, already." A now familiar fluttering in her belly distracted her, and she brushed crumbs from the skirt of her pale blue dress. "And I am so grateful."

"I hesitate to remind you, because a gentleman would never do so." For a scarce second, he studied her mouth, and then he met her stare. "But I am not interested in your gratitude, my lady."

"Then take my heart, as it is yours." And then Daphne bit her tongue, as she had not planned to make her declaration at that moment. There, amid the pink and white chintz wall coverings and matching tablecloths, she had made her stand for the future she desired. To her amazement, the surroundings seemed to fracture, her ears pealed, and she only had eyes for Dalton. For a while, her future husband simply gazed at her, shock investing his boyish features. When she could bear no more, she blurted, "I love you."

"I know you do. Why else would you accept my proposal? And I believe I love you, too." Furrowing his brow, he glanced surreptitiously about the crowd, as he rested her palm to his thigh and caressed the delicate flesh between her fingers, through her gloves, and she shivered. "At least, I think I do, but I am unfamiliar with such emotions. Yet I care for you, more than you realize."

"Will you tell me when you know for certain?" Yes, she was disappointed by his not so ardent attestation, but she recalled the brooch's mystical powers, her visions, as well as Lady Amanda's assurance, and in silence Daphne pledged to persist. "As I would know when you share my devotion."

"You have my word, although I am not sure I will recognize such attachment." Despite his prosaic proclamation, she remained resolute. "Never have I experienced that singular sentiment, but if I could ever love anyone, it would be you."

"Well, that is something." No, his was not the commitment she had sought, but her circumstances had changed, and so she had to alter her expectations, but she had not ceded the fight.

"My, my, what a fetching sight." With a cat-that-ate-the-canary grin, Lady Moreton stared down her nose at Daphne. "If it is not the black sheep and the rustic ragamuffin."

"Better that than a low-rent doxy." The soul of feminine deportment, Rebecca daubed the corners of her mouth, and Daphne could not stifle a snort.

"Well, I never." The troublemaker humphed and drew herself up with regal hauteur.

"That is not what I heard." The former spy inclined her head and arched a brow. "And I would thank you not to intrude on our family gatherings, as you are not welcome."

"Why can you not leave us in peace, Almira?" Dalton

stood. "Why can you not be happy for me? What did I ever do to you? And, as I told you, our arrangement is ended."

"You do not throw me over, Sir Dalton." Lady Moreton lowered her chin. "I am a lady of noble blood, widow of a great man, and you are nothing more than a second son."

"You dare call yourself a lady?" Daphne shot to her feet. "Given your shameful behavior with Lord Sheldon and Sir Dalton, I wonder how you refer to yourself as such and maintain your composure. And I may be a backwater girl, but I would rather hail from a dignified if unfashionable Portsea Island upbringing than a cosmopolitan lifestyle that ranks iniquitous self-gratification above honor and respectability. Now I say good day to you, ma'am."

Clutching a hand to her throat, Lady Moreton gasped, and her mouth fell agape. It was then Daphne noted the hushed whispers, as the patrons remarked on the confrontation. Unsure how to respond, she glanced at Dalton for reassurance, but he appeared too shocked to respond.

Without a word, Lady Moreton fled the establishment, and the murmurs grew louder. To the right, a group of older women stared at Daphne, and then one raised her glass, in toast.

"Well she will think twice before tangling with you again." Rebecca beamed as a proud mama. "Nicely played, Daphne."

"That was bloody brilliant." Dirk clucked his tongue. "By God, but our mother could not have done better."

"Are you positive she would approve?" Daphne reclaimed her chair, as the business resumed normal service in the wake of her brief contretemps, and Dalton had yet to offer his perspective of her exchange with Lady Moreton. "As I let my emotions get the best of me, and I should apolo-

gize. In my defense, I was born a Harcourt, and we are notorious for our quick tempers."

"You were born to be a Randolph." To her surprise,
Dalton came alert, brought her hand to his lips, and pressed
a chaste kiss to her knuckles. "And I should gift you
diamonds, as I am in your debt, in more ways than one."

"I beg your pardon?" In confusion, Daphne blinked, as
he owed her nothing. "Given our arrangement, how could
you be obligated to me?"

"Because you may have just rid us of the importuning
Lady Moreton, once and for all."

THE EDDINGTON'S massive ballroom reigned as a favorite of
Dalton's, because it contained a vast array of nooks and
crannies perfect for an illicit tryst, and in the great hall he
had engaged in numerous clandestine rendezvous amid the
shadows. But on that night he had promised himself to
remain on his best behavior, for Daphne's sake, as they
returned to the *ton*'s stage, as a dubious pair.

As he had anticipated, many partygoers, most he would
describe as hypocrites, gave him a wide berth. Whispers
and hushed murmurs greeted their arrival, and several
women turned their backs on Dalton and Daphne, but his
resilient rustic wavered not an inch. When he spied his
newfound enemy, he flinched.

"What in bloody hell is Lady Moreton doing here?" He
anchored Daphne at his side. "I do not like this. Almira is
up to something."

"Perhaps she received her invitation prior to our
confrontation, and the Eddington's did not wish to offend
her." Daphne peered at him, frowned, and flexed her

fingers as she clutched his arm. "Is that not why we enjoy the same hospitality, because Lord Eddington could not rescind the summons without committing a breach in social etiquette?"

"I suppose that explains her presence, but we are welcome because Lord Eddington is a very good friend of my brother's." The termagant lurked as a jungle cat preparing to pounce, and he raised his defenses, as he scanned the vicinity for Lord Sheldon, given the two were thick as thieves. "Promise me you will remain with a member of our family, in my absence, for the length of the celebration."

"But I am not afraid of her," Daphne declared in a low voice. "As we have no more secrets between us, she can not hurt us."

In the four days since the confrontation with Lady Moreton, Dalton had conferred with his bride-to-be and divulged every dirty tale of debauchery and devilry, going back to his years at Eton and Oxford, and including his particularly licentious tenure as a midshipman. While it had been painful to catalogue his nefarious capers for the gently bred virgin, and she had consumed impressive amounts of brandy during his bawdy recitations, he had been determined to spare no detail, which might function as an impediment to wedded bliss.

"Sweetheart, trust me. There is much mischief she can instigate, given we are minus a few allies." Everett and Sabrina remained at home, with their new baby. And just prior to departing for the festivities, Dalton had received word that Cara had gone into labor, and Lance had opted to forgo the party and stay with his wife. Yet he could not blame his family for his predicament. For the umpteenth time, he wondered whatever possessed him to get involved with the widow, but he could not undo the past. "And Almira Moreton is a master of manipulation."

"But you said we were rid of her, so why would she target us?" Daphne fidgeted with her diamond necklace, which he had gifted her in the wake of the set-to with Lady Moreton. True to form, his pretty provincial had protested the extravagance, until he threatened to throw the expensive bauble in the refuse. Only then had she acquiesced and accepted the matching earrings and bracelet, too. "And everyone watches her."

"So I had presumed, but I can think of no other reason for her attendance." And he could not shake the overwhelming sensation that Almira would seek vengeance. "In light of your haphazard revelation concerning her involvement in my discreditable activities, she needs no reason to fix on you. And Lady Moreton can hold a grudge like no one's business. Do not be fooled by her delicate appearance, as she is a formidable adversary."

"Then I shall be vigilant and do exactly as you suggest." Despite her charming smile, the rigid set of her jaw betrayed her discomfit, and he hated ruining the otherwise fanciful evening for her. "Am I, at last, permitted to save all my waltzes for you? Is it permissible to make that statement, given our intent to wed, as I would rather eschew any other man's embrace?"

"My angel, I command it, as I could not bear to see you in another man's embrace." To his inexpressible joy, she glowed. "And I might be persuaded to give you a tour of the Eddington's library, if you are good."

"Define 'good,' my gallant knight." With a flirty titter, she licked her lips. "And I shall do whatever you wish."

"Careful, my dear Miss Harcourt." He bit back a groan, as everything inside him came alert at her innocent but inspiring proclamation. "I would not compromise you until the vows have been spoken, but you test my fortitude."

"Am I so special?" The initial notes of the first waltz signaled the crowd, and he escorted her to the dance floor. "Given your extensive experience?"

"Would it shock you were I to admit I have wanted you since you bent over the tea stores in the *Siren's* hold?" He arched a brow and hugged her tight about the waist. "Have I scandalized you?"

"Hardly, as I am well acquainted with your comedic nature, Sir Dalton." Daphne squealed, as he twirled her in the rotation. "If you recall, I wore a hood, so my face was shrouded. How could you know anything of me?"

"I knew more than enough that night." As always, he could not contain his laughter, when her arresting naïveté charged the fore. "Especially with you sporting those tight breeches, and I look forward to our honeymoon and a lengthy survey of your delectable derriere. Never let anyone tell you to be ashamed of your figure, angel."

"*Dalton.*" Her attempt at reproach failed when she grinned. "So that is where your interest lies? And I had thought you partial to my mind."

"Oh, I want that, too." He reversed course. "I want to possess every part of you, my angel."

When the dance ended, he led his lady to the edge of the throng. As the sea of bejeweled revelers parted, he noted a familiar visage and steered for the entrance.

"Where are we going?" Daphne inquired. "Your family is gathered in the back."

"There is someone I want you to meet." Standing before the grandest dame of the *ton*, Dalton drew up short, clicked his heels, and pulled Daphne to his side. "Miss Daphne

Harcourt, may I present Lady Elizabeth, dowager viscountess of Wainsbrough and my mother."

"OH, MY." Daphne jerked, half-bowed, and then sketched a proper curtsey. Why had Dalton given her no warning? "Lady Elizabeth, I am so honored to make your acquaintance."

"Are you not a delightful little thing. Please, you must call me Beth, as my son tells me we are to be family." The poised noblewoman inclined her head and smiled. "And I wager I am far more excited to meet you than you are to meet me. Perhaps we can get to know each other, over tea, tomorrow."

"I would love that." In an instant, Daphne decided she liked her future mother-in-law.

"Wonderful." The dowager extended a hand and flicked her fingers. "But now I would ask my youngest to favor me with a dance."

"Of course, Mama." Just as fast, Dalton jerked and glanced at Daphne. "If you will permit me to return Miss Daphne to—"

"Stuff and nonsense." Daphne shooed her overly protective one true knight. "Indulge your mother. I know where to find Elaine and Celia, so I will be fine. And we are in the middle of a crowded ballroom. What could possibly happen?"

With that thought swirling in her brain, Daphne turned on a heel and weaved through the crush. After admiring a massive spring arrangement, which boasted a mix of roses, daisies, and snapdragons, she ventured into the shadows, where she located the youngest and quietest member of the odd extended family.

"Lucien claimed Celia for the quadrille." Elaine drew Daphne behind a large bust perched atop a pedestal. "Do you see them? I feared Celia might burst, she was so excited."

"How marvelous." Daphne glimpsed the happy couple, and Celia emanated unutterable elation, as she gazed at the young sea captain. "Oh, no. She tripped."

"She refuses to admit it, but she is smitten with him." Elaine scooted lower. "And he is interested in her."

"How do you know?" She craned her neck to gain a better vantage. "Have you heard something?"

"That is the benefit of blending into the background, as people do not hide what they believe others neither perceive nor detect. Watch and learn, my pretty friend." With a muffled chortle, Elaine tugged Daphne to the other side of the column. "Men are not so difficult to read, as the clues are in their conduct. See how his fingers linger with hers, he licks his lips, when he meets her stare, and look how he admires her, when he thinks her unaware. She has caught his special attention, though he may not yet know it."

"Does Dalton act in similar fashion, with me?" Daphne searched her memories for any relevant hints. "Have you noted any singular habits?"

"Indeed." And then Elaine remained silent.

"Well?" Daphne shook Elaine. "What have you noticed?"

"Check his bearing." The serene noblewoman pointed. "He searches for you, even in the company of Lady Elizabeth. When in deep conversation with the boys, Dalton adores you with his eyes. And when you stand within arm's reach, he can't stop himself from touching you, however brief the contact. I have witnessed such behavior, before, with my married brothers."

"He cares for me." It was a statement, not a question, and her knees buckled. Crouched in the Eddington's ballroom with Elaine, Daphne realized Dalton had spoken the truth, when he claimed an emotional attachment. No, his had not been an attestation of undying love, but her one true knight harbored *something* for her, and that was better than nothing. In that moment, her heart sang.

"There is Sir Ross." Elaine lurched upright and grabbed Daphne's hand. "I would speak with him, but I promised Dalton I would not leave you alone."

"Go to him." Daphne grasped Elaine by the shoulders and gave her a gentle push. "As I can manage on my own."

As the orchestra segued into an allemande, Lady Elizabeth patted Dalton's cheek and then exited the grand hall. The gallant knight peered left, then right, and started in Daphne's direction. So when Lady Moreton threw herself into his path, Daphne came alert. The nettlesome woman gestured with wild and frantic movements, while Dalton attempted to evade his nemesis, but she yanked hard on his coat sleeve. Conscious of the multitude of witnesses, her beau rested fists on hips and thrust his chin. Just as Daphne considered intervening on Dalton's behalf, someone covered her mouth with a palm, slipped what seemed as an iron band about her waist, pinning her arms, and lifted her feet from the floor.

In the dark, she struggled in vain, as her unknown assailant carried her along the back wall and navigated a small passage. At last, they slipped into a dimly lit chamber, which Daphne surmised was the study, because of the furnishings and the faint smell of cigar smoke.

"Now I am going to put you down, and if you raise the

alarm, I will quiet you in a manner you may or may not enjoy, Miss Daphne." In a flash, she recognized the voice and calmed. "Do you understand?"

She nodded.

"My but you look rather fetching tonight, in your cream ensemble." Her kidnapper set her on terra firma, then trailed a finger along the curve of her breast, and she stomped his booted foot and wrenched free. "What a spit-fire. No wonder Randolph favors you."

"Lord Sheldon, why have you brought me here?" Daphne retreated a step and inhaled a shaky breath. "What do you want with me?"

"Can you not guess?" He studied her from top to toe. "Or are you that naïve?"

"Pray, I comprehend nothing in your outrageous manners." Hugging herself, she withdrew and added more distance between them. "Why am I the unfortunate bene-factor of your unwelcome flattery, sir?"

"Lady Moreton has a score to settle with you." As if guessing her thoughts, the scoundrel positioned himself in the path to the door. "She asked for my assistance."

"And you champion her spurious cause?" To her frus-tration, she could identify no other exit. "Have you no sense of decency?"

"No, I am not so encumbered." He laughed, as he moved in her direction. "I am in it for the sport."

"Is that what I am to you?" And then his heinous purpose dawned, and she shuddered. "You intend to compromise me."

"My dear, I am many things, but I am no rapist. Almira merely requires me to give the impression that I have ruined you, and I am more than adequate to the task." The devas-tatingly handsome but unscrupulous rogue cast a lazy smile, and she feared she might vomit. "But I caution you not to reject the meal, when you have yet to sample the main dish."

"And what does she hope to achieve, aside from my embarrassment?" In a swift maneuver, Daphne skittered behind the massive desk, achieving a modicum of security. "As I am a provincial, I do not value society's good opinion."

"She suspects Dalton wishes to marry you." He lunged, but she avoided him. "I am to ensure that never happens."

"No matter what you try, you will fail." In that second, Daphne's confidence soared, as the reprobate could never succeed. "Because I love Dalton, and he cares for me. So do your worst, sir. You cannot hurt us."

Lord Sheldon opened his mouth and then closed it. For a few seconds, he simply gawked at her. Then, to her surprise, he sat in the leather chair near the hearth. "Has Dalton told you of the time he cuckolded Lord Walton?"

"At Lady Darrow's, after a visit to the theatre?" Daphne sank into the plush seat at her left and rested her elbows atop the blotter, as she fretted she might swoon. "Yes, I know the whole of it."

"And what of the Heath affair?" Lord Sheldon fixed his stare on the ceiling. "When we got foxed and—"

"You seduced the Howard twins and then traded partners." Daphne sighed. "I have heard the story, as Dalton shared the entirety of his history with me."

"And it does not bother you?" The wicked man met her gaze and furrowed his brow, as his astonishment was evident in his tone. "You forgive him?"

"In the grand scheme, it does not signify." Emboldened anew, she soared on a wave of unshakeable conviction, as she recalled her conversation with Lady Amanda. "As the events occurred prior to our meeting, they matter not to me, so there is nothing to forgive. And as I apprised you, I love Dalton."

"How very old-fashioned of you, Miss Daphne." Lord Sheldon scrutinized the shine of his boots. "I had thought to stun you into submission, to incite your anger and then use revenge as a catalyst for a pleasurable tryst."

"It will not work." And then she fretted for her knight. Had Lady Moreton lured him to an equally remote location? Regardless of the outcome, Daphne vowed to support her future husband. "Dalton is the only man I have any interest in touching—or having touch me."

"And do you think such a creature exists for me?" He frowned. "Is it possible for someone who has wreaked so much havoc in this world, and destroyed untold marriages, to find love?"

"Of course, it is possible." Unafraid, Daphne stood, walked to the center of the chamber, and claimed the chair beside his. "You need only earn the lady of your dreams with honesty and a true heart."

"What of you?" He shifted to face her. "My fortune is greater than Randolph's, and although I, too, am a second son, my father is an earl, so you would be Lady Sheldon, if we wed."

"Thank you, for the gracious offer, but I do not set store in such trivial titles, sir." She studied the flames in the fireplace. "And I have found my mate."

"Indeed, you have, and I should return you to him, as you have made a dolt of me." Lord Sheldon checked his timepiece and shot forth. "Bloody hell, Almira will be here, at any second."

"Oh, no." She leaped to her feet. "What shall I do?"

Just then, the door flew open, and Dalton loomed in the entrance. He glanced at Daphne, glared at Lord Sheldon, and kicked shut the oak panel. Before she could utter a word, her knight stormed across the room, clutched the lapels of Lord Sheldon's coat, and slammed him against the wall.

"If you put your hands on her, I will kill you." Dalton bared his teeth. "I will see you at dawn on Paddington Green."

"Dalton—no." Fearing for her knight, Daphne framed his face and forced him to look at her. "Nothing happened. In fact, Lord Sheldon intervened on our behalf, after Lady Moreton hatched a plot to compromise me. But he could not go through with it."

"Oh, come now." Dalton scowled. "Do you really expect me to believe this leopard has changed his spots?"

"Yes." Daphne leaned against him. "Will you hold me? Lady Moreton planned a horrible scheme, but Lord Sheldon confessed the entire stratagem."

"Darling." A sudden shift in Dalton's demeanor coincided with a growl, as he thrust aside Lord Sheldon and then enfolded her in a gentle embrace. "Are you all right? I feared the most awful things, when I could not find you."

"I am fine." She lifted her chin, and he bestowed upon her a tender kiss. "And I am better, now."

"Uh, I hate to break up this sickeningly sweet reunion, but Almira should have already found us, so I would not delay." Lord Sheldon paused at the portal, which he eased ajar. Without ceremony, he retreated. "Hell and the Reaper, she comes down the hall, with Lady Howard and Lady Eddington as witnesses."

"What can we do?" Daphne gulped.

Lord Sheldon sprinted behind the desk and said, "Randolph, you owe me for this." Then he pushed the chair aside and dove beneath the piece of furniture.

"Follow my lead, sweetheart." To her infinite amazement, Dalton dropped to one knee and pulled a small box from his pocket. When he lifted the lid, he revealed a diamond ring nestled in a bed of cotton. "I have been carrying this with me, waiting for the perfect moment to gift your betrothal band, since the jeweler delivered it. When Lady Moreton opens the door, shout, 'yes.'"

As if on cue, the nasty woman thrust the oak panel, and Daphne cried, "*Yes.*"

"Oh, my." Lady Howard blinked and sputtered. "It appears we have intruded on a romantic interlude."

"And what a momentous occasion." Lady Eddington pressed her clasped hands to her bodice. "While I must apologize for the interruption, may I extend my deepest congratulations, my dears?"

Dalton slipped the understated bauble onto Daphne's finger and then kissed her knuckles, before he stood. "I beg your pardon, Lady Eddington. Given our close familial ties, I thought your venue the perfect opportunity to surprise Miss Harcourt with a proposal. I hope you are not angry that I commandeered the study for the private ceremony."

"Sir Dalton, I am honored." Lady Eddington approached and whispered in his ear. "I should be uncontrollably excited, and my ball would be the talk of London."

"What an excellent notion." Dalton bowed. "Lead the way, Lady Eddington."

As Lady Eddington and Lady Howard disappeared into the hall, Lady Moreton clutched Daphne's arm and whispered, "As long as you live, you will never satisfy him as I satisfied him."

"Do not intrude on my person, again, as I may be moved to violence." Daphne wrenched free and lifted her chin. "And that is me being nice."

"Leave us alone, Almira." With that, Dalton ushered Daphne to the ballroom.

Following in their hostess's wake, they strolled straight to the orchestra, where Lady Eddington indicated she wished to address the revelers. After flagging down a footman, she claimed a crystal flute of champagne and sent additional portions to Dalton and Daphne.

"What is happening?" Daphne's heart beat a salvo in her chest.

"Smile, my angel." Dalton winked. "There is nothing the *ton* loves more than romance."

"My lords, ladies, friends, and family, I am so pleased to announce the impending nuptials of two of our brightest young people, and we are the first to share the stupendous news. So raise your glasses in toast." Lady Eddington paused for effect. "Sir Dalton Randolph, brother of Viscount Wainsbrough, is to wed Miss Daphne Harcourt."

CHAPTER ELEVEN

*H*ad Dalton known how quickly polite society would forgive and forget his foibles in the wake of his engagement; he would have sought a bride much sooner. Given only one woman had ever inspired thoughts of marriage and a trip to the altar, such revelations mattered not. In a mere sennight, he and Daphne had gone from being the pariahs of the *ton* to the most marvelous couple in London. For good or ill, his course was set, and Miss Daphne Harcourt would be his bride in a fortnight. It was that fact, alone, which had brought him to White's; in search of information he never thought he would solicit.

"Gentlemen, each of you has survived my current predicament and now enjoys a happy union, which is why I have asked for this meeting." Stretching his legs, he reclined in his chair and ignored the sea of smirks. "So how do I make love to a virgin?"

"Very carefully," Everett replied. "As it can be a traumatic experience for both of you."

"Which has been known to cause some fledgling wives to leap from moving carriages, to escape the ordeal." Trevor gurgled, and in unison, the gathered Brethren husbands, save Lance, who remained at home with his wife and new son, burst into laughter.

"How did I know you would toe that same tired mark?" Everett rolled his eyes. "And this from a man who mistook his blushing mate for a seasoned doxy."

"Watch it, old chum." Trevor sobered. "It was an honest miscalculation, on my part. And who would have ever guessed I would find a naked but unspoiled dove in Dalton's cabin? But if I could travel back into the past, and have my chance again, I would have taken my time and savored the moment, committing every caress and kiss to memory, because it happens but once, and then it is done. However unintended, in my haste to have Caroline, I took her as a tried courtesan, and I hurt her. Had I known of her delicate state, I would have prepared her, as most maiden's discomfort stems from nerves."

"Point taken." Everett stared into his glass of brandy. "And Trevor is correct, in some respects, as there is nothing like the deflowering of the woman who claims your heart. It is not something you do in a rush. Rather, you should recognize the achievement and relish the significant event in your life, as a couple. It sets the tone for your conjugal bed, and that could be a blessing or a curse, depending on how you handle it."

"I concur with Everett." With a half-smile, Jason leaned on the armrest. "Given we were none of us green lads for the singular occasion, we can attest to the certainty that, while the anatomy remains the same, there is something altogether special about sailing your wife's uncharted harbor, when you ponder the fact that no other man has lain between her thighs. And although the mechanics do not differ, nothing feels as you expect it, when your affections are engaged. Prior to our marriage, I will admit I lusted after my Alex, but love tempers some aspects of coitus, such as the baser instincts centered on self-gratification and release, while amplifying others, which defy explanation. Simply put, nothing compares to what I share with my bride, and she holds my unreserved and exclusive attention. I will have no other, as I desire no other."

The men grew quiet, as palpable tension hung heavy in the air. Pondering the heady conclusions his brothers had disclosed, Dalton rubbed his chin and wondered how to maintain control in the throes of passion, as he nursed a powerful hunger for his blonde angel. To Dirk, he asked, "Was it the same for you?"

"Aye." His always-refined elder sibling gazed at the floor and grinned. "While I wanted to wait until the vows had been spoken, my spy had other plans, and she would not be denied. When I took her, it was all I could do to manage her enthusiasm, without embarrassing myself, but the trick is in the focus. You must place her needs before your own. Endeavor to bring her fulfillment, which will help her relax and minimize her pain. In regard to completion, you need not worry about yourself."

"Oh, I say. He is right." Everett grimaced. "You must summon dispassionate thoughts, else you are done for, and I would know. My Brie provoked me, and I rode her, hard and fast, as an unbroken horse, though I am not proud of it."

"Bloody hell, it can be mortifying for a reformed rake." Trevor downed his brandy, signaled for a refill, and winced. "Think back to your days as a randy lad, when the softest breeze could load and fire your cannon, and then double it. And while Caroline and I have been married these past four years, and we have produced two healthy sons and have another child on the way, I still want her every bit as much as I did the night I claimed her."

"In that I would not argue, as it is all I can do not to ravish my Becca at every turn." Dirk chuckled. "Brother, in the early tenure of our marriage, we made love every morning, noon, and night, and several times in between. And my wife shows no signs of slowing her carnal crusade. To date, we have christened each chamber and parlor in Randolph House and worked our way through the larger portion of apartments at Lyvedon, but we will persevere."

"But our ancestral home has over one hundred rooms." The logistics, alone, impressed Dalton, and he drew his lucky coin from his pocket and flipped it in his palm. "Never knew you had it in you, old boy."

"You will be amazed by what a cherished wife can inspire." Dirk waggled his brows. "Best aphrodisiac known to humanity, in my humble opinion."

"And then there is the dreaded declaration." Trevor elbowed Everett, who nodded his assent. "You may avoid it, in the beginning, but sooner or later, you must proclaim your love, as Daphne will need it."

"And do so without turning green in the face." Everett snickered.

"I resent that, Everett. Really, I do." With a mighty scowl, Jason folded his arms. "I succeeded, eventually."

"How long did it take?" Everett clucked his tongue. "Come, now. We are friends."

"It was almost two blasted months, before I could pledge my heart without vomiting, and I will thank you not to harp on it." Jason glared at Dalton. "Though I am loathe to concede, Everett is right—"

"Oh, I love it when you say that." Everett gave vent to a

growl of triumph. "But I am no better, as I believed, in a moment of sheer lunacy, that I could win Sabrina without a declaration, and my err almost cost me everything I hold dear."

"But I have already told Daphne I love her." Dalton rubbed the back of his neck. "Though I am not sure my emotions are so engaged, and I apprised her of that."

"What?" Dirk stiffened his spine. "You proclaimed your love and then qualified it?"

"Yes." Dalton leaned forward and rested elbows to thighs. "Why do you ask?"

"How did she take it?" Jason queried. "As my Alex would have lopped off my—never mind. But she would have been a vast deal more than unhappy with me."

"Did you have to go there?" Everett shuddered. "The mere suggestion gives me collywobbles, as my Sabrina would have done the same thing."

"How do you mean?" Dalton shrugged. "Given Daphne gifted me her heart, she accepted my tempered pledge with unimpaired aplomb, though she has requested I inform her once I am assured of my feelings."

Slack-jawed, Dirk peered at Trevor, who glanced at Everett, who stared at Jason.

"I have nothing." With an owlish expression, Trevor blinked.

"I am at a loss." Everett retrieved his handkerchief and daubed his temples. "As such revelations defy the limits of perspicacity."

"And that was the *coup de grâce* in this group's repertoire." Jason snorted and glared at Trevor. "Now what do you suggest, Mr. 'I am the veteran of four wicked campaigns?'"

"Five, including yours." Trevor held up a hand with

fingers splayed. "And as I recall, you swept the pool, when it comes to self-made disasters."

"We are not here to discuss my courtship of Alex." Smacking a fist to a palm, Jason scowled.

"You call that a courtship?" Everett scoffed. "I have seen better pursuits from the Kleinfelds."

As his fellow Nautionnier knights argued the salient points of women, love, and relationships, Dalton mulled the situation regarding Daphne. Making his declaration worried him not, as he cared for her. But how would he know when his heart was engaged, given he hardly knew himself? After years of pretending to be something he was not, would he even recognize what remained of Dalton Randolph?

"Brothers, I appreciate your expertise and counsel." Then he raked his hair and braced for their reaction. "But I intend to follow my instincts, where Miss Harcourt is concerned."

"So WE HAVE POSTED the banns, contacted the modiste, the milliner, the hosiery, and Damian's cook." Lady Elizabeth checked off an imaginary list. "Has Dirk submitted the papers to secure the license?"

"He has," Rebecca responded. "We should receive the requisite documents in plenty of time. And everyone has circulated the *on-dit* that the hasty nuptials take place at Penhurst, due to the governor's rapidly declining health, which forbids him from journeying to London for the ceremony. Damian explained the situation to Mr. Catchpole, and the vicar has agreed to maintain the ruse."

"And Richard will travel to Penhurst, with Hicks and

Mrs. Jones, but Robert will stay on the Continent, as Beresford refused to grant leave on such short notice." Daphne toyed with the betrothal ring, as nerves got the best of her. "Then that covers everything."

"Which allows us to depart on Friday, for a Sunday ceremony, as planned." Rubbing her eyes, Alex yawned. "Forgive me, but my bargain with Jason has left me exhausted, as he exercises my imagination, among other things, with his daily boon."

"But I had presumed that ended, given Dalton proposed." With baited breath, Daphne awaited a private dinner with her fiancé, which she looked forward to ever since she had received his sweet note. With all the excitement surrounding her wedding, they had enjoyed little time together, and he had requested an audience, which had set her thoughts racing in various directions. "Their job is done, is it not?"

"Oh, but you forget my husband's stipulation that our pact continued until you married." Alex reclined amid the pillows and sighed. "I should have known better than to tangle with the captain of my heart, as he is a past master at licentious stratagem, and he indulges in his installments for hours, on end, but that is an observation, not a complaint."

In concert, the ladies giggled.

"Beth, this younger generation never ceases to amaze me. Secret alliances and recompense to win a man, and all I had to do was seduce Mark. And when I seduced him, he stayed seduced." Poised and polished as ever, Lady Amanda ignored the laughter and smiled, as she perused a sampling of wall coverings, which the interior designer had delivered that morning, after Dalton had employed a small army of experts to redecorate Courtenay Hall. "And I believe I am partial to the navy flock with the damask pomegranate designs, for the drawing room."

"That was my choice, too." With cheeks burning, given Lady Amanda's statement, Daphne nodded. "And I ordered two Hepplewhite chairs, in a cream textile. I had intended to select a softer hue of blue for the sofa and *chaise*."

"Sounds marvelous." Rebecca flipped through a collection of swatches. "And what shade did you select for your apartments?"

Now that was one aspect of the renovations Daphne had thought about long and hard, and her decision had been finalized the previous afternoon, with a brief but concise directive to the contractor. Borrowing from Sabrina, as well as the other wives, Daphne had instructed the foreman to make some last minute changes to Courtenay Hall, which she had not discussed with Dalton.

"May I impart a secret?" Daphne scooted to the edge of her seat. "I am having the wall between the master suites torn down, so we will share a much larger space, and the entire chamber will be trimmed in Dalton's favorite color. However, as our schedule is tight, I delayed that portion of the project until after we return to London."

"Nice move, Daphne." Beth winked. "Like I said earlier, I believe you will do very well with my son."

Just that morning, Beth and Daphne had taken breakfast in the dowager's sitting room. During the casual meal, Dalton's mother had detailed some disturbing news of his childhood, which had brought Daphne to tears.

A mean-spirited nanny had denied basic nourishment and care to a newborn Dalton, in favor of spoiling the heir. Given Dalton was but a babe, the abuse had been well hidden. As a result of the neglect, the second son had failed to thrive and become quite ill. It was in Dalton's third year that a physician had suspected maltreatment, the injury had been discovered, and the evil woman had been fired, but the damage had been done.

"I hope so." When Beth catalogued Dalton's misfortune, Daphne ached to hold him. A quick check of the mantel clock declared the appropriate hour grew nigh, and she trembled with anticipation. "And I do wish to please him."

As if on cue, someone knocked at the door.

"Come." Rebecca peered over her shoulder.

"Have you finished your business, love?" Dirk sauntered into the room. "As Jason is just arrived to collect Alex."

"Where is my beautiful bride?" The blonde captain strutted to the fore and grinned, when everyone noticed Alex had drifted off, sitting upright, and nestled in the cushions. Jason pressed a finger to his lips and tiptoed, yes, the giant tiptoed to his wife. With great care, he lifted her in his arms and kissed her forehead.

"Captain of my heart, am I dreaming, or are you here?" Cupping his cheek, Alex sniffed. "Even if I wished to, I do not think I could muster sufficient energy to walk. I am so tired, Jason."

"You are not dreaming, darling." As he adjusted his hold, he chuckled. "And I shall take you home, feed you, and put you to bed, straightaway, as you have earned your rest."

"And I should be going, as Mark will be expecting me." Lady Amanda stood and smoothed her skirts. "So we are to attend the wedding in Penhurst, the funeral in Portsea, and the family dinner that I will host, once we return to London."

"In that order." Beth clutched Lady Amanda's elbow, as they walked into the foyer. "And I am so glad you are feeling better.   Did Dr. Handley know what caused the sour stomach?"

"Oh, yes. And I am in fine fettle." Lady Amanda cast a pointed stare at Daphne, and she dipped her chin. "But we can talk more, when we are all together."

"And my brother paces in the back parlor, Miss Daphne." Dirk smirked, has he hugged Rebecca. "I do not think I have ever seen him so nervous, so you should take pity and put him out of his misery."

"How do I look?" Wearing a sapphire silk gown, which she had purchased just for her one true knight's delectation, Daphne rotated. "Will Dalton consider himself fortuitously matched?"

"Given you sport his favorite color, he will fall at your feet." Then Dirk nipped the tip of his wife's nose. "As do I, when my bride captivates me with something fetching from her wardrobe in my shade of choice. Oh, I almost forgot, Hughes gave me a message, which is addressed to you."

"Thank you." With a half-curtsey, Daphne swiped the envelope, slipped it into her side pocket, and squealed.

In the hall, she turned right and walked to the appropriate portal. A footman opened the door, and she crossed the threshold and gasped in surprise.

What she had previously known as the back parlor had been transformed into an oasis filled with red roses and a smattering of candelabra, which lent a warm, soft glow to the room. Some of the furnishings had been relocated to make space for a small table for two, which had been set in the center of the room.   Standing before the hearth, bedecked in his gentleman's garb, featuring a fawn waistcoat and a coat that matched her dress, her dashing sea captain favored her with his shy grin. When the latch clicked shut, she gave vent to a smothered sob and sprinted into his embrace.

For a long while, Dalton held her, and though no words were spoken, they conveyed a wealth of meaning in gentle caresses and sweet kisses. Again and again, they came together, tongues twining, lips converging, and hands groping in an enchanting symphony of desire, and Daphne wanted more, as everything inside her seemed to twist and turn. When he attempted to set her free, she moaned an injunction of protest, and he steered her into heretofore-unknown bliss.

How they made it to the sofa, she neither knew nor cared. But when he settled her in his lap and loosened her bodice and the chemise, she retreated a hairsbreadth and inhaled a shaky breath. "What are you doing?"

"May I?" Recalling his troubled infancy, she could not comprehend how anyone could have hurt him. Endearing to a fault, he had been blessed with endless charm, and she could not resist his lure, so she nodded her assent.

"If you wish me to stop, you need only say so." Then her knight bared her breasts. Whereas she had expected some semblance of awkwardness, the heat of his stare emboldened her, and she relaxed. "You are beautiful, Daphne."

"I am so glad to know you are pleased with me." As he cupped her tender flesh, she shifted her hips, as foreign sensations assailed her.

"Pleased? The word is insufficient, sweetheart." To her minor discomposure, he admired her without restraint and drew small circles on a peak. "Watch your nipple. See how it responds to my touch? It grows hard."

"Yes." A strange fluttering in the pit of her belly, and lower, snared her attention. But when Dalton licked his finger and brought the warm wetness to her pebbled tip, she emitted a muffled cry.

"Do you know what this means?" he inquired a husky tone. When she shook her head in reply, he smiled. "You are aroused. It means you want me, as I desperately want you."

"In that, I must trust you, as I have no experience in such matters." Despite her nudity, she sank against him and nuzzled his chest. "How I have missed you. I long for the simple days, on Portsea, when you joined me on my charitable visits."

"My back may never recover, given I chopped more wood in those few hours than I have in my entire life." In that instant, he bent and suckled her nipple, and Daphne thought she would surely melt. "Just as I presumed. You are pure honey, my angel."

"Will it be like that again?" She struggled to focus, as fire simmered in her veins, and her heart beat a rapid salvo. "The companionable walks and easy talks, with just the two of us?"

"I hope it will be better." He grazed her with his teeth, and she closed her eyes. "I want you to be happy, Daphne. But if you have any second thoughts or regrets, you may tell me, and I will release you from our engagement."

"What?" She lurched upright, as sheer panic replaced the contentment. Clutching her gown, she retied the chemise and secured the bodice. "You do not wish to marry me?"

"You did not listen to me." He kept her in check, when she tried to push away. "I seek to give you a way out, if you so desire it, because you know my faults. As for me, you are the only woman I would ever wed, but I would not hold you to our arrangement, if you valued your freedom. You need not concern yourself with money, as I would take care of you, regardless."

And there it was, his vulnerability on full display, just as his mother had explained. He considered himself less than honorable, when nothing could have been further from the truth. At that moment, she framed his face and kissed him with all she had and for all she was worth. When, at last, they came up for air, she rubbed her nose to his.

"I will not let you renege on your proposal, Dalton Randolph." At her proclamation, he squeezed her so tight she gasped. "And if you try to leave me, I will hunt you down, sir. You would never escape me, because I love you. So you are saddled with me, till death do us part."

"All right, sweetheart." Without ceremony, he retrieved a long but thin box from his coat pocket. "Then I would ask a favor. For our wedding, I would have you wear something special to mark the event."

"Dalton, not more jewelry." He had already gifted her diamonds, after the awful confrontation with Lady Moreton, and Daphne was unaccustomed to such demonstrations of wealth. "I feel guilty, as I have nothing to give you, in return."

"Oh, I don't know about that, as I count your kisses as priceless treasures, love." As if to prove the point, he claimed a quick buss. "Humor me, for the occasion."

"You spoil me terribly." With a frown, she lifted the lid —and burst into tears. "Mama's pearls."

Hugging the much-cherished family heirlooms to her chest, she collapsed, as the stress of the impending nuptials, the remodel of Courtenay Hall and her room at his bachelor lodging, and the contretemps with his former mistress had taken their toll.

"Daphne, please, do not cry." As she wept and sobbed,

divesting herself of the tension that had plagued her since arriving in London, her knight massaged her back and offered unshakeable support. "I had intended the senti-mental gesture to make you smile."

"You have no idea what this means to me." With a roll of her shoulders, she laughed and burrowed close to him. "But how did you know about the pearls? I surrendered them to pay a portion of papa's debt."

"I know." Dalton cupped her chin and brought her gaze to his. "I was in your father's study, hiding behind the drapes, when you gave them to Mr. Allen. I knew you were in trouble, and I wanted to help you. After the ball, I sent two of my men to locate him and purchase the baubles, so I could restore them to you. That is the effect you have on me. You make me want to be a good man."

"But you could never be a good man." She pressed her forehead to his and sniffed. "Because you are a great man, and I am fortunate you found me."

"Sweetheart, I thank my lucky stars, every day, that you chose to board my ship." It was just as Elaine had said, he could not stop touching Daphne, and she reveled in the attention. "And I never thought I would be grateful to your brother for stealing the brooch, but I am obliged, because the theft led me to you."

"Then let us toast our auspicious fortune." With that, she eased from his hold, pulled on his wrist, and led him to the table. "Because right now, I want to celebrate."

The meal passed in relative calm, as she learned the simple fare of roasted pork and apples, with a side of maca-roni and cheese, was Dalton's favorite. For dessert, ah, dessert was a marvel of unimaginable delight, as her one true knight fed her a spectacular whipped syllabub. Then it was her turn to offer him spooned bites of the creamy concoction, interspersed between sugary kisses, which she had indulged from the now-familiar cozy perch of his lap.

All too soon, the long-case clock chimed the late hour, and her fiancé stood to depart. But another thirty minutes had passed before she walked him to the door.

"So we journey to Penhurst on Friday, lady mine. And on Sunday, you shall be Mrs. Dalton Randolph." With a sly grin, he drew her close and set his mouth to hers, and she flicked her tongue to his, just as he like it. "Thank you, for a lovely evening."

"Oh, I dearly love the sound of that." Wrapping her arms about his waist, she rested her head to his chest and sighed. "Tomorrow, after I inspect my quarters at your home—"

"Our home." In play, he tapped her nose. "And I want everything to be perfect for you."

How disappointed she had been, when he gave her a tour of his town residence. When Daphne had envisioned their happily ever after, it had not included separate bedrooms, and she wondered how he would react to her secret renovations at Courtenay Hall.

"In any case, I shall practice writing my new name." Just the prospect gave her gooseflesh. "Until I see you again, I will miss you."

"Then dream of me, tonight." He pressed his lips to her bare knuckles. "As I will conjure naughty fantasies of you, angel. Now go upstairs, before I break my promise to be good and have my wicked way with you."

THE NEXT MORNING, after a relaxing breakfast in bed, in her private apartment, Daphne stretched long, as the lady's maid shook out the sapphire blue gown and hung it on a peg in the armoire.

"Miss Daphne, an envelope fell from the pocket of your dress." Mary set the missive on the tray. "Will there be anything else? Would you like more tea?"

"No, thank you." Daphne poured a third cup of the steaming brew. "I shall lounge for another hour, and I will ring for you when I am ready for a bath."

"Very good, Miss Daphne." The maid curtseyed and exited the room.

Reclining against her pillows, Daphne tore open the letter and unfolded the parchment. As she digested the contents, she cried out in shock.

Miss Harcourt,

If you value your life, do not marry Dalton Randolph. Heed this warning, and call off your wedding. If you do not do as I advise, you will be sorry.

There was no signature, and neither the stationary nor the handwriting yielded hints of the sender. Of course, Daphne had her suspicions, and she pondered whether or not to apprise Rebecca and Dalton of the threat. As the obvious culprit was Lady Moreton, Daphne saw no reason to permit the harridan a victory, of sorts, by spoiling what should reign as a happy occasion. And what could the widow do in so little time?

Resolved to stay the course, she tucked the envelope into her journal and opted to pen an entry describing the evening with her one true knight. For good or ill, she had given him her promise, and she would not go back on her word.

CHAPTER TWELVE

$\mathcal{I}$t had taken two days to journey to Penhurst Castle, the ancestral seat of the Weston dukedom, so Dalton's last night as a bachelor had been spent in a dank tavern in the village, surrounded by his fellow Brethren of the Coast, save Everett and Lance, who remained in London with their wives and newborn children. As he peered out the window of his chamber, which had been prepared to accommodate his bride for their wedding night, he admired the impressive vistas of the Channel.

"Brother, it is time." Dirk came to stand beside Dalton. "Are you ready?"

"Yes." That was putting it mildly, because he had not slept much, as all he could think of was his blonde angel and the consummation of their vows. Never had he wanted a woman, as he desired Daphne. "Is it true? Does the drawing room look like a hothouse run amok?"

"You never should have told Damian that Miss Daphne favors roses, as he may have secured every bloom in England, for the occasion." Dirk chuckled and chucked

Dalton's shoulder. "Alex believes her brother lavishes on your blushing bride the trimmings he had intended for his sister, as he has thrown himself into the planning and decorating with unrivaled gusto, and even mama is irritated."

"Bloody hell. But I cannot complain, as he aids our cause." Dalton swaggered to the long mirror and assessed his appearance. After adjusting his cravat, he smoothed the lapels of his coat made of Bath superfine and sighed. "By the way, thank you, for the suggestion regarding my formal-wear. As you warned, the old Jolly Roger is primed for battle, in anticipation of tonight's consummation, and I would not frighten my bride or scandalize the vicar and mama."

"I understand." With a snicker, Dirk inclined his head. "Suffered the same affliction until I bedded Rebecca in my bunk aboard the *Gawain*, and I had already sailed her harbor, so I can't even begin to imagine your misery, at this point."

"Trust me, you do not want to know, as I may be erect until the holidays." He stepped into the hall, with his sibling in tow, and navigated the landing. In seconds, he skipped down the grand staircase. In the foyer, he turned left and strolled through the double door entry. "Good afternoon, Conrad."

"Good afternoon, Sir Dalton." The butler bowed. "May I extend congratulations on behalf of the entire household, as we are honored to serve you during this most felicitous event."

"And my soon-to-be-wife and I thank you." As he tugged on the lace trim of his shirtsleeve, he cleared his throat and entered what he had previously known as the drawing room. "Upon my word. What in God's name has Damian done?"

Crimson blooms festooned every conceivable surface, and tapered candles dotted the chamber. Some sort of sheer white material bedecked every stick of furniture, and a haphazard arch had been constructed of branches and boasted the same textile and flowers. While he understood the female sex lived in expectation of their wedding day, in all its pageantry and splendor, he could think of nothing more than the moment when he rested between Daphne's creamy thighs, savored her untried flesh, and the two became one.

"Is it not fabulous?" Alex rocked on her heels and cast Jason a dreamy expression. "Do you remember our own nuptials, in this very space, Captain of my heart?"

"Trust me, I will never forget it." Jason blanched. "I was certain Damian would kill me, after the ceremony had ended, and I had given you and our babes my name."

"Stuff and nonsense." With a gentle nudge, Alex teased her spouse. "My brother adores you—*Oh*, there is Hicks. Let us take our respective places, as the bride is just arrived."

"I say, good luck, Dalton." Over his shoulder, as Alex dragged him away, Jason imparted, "Though you will not need it, as your fiancée is of an agreeable disposition."

"Indeed." With a wink and a smile, Dalton nodded acknowledgements to his family and assumed his prearranged position. In that instant, nerves set in with a vengeance, and he inhaled a deep breath. Myriad memories flashed in his brain, as a sentimental journey: Daphne eluding him aboard the *Siren*, Daphne walking along the lane in the Portsea countryside, Daphne bound and gagged in his bunk, Daphne garbed in various sapphire gowns, and Daphne seated in his lap as he fed her a sumptuous syllabub.

But it was the vision of his provincial angel, standing in

the entry, with a halo of blonde curls backlit by the afternoon sun, and gowned in another spectacular creation fashioned in his signature shade and trimmed in old gold, which he would carry to the grave and beyond. When she met his gaze, she glowed, as she fingered her mother's pearl necklace, and unfamiliar but not unpleasant warmth spread from his chest, suffusing his muscles in soothing heat, which eased the tension investing him. Holding a bouquet of lilies clustered with red roses, and with Richard and Hicks at either side, as the string quartet played a tune he barely heeded, she promenaded in his direction.

"Please join hands." Looming before the makeshift altar, Mr. Catchpole flipped through the Book of Common Prayer. "Dearly beloved friends, we are gathered here…"

As Dalton twined his fingers with Daphne's, he bent and whispered, "Nice dress."

"I had it made just for you." She stuck her tongue in her cheek, and an endearing blush colored her countenance.

"I never would have guessed." With his thumb, he caressed her palm, and gooseflesh covered her arms. Desire surged, potent and palpable, and he swallowed hard.

"…I require and charge you, as you will answer at the dreadful day of judgment, when the secrets of all hearts shall be disclosed, that if either of you do know any impediment, why you may not be lawfully joined together in matrimony, that you confess it." Mr. Catchpole adjusted his spectacles and turned the page. "Sir Dalton Philip Arthur Randolph, will thou have—"

"Wait." The youngest Harcourt elbowed Dalton and wrenched Daphne. "Sister, you do not have to do this. You need not sell yourself for our family, as Robert is commissioned, and we can survive, on our own."

"Richard, what are you doing?" As she paled, Daphne

pulled free of her brother. "Are you out of your mind? I am not selling myself. I love Dalton, and I would have you wish me merry, not interfere where you have no right."

"I have every right, as your blood relation." The gadling sneered at Dalton. "And you are grateful to him, because he gave us food. He bought you, in exchange for fancy decorations and new carpets in Courtenay Hall."

"Should we give you a moment?" Mr. Catchpole shuffled his feet. "If you would prefer to discuss this in private—"

"I would not." Daphne wiped a stray tear, and Dalton wanted to spank her sibling for making her cry. "How could you do it? How could you spoil my special day? You had every opportunity to speak with me, last night, if you had concerns. Why would you hurt me with your shameful behavior, now, of all times?"

"I am sorry, Daph." The scamp shifted his weight and shot Dalton a sheepish glance. "I just needed to be sure you were happy."

"I was—until you embarrassed me in front of our guests." When she faltered, Dalton wound his arm about her waist.

"Are you all right?" He pressed his lips to her forehead. "Do you wish to continue, or would you rather postpone the ceremony?"

"I will marry you—now." At her command, he leashed his temper. "And my brother has nothing further to add, so he will stand silent."

"Then let us put this vexatious business behind us and continue." Mr. Catchpole drew a handkerchief from his coat pocket and wiped his temples. "As I would dearly love to preside over an unremarkable service, just once, in this household."

Alex giggled, Jason groaned, and Dalton burst into laughter. Soon, the entire gathering of family and friends collapsed in unrestrained mirth, which reversed the tone Richard had set with his impromptu objection. Just when things quieted down a tad, another fit of hilarity plagued the group, especially when Alex cooed at Jason, and he rolled his eyes.

"Well, then. It would appear we are, at last, ready to proceed. Please, take your respective places, so we might conclude this most auspicious event, as I am in serious need of a refreshing libation from His Grace's best stock." The vicar marked his spot in the text and huffed a breath. "As I was saying, Sir Dalton Philip Arthur Randolph, will thou have this woman to thy wedded wife, to live together after God's ordinance in the holy estate of matrimony? Will thou love her, comfort her, honor and keep her, in sickness and in health? And forsaking all others, keep thee only unto her, so long as you both shall live?"

"I will." And so it was done. In that moment, with two simple words, unexceptional on their own, but uttered together as a whole, he had undertaken the single most important commitment of his life.

While Daphne made her vows, and responded in kind, Dalton gazed into her baby blues and fell under her spell. Yet he could not discern the depth of his affection for her. Was what he harbored for her anything near the powerful connection Dirk enjoyed with Rebecca?

And then Daphne faced him and pledged, "From this day forward you shall not walk alone. My heart will be your shelter, and my arms will be your home."

"And now I pronounce you husband and wife." Sweating profusely, Mr. Catchpole dragged his sleeve across his brow. "Sir Dalton, you may kiss your bride."

Had they married in St. Georges at Hanover Square, he might have moderated his enthusiasm. Given the audience consisted of his immediate and extended family, that knowledge fueled the desire simmering beneath his respectable attire, and he could summon no restraint. Dalton grabbed Daphne, tipped her head, and covered her mouth with his. All but crushing her against him, he suckled her succulent flesh between his lips, and she drove him into frenzy, when she speared her fingers in his hair. Fire erupted in his loins, and he pulled her even closer.

A hearty chorus of hoots and hollers penetrated the intoxicating aura, and with great reluctance, he retreated from his wife. Then the Brethren ladies surrounded Daphne, and he turned to Dirk and expelled a sigh of relief. "Well, it is done."

"Congratulations, brother." Dirk extended a hand. "How do you feel?"

"Better than I had imagined, despite the unexpected intrusion." Dalton scanned the vicinity and realized Richard had left the drawing room. "But it matters not, in the grand scheme."

"Most honored guests, may I have your attention?" Damian clapped twice. "What say we adjourn to the dining room for refreshments and an early dinner, so our newlyweds might retire at a reasonable hour, as they have much to be about."

"By all means, lead the way." Strutting to his wife's side, Dalton offered his escort. "Mrs. Randolph, shall we?"

"Oh, just the sound of that gives me delicious shivers." Emanating inexpressible elation, she beamed, as she pressed her palm to the crook of his elbow. "And I will never grow tired of hearing it."

"Very well, Mrs. Randolph." He chuckled, as she

squealed with unveiled delight. Ah, it was good to be a husband.

AT HER WEDDING DINNER, Daphne basked in the dramatic decorations Damian had ordered for the festivities. Crisp white linens trimmed in old gold bedecked the longest table she had ever seen. And as in the drawing room, huge crystal vases filled with red roses mixed with white lilies rested on every surface, and matching arrangements had been situated at equal distances across the table.

Running the length of the dazzling chamber, floor to ceiling windows offered unrivaled views of the Channel, and she and Dalton had been placed at the center of the gala. As they took their seats, she attempted to shrug off the depressing thoughts surrounding her brother's protest, and she noted Richard's absence with a heavy heart. Yet his was not the only unwelcome surprise, in relation to her nuptials.

The day before she had departed London, she had received another mysterious missive, which portended doom should she pursue marriage with Dalton. Twice, she had attempted to broach the subject with her one true knight, but her courage had faltered, as she feared losing her husband before they spoke their vows.

As long as you live, you will never satisfy him as I satisfied him.

How unfair was it that Lady Moreton's prediction had haunted Daphne's slumber, ever since that heated confrontation at the Eddington's ball? And although the Brethren wives had been all too ready to impart sage advice regarding the consummation, Daphne had not been able to escape the nagging worry that she would fail her cosmopolitan, worldly man of the sea and share her mother's fate.

"Hungry, sweetheart?" Dalton drew imaginary circles on her bare knuckles, as the footman held a platter of beefsteaks. "Should I serve you, Mrs. Randolph?"

"Please, do so." Every time he called her by her new name, her gut clenched. "As I am quite famished."

"Eat plenty, darling." Dalton leaned near and whispered, "You will need your strength for the night I have planned."

"Oh?" She gulped, as a tidal wave of apprehension swamped her. "Pray tell, what have you arranged for us?"

"Naughty wife, I like your spirit." The minute her spouse gave his full attention, she discovered the error in her innocent query, and she gulped, as he looked on the verge of taking a bite of her. "Should I tease you? Should I tempt you? Should I offer you a glimpse of what is to come?"

"Is that possible, amid company?" When he claimed her hand, she started. But then he massaged the soft flesh between the bases of two fingers, rubbing in a monotonous rhythm, hinting at the act that would complete their nuptials, and Daphne thought she might swoon.

To prolong the meal, she consumed a second beefsteak, ample portions of brown onion soup, mashed turnips, green peas, and Salamongundy. By the time the cook rolled a trolley bearing the cake and a pyramid of grapes, nectarines, peaches, and strawberries, into the dining room, Daphne was positive she would bust. To delay the inevitable, she shoved two pieces of the frosted confection into her already unstable belly, and her nerves grew in epic proportion with the lateness of the hour and her girth.

"My dear family, if I might, I would say a few words."

With a champagne flute in his grasp, Dalton stood and drew her with him. "On behalf of my wife and I, know you have our utmost gratitude for everything you have done to see us to this most blessed day. And now we will leave you to—"

"Wait." Teetering on the precipice of some perceived danger, neither real nor facetious, Daphne clutched at a last ditch means of escape, however brief. "I have a surprise for you, my cherished husband. I packed my lute, and I would like to play for you."

"What a wonderful idea." Although Dalton had said one thing, his frown and rigid features conveyed an altogether different message. "Perhaps we should send Conrad to—"

"Oh, I will fetch it." Daphne tore from his side but slowed, when Conrad stepped into her path. In the hall, she teetered, as her stomach lurched. "Yes, Conrad?"

"Mrs. Randolph, your belongings have been moved to what His Grace designated as your honeymoon suite." The genial butler bowed. "Given the size of Penhurst Castle, please, permit me to show you the way, as you could, very well, get lost."

"Of course." But as she navigated the massive stone structure, with its mahogany trim and casements, it dawned on her that, if Dalton could not find her, she could not disappoint him. After ascending the huge staircase, they strolled through a colossal gallery, which she had not had the opportunity to tour, in her rush to the altar. Wending between the sea of sculptures and busts perched atop pedestals, with the eyes of Damian and Alex's ancestors seeming to trail her march, she followed Conrad down another long hallway.

At a double-door entry, Conrad set wide an oak panel. "Continue to the other end of the sitting room, where the opposite portal opens to the bedchamber, and I shall await you, here."

"Thank you." Her padded footfalls, muted by the thick burgundy carpet, sounded a dirge, of sorts. When she found herself face to face with her doom—an enormous four-poster fit for a king, everything seemed to spin out of control. Draped over the footboard, a sheer nightgown and a matching robe almost mocked her.

As long as you live, you will never satisfy him as I satisfied him.

Covering her ears, Daphne closed her eyes. "No."

But her shaky belly paid no heed, as it rebelled in the worst way. She jerked alert, scanned the area, located the washstand, hiked her skirts, sprinted to the back corner, bent, and revisited her wedding feast. After a series of wicked bouts of retching, she leaned on the edge of the bowl and gasped for breath. When she stretched upright, she swayed.

"Careful, Mrs. Randolph." Providing unfailing support, Conrad conveyed her to a *chaise* and then wet a cloth, which he pressed to the back of her neck. "Relax, while I retrieve your lute, as the maid put it in the adjoining dressing room."

"I am so ashamed." She unfolded the towel and wiped her cheeks. "You will not tell anyone, will you, Conrad?"

"Never." Carrying her instrument, he smiled. "Your apprehension is quite normal, if I may be so bold, Mrs. Randolph. Daresay you are not the first newlywed to suffer such malady in advance of your wedding night. Now, there is fresh tooth powder and soap, and I shall have the maid empty, clean, and replace the basin, with none the wiser."

"Mr. Conrad, I could kiss you." Refreshed, to an extent, she made quick use of the opportunity to calm her nerves, as she cleaned her teeth and washed her face. Later, poised and confident, clutching her lute to her chest, she returned to the dining room.

"There you are." Dalton vacated his chair and approached, and intense terror reared its ugly head. How could her greatest ally have become her worst fear, when all he had done was feed and clothe her and her family, restore Courtenay Hall, pay papa's debts, and give her the security of his name? "I had thought, perhaps, you had got lost in the castle."

"Oh, no." She forced a laugh. "I could not locate my lute, and I had to search my things."

"So you are going to serenade me, again?" He rocked on his heels and winked. "I should like you to do that, some-day, in the privacy of our apartments. But I shall content myself with tonight's performance. So what will you play for us, love?"

"I had thought an old folk ballad, 'The Knight and the Shepherd's Daughter,' appropriate for the occasion." Of course, Daphne neglected to mention the song had seventeen verses.

"OH, DAPHNE, YOU LOOK WONDERFUL." As Alex placed the silver-backed brush on the vanity, she smiled and admired her handiwork. "Dalton will fall at your feet when he sees you."

"As well he should, which is a good place to keep him." After hanging Daphne's wedding dress on a peg in the armoire, Rebecca folded her arms and inclined her head. "Now then, do you remember everything we told you?"

The previous evening, while the men congregated in the village of Penhurst, the women had gathered to impart the detailed history of the Brethren of the Coast, a secret order of nautionnier knights descended from the Templars, after Dalton's haphazard explanation, which had left Daphne filled to the brim with numerous unanswered questions. She had assumed there had been more to his character than he had admitted, and she had been correct, but she had never fathomed a jaw-dropping narrative of daring deeds and military prowess that counted Vice Admiral Nelson among the ranks.

"Given this is your first time, you should let him set the tone and pace." Toying with her diamond necklace, Caroline averted her gaze and sighed. "Trevor was wonderful on our honeymoon, so thoughtful and patient. It was a far cry from my deflowering, when he thought me a practiced courtesan, and he came at me as if he had just returned from a long voyage."

The Brethren wives chatted about all manner of spousal enjoyment, which she suspected they intended to soothe virgin's anxiety, but their voices came to Daphne through a haze of rock-solid, almost impenetrable apprehension. In light of her lengthy performance, and the requested encores, which she had been more than willing to accommodate, the hour had grown late, to her husband's expressed consternation. But she had stalled as long as possible and now loomed on the precipice of the most dreaded event.

"My dear, are you all right?" Rebecca studied Daphne and then led her to a chair. "Sit, as you are white as a ghost."

"Do you really think Dalton will like me?" She bit her lip, as she pondered the humiliation of a rejection. "What if I fail him? What if he finds no joy with me? What if—"

"Sister, calm yourself." Caroline bent and cupped Daphne's chin. "Dalton worships you. I would wager you could lie abed and do nothing more than blink and breathe, and he would still find release."

"Indeed, recall our counsel. Men are easily managed once you bridle the beast below their belly button." Alex snickered. "Captain of my heart complained of the journey, as he wished to return to Stratfield Manor, until I suggested we have a second go at our wedding night in my old chambers, and now he is the soul of cooperation. So I should leave you, as I must change for the occasion, and I purchased something to inspire him, though I will not need it. Words of warning, if you hear a scream do not sound the alarm."

"Very good, Alex." Rebecca tittered. "And we should vacate the room, as the groom will soon arrive."

The elegant allies exited, and Daphne found herself alone. The constant ticking of the mantel clock played an accompaniment to the steady drumbeat of her pulse, which echoed in her ears. She stood and walked to the long mirror, to check her appearance, and shrieked.

The sheer sapphire nightgown and matching robe concealed nothing of her body. Then she turned and discovered the cleft of her bottom visible through the diaphanous material. Trepidation burgeoned into raw fear and panic. While the Brethren wives possessed a wealth of knowledge regarding a sated spouse, they had nothing to impart about a disappointed mate. In a flash, she flew into the dressing room, in search of protection. When she returned to the bedchamber, she found her husband standing in the entry, and she screamed.

"Well that will give our brothers something to talk about." As he untied his cravat, he scrutinized her appearance and frowned. "Going somewhere?"

"No." Confused by his rather odd query, she curled her toes into the thick carpet. "Why do you ask?"

"Because you are wearing your pelisse."

Clutching the wool as a shield against salacious invasion, she retreated. "I am cold."

"I can take care of that." After doffing his coat, waistcoat, and boots, Dalton unbuttoned the collar of his shirt. "Come here."

As long as you live, you will never satisfy him as I satisfied him.

"What for?" Despite her best efforts, she trembled. "As I am fine, right here."

"Indulge me." He flicked his fingers in entreaty. "Come here, darling."

Whereas some ladies might have seen a handsome rake bent on seduction, she considered him something more akin to an executioner—her downfall. It was with that thought swirling in her brain that she neared. When he unhooked the fastener at her throat and let her coat drop to the floor, she emitted a soft sob and crossed her arms to cover herself from his heated stare.

"Are you afraid, sweetheart?" With his brow a mass of furrows, he settled his palms to her hips and pulled her close. "Relax."

"Easier said than done." When he cupped her bottom, she shrieked, jerked free, and ran into the sitting room. "Would you like some wine?"

"Daphne, what is wrong?" On the surface, his was a simple query, but the answer eluded her, just as she evaded him. "Have I done something to disturb you?"

"Of course, not." She responded with a high-pitched giggle and poured a full glass. But when he moved toward her, she sprinted behind the sofa. Oh, why had she listened to the Brethren wives, as they shared stories of their triumphant unions, when the end result, for her, had been monumental stress? How could she possibly live up to his expectations? "Remain where you are, sir. Else I may be forced to inform your mother of your inappropriate advances."

"Easy, love." With hands up and splayed, he rounded the chair. "I am not going to hurt you. And, for us, there is no such thing as an inappropriate advance, as we are married, and we must consummate our vows. But we can take it slow."

"If that is true, then stay there." Her gaze lit on his crotch and the source of her consternation. The black wool tented with proof of the one-eyed pirate Alex referred to as the perky but proud Jolly Roger, and Daphne's knees buckled.

"Sit, angel." Spearing his hair, he shifted his weight. "You look unwell."

"Must you have said that?" To her utter humiliation, her tempestuous belly rebelled again, and she covered her mouth. Retracing her earlier steps, she made it to the wash-stand with no time to spare, as she bent and vomited violently.

"Do not fight it, Daphne." At her side, Dalton held her long locks out of the line of fire, as she heaved. "Poor little thing, you have nothing to fear, as I know what I am doing, and I would never cause you pain."

"But that is the problem." Mortified, she buried her face in a towel. "You know so much, and I know nothing. How am I to please you?"

"On that account, you need expend no effort." Dalton chuckled and massaged her shoulders. When he skimmed her bare arms, she flinched and lurched.

"Stop." Daphne scampered to the opposite end of the chamber, and the four-poster lay as a very real barrier between them. He veered left, and she darted right. "Dalton, please. This is ridiculous."

"This is your game." With his chin lowered, he grinned. "You wish me to pursue you, angel? Believe me, I am more than ready to give chase."

"No." Before she could utter another word, he dashed over the mattress, and she bolted into the sitting room and sheltered behind the *chaise*.

"I will catch you." He bounded to the fore, and she scrambled toward the door, but he executed a brilliant flanking maneuver, which had her racing back to the interior apartment.

"Go away." With the oak panels shut, she tried to set the bolt against her husband, but he shoved hard, and she stumbled. "Leave me alone."

"Daphne, cease your nonsense, this instant." Breathing heavily, he stared at her and shrugged from his lawn shirt, which he flung aside. "You are my wife, and I am no stranger, so I find your behavior perplexing. Did my sisters not prepare you?"

"Actually, they explained quite a bit." As she glimpsed his incredible chest for the first time, her insides balled into knots, and her cheeks burned. "But I have no experience, and you have more than I wish to know."

"My dear Mrs. Randolph, would you prefer an uninformed clumsy dolt who might cause you untold discomfort or a seasoned man of the world possessed of the ability to play your body as a finely tuned instrument?"

"I am unsure."

"You must be joking."

"It would be nice to have someone with whom I could sympathize."

"You think me insensitive to your needs?"

"You stalked me."

"Point taken. But in my defense, it is our wedding night."

"And you wish to consummate our vows."

"Very much."

She dreaded what he desired. How on earth could they reconcile their differences? Squared off, as two combatants on the field of glory, she zigged, he zagged, and she sought escape via the bed. But her one true knight dove over the footboard and snagged her ankle.

"Let go." She kicked hard.

"Not a chance." He squeezed her calf and blazed a trail to her thigh, with his naughty fingers. "Do not fight me, angel. I promise, you will enjoy it."

But could she say the same for him?

As long as you live, you will never satisfy him as I satisfied him.

With that thought taunting her, she wiggled loose and toppled to the floor, whereupon she crawled to her vanity. When she jumped to her feet, with fists at her sides, Dalton mirrored her stance.

Given all her dreams and fantasies, which had culminated in a mystical joining that defied the temporal plane, Daphne peered at the patterned rug and sobbed. "This is not how I had envisioned this moment."

"Believe me, that makes two of us." Her husband exhaled in unmistakable frustration, and her already flagging confidence sank to new depths.

"Perhaps, we could talk." Her mind raced in search of a solution. "If you would—"

"What would we discuss that had not been covered?" In a flash, he rushed her fences.

Locked in the throes of nervous agitation, she sought a diversion—and nothing more, as she seized upon her silver-backed brush. Before she realized she had moved, she flung the refined lady's accouterment at Dalton. To her horror, the heavy utensil struck him in the forehead. With a countenance of unutterable shock, he dropped to the floor.

CHAPTER THIRTEEN

A wicked headache penetrated his sleep, suspending a rather ribald reverie featuring Daphne as the star participant, and Dalton groaned. Massaging his temples, he stretched long, came alert, and recalled his wedding. Then a series of images composed a visual tapestry that devolved in rapid succession from elegant to disastrous. Daphne gowned in sapphire. Daphne singing like a nightingale, as she played her lute. Daphne paralyzed with fear. Daphne vomiting in the basin. Daphne fleeing in fear. Daphne assaulting him with what he had considered nothing more than a harmless hairbrush.

"Bloody everlasting hell." He opened his eyes and glanced at what should have been his wife's side of the bed and found nothing but space and silence for company.

"Feeling better?" Dirk inquired in a low voice.

"Please, kill me." When he tried to sit upright, the world spun out of control, and he sagged amid the pillows. "Where is Daphne?"

"Reinstalled in her guest quarters, as she was hysterical, when she ran for assistance." Occupying a chair beside

Dirk, Jason scratched his chin. "Dr. Meade prescribed an uninterrupted night, and Alex guards your lady."

"Of course." Dalton remembered her panicky pleas for forbearance and his stubborn refusal to heed the depth of her distress. "How is she?"

"Rebecca informed me that your bride dozed, at last, after the physician dispensed a healthy dose of laudanum, to Daphne's protest, but she should be fine." His elder brother scrutinized the shine of his boots. "Given we found you half-naked, unconscious, and bleeding on the floor, I take it you never consummated your vows."

"What do you think?" Sunlight peeked through a separation in the closed drapes, and he rubbed the back of his neck. "But I ought to be horsewhipped for what I provoked here."

In that instant, Trevor and Jason fumbled in their pockets and then passed a few pound notes to Dirk.

"I do not believe it." Seething ire flourished, only to be quenched by steely humiliation, as Dalton propped on an elbow. "You wagered against me?"

"Because I know you too well, you are damn right I did." With a grin, Dirk counted his winnings. "You could not wait to make feet for children's stockings, before we departed London. As I am well aware you never put much store in delayed gratification, I even bested my lady spy. In fact, Becca swore you would rout Daphne's privy-counsel prior to your nuptials, but I declared otherwise."

"But how could predict my founder?" Narrowing his stare, Dalton mulled the possibilities, which made no sense. "Daphne is a stranger to you."

"You forget those few days I passed in her company, as I audited the estate ledgers, while you moved the *Siren* to Portsmouth." Dirk tossed Dalton's lucky coin. "That wisp of a girl ran Portsea Island, and kept her household together, while her father gambled away their legacy, invested the larger portion of his monthly stipend in wenching, drowned his sorrows in a bottle, and took his own life rather than face the consequences of his actions, leaving her to pick up the pieces. Like my Becca, your Daphne is formidable, and she will do very well in our family. And although you possess a vast deal of knowledge of the fairer sex, when it comes to seduction, you know nothing of wives. Trust me, they are as different as ebony and ivory."

"So you bet on her." He ignored Trevor and Jason's smirks.

Proud as punch, Dirk thrust his chin. "I did."

"And how much did I add to your purse, with Rebecca's ante?" he asked, as he ought to have collected half of Dirk's stakes, in recompense for the nasty injury.

"Oh, I chanced something far more precious, with my agent provocateur, and I aim to savor the payoff—tonight." With a chuckle, Dirk folded his arms. "Now, may I dispense a bit of advice to smooth virgin waters, given you struck breakers on your initial attempt to dock in her harbor?"

"Am I ever going to hear the end of this?" Dalton rolled his eyes.

"Not if we can help it." Trevor elbowed Jason in the ribs, and they burst into laughter. "Damn, but I wish Everett was here, as Daphne's attack by affected arsenal has topped Sabrina's leap from a moving coach, and I never thought that would happen."

"I say, gives a whole new meaning to 'having a brush.'" Jason tapped his cheek.

"Or 'taking a flyer.'" Trevor pointed for emphasis.

"Ah, I have another." Jason snapped his fingers. "What about 'making a stitch?' Or, in this case, several stitches."

With a sly smile, Jason nudged Trevor, and the two collapsed in another fit of mirth.

"I am so happy to provide you with comedic sport, brothers." While he would rather go to his grave than admit Dirk was right, Dalton could not ignore his present circumstances. "Instead of mocking my shame, I would much prefer you offer sage counsel."

"Might I suggest next time you duck?" Trevor replied and then snorted.

"Or I could loan you the helmet to the suit of armor that graces the foyer at Stratfield Manor." Holding his belly, Jason snickered, and Dalton reclined and pulled the covers over his head, but even the thick bedclothes could not temper the blonde knight's boisterous rumbles. "But you might frighten the poor girl. Wait—you already did that."

Dalton braced for the forthcoming levity, and his fellow Nautionniers had not disappointed him, as the room reverberated with their merriment. If only he could join in their amusement, yet his wife occupied his thoughts. What could he do now? How would he ever earn Daphne's trust?

"Are you still with us?" Dirk drew back the counterpane and winked. "However late, I am glad you were not seriously injured. Dr. Meade assured me that you would recover, as long as you avoid physical exertion, for a fortnight, or so."

"That should not be too difficult," Jason quipped.

"*Enough.*" Dalton winced, as his temples throbbed. "I made a mess of my wedding night, and now I suffer some strange burning agony, which has taken residence deep in my chest, such as I have never known. Is that what you want to hear?"

To his relief, the chamber grew quiet as a tomb.

In the suddenly unwelcome solitude, he reminisced of

his original strategy and sighed. Breakfast was to have been a singular triumph, after a night of heretofore-unrivaled passion. He had plotted, planned, and ordered a sumptuous repast, which he had aspired to partake of with Daphne nestled in his lap.

"Brother, how well we know your pain, as each of us stumbled on our way to the altar." Leaning forward, Trevor wiped his face and grimaced. "We are none of us perfect."

"Some of us fell flat on our face, even after the ceremony." Jason whistled in monotone. "It took me months to gain ground with Alex, and I would spare you such extended torment, so I will share my secrets to success. Poetry. Alex collects my original compositions in a leather-bound journal, which she takes with her, whenever we travel. And she never fails to express her appreciation in the manner I favor most. Also, try your hand at floral arrangements. At Stratfield, I often raid the rose garden, to create custom offerings to my wife's incomparable beauty, and Alex raves of my talents."

"I am not so creative as Collingwood," Trevor revealed, with a frown. "My advantage was born of seclusion. I took Caroline to my beach cottage, so we could spend time, alone. Without doubt, I suspect we conceived all three of our babes in the modest structure, as there is little else to occupy the hours at our remote hideaway."

"And I won Rebecca by offering her something she never presumed possible—a loving family and a home." Dirk shifted and straightened his lapel. "Therein lies the key. Every woman is unique, and what she covets is equally distinct. You know Daphne. What appeals to her? Identify what entices her, and give it to her. And then let her come to you, as she will do that, when you least expect it."

Dalton relaxed in bed long after his brothers had

vacated the honeymoon suite. After revisiting cherished memories of their first encounter aboard the *Siren*, and their subsequent days on Portsea Island, he seized upon the answer to his conundrum.

Flinging aside the sheets and blankets, he swung his legs over the side of the mattress and stood. Just as quick, he landed back in the four-poster. On his second try, he moved slow and steady. Still wearing his breeches from the previous evening, he staggered into the dressing room and located a robe.

Draped in black satin, he cinched the belt at his waist and ambled from the chamber. In the hall, he gathered his bearings and strolled to the wing in which Daphne had been accommodated. At her door, he considered knocking, but if she slept, he did want to disturb her. So he turned the knob and peeked into the dark quarter.

The sitting room boasted a wide expanse of windows, which shielded the open portal to the inner boudoir. As he neared, he spied Rebecca.

"Dalton, what are you doing here? Dr. Meade gave explicit instructions, and you were not to be about so soon." His sister-in-law vacated a bedside chair and rushed forward. "Are you all right? You gave us a terrible scare."

"I am quite well." He shuffled his feet. "Daresay the worst injury is to my pride. May I have a moment with Daphne?"

"Of course, as she is your wife." Rebecca patted his cheek. "I will wait in the hall, to give you privacy, but I would caution you not to wake her, as she drifted off just as the sun rose above the horizon. She cried for hours, Dalton."

"I promise, I will not disturb her." The fact that he had reduced his new bride to tears tore at his gut. As he gazed upon her still form, with her angelic features sublime in repose, he noted the swelling about her face and her red nose, and he cursed himself. How ironic was it that a provincial virgin had capsized one of the most notorious rakes in London? "Worry not, sweetheart. Everything will work out, in the end, because fate favors the lucky."

FOUR DAYS LATER, beneath the shimmering sun on a warm June morning, after her family had announced the governor's untimely demise from an infectious fever, Daphne stood at graveside in Portsea and let loose the grief, so long locked deep inside, and it flowed as the incoming tide. No, her father had not been a very good man, but he was her sire nonetheless, and so she had ached to honor his memory. Garbed in the somber black attire of mourning, she flung a single rose atop his grave, above which Hicks and Dalton had broken the earth, to give the allusion of a fresh dug resting place. So paradoxical an end it was, that her father would remain at her mother's side, for all eternity, in death, when in life he had scarcely regarded her.

Owing to a fear of contagion, she had not permitted the governor's casket to lie in state at Courtenay Hall. The locals commended her, for her customary prudence in such matters, and so they abided and respected her request to gather on a nearby rise, while the immediate relations congregated in the fenced plot, and the hastily sketched ruse played its final act.

How different it was from the original midnight internment, five months ago, in the glow of a full moon, after Hicks and Robert had constructed a modest wooden coffin, with only Richard and Mrs. Jones for company. Now,

Daphne leaned on her husband and wept, without shame, as the others had retired to the house, in preparation for an afternoon visitation.

"It is done, darling." Cradling her head, Dalton hugged her close. "For all intents and purposes, he is safely in the ground. You need carry this burden no more."

"I can hardly believe it is over." When he pulled her fully against his chest, she broke.

For a while, he simply held her, as she lamented for her parents. But it was the deplorable deterioration of her fledgling marriage that really hurt. She shifted in his grasp and gazed at her mother's headstone. Friends had always said she was just like mama, and Daphne had considered such praise a high compliment. Given her fractured union, she rued the similarity.

"Oh, Dalton, I am so sorry." They had barely spoken in the wake of their disastrous wedding night, and she blamed herself for everything that had gone wrong. "I know not what got into me. Can you ever forgive me?"

"Sweetheart, there is nothing to forgive." Trailing the curve of her cheek with a finger, he bestowed upon her a sweet kiss and then led her from the Harcourt graveyard. Pausing beneath the thick canopy of an old oak tree, he turned and drew her into his embrace. "I owe you an apology, love. As the more experienced party, I should have recognized the extent of your distress and responded as would a gentleman. Instead, I compounded your anxiety, and I assume full responsibility for the resulting fiasco. I let you down, and you are faultless."

"Do you really mean that?" Though she suspected otherwise, she would not argue with him, as at last they were conversing. "As I never aimed to cause you injury."

"Evidence to the contrary. Actually, I am quite

impressed, as you are a devil of a shot." Favoring her with his boyish grin, he chuckled. "In future, I should remember that, whenever we have a row, and ensure there are no hair-brushes within reach."

"Stop it." Comforted by his jovial demeanor, Daphne sighed in relief. "And regardless of your indulgence, I am ashamed of my behavior. If you wish to try again, I will not fight you."

"Darling, so much has happened in so little time, and you have every right to feel rushed." Framing her face, he rubbed his nose to hers and then touched his lips to hers in a whisper of a buss. "When you are ready, come to me. Until then, I will wait."

"What?" He sounded so methodical—nothing like the flirty knight who claimed her heart. "Do you not want me?"

"Of course, I want you." She nestled close and inhaled his signature spicy scent. "But I would not hurry you. Let us take a brief respite, spend a few days in Portsea, and dispense with your father's final affairs. When we return to London, we are booked for dinner with the family, and I received orders to commence transporting wounded soldiers from the Continent, as soon as the *Siren* is out of dry dock. Given we are officially in mourning, we may forgo the few remaining engagements of the Season and keep to ourselves. Would that please you?"

"I must confess it is my fondest wish." Save their residence in the city, which she still viewed as his bachelor lodging, and she abhorred it. How many women had he seduced under that roof, she knew not, yet she had not wanted to join their ranks. She wanted to be *the one*, not the one of many. "Excepting the Brethren, I care not for London society."

"I believe I figured that out, love." Shifting her in his

hold, he rested his chin atop the crown of her head. "And is there anything I might do to put you at ease, where we are concerned?"

"Are you asking in earnest?" Oh, she hoped so, as she needed his kindness.

"Indeed." He caressed the small of her back, and she shivered, as he had that effect on her, despite their unpropitious wedding night. "Given we enjoyed a favorable start, I would recover the precious ground we somehow lost."

"You truly wish to know what attracted me to you?" she inquired, as she toyed with his black armband. "You want to know why I accepted your proposal?"

"You said you love me." He exhaled audibly. "I suppose that had something to do with it."

"It was our conversations that caught my attention. Our first, over dinner at the inn, when you detailed the history of the brooch, reigns supreme as a most cherished memory. And then there was our shopping excursion to fill my community pantry, and the day you accompanied me on my charitable visits." Daphne inched back, adjusted his cravat, and met his stare. "I like how you talk to me, with deference and directness, as an adult. And you cover a wide variety of topics, which is never dull. That is how you won me."

For a minute, he gazed into her eyes, with a quizzical expression. Then he sobered. "You are serious." It was a statement, not a question.

"Yes." That he had ceased their dialogues had stung, and his withdrawal had rendered her confused and second-guessing every move. "And I dearly miss our chats."

"I am blessed with many skills, but never had I counted verbal exchange among them." He scratched the back of his neck and frowned, and it was clear she had stumped him. Could it have been possible that she knew him better than he knew himself? "So you are telling me I have a talented tongue?"

"In more ways than one, sir, but I believe you know that." Glancing at the family plot, she vowed never to suffer the same fate as her parents. Her marriage would be a success. "And there is something else you could do to allay my trepidation."

"Name it, sweetheart," her true knight proclaimed without hesitation.

"From the onset of our acquaintance, we shared some tender moments when we were alone." She gulped, and her cheeks burned with embarrassment. "But when we journeyed to London, you terminated such solicitous...attentiveness. Do you understand what I am asking?"

"I think I do, but I want to hear you say it." Now he had the audacity to wink. "So what is it you want from me?"

"I want you to kiss me." There. She had proclaimed it, loud and clear, in no unmistakable terms. "Your lips present a powerful diversion, such that I can scarcely think, let alone suffer fear or anxiety, and had you applied yourself with diligence the other night, we would have consummated our nuptials."

"My beautiful wife, the reason I ceased such activity when we ventured to the city was because societal dictates demanded restraint, as we were not wed, and I would not damage your reputation. The provincial Portsea community commanded no similar limitations, and I took liberties, as I could not resist you." He tipped her chin. "Now we are married, we are free to luxuriate in each other's company, and the gossipmongers will say we benefit from a felicitous union."

Before she knew it, Dalton bent his head and set his mouth to hers. Fire ignited from the point of contact, and she delighted in it, as his particular brand of intoxication quelled all distress. Searing heat blazed a path from top to toe, and she relaxed against her husband. In seconds, gone was the cold chill that had pervaded her chest since the disaster at Penhurst, and in its place was only warm contentment.

THE SUN HAD NOT YET SURPASSED the yardarm, when Dalton loitered at the foot of the front entry steps before Courtenay Hall. Checking his pocket watch, he rolled his shoulders, as uncharacteristic and unwelcome nervousness plagued him.

It was only yesterday that he had queried Mrs. Jones and Hicks, regarding his wife's usual habits, and had learned of her morning walks along the beach. As if on cue, the front door opened, and Daphne emerged. When she spied him, she halted.

"Dalton, what are you doing up and about, at this early hour?" Gowned in a heavy black mourning creation, which still set his blood boiling, she bestowed upon him a glowing smile.

"Good morning, love." Recalling her sweet confession beneath the oak tree, he charged if only to hold her. With his arms about her waist, he hugged his wife and then claimed her mouth. Had he known of the power his kisses wielded over his backwater bride, he would have engaged in all manner of questionable clinches with his angel, prior to their nuptials.

With unmasked enthusiasm, she moaned, as he suckled her little pink tongue, and his loins went up in flames, despite his crude handiwork, to which he had resorted in the wee hours. Again and again, he nibbled her succulent flesh, as he remained on guard for the minutest amount of fear. When she speared her fingers through the hair at the nape of his neck, pulse points blazed to life, and every muscle tensed, as never had he desired any woman as he desired Daphne.

"Oh, dear." Gasping for breath, she nuzzled his chest. "Perhaps I should not have apprised you of your singular appeal, as someone might see us."

"Relax, darling." How quickly she reverted to his naïve provincial. "Remember, we are married, so our behavior is state-sanctioned. But my plan was to join you for your customary stroll, not to ravish you, though I am at your service, if you choose otherwise."

"Well, I cannot complain, as I wedded a rake." Though she giggled, it was high-pitched, and her subtle flinch betrayed an inner turmoil, so he withdrew before she conked his noggin.

"Former rake." He arched a brow. "As I belong to you, now."

"And I am yours." With a girlish squeal, she jumped and smacked her lips to his. Then she grabbed his wrist and yanked him to the driveway. "Hurry, as June is the perfect month to collect wildflowers on Portsea."

"I did not know you collected wildflowers." He marked that for future reference. "What do you do with them?"

"Mama taught me to press and frame them." Marching forth, as a woman on a mission, Daphne led him to a narrow path amid the tall grass. "I want to find some nice specimens, to make gifts for the Brethren ladies."

"How very thoughtful of you, my angel." All of a sudden, she halted, and he almost knocked her to the ground.

"Is that your pet name for me?" Without warning, she

whirled about and cast him an expression of hopefulness. "As I have always wanted one."

"It is, indeed." Given her parents' unhappy union, he guessed her query disclosed a real concern in that respect, and he understood her apprehension. "Do you recall our initial meeting, in the study at Courtenay Hall? You wore a pale yellow dress, with your blonde curls fashioned as a crown, of sorts, and when you stood by the window, the sunlight caught your hair, and it appeared as a halo."

"You recount so much detail." Emanating unutterable joy, she bared her teeth as she smiled, and he found her enchanting. "Was that instance so special?"

"It was life-changing." How he loved it when she bounced. "Because that was the first time I set eyes on my future wife."

"Oh, Dalton." When she came at him, he could have cried. Framing his face, she offered her rosy lips, and he took what she gave—but no more, as he would not frighten her. But, God, she was delicious, and he was hungry.

As the situation spiraled out of control, and Daphne's maidenhead hung in a fragile balance, Dalton broke their kiss and set her at arm's length. "Easy, angel, else you will lift your ankles for me right here."

"Did I do something wrong?" She snuggled to his side, and he marveled at her innocence.

"No, love." Oh, she had done everything right, the marauder below his belly button poised for attack, and Dalton would have to deploy four fingers and a thumb upon return to the estate house. At that rate, he would develop calluses. "But let us continue on your search, as I see a cluster of blooms near the bend."

"That is a perfect yellow horned poppy." How fast she

shifted directions, as she ran down the verge. "I will need several more, but this is an excellent start."

"What about the pink thatch by the large rocks?" He pointed to the west. "Over there."

"Upon my word, but you have a keen eye." After making her selection, which she spread atop her handkerchief, she jumped to her feet and sprinted to the next target. "This is red valerian, and it is my favorite."

"I should make note and present it to you, often." And then something occurred to him, and he asked, "Did you save any of the roses I gave you?"

"Every one of them." With her back to him, she had missed his shudder of shock. "And I would prefer you pick the wildflowers, as they are far more colorful than the hothouse varieties."

"Wait a minute." He stretched upright. "You kept all of them?"

"Why would I not?" She shrugged. "In fact, the two dozen that decorated the table for our dinner at the inn is now framed, and the complete set graces a wall in my bedchamber." To his surprise, she turned and glanced at him, and her welling tears gave him pause for reflection. "When I pressed the buds, I had thought, at some point, they would be all that remained of you in my life, and I dreaded that day."

"Daphne." He spread wide his arms and exhaled in relief, when she came straight to him. "You humble me, angel. I had no idea how much my simple display of affection meant to you, but I will never forget."

"May I make a confession?" She sniffed. "My greatest cause for concern is that I might suffer my mother's ill fortune. To my knowledge, her father negotiated her marriage contract, including a healthy dowry, to give her social standing, as my sire was destined to assume the governorship. Love never entered the equation. And were it not for my engaged affection, I would have rejected your proposal."

"In good faith, I should admit your concern was no secret." But her spontaneous admission inspired the strange but not unpleasant response he had come to expect. Looking inward, he searched his soul. What he discovered remained shrouded amid a nebulous haze of indecision, so he let it go for the moment. "Fret not, angel. Despite our dubious beginning, we will sort it out, as all Brethren marry for love."

"Do you know—yet?" she asked in a small voice.

"No." But it physically hurt him to acknowledge it.

"Then let us continue our walk." With that, she pushed free, retrieved her handkerchief with the floral booty, and resumed her search.

For the ensuing hour, Dalton escorted his bride along the dunes, until they neared the coastline, when she shed her slippers and hosiery to stroll at water's edge. After numerous pleas, which he pretended to disregard, because he adored her entreaties, she persuaded him to doff his boots, and they frolicked in the ebb and flow of the ocean.

When a rather loud grumble announced her hunger in less than graceful fashion, he could not help but laugh. "My angel, let us return to Courtenay Hall, as we have yet to break our fast, and it sounds as if you require sustenance."

"Might I prevail upon you to forgo the dining room and partake of your meal in my sitting room?" With their clothes righted, they climbed the dune, and she took his hand. "I have so relished your company that I am loathe to share you with anyone."

"What a wonderful idea, and I like the way you think."

In play as his mood was light, he patted her bottom, and she favored him with a coquettish giggle. "I shall make you a bargain. You tend your bounty, I will order our repast, and we can meet in your quarters in forty-five minutes."

"My one true knight, I shall await your arrival with baited breath." In the courtyard, she hiked her skirts and broke into a run. As she skipped up the entrance stairs, he caught a glimpse of her shapely calves and salivated.

As he stepped into the foyer, he noted her thunderous jaunt to the second floor, and he grinned. "Hicks, your suggestion was a stroke of genius, and my bride and I will take our morning meal served in her sitting room. And, by any chance, do you have strawberries leftover from the funeral reception?"

"I do, Sir Dalton." The butler narrowed his stare. "And Mrs. Randolph is quite partial to clotted cream, as well. Of course, for her main dish, she prefers scrambled eggs, ham-steak, and toast."

"Then I shall have the same." Was it too soon to hope, or had he turned a corner with his wife?

"Very good, sir. Also, the contractor, as well as his fore-man, is here to review the last minute changes to the renova-tion, and the gentlemen are in the drawing room." Hicks bowed. "And there is correspondence just delivered from London."

"Thank you, Hicks." Dalton strolled into the redeco-rated chamber, which boasted his signature sapphire hue as the primary focus, much to his amusement. As Rebecca had appealed to Dirk's predilections, so, too, had Daphne appealed to her husband's preferences. "Mr. Benson, Mr. Dumas, to what do I owe this visit?"

"The remodel has exceeded the budget, due to your wife's additions." The contractor fumbled with a sheaf of documents, which he passed to Dalton. "Those are the updated costs, as well as the rendering of the new master apartment."

"What new master apartment?" He perused the drawing and discovered the current separate bedrooms were to be combined into one large accommodation.

"Mr. Benson, it was to be a surprise." The foreman shot Dalton a sheepish glance. "I beg your pardon, sir. But Mrs. Randolph bade me not to show you the plans."

"That is all right." Clenching his jaw to stave off laughter, he studied the images and knew just where she had got the idea.

Everett had started the trend, when he removed the beds from Sabrina's quarters. Then he took things a step farther, when he had the walls separating their rooms torn down. Trevor and Dirk had followed suit and had nothing but praise for the practice. So it appeared Daphne wished to share a single space, and it was an aim he would not countermand, given the inevitable conclusion.

"As we have not begun the demolition, we can modify the alterations, sir." Mr. Benson tugged his cravat and resituated himself on the sofa. "And I can always—"

"I shall direct my solicitor to remit payment for any extra expense." He rolled up the sketches. "And you will adhere to Mrs. Randolph's demands and say nothing of my knowledge thereof."

CHAPTER FOURTEEN

A sennight had passed, since Dalton and Daphne had returned to London, and she already longed for the security of Courtenay Hall. In full mourning, society expected her to avoid the limelight and eschew public events, which suited her, given recent troubling events.

Ensconced in the back parlor of her husband's bachelor lodging, she examined the third threatening missive, which he had unwittingly delivered on that spectacular morning, wherein they had enjoyed a delicious breakfast, and he had fed her strawberries and clotted cream, as she nestled in his lap. Later, he had kissed her for the better part of an hour, and the memory precipitated a foreign ache, even now.

Yet the nefarious note intruded on her pleasant reverie, as it carried an identical intimidating ultimatum:

If you value your life, do not marry Dalton Randolph. Heed this warning, and call off your wedding. If you do not do as I advise, you will be sorry.

The unfamiliar franking bore a date that indicated the letter had been posted prior to her nuptials, but she could glean nothing beyond the pedestrian information. A knock at the door brought her alert. "Come."

"Mrs. Randolph, the carriage awaits." Merton bowed.

"Thank you." Standing, she tucked the ominous directives into her reticule and followed the butler to the foyer, where he held her black shawl and gloves. "I expect to be home by three, and I should like dinner served at six, as Mr. Randolph expressed a desire to retire early."

"Yes, ma'am." Bearing a wrapped package, he loomed in her wake, as she settled into the squabs. Then he placed the parcel on the opposite bench, closed the portal, and stepped to the sidewalk. "Drive on."

After a short ride through Mayfair, the sumptuous equipage halted before Caroline and Trevor's townhouse. A footman rushed forward to provide assistance, and he handed her to the road.

"Will you please retrieve the bundle?" In the grand entryway, she tugged off her gloves, untied and removed her bonnet, and then shrugged from her light wrap, which she passed to the butler. "I am here to see Lady Caroline."

"Yes, Mrs. Randolph. Her ladyship is in the morning room, and I shall take you to her." The manservant bowed and accepted the package from the footman. "If you will follow me, ma'am."

As was the case with the other Brethren properties, the Lockwood residence blended expensive textiles and refined accessories, to create an overall elegant abode. So how was it that Dalton's décor seemed more suited to a house of ill repute? Of course, she had no experience with such places, but the bold red and gold that covered everything struck her as altogether discordant with the image his family portrayed.

"Mrs. Randolph is just arrived." The butler placed the parcel on a table and bowed. "Will there be anything else, your ladyship?"

"No, thank you, Roberts." Caroline waved a welcome. "Daphne, it is so good to see you. Rebecca, Alex, and I were just talking about you. Sabrina and Cara will not be joining us, as they are reluctant to leave their new babes, and Elaine is shopping with Celia, so it is just the four of us. And what have you brought?"

"I come bearing gifts." Daphne untied the twine and unfolded the brown paper. "My mother taught me to press flowers, and I created collections from Portsea's native growth, to commemorate my wedding, since you stood as witnesses."

"This is gorgeous but entirely unnecessary." Alex held up her frame, as she admired Daphne's peculiar talent. "You are quite skilled."

"I would call her an artist." As she studied the blooms, Rebecca smiled. "It is lovely, Daph. I will hang it in a position of prominence at Randolph House, and perhaps I can persuade you to construct another for Lyvedon Hall."

"It would be my honor." Basking in their praise, Daphne ignored the consternation surrounding the threatening missives, as she could reflect on that, tomorrow. After all, the letters had preceded her nuptials. Now that she was married, what could the sender do to her? "And I am so glad you like it."

"Well I love mine." Caroline propped the display of viper's bugloss and sea radish on a sideboard. "When Trevor comes home, I shall ask him to help me select a conspicuous place in the drawing room, so all our guests will view it."

"So how are you, sister?" When Rebecca narrowed her stare, Daphne feared the former spy might have seen more than Daphne was prepared to reveal. "Regardless of your attempts to the contrary, you strike me as a tad out of sorts. Have you mended the rift with Dalton?"

"To a degree, yes." It was Becca's directness that Daphne both welcomed and rued, as the secret agent never minced words. "I apologized for knocking him unconscious, and he expressed remorse for frightening me. We have made a serious effort at détente, but we have not...that is to say...I cannot—"

"You have not consummated your vows." Rebecca lifted a teapot but halted mid-pour. "Is this the chamomile?"

"Yes." Caroline nodded at Dirk's wife. "Daphne, I fear we owe you an apology."

"Oh—how so?" Curious, she inclined her head and summoned calm. "As you have done nothing but support me with your vast knowledge and experience."

"That is one way to look at it." Biting her lip, Alex lowered her chin and sighed. "But we misled you, in a manner of speaking, when we neglected to share the difficulties that preceded the eventual development of our, for lack of a better term, and forgive my forthrightness, propitious coital relationships."

"Precisely." With a sorrowful visage, Rebecca compressed her lips. "The night I approached Dirk, he rejected me and bade me vacate his bedchamber."

"After I gave Jason my bride's prize, he accused me of trying to trap him, and he refused to marry me." Wiping a stray tear, Alex sniffed. "I was alone, pregnant, and so afraid. When he returned to our shores, and Damian forced Jason and I to marry, I punished my husband by withholding my favors. It took months to set things right."

"And even after Trevor and I made our vows before the archbishop, my stubborn spouse did not trust me." As she twirled a lock of her hair, Caroline averted her gaze. "Later, he charged me with having an affair, with a former beau, Lord Darwith, and Trevor left me. In comparison, your only difficulty is the retention of your maidenhead. So we are none of us perfect here."

At Caroline's innocent proclamation, Daphne peered at her reticule. Should she apprise them of the threats, or had she lent too much weight to a harmless prank? As she had celebrated her wedding almost a fortnight ago, and had suffered nothing more than her self-made disaster, should she worry the pregnant Brethren wives?

"I hope you do not take this the wrong way, but I find your stories rather reassuring. In light of your deleterious beginnings, how did you establish yourselves as you are now?" She reminisced of their seaside walks in Portsea and their new customary practice of breaking their fast in her sitting room, wherein they always spent several minutes engaged in heated kisses. "Dalton told me to relax. When I am ready, I am to go to him, so he will not initiate the deflowering, and I am at a crossroad."

"But that is perfect for our cause." Rebecca glanced at Alex. "As our recommendation is unanimous. You must adhere to our example and take charge, as that is how we won our men."

"How so?" At the prospect, Daphne gulped. "Because the last time I took the lead, I knocked Dalton unconscious."

"True." Caroline furrowed her brow and then snorted.

"But that was a spectacular comeuppance, and that can be a good thing, as grooms should fear their brides, a little."

"What if I do not please him?" To her chagrin, Lady Moreton's crude pronouncement echoed in her brain. "Dalton has had so many women."

"But therein lies your primary advantage, as Dalton has never had you." Rebecca tapped a finger to her chin. "And there are countless variations of virtue, my dear. Prior to meeting Dirk, I performed questionable acts with men, targeted because they possessed vital war secrets, who were strangers to me. However my sweet viscount did it, he surmised I was not so pure as the typical London debutante, but it mattered not in the grand scheme. When he rebuffed me, he did so because he wanted to distinguish our love-making from our prior liaisons with other people. In that respect, Dalton is every bit as much a virgin as are you, and I would wager he is equally anxious."

"I concur." Scooting to the edge of the *chaise*, Caroline swiped a square of shortbread. "Trevor and I consummated our vows aboard the *Hera*, as he later admitted he required his trusty bunk to feel at ease."

"As did we, on the *Gawain*." Rebecca snapped her fingers. "Since the *Siren* is dry-docked in Portsmouth, you must choose your moment and your locale, and you must do so wisely."

"And do not attempt a full-scale seduction on your first strike." Alex pointed for emphasis. "Have you glimpsed his one-eyed helmeted buccaneer?"

"Not yet." Daphne shook her head. "And the unknown terrifies me."

"Then you must make your move, when you are ready." Alex seemed so certain, and the force of her conviction gave Daphne hope. "Take him in hand, to build your confidence. Give him a stout yank, just as we taught you, and count the number of tugs necessary to fire his shot. If he reaches completion in five or less jerks, you are a veritable Delilah."

"Well I am impressed, as you make that sound almost scientific, Alex." Caroline reclined amid the pillows and stretched her legs. "You know, after a long voyage, I need only expel my breath to the tip of Trevor's Jolly Roger, and he lets fly a virile barrage."

"Oh, dear." Daphne swallowed hard. "I pray you do not think less of me, but I do not possess the courage to use my mouth."

"Now do not let that scare you." Rebecca patted Daphne's shoulder. "We tell you this so you might understand that men are not so difficult as you imagine. They are maneuvered by their most protuberant part, just as a rudder navigates their ships, and nothing you do will miss the mark."

"Trust us, Daphne." Alex pressed a palm to her chest. "We would not steer you awry."

"All right." Riding a wave of newfound courage, Daphne waved her fist in the air. "I will do it."

And with bold visions swirling in her mind, she returned to Dalton's bachelor lodging, determined to initiate a tryst with her husband, after dinner. In the foyer, she doffed her shawl, bonnet, and gloves.

"There is a missive for you, Mrs. Randolph." Merton held a silver salver, and a crisp white envelope with now familiar handwriting mocked her.

"Thank you, Merton." Her heart sank, as she stifled a cry of despair, and she studied the same peculiar franking she had come to dread. "Is Sir Dalton in residence?"

"No, ma'am." The butler bowed.

A chill crept from her toes, seeped into her calves, pene-trated her thighs, pervaded her gut, and invested her chest with a sense of powerful foreboding, as she strolled into the drawing room. Sitting in an overstuffed chair near the hearth, she tore open the note, unfolded the stationary, and sobbed.

I know the truth, and Dalton Randolph cannot save you. You should not have married him, as you will live to regret it.

"EVERYTHING WAS GOING WELL—UNTIL it was not." Frustrated and aroused beyond words, Dalton wanted to pound someone to a pulp, given he could not make love to his wife. "Daphne hides something from me, and I have, thus far, failed to induce her to share her worries."

"It is a delicate business, as you do not want to rush her, again." Dirk refilled the brandy balloons and returned to sit by the hearth in his study. "As the woman is blessed with lethal aim, and you may not be so lucky, next time."

"Very funny." Dalton rolled his eyes and pictured his wife, as she skipped along the water's edge at Portsea. The priceless reminiscence conflicted with her current demeanor. "We break our fast, every morning, together, and discuss our schedules. And tonight we dine in her sitting room, but she displays no interest in our marital bed, and I promised I would let her come to me. But at this rate, I could go to my grave with a wicked erection, and moun-tainous calluses, as my wife shows no signs of surrender."

"Perhaps it is just a severe case of nerves, and she requires a period of adjustment." His elder brother leaned on an armrest and averted his stare. "No doubt, she regrets what happened and wishes to make amends, but she could be unsure how best to achieve reconciliation. Are you positive you are not making something of nothing?"

"No, I am not." He sifted through the memories of recent days and frowned. "Daphne has always been a woman of lighthearted spirit. Yet, only yesterday, I came upon her in the garden, her brow a mass of furrows and her exquisite features invested with sorrow. On normal occasions, the sight of my beautiful bride in repose inspires peculiar warmth in my chest. But in that moment, I struggled with a chill of unease, and my instincts tell me she is in some sort of trouble."

"Indeed, I know well your unrest." Dirk huffed. "So I sympathize."

"Nightmares continue to plague Rebecca?" Dalton had been so focused on his problems, that he had ignored his sibling's difficulties. "And she still refuses to reveal their content?"

"Aye." With a mournful sigh, Dirk rubbed his eyes. "Every night is the same. She wakes me with bloodcurdling screams and insists she is drowning, until she is fully *compos mentis*. I have been gentle with my queries, but she insists I am overreacting. Yet I know she battles unknown demons from her past, and I cannot fight what I cannot identify."

"I am sorry, brother." Wound tight as a clock spring, he shoved from his seat and paced before the windows. It was a habit he had never practiced, as he thought it symptomatic of control run amok, and that was not his character. At least, it had not been in his nature—until he met Daphne. "Is there anything I can do?"

"You already have." Dirk raised his glass in toast. "Misery loves company."

"And we are a fine pair." For a second, he forgot about his injury and winced, when he scratched his forehead and caught a suture. "So tell me the truth, how did you foster such an harmonious conjugal relationship with Rebecca?"

"Allowing for discretion, I must admit I cannot assume credit for our rapport between the sheets, as I was not exaggerating when I explained how Rebecca pursued me." Dirk pinned Dalton with a steely glare. "If you ever betray my confidence, I will tie you to the *Gawain's* rudder and haul your traitorous arse across the Channel. But suffice it to say on the night I claimed my wife's most intimate gift, she launched an invasion of my private apartments, insisted I take her, and brooked no refusal, despite my initial rejection."

"You were not joking?" Why could Dalton not be so fortunate? After all, he was the lucky one. "And *you* rejected *her*?"

"I plead temporary insanity, as my Becca, naked as the day she was born, could drive a sane man mad as a March hare for want of her." Chuckling, Dirk grinned. "God, but she was glorious, brother. In vain, I tried to rebuff her advances, because I wanted to wait until the vows were spoken, but my heretofore-vaunted self-restraint yielded to the strength of her desire."

"So you took her." Dalton had always suspected as much, but that had not diminished the weight of the revelation, given Dirk's oh-so-noble reputation.

"Because I love her, as she loves me, I acquiesced to her demands." Dirk clucked his tongue. "Our intimacy was superb, unlike any I had ever enjoyed. And it was all I could do to focus on her needs. Summoning the patience of a saint, I brought her to release and breached her harbor, as she savored completion. It worked perfectly, and we have benefited from an abiding ardor, ever since."

Filing the information for future use, Dalton contemplated his next move. He desperately wanted to aid Daphne, but he could not broach the subject without trampling what little trust they had forged. For good or ill, he had to retrench and wait for his wife to come to him. And when she vouchsafed her secrets, he would accept them with unimpaired sangfroid.

"I appreciate your frankness, brother." Dalton downed the last of his brandy and set the balloon on a nearby table. "But I should—"

"Am I intruding on anything of significance?" Rebecca strolled into the study. "Oh, please, do not stand on my account, my sweet lord." As she pushed Dirk back into his chair, she peered at Dalton. "Your wife made the loveliest gift. What a thoughtful woman you married."

"Thank you." To his embarrassment, the burn of a blush seared his cheeks, and he shuffled his feet. "Daphne is a kind and most generous lady."

"Becca, what are you about?" Dirk narrowed his stare, as she stepped about his legs and eased to his lap. "I should see Dalton to the door."

"He knows his way out, as he grew up in this house." She wound her arms about Dirk's neck. "And I would take a short nap, as we have an hour before the dinner bell sounds. Would you refuse me?"

"Never." Dirk nipped her nose. "Brother, I bid you farewell and much luck."

"Good evening." He sketched a bow and headed for the exit. In the hall, he turned to close the oak panel and discovered Dirk and Rebecca sharing an amazingly thorough kiss. Polite decorum demanded he avert his gaze, yet he found their tender exchange riveting.

How he envied their reciprocal passion, and he wanted that with Daphne.

In mere seconds, Dalton collected his curricle and steered for home and his wife. Thoughts of their prearranged appointment to partake of their meal in her sitting room filled him with anticipation, and fiery zeal rode hard in its wake. Minutes later, riding a wave of fervor, he skipped up the steps and entered his residence.

"Where is Mrs. Randolph?" he inquired of his butler, as he doffed his hat, coat, and gloves, and adjusted his cravat.

"Mrs. Randolph asked me to convey her regrets, as she is unwell and unable to keep her commitments, tonight." Merton bowed. "Shall I tell Cook to prepare a tray, sir?"

Overwhelming disappointment settled as a lead ball in his belly, and Dalton grimaced. "No, as I am not hungry. That will be all, Merton."

Despondent, Dalton trudged upstairs and halted on the landing. Upon their arrival from Portsea, his bride had vacated the large chamber that adjoined his and moved to a small guestroom at the other end of the hall. At first, he had wanted to rain holy hell, but he had said nothing, after recalling the debacle that had been his wedding night.

Carrying a candlestick, he tiptoed into her quarters and found her asleep. The room was quiet, save the ticking of the mantel clock and his heartbeat, which seemed to keep rhythm. To the undiscerning observer, nothing appeared amiss. But what struck him was her tearstained face. She had been crying, but—why? What had happened? And why had she excluded him from her anguish? Sitting at the edge of the mattress, he adjusted the covers, pulling them to her chin. Daphne vented a soft sob indicative of some inner torment, and he ached to console her. Hours had passed before he left her.

"BROTHERS, we are gathered here to welcome two new Nautionnier knights into our distinguished order. Captain George de Vere, Viscount Huntingdon and my nephew, and Captain Lucien Wentworth, sixth Earl of Calvert and Rebecca's elder brother." Admiral Douglas perched at the edge of his desk. "Despite the Treaty of Fontainebleau, the restoration of the Bourbon monarchy and Louis XVIII, and the exile of Napoleon to the island of Elba, Wellington does not believe we have seen the last of French aggression, so we increase our ranks to serve His Majesty. To that end, I anticipate a plethora of assignments from the Lord High Admiral, any day."

"Hear, hear." Blake slapped his thigh. "Now pass the brandy, and let us commence the celebrations."

"Knights, at the ready." Damian corralled the veteran seamen. "Love, honor, and devotion were the beginning of our Order. Bonds of kinship and friendship, all-important. We uphold these principles embrace for embrace, desire for desire, for one, for all. For King and Country we stand, for love and comradeship we live."

In unison, the group shouted, "*Nulli Secundus.*"

As his fellow Brethren of the Coast toasted and roasted the latest additions to the famed order descended of the Templars, Dalton found no joy in the festivities. His thoughts centered on his wife, who had closeted herself in her chamber and eschewed their breakfast ritual, to his monumental disappointment. It was only when they were scheduled to depart for the family dinner that she appeared in the foyer.

In the coach, as they drove to Upper Brooke Street, Daphne had not uttered a word, and she looked pale. And although Lady Amanda had planned a tempting menu with not one but three of Daphne's favorite dishes, his bride had hardly ate a bite.

"Shall we rejoin the women, as Cook prepared apple snow, and I am quite fond of it?" The admiral clapped twice, and the rowdy sailors quieted. "And Amanda and I have another announcement to make."

As usual, immature ribbing continued in the hall, and Dalton hugged the rear, given his sour mood. In the drawing room, the ladies chatted, and Daphne sat alone, near the hearth, gazing at the flames. He grabbed a cup of tea from the trolley and weaved his way to her.

"For you, darling." He was glad, when she accepted the steaming brew. "I missed you, this morning."

"I missed you, too." She avoided his stare, which spoke volumes, and none of it boded well. "I wondered if I might—"

"Our dear family, if we could have your attention, Mark and I would like to share a bit of news." Lady Amanda peered at the admiral and nodded. "And we do hope you are thrilled for us."

"What Amanda is trying to tell you...we want you to... recently we discovered...oh, bloody hell." The admiral snatched the brandy decanter from the trolley and drank from the bottle. The venerable naval legend wiped his mouth on his coat sleeve. "We are expecting our third child."

A chorus of gasps pierced the solitude.

"But—how is that possible?" Everett blinked.

"How do you think?" Admiral Douglas arched a brow, and Dalton was grateful for the distraction, as it afforded the opportunity to scrutinize his reticent bride.

"Sorry." Everett bowed his head.

"Well I am impressed." Trevor winked. "Did not know you still had it in you, old boy."

"Mama, are you all right?" Cara glanced at Sabrina. "I mean, is this normal?"

"It is perfectly normal." Lady Amanda laughed. "Upon my word, but why the long faces? My situation is not unheard of, and Dr. Handley assures me everything will be fine, if I am careful."

"And you will be *very* careful." The admiral frowned. "In fact, I am taking you to the country, for the remainder of your confinement, as I would preserve your health and that of our unborn babe."

As the group digested the recent revelation, Dalton studied Daphne's reaction. "You knew."

"Yes." She clutched his hand and squeezed his fingers. "I guessed, when I visited her, after the contretemps with Lady Moreton and Lord Sheldon."

"You are excellent at keeping secrets." When her smile faded, he said, "I am teasing, angel."

"Are you angry that I did not apprise you of the impending addition to their family tree?" Her countenance of concern gave him pause, as he realized that, despite her direct query, she was asking in the general sense. "Have I displeased you?"

"No, angel." In his brain, he formulated a response intended to reassure her. "Everyone has secrets, but I value honesty. It is very easy to be angry with someone who lies to me, but it is difficult to be mad with someone who tells me the truth, however late."

"I understand, and I admire the sentiment." Then she started. "What on earth is Blake about?"

"We need a little levity in this somber lot, as it has grown far too serious for my taste." Always the life of the party, Blake snickered, waggled his brows, and then gave the group his back. "What do you think of my new disguise for Buccaneers and Bluejackets, with my nephews?"

The usually hotheaded duke pulled on a black hooded mask and charged Caroline, who cringed. "Blake, you can't be serious. Welton will be three this November, and he is too young for such games."

A loud crash had Daphne jumping from the chair to stand at his side, and he noticed Rebecca had dropped her crystal dish of apple snow, and the delicate bowl shattered when it struck the tea service on the trolley, as she fixated on Blake. But it was her wide-eyed visage of terror that brought Dirk to her aid.

"Becca, what is wrong?" Dirk eased her to the sofa, sat to her right, and draped an arm about her shoulders. "What is it?"

"*Varringdale.*" At the former spy's exclamation, Dalton shuddered.

A double agent for the Counterintelligence Corps, Lord Varringdale had betrayed Rebecca and her partner in espionage, Collin Eddington. Varringdale had tortured Rebecca, and Dirk had killed the traitor, with his bare hands.

"I apologize, Dirk." Blake removed the mask and compressed his lips. "I meant no harm."

"It is all right." Dirk cupped Rebecca's chin, as she wept. "Talk to me. Tell me of your distress."

"Should we give you the room?" the admiral asked.

"No." With an upraised hand, Dirk shook his head, as

he remained focused on Rebecca. "There is no shame in her tears."

For a while, Rebecca said nothing. Then she inhaled a shaky breath. "After I lost our baby, Varringdale tied me to a table. My wrists and ankles were strapped down, and another band, which was attached to a panel, crossed my forehead, so I could not move. When unlatched, the board dropped, which enabled him to pour a torrent of water over my nose and mouth. At one point, he draped my face with a cloth, and I was certain I would drown, as I eventually lost consciousness."

"Hell and the Reaper." In a low voice, Dirk inquired, "And is that what haunts you, in your nightmares?

Rebecca nodded and then broke.

"I figured as much." Dirk lifted her to his lap. "And now that I know the whole of your trauma, we can fight your demons together, sweetheart."

"I am so sorry, as I should have told you," Rebecca cried. "I should not have kept the details from you."

"You did it to spare my feelings." Dirk caressed his wife's cheek. "So there are no apologies necessary, love."

As had the other Brethren husbands, Dalton pulled Daphne into his embrace, and she shivered. Regardless of their difficulties, he needed to hold her. Never had he comprehended the depth of Dirk's fury, in regard to Rebecca's ordeal, until that moment. Until that second, when he imagined someone hurting Daphne.

The urge to protect her, to keep her safe from harm, was compelling. Of course, she was no spy, and no turncoat stalked her, but he could not tolerate the mere thought of someone harming his wife. It made him angry.

"Dalton, I want to go home." Daphne burrowed into his chest. "I wish to return to Portsea Island."

Stunned by her declaration, because he had presumed she referenced their townhouse, he knew not how to respond. "Admiral, could you have your man bring around our carriage?"

"Of course." The admiral signaled the butler.

Myriad possibilities echoed in his brain, as Dalton feared she planned to leave him. By the time they had collected their gloves and outerwear, he was submerged in a miasma of confusion mixed with pain. But no matter what she asked of him, he vowed to bear it. He would neither shout nor rave. He would relent. He would accept her choice, if only to make her happy.

When Daphne shifted in the squabs to lean against him, he kissed her crown of curls, and she said, "Dirk and Rebecca have known so much sadness."

"More than anyone deserves." The clip-clop of the team beat in harmony with his pulse, and dread permeated his muscles. What would he do without his backwater bride? How would he persist without her? "But they have survived, because they work as a couple."

"And he supports her, without condition." She snuggled close. "Even though she hid the full extent of her torture from him."

"Well, Dirk loves Rebecca." And Dalton believed he felt the same for Daphne, but he remained uncertain. "And as I said before, all that matters is she told him the truth."

When the carriage halted, he handed Daphne to the sidewalk. Various propositions danced on his tongue, and he considered offering her a brandy. Then again, she had choked on the amber intoxicant the last time she had consumed it, so he nixed the idea. Perhaps she would have preferred a glass of wine, or he could order a pot of tea.

In the foyer, he nodded an acknowledgement to Merton.

"How was your evening, sir?" The butler hung Dalton's coat on the hall tree.

"Interesting." That was putting it mildly. Then it dawned on him that his wife often requested warm milk before retiring. Though the prospect seemed not so palatable, he would sacrifice his stomach if it afforded him the chance to persuade her to stay in London. In that instant, Dalton turned to discover Daphne gone.

CHAPTER FIFTEEN

arching into her guest room, Daphne crossed the floor and walked straight to her armoire. After a brief search, she located the reticule in which she had hidden the ominous notes. In the long mirror, she caught sight of her reflection, and she studied her appearance for signs of her distress.

Had Dalton detected her unrest? Had he suspected her of deceit? Given Rebecca's revelations, and Dirk and Dalton's reaction to her sin of omission, Daphne had everything to gain by taking a stand. So she had nothing to lose by making her confession, and she had tarried long enough. Once again, she would trust her husband and bare her soul. She would share her secrets, she would withhold nothing, and he would help her. With conviction as a shield, she trudged forth.

But the walk to his apartments seemed never-ending.

Without knocking, she twisted the knob and entered his sanctuary, which she had never visited. In stark contrast to the remainder of his bachelor lodging, Dalton's private apartment sported his favorite sapphire shade trimmed in mahogany. Absent the excess knickknacks, his personal surroundings boasted only nautical tools, some of which appeared ancient. And, to her abiding delight, the small framed assortment of yellow horned poppy, red valerian, viper's bugloss, and sea radish, which she had created to commemorate the first time he accompanied her on her morning jaunts, held pride of place on a small stand, atop his bedside table. That sight, alone, girded her resolve.

Voices from the closet snared her attention, and she cleared her throat. "Dalton, are you there?"

"Daphne?" Wearing his breeches, boots, and shirt, which sat open at the throat, Dalton emerged from behind an oriental screen. "What are you doing here?"

"I need to speak with you." With fists at her side, she vowed to prevail.

"Right now?" Her husband appeared shocked, as he blinked.

"Yes." Before her confidence faltered, she took two steps, as she would not be denied. "This very instant."

"Can it not wait until the morning?" With a mighty frown, he folded his arms. "You have my word, as a gentleman, I would honor your request, whatever you require."

"No." She advanced further into his domain, as, in the spirit of the Brethren wives, she would not be rebuffed.

"All right." To her chagrin, he retreated, but her concerns were allayed, when Dalton said, "You are dismissed, Bowling. I shall see to the rest, myself."

Nervous, Daphne chewed her lip and tapped her foot, until her husband returned. For several seconds, they just stared at each other. In no uncertain terms, she had the floor, but the perfect entreaty failed her.

At last, her knight sighed. "Angel, what are you about?"

Silent, she thrust the bundled letters at him.

"What is this?" He untied the twine and flipped through the envelopes. "But this correspondence is addressed to you. Yet you wish me to read them?"

Fear locked as a vise about her throat, so she nodded her assent and prayed for strength.

Shifting his weight, he unfolded the top note, perused the brief but disturbing content, and snapped to attention. In rapid succession, he digested the remaining three missives and then pierced her with his stare. "Where did you get these?"

"The first two were delivered to Randolph House." Wringing her fingers, she cursed the urge to weep. "The third was redirected to Courtenay Hall, after our wedding."

"Which I unwittingly conveyed to you." Dalton closed his eyes and bowed his head. "Over breakfast, after our stroll among the dunes."

"Yes," she said in a small voice. "And the fourth arrived yesterday."

"Which is why you canceled our dinner, retired early, and cried yourself to sleep." He tossed the stationary to his bed and paced.

Shocked by his revelation, she gasped. "How did you know?"

"Because I sat with you into the wee hours." He halted and confronted her. "Why did you not tell me someone had threatened my wife? Do you imagine I will stand idly by while an unknown villain assaults you? How dare they."

As he ranted and raved, Daphne heard nothing but his simple yet compelling admission, over and over, as a sweet refrain.

Because I sat with you into the wee hours.

In that moment, he won her heart, once again. As tears streamed her cheeks, she resolved to concede. Whatever he desired, even if he decided to send her away, she would obey. No matter what he asked of her, she vowed to bear it. She would neither shout nor protest. She would relent. She would accept his choice, if only to make him happy. But when Dalton quieted and charged her, she trembled.

"Oh, sweet Daphne." With his arms about her waist, he lifted her from the floor and held her so tight she could scarcely draw breath. "My cherished backwater bride, I will let no one take you from me. And I will sort this out, I swear."

"So you are not angry with me?" Nuzzling his neck, she pressed her lips to his warm flesh and drew comfort from his mere presence. "And you will not leave me?"

"What do you mean?" Relaxing his grasp, he let her slide down the front of him, and she discovered him aroused. "Of course, I am not upset with you. But I am livid with those who would cause you harm. And we are married, till death do us part, so I will never surrender you without a fight, my angel. If someone wants you, they must first go through me."

At his priceless admission, everything inside her flip-flopped and clenched. Daphne gave vent to a half-strangled sob, as a valiant rallying cry, and came at her husband with a force she had not known she possessed, and he stumbled backward but never broke their point of contact. Twining her fingers in his hair, she bit his lip and then besieged his mouth. Like a firestorm, they ignited.

When Dalton settled his palms to her bottom, and pressed her hips to his, she moaned, as delicious heat simmered beneath her skin and quelled the chill of fear that had plagued her for more than a fortnight. As some sort of addictive intoxicant, he bestowed upon her intimate kisses, with his tongue delving deeper than ever before, and she craved more.

A foreign hunger blossomed in the pit of her belly, and she yearned to assuage the heady appetite. Now she understood the temptation of desire, which the Brethren wives had recounted. Without doubt, she wanted her husband, longed to reap the rewards of his expertise, of everything he could teach her, and pleasure him, too. The knowledge worked on her in ways she could not defend against, given her innocence, and her knees buckled.

"Easy, love." All of a sudden, Dalton bent and swept her into his arms. "Do not be afraid."

In a flash, he carried her to his bed and eased her to the mattress. Stretched alongside her, he nudged her legs apart, as he wielded gentle caresses in a delicate invasion, and she followed his lead. But when he shifted and flicked up her skirts, she gasped.

"What are you doing?" She tensed, when he placed his hand on her bare thigh.

"Please, sweet Daphne. I will not hurt you." He nipped her nose. "Permit me to feed you a taste, just a morsel, of the delights we can share."

"You promise, it will not hurt?" Pining for what she knew not, she clung to him.

"You have my solemn vow." To her lips, he said, "Please, angel."

His appeal, captivating in its simplicity, arrested her, and she could not refuse his elementary petition. And she had not wanted to refuse him. Opening to her knight, she told him with her body what she lacked the courage to say with words, and Dalton rewarded her with a lusty growl, as he took the helm and steered her into a mystical realm, where she floated beyond her mortal coil, and sight and sound yielded to touch.

As she sampled his desire, a potent elixir not unlike the brandy that rendered her dizzy, she wallowed in the luxurious heat suffusing her in peaceful euphoria—until Dalton touched her most tender flesh.

"Wait." The ugly reality of her locale struck her as a cold-water bath. She jerked free and rolled to the opposite side of the bed. "I can't do this—not here."

"What did I do, darling?" The sadness investing his boyish features tore at her heart. "Tell me what you want me to do, and I will do it. Just do not turn me away."

"But I am not rejecting you." Somehow, she had to make him understand her perspective. Had he not demanded honesty? Had he not claimed he valued the truth? Daphne stiffened her spine and inhaled a fortifying breath. "I hate this house. I detest it and everything that happened here, before we met."

"I beg your pardon?" Her husband sputtered and stuttered. Then he rubbed the back of his neck and stood. "Pray, explain yourself."

"I want to be yours. I want to make love to you—I want it all." Cresting on a tide of conviction, she lifted her chin. "But not here."

"What is your objection?" He glanced about the room. "What is wrong with my home?"

"That is the point. This is your bachelor lodging, where you have taken any number of women, of whom I am jealous, and it pains me to admit it, but there it is." There was no going back, so she clenched her fists. "I have no wish to join the ranks of the many. I want to be *the one*."

Dalton opened his mouth and then closed it. "Am I to

understand you have no quarrel with me, and your issue is with our current location?"

"Yes." Rounding the footboard, she smiled. "I long to be yours, but it will never happen in this place. And I do not want to live here. I would have something that reflects our combined tastes, as a couple. I would have what is ours."

"Is that your sole complaint?" He sauntered to the bell pull and tugged hard. "Have you any other grievances?"

"No," she replied without hesitation.

"Well, then." To her confusion, her husband returned to his closet. When someone knocked at the door, Dalton reappeared, wearing a tan waistcoat and shrugging into a dark green coat. "Come."

Merton peered around the edge of the oak panel. "You rang, sir?"

"Have the carriage readied, as Mrs. Randolph and I depart in twenty minutes." Her knight seemed so calm, and she was anything but, as he tied his cravat.

"Yes, sir." The butler rushed to convey the directive, and Daphne gulped.

"Where are we going?" She scrutinized her dress and slippers. "Should I change my gown?"

"No, angel." His answering smirk gave her delicious shivers. "And where we go, you will need no clothes."

Before she could respond, he clutched her wrist and led her into the hall, down the stairs, and into the study. At the side table, he lifted the brandy decanter and poured a glass of the stiff drink. Mid-air, she grabbed the balloon, drew a healthy draft, and choked as the intoxicant burned her throat.

"Easy, sweetheart." Dalton chuckled. "I want you fully alert when we consummate our vows."

At his casual statement, she almost swallowed her tongue. "Are we to take a room in a hotel?"

"Sir Dalton, the coach is here." Merton bowed.

In the foyer, Dalton draped her shawl over her shoulders, and she tugged on her gloves. Then he steered her out the door and into their equipage. After a few brief comments to the coachman, her one true knight plopped into the squabs and hauled her into his lap.

"Angel, do not worry." He kissed her temple. "I will protect you, and in my absence, our family will guard you. No one will harm you. And tomorrow I will summon assistance in the matter. We will uncover the villain threatening you and bring them to justice."

"Dalton." She framed his face. "I love you."

"I know you do, sweetheart." He tickled her jawline with the tip of his nose. "And I truly believe I love you, too."

"Yet, I hear uncertainty." And she was more than a little deflated. Daphne knew, without doubt, that her husband loved her, but she needed him to know it. "So you will tell me when you are positive?"

"Can anyone be assured of anything?" He sighed. "I care for you, of that I am satisfied. Why is that not good enough for you?"

"Because I want more, and I will have it." The streets of Mayfair passed in a blur, until familiar surroundings struck her. When the coach came to a halt, her question had been answered. "We are to spend tonight at Randolph House?"

"Indeed." Without waiting for the footman, Dalton leaped to the sidewalk and then handed her down. "It meets your requirements, as never have I brought any woman to my ancestral home. And you shall be the only lady to grace the sheets of my bed."

D<small>ALTON</small> <small>HAD</small> <small>LINGERED</small> in Dirk's study long enough for Hughes to light the fireplaces and inspect the accommodations. Once Dalton had Daphne alone in his apartments, he gave her the bedchamber to prepare herself, while he untied his cravat, tossed the yard-length of linen to a chair, doffed his coat and waistcoat, and sat to pull off his boots, in the sitting room.

To his amazement and mortification, he was as nervous as a giddy green lad with his first woman. On the tallboy, the brandy decanter called to him, as a sultry summons, but he opted to forgo the liquid courage, as he required all his faculties and what remained of his tattered self-control, to survive the deflowering he had planned. And he wanted nothing to dull his senses when he docked in her honey harbor.

"Hello, my one true knight." His wife loomed in the open entrance to the inner sanctum, and once again she stunned him.

Barefooted, wearing nothing but her sheer chemise, with her blonde curls draped about her shoulders, she could have been mistaken for a practiced seraph, if not for the telltale wringing of her hands. And never had he known a lady could blush from top to toe, but his provincial bride colored beetroot red, and he could not help but laugh.

"You are beautiful, my angel." When he eased to the edge of the *chaise*, she halted him with an upraised palm.

"Please, do not get up on my account, as I would join you." Confused, he reassumed his position amid the cushions, as she sat beside him. "Might I ask a favor?"

"Sweetheart, you may have whatever you wish." He winked. "As I am in a mood to indulge your every fantasy."

"Perfect." She scooted closer, until she nudged his thigh with hers. Then she settled her gaze on the robust bulge at his crotch. "I have never seen a naked man before."

"I would hope not." Her fascination fueled an already wicked erection, and he shifted his hips beneath her ardent scrutiny. "Our bodies are rather different, but we are fashioned to link as one, and the union is quite natural."

"Will it hurt?" She bit her lip, and he almost spilt his seed.

"No, angel." It was, perhaps, a testament to the depth of his regard and her influence over him that the mere discussion of coitus had him teetering on the brink of sweet release. And her surprising but most welcome curiosity only fed his hunger. "If you follow my lead, and do exactly as I say, you should feel only pleasure, as most virgin's pain stems from anxiety."

"That is what the Brethren wives said." How earnest she seemed, as she studied him. "May I?"

Now that request he had never seen coming.

Incapable of forming a coherent response, he nodded. To his shock, he damn near exploded, when she unhooked his breeches and drew back the placket.

"Goodness, now I know why Sabrina calls it the one-eyed pirate, as it looks rather angry." That gem of brilliance was just the levity he needed to break the tension investing him. As she inclined her head and made an in-depth study of his most prized protuberance, he gritted his teeth. "Might I touch you?"

She was going to kill him.

"My dear, I am yours to do with as you will." Brave words from a man on the verge of shaming himself and his sex. When she grasped his length, he tensed and groaned, and she recoiled.

"Was that bad?" She fidgeted. "Did I injure you?"

"No, sweetheart." He wrapped an arm about her shoulders, toyed with a lock her of guinea-gold hair, and kissed her temple. "It is just that I have dreamed of you, like this, so many nights. Now that you are here, I can scarcely believe the reality."

"And what is this?" She smeared the drop of moisture about the plum-shaped tip. "Is this normal?"

"It is perfectly normal." He closed his eyes. "And it means I desire you, so very much."

To his infinite thanks, she emitted something between a sob and a sigh and set her mouth to his in an inexpressibly endearing affirmation—just as she worked him. With her fledgling assault, he grabbed her wrist. On the second tug, his gut clenched, and on the third, he let fly an effuse volley, which shot forth in a jetting rush. Covering her hand with his, he dropped his head against the back of the *chaise* and taught her how to milk him dry, as he grunted and groaned in blessed relief.

After what seemed as hours but was only a few blissful minutes, he resurfaced from the exhilarating oblivion to discover his wife smiling at him.

"I did it." Spattered with the proof of his ardor, she all but bounced with enthusiasm. "I am a veritable Delilah."

"Oh, I would say you did it, all right." Dalton chuckled, as her good humor was infectious. "And you have no idea how much I needed that."

"And now I know I can satisfy you." Was it his imagination, or had she appeared proud of her accomplishment? "I feel so powerful."

"Did you ever doubt it?" When her ebullience faded, he sat upright. "Daphne, you must know I desire you."

"But Lady Moreton said I could never satisfy you as she satisfied you," she murmured.

"Angel, I hope this does not make you think ill of me, but I am aroused by the mere sight of you." Standing, he secured his breeches, shrugged from his shirt, pulled her from the *chaise*, and led her to the bedchamber. "The subtle rush of your breath, the gentle lilt of your voice, the slightest glimpse of your blue eyes, and I am inspired to the heights of passion such as I have never known. I would argue the opposite is true, as no woman could ever satisfy me as you satisfy me, and we have yet to make love." In seconds, he untied the ribbon and whisked the soiled chemise over her head. Then he knelt before her and pressed his face to her belly. "I am your most unworthy servant, Mrs. Randolph. But I shall endeavor to deserve you, every day, for the rest of my life."

"My one true knight, you are more than worthy." In that moment, his wife bent and caressed his cheek. Then she retreated, eased to the mattress, and flicked her fingers in entreaty. "Now make me yours."

Again, she astonished him with her overt surrender, but he should have expected no less from his bride. Dirk had called her formidable. Surely, that was an understatement. After divesting himself of his breeches, he sat on the edge of the four-poster and brushed the hollow between her breasts with his knuckles.

"I need you to listen carefully, as I want you to know what I am going to do, so I will not startle you." Dalton glanced at the table, collected all manner of items that might function as projectiles, and either deposited them in a drawer or relocated them to the dresser. "In order to prepare you, I am going to kiss you, right here." With caution, he grazed the supple flesh at the apex of her thighs. "Have I shocked you?"

"No." Despite her response, she appeared nervous. "Rebecca insists there is much to recommend it."

"She discussed such behavior with you?" Bloody hell, he needed to attend more tea parties. "And your actions in the sitting room—who told you of that?"

"The Brethren wives sought to allay my concerns, and I am grateful for their counsel, else I might have swooned just now, so do not be angry with them." She squirmed. "And Alex swears Jason raves about what she calls naughty finger work."

"Upon my word." At that, Dalton burst into laughter. "But I never knew my sisters engaged in such licentious conversations."

"You would be surprised." Her eyes flared, as he assumed a comfortable position between her legs, which he pushed further apart.

Slowly, he bent and expelled his breath to her soft little curls, and she shrieked. Watching his every move, she moaned, as he flicked his tongue to her taut nub. But when he probed her pliant folds, and delved deeper still, she grabbed a pillow and hugged it over her face. Savoring her unique essence, he licked her slowly, in a monotonous cadence, letting her adjust to his tempered invasion.

A series of muffled sighs played an arresting accompaniment, and he worked himself, in concert. At last, she relaxed and stretched her limbs, heavy with diverting languor, and he knew she was with him.

Dalton reached up and slid the pillow from her grasp. With her lips parted, her breathing had slowed, and her lushly lashed lids were closed, so she had not noticed he had removed her makeshift shield. Fastening his mouth to the jewel of her desire, he suckled hard. She cried out, and he flipped her onto her belly, so he could pay homage to her shapely backside, which he had admired the night of their initial acquaintance aboard the *Siren*. How he cherished the memory of her glorious derriere, as she had bent over the stores in the hold.

Sparing not an inch of her succulent bottom, he indulged every fantasy he had conjured during their courtship. And again, his wife serenaded him with a priceless audial tapestry of pants and sighs he would carry to the grave. When he feared he could take no more, he rolled her onto her back, closed his lips about her tender core and pressed on her a decadent massage intended to entice and arouse. With every swirl, swish, and swipe of his tongue, she all but melted into the downy surface, until telltale rigidity signaled she had soared into rapturous paradise.

Moving swift and sure, Dalton rose above her to witness her virgin release, and uncharacteristic tears blurred his gaze, as Daphne stared at the canopy, clutched her throat, and emitted an achingly sweet scream. Settling his hips to hers, he bent and kissed her rose-tipped breasts, as she whimpered, lost amid the throes of ecstasy. Perfectly positioned, he claimed her in a single powerful thrust.

And so it was done.

Forever, Daphne was his, and her untried sheath enveloped him in scorching slick heat. Summoning patience, and resting on his elbows, he framed her face and set a slow and steady rhythm, as he waited for her to join him in the dance.

At last, she peered at him. "So I am yours?"

"Yes, angel." He rubbed his nose to hers and showed her how to lift her heels and hug him with her thighs. "You are mine, and I am unequivocally yours."

With an expression of wonder, she wound her arms about his neck and bestowed upon him a feminine smile, and Dalton Randolph, rake, rogue, Nautionnier knight, and the lucky one, was lost.

A RAY of shimmering sunlight peeked through the heavy drapes, as Daphne rubbed her eyes and sat upright. Clutching the sheet to her chest, she glanced at the left side of the four-poster and discovered her husband gone. Naked, she shimmied to the floor and winced, as she ached in places she had never known she could ache. Then she walked to the washstand.

After scrubbing her face and cleaning her teeth, she strolled to the window and peered at the world beyond the glass. The sky boasted a brilliant cerulean backdrop dotted with puffy white clouds. And then memories and bits of time flashed in her brain. Bodies bumped and ground, hands caressed, lips met, and tongues tasted, accompanied by a heady concert of Dalton's husky grunts and groans and her feminine pants and sighs. Revisiting cherished memories of all her husband had done to her, all he had given her, she hugged herself and smiled.

"Good morning, my gorgeous wife." She started and whirled about, just as her husband, bare-footed and wearing only his breeches and a navy silk robe, rolled a trolley into the room. "And it is a very good morning, indeed. Hungry?"

"Starving." Prior to last night, she would have been distressed, to say the least, by her state of utter nudity, but her knight had made it clear he preferred her sans clothing. And the heat of his stare, even now, galvanized her courage, and she thrilled to the power she wielded over him. "What is for breakfast?"

"You mean lunch?" He lifted the silver domed covers, to reveal slices of ham, gooseberry cheese, Bath buns, black butter, and white grapes. "It is almost two, my sleeping beauty."

"What?" She returned to the bed, as he prepared a tray with two plates. "I have never slept so late. Then again, we were awake for the better portion of the night, engaging in your favorite activity."

"And I intend to lock you in here, today, as I have yet to sate my senses with you." He poured a cup of tea, served her, and then sketched a bow. "So eat your fill, as you need to replenish your strength."

"You are shameless." Her pronouncement might have been convincing had she managed to stifle her grin.

"That is not what you said last night." Dalton swaggered to his side of the bed, stripped from his robe and breeches, and joined her. With a quick swipe, he nabbed a plump grape, bit it in half, and offered the juicy morsel to her with his lips. Of course, the simple gesture soon spiraled out of control, as he kissed her—and kept kissing her. And then her belly grumbled. "Bloody hell, it sounds as if you swallowed a monster."

"I did, in the wee hours, with your precipitate tutelage." And in the heat of the moment, she had forgot Sabrina's instruction, using a rather large banana, and had scraped his stout pirate with her teeth. That had brought their close action to an abrupt halt, but he had compensated admirably, with a rapidly deployed diversion. Despite efforts to the contrary, Daphne giggled. "I hope I did not cause permanent damage."

"Not at all, as I am rock-solid whenever you are within

reach." He tempted her with a bite of ham. "And to show you I hold no grudge, we can attempt another lesson, after we eat."

She cooed. "How magnanimous you are, my handsome husband."

"Sweetheart, you have no idea. And I intend to be generous with my knowledge and expertise, well into the evening." Waggling his brows, he smeared strawberry jam over her nipple and proceeded to lick her clean. "While I am loathe to spoil our wonderful meal, I must apprise you of the arrangements I have made on our behalf."

"Oh?" She returned her cup to the saucer. "What manner of naughty business have you been about?"

Dalton opened and then closed his mouth. "My saucy wife, I like the way you think. But I am in earnest, as I would keep you safe from harm, and we have yet to identify the blackguard threatening you."

"I am so sorry." The ugly reality of her predicament intruded on their sanctuary, and her appetite waned in an instant. "Would you think me silly if I said I wished we could stay here, in your private apartment, forever?"

"On the contrary, I find you unutterably alluring and winsome." He fed her a nibble of bread. "And it is all I can do to grant you a brief respite, as making love to you is my new favorite pastime. With the goal of increasing my proficiency in said hobby, I directed my solicitor to sell the townhouse, and I engaged a broker to help you select our next residence, as I will purchase nothing that makes you unhappy."

"But what of you?" Given the significance of his gift, her heart sang. "Have you no requirements? And where shall we stay, in the meantime, as it could take weeks to find a new home."

"I have but one demand, my angel." Grasping her wrist, he drew her hand beneath the covers, whereupon she found him hot and hard. "We will share a master suite. However, if your choice does not meet my stipulation, we will hire a contractor to make the necessary renovations, if you approve. And Dirk and Rebecca have invited us to remain at Randolph House until we locate a suitable property."

"Then everything is settled." Daphne pulled free, pushed back the counterpane, lifted the tray, and conveyed it to the trolley. Then she paused, glanced at her gallant knight, and retrieved the porcelain jam pot. Driven by bold-ness learned in his ardent embrace, she returned to the bed and scooted next to her husband.

"What have you there?" Dalton narrowed his stare, and she lowered her chin and smiled.

Without a word, she shoved aside the sheet, exposing his most elementally male aspect, which no longer frightened her, as she craved the pleasure he brought her. After scooping the thick strawberry compote with a finger, she set the bowl on the side table. Leaning forward, she kissed her man with all she had and for all she was worth. Spreading the tart preserve to his prized protuberance, she whispered against his lips, "Now about that lesson..."

CHAPTER SIXTEEN

The sun had risen above the yardarm, when Dalton heeled his bay and raced along the sandy track in the park, as excitement surged in his veins. Sweet reflections, spectacular reveries flashed in his mind as a siren's serenade, and Daphne's creamy flesh, supple thighs, and luscious lips called to him. But he owed her a respite, however brief, as she had earned it, so he sought distraction. Wild and reckless, he jumped a low-lying hedge and veered toward a copse of oaks. When he spotted a familiar figure, he drew rein, eased his mount to a canter, and steered for the verge.

"Good morning, brother." He saluted.

"Finally found your way out of your bed, I see." Dirk shifted in his saddle and clucked his tongue. "Is it safe to presume an annulment is now out of the question?"

"That is putting it mildly." He snorted. "By God, but Daphne is wondrous, and it is just as you said. The anatomy is the same, yet nothing is as I expected. Somehow, some way, everything is different. What I thought I knew seems altogether foreign, as if I am learning the feminine terrain all over again."

"As a virgin?" Inclining his head, Dirk snickered. "You are in love."

"How do you know?" How calm his brother appeared, whereas the prospect bloody well scared Dalton to death. "How can you be certain?"

"How does anyone know anything? I just know." Dirk shrugged, and it dawned on Dalton that he had said the same thing to Daphne, two nights ago. "Do you doubt it?"

"I am unsure." And the proposition had kept him awake, long after Daphne had drifted into dreamland. "But she captivates me, brother. She holds my attention, unreservedly, and I find the sensation rather discomposing."

"You will get used to it—welcome it, even. And where is your fetching bride?" Dirk inquired, arching his brow. "If I may ask?"

"Sleeping the sleep of the sated." Envisioning her as he had left her, with her hair splayed across her pillow, and her cheek resting to her hand, after he rode her hard and fast, he growled. "And Rebecca?"

"Same, and she is nightmare-free, I am happy to report." Dirk thrust his chin. "Ah, it is good to be married, is it not?"

"It is more fulfilling than I had imagined, now that I have charted my wife's pristine waters." His horse sidled up to Dirk's stallion, and Dalton stretched his back. "And I am grateful for your advice, because I followed your directives, and you were correct. Whatever I teach her, Daphne accepts it as natural, insofar as I tutor her with unimpaired aplomb, though such lascivious training seems a tad manipulative, given her innocence."

"But I would argue you do nothing wrong, brother." With a ghost of a grin, Dirk averted his gaze. "Regardless of who initiates and imparts the instruction, anything you indulge with your mate, in the privacy of your home, is state-sanctioned. You have a license to prove it."

"True." But he would wager his elder sibling would think otherwise, were he privy to Dalton's escapade, in the wee hours. In a flash, he pictured Daphne on her knees, bent over, with her ample derriere in the air, and hugging the cushioned footstool in his sitting room, as he knelt behind her and sailed her back channel for the first time. Anticipating a hailstorm of protestations, he had braced for her reaction as he explained the controversial act, which polite society had deemed anything but polite, yet his provincial bride had assumed the position, sans complaint or question. Her surrender, without hesitation and unutterably arresting, had moved him more than he was willing to admit. With tenderness of which he had not thought himself capable, he had taken her bottom. "And she trusts me, because she loves me."

In that fraction of a second, he shuddered, as the full import of that statement, haphazardly spoken, hit him in a tidal wave of emotion mixed with conviction, and he gasped for breath. It had not occurred to him what she meant, when she declared herself, as he took her on face value. But the undeniable fact was he owned his wife's heart, and he vowed, then and there, to gift his, in kind.

"Good morning, gentleman." Admiral Douglas drew nigh and tipped his hat. To Dalton, the admiral said, "I was on my way to see you, after receiving your summons. My boy, I am more sorry than I can say for your troubles, and I am at your service."

"Perhaps we should repair to my study." Dirk checked his pocket watch. "Sir Ross should arrive on the hour."

"Then let us make haste." Dalton heeled the flanks of

his mount and steered for Randolph House, with Dirk and the admiral in his wake.

"Sir Ross Logan awaits you, in the drawing room, your lordship." Hughes hurried to collect the outerwear.

"Thank you, Hughes." Dirk dusted off his lapels and adjusted his cravat. "Will you send for her ladyship and Mrs. Randolph to join us?"

"Right away, your lordship." Hughes bowed.

"You intend to involve Rebecca in our predicament?" Dalton asked.

"Do you honestly think we can keep it from her?" Venting a snicker of pure skepticism, Dirk rolled his eyes. "You have enough trouble on your hands without angering my viscountess, and despite her departure from espionage, she remains sharp as a tack, and I would make use of her instincts, which is a damn sight smarter than offending her."

"I beg your pardon, Sir Dalton." Holding a now familiar envelope, Hughes frowned. The staff had been apprised of the threats to Daphne and, as such, was on full alert. "Your man delivered this message while you were in the park. It was found on your doorstep, early this morning."

"Bloody everlasting hell." The addressee and accompanying inscription seemed to mock him, and he snatched the offending letter. "I swear when I discover who is behind this vile business, I will rip the bastard's throat out with my teeth."

"Let us confer with the expert, brother." Dirk chucked Dalton's shoulder. "And we shall remand the villain to the proper authorities, that your lady might enjoy a measure of justice."

"I would dispense my own justice." Rage, compelling and pure, simmered beneath his gentleman's attire, and he ached to hurt to unknown scoundrel. But when Daphne descended the stairs, gowned in grey silk, with her saffron locks piled in loose curls atop her head, as an angel on high, the emotions wreaking havoc within him pooled in his chest. And an altogether different sensation burned bright as the sun, bathing him in soothing but nonetheless riveting sentiment.

It was at that precise moment that he realized he had spoken the truth to his wife. He loved her. He did not know how he knew it, but no one could convince him otherwise. And at the first opportunity, he would make sure she knew it, too.

GATHERED IN THE DRAWING ROOM, with Admiral Douglas, Sir Ross Logan, Dirk, Rebecca, and Dalton, Daphne sat beside her husband on the sofa, as the mysterious head of the Counterintelligence Corps, and Elaine's secret beau, opened the latest peculiar letter. After unfolding the parchment, which matched the others in her puzzling collection, he scanned the contents, and she held her breath.

"Well, at least now we know what the villain wants, in exchange for not revealing the truth behind your father's death." Sir Ross passed the note to Dalton. "Who is aware of the actual circumstances surrounding Governor Harcourt's demise?"

"At first, only myself, my brothers Robert and Richard, Hicks, and Mrs. Jones." Daphne searched her memory. "Later, I confessed the sum of the facts to my husband and Dirk." She peered at the note and gasped in horror. "Five thousand pounds? Where am I to get such funds?"

"Worry not, my angel." Dalton draped an arm about her

shoulders and pulled her close. "It is but a drop in a very large bucket, but it will not come to that, as I will protect you."

"What of my brothers?" At the mere thought of someone hurting her younger siblings, her gut clenched. "And the only other persons involved are my husband's family. Surely, you don't suspect them?"

"I suspect no one and everyone, Mrs. Randolph." Rubbing his chin, Sir Ross averted his stare, and something in his manner troubled her. "But I think it safe to rule out the relations, which leaves—"

"*No.*" With clenched fists, she leaped to her feet, and Dalton followed suit and enfolded her in his embrace.

"Daphne, we must leave no stone unturned," Dalton stated with grim finality.

"And people behave altogether strangely, when money is involved." With a sigh, Sir Ross frowned. "How long have you known Hicks and Mrs. Jones?"

"All my life." Given the prospects, something inside her shattered, and tears welled. But her every instinct told her the venerable spy was wrong. "And I refuse to believe either of them would betray me. They could have left us, after my father died, as I could not pay their salaries, but they stayed, even though food was scarce. Does that sound like the blackguard you describe?"

"Darling, I know it hurts." Dalton kissed her forehead and dried her cheeks with his handkerchief. "But we have no one else, and we must consider all avenues."

"But what of Lord Sheldon or Lady Moreton?" She sniffed and rested against his chest. "Why can it not be one of them, as they certainly do not wish me well? Why must you accuse Hicks and Mrs. Jones, who are as family to me?"

"Because Sheldon and Almira have no direct knowledge

of your situation on Portsea." As she wept, he squeezed her, and she gleaned strength from her true knight. "How would they have discovered the facts?"

"It must be someone with intimate information regarding your private affairs," Sir Ross implied, as though imparting a critique of the weather. "Thus far, my investigation has revealed no concrete evidence pointing to any one person. Indeed, the franking suggests the perpetrator has gone to great lengths to confuse us, as each dispatch was posted using a different packet service, so it is impossible to trace the sender to any single location."

"What I find interesting is the absence of conveyance details." Admiral Douglas scanned the note. "How does our villain expect to gain his very unjust reward, when he designates no courier?"

"That *is* interesting." Hugging her round belly, Rebecca cast an expression of sympathy. "It is as if the rogue expects you to go to him, as if such commands are unnecessary."

"Which suggests the criminal anticipates Daphne's return to Courtenay Hall, wherein he shall strike." Sir Ross flipped through the bundled communiqués and grimaced. "And that may be his mistake, as the smaller population on the island could work to our advantage."

"Were you planning to return to Portsea?" Admiral Douglas asked.

"No, at least, not yet." Dalton met her gaze. "I had thought to take Daphne home, before I sail on my next mission, presuming there is a next mission, given the peace in the wake of Napoleon's exile. Otherwise, we had contemplated a journey, once the renovations are complete."

"How soon might that be?" At that instant, Sir Ross pulled a small square of paper and a pencil from his coat pocket and jotted a list.

"I had an update from Mr. Benson, and the remodel should be finished within a fortnight," Dalton replied, and she wondered if that timeline included her additional changes to the master suite. "What do you suggest, Sir Ross?"

"That you take your wife to her childhood home for an impromptu holiday." Then Sir Ross pinned Dalton with an unflinching glare. "And you take your new valet with you."

"His new valet?" Daphne blinked.

"Of course." Rebecca snapped her fingers. "What a stroke of brilliance, though I have a hard time envisioning you acting as Dalton's manservant. How are you with babies?"

"Very funny." The handsome man grinned, revealing a single dimple, and Daphne understood his appeal, which Elaine had lauded. "Given my relative obscurity in the back-water, we should have none the wiser, when we spring our trap."

For the next half hour, the group strategized and plotted, until the course was set. And each had their part to play, save the admiral, who declared his intent to depart for Kent with Lady Amanda, given her delicate condition. But when Rebecca proclaimed a desire to assist Dalton and Daphne, Dirk protested.

"Rebecca, you are with child. If you think I will risk one hair on your lovely head, you are seriously mistaken." The viscount folded his arms. "I admire your courage and willingness to help, but I put my foot down."

"Excellent." Rebecca stood. "I will be too happy to tell you just where to put your foot."

"Er, perhaps we should leave you alone?" Sir Ross scratched his temple.

"That is not necessary, as we journey to Courtenay Hall." Rebecca stomped the floor.

"No, we do not." Dirk rested hands on hips. "They do not require our assistance, and we would only get in the way."

"We could extend much needed support, and there is safety in numbers." The viscountess lowered her chin. "And we would provide two additional voices to sound the alarm. How can you turn your back on your own brother, when the life of his wife hangs in the balance? Did Dalton not ride to my rescue, at your side, when Varringdale kidnapped me?"

"You will not let this go, will you?" Dirk exhaled in obvious frustration.

"When hell freezes." The former spy met Dirk toe-to-toe and never flinched.

"Oh, I say." Sir Ross slapped his thighs and chuckled. "But that is your bride, Wainsbrough."

"And I blame you for her willful nature." Dirk frowned, until Rebecca kissed his cheek, at which time he drew her near. "If we do this, you must abide my dictates, without fail. And as such, I forbid you to leave the estate without me. You must remain at my side, at all times, unless I am called upon to pursue the blackmailer, in which case you will stay inside Courtenay Hall. And if you violate any one of my commands, I will heat your posterior, regardless of your condition, and you will not sit comfortably for a fortnight. Do I make myself clear?"

"I love it when you talk tough." With a flirty titter, Rebecca gave him a gentle nudge, and Dirk blushed.

Daphne sighed in relief, as she hated causing marital discord, and she feared the horrible affair had claimed more victims.

So the meeting adjourned, and she pondered the future of which she had dreamed. What if their scheme failed? What if Dalton was injured, or worse, in their attempt to uncover the scoundrel?

In the foyer, Dalton caught her by the wrist. "May I speak with you, in private, sweetheart?"

"Of course." As she admired her beautiful husband, Daphne shivered with dread of the unknown, and she desperately yearned for the comfort of his body. "May we withdraw to our chamber, as I would not share you with anyone, just now."

"As you wish." With a dramatic bow, Dalton winked and offered his escort, which she accepted.

The epitome of grace and elegance, they climbed the stairs and veered right at the landing. A long hall led to the west wing of the huge mansion. When they passed through the double-door entrance to their sitting room, she turned on a heel and flung herself at her man.

Twining her fingers in his thick brown hair, she suckled his bottom lip and then launched a full-scale assault on his mouth. When Dalton broke her hastily initiated kiss, she sobbed.

"Did I do something wrong?" Lost in a vortex of panic, as she pondered their impending date with fate, she could not bear his rejection.

"No, angel." To her surprise, he walked her to the *chaise*, sat, and then pulled her into his lap. "While I savor your impulse, and am humbled by your desire, there is something I must tell you, and I would do so before we retire to our marital bed, as I may not let you out of it until tomorrow."

"Oh?" In light of his sober countenance, Daphne

conjured the worst conclusions imaginable. "Have you no confidence in Sir Ross's plan? Do you doubt our success?"

"On the contrary, I have faith in Sir Ross, and fate favors the lucky." He took her hand in his and brought it to his lips. "But I will waste not a single second more and allow you to labor under a misapprehension. My darling, I love you."

His declaration, stark in its simplicity, rang clear with conviction, and her spirits soared. "Will you say that again?"

Dalton favored her with his boyish smile, which melted her heart. "I love you, Daphne."

"I know you do." Resting her forehead to his, she rubbed her nose to his. "I needed you to know, as I have always believed in you."

"Am I so worthy?" He squeezed her so tight she could hardly breathe. "Do you honestly think I deserve you?"

"I would argue the more appropriate question is whether or not I deserve you, and I adore it when you blush." She poked him in the ribs.

"I do not blush." And then he compounded his appeal with an endearing pout.

With that, she wiggled from his lap and stood. "Shall we continue this discussion in bed, as I want to be near you."

"Angel, I am most definitely at your service." Dalton shrugged from his coat, when a knock at the door diverted him, to her chagrin. "Just a minute, sweetheart. Let me take care of this, while you get rid of your clothes."

He patted her bottom, and she kissed him hard and fast, before sprinting into their inner quarters. Kicking off her slippers, she reached around, grabbed her laces, and tugged them loose. After a few wicked twists and turns, she yanked her dress over her head. Then she bent, unhooked her garters, and removed her hose. At last, she stripped from her chemise and turned to discover her husband, holding a bouquet of roses presented in a crystal vase and watching her with unveiled intent.

"That was some performance, Mrs. Randolph." Basking in the heat of his admiration, she rotated for his delectation.

"What beautiful flowers." And a new framing alignment struck her.

"They are but ordinary blooms, in comparison to my wife, and I ordered them this morning, to please you." He removed a single long-stem bud, put the arrangement on the dresser, and then approached. "I know you well enough to surmise you are already planning to press the crimson blossoms, and my gift is yours to do with as you will, but this is mine." With the soft petals, he teased her nipples, brushed her belly, and caressed her shoulder. Strolling in a circle about her, he visited each peak and valley of her body with the rose, until he wrapped his arm about her waist, from behind, and she leaned against him. "I would ask you to preserve this bud, in one of your special creations, which I would carry with me, whenever we are apart, to commem-orate the day I made my declaration."

"Oh, Dalton." Accustomed to his moods, she knew the beast was hungry and just how to feed him, so she framed his face. "You are so sweet. How anyone could know you and not love you is unfathomable to me."

"I do not give a damn what anyone else thinks. All that matters is you." He set the rose on the bedside table and turned, just as she launched herself at him. An awkward dance ensued, as he fought to touch her, and she struggled to rip off his clothes. Naked and aroused, they sank into the downy mattress.

Their limbs twined, as he gave her his weight. He took her lips and then claimed her mouth. Just when Daphne thought she could withstand no more, and she would explode from need, he deepened the kiss, and the bond spiraled to the heady heights of passion. And then he joined their bodies in a single forceful thrust.

As he moved over her, on her, and within her, Dalton whispered praise and encouragement. He told her what she had done to him, how she had affected him, and, most importantly, how he could not live without her. And she clung to him, coveting the vibrant beat of his heart, which fed a compulsive urgency impossible to deny, and she knew he felt it, too.

Minutes stretched into hours, as they savored the touch of skin to warm skin, of hands exploring, of hips coming together to form an intimate connection, in perfect alignment, until time suspended. The world stood still, as they lingered on the precipice of heaven on earth, and then they plunged, headlong, into paradise.

IN THE WEEKS leading up to the journey to Portsea Island, Dalton spent his days at Randolph House, forgoing his weekly pugilistic exercise and evening brandy at White's in favor of extended maneuvers, intended to broaden his bride's horizons, in his bed. As the Season ended, and the *ton* retired to their country estates for the summer, the streets of London, and Mayfair, in particular, were noticeably less crowded. But he remained on heightened alert for any sign of trouble, especially after another threatening letter, with the same demands, arrived for Daphne.

After hiring additional footmen to guard her, he forbade her from leaving the residence, which his provincial wife accepted without complaint. Given her good humor, he purchased a new lute and invited those members of his family still residing in the city for an impromptu musicale, with Daphne as the star, and how she shined. Later that same night, she gave a private performance, sitting at the end of their bed, wearing nothing but a smile, just for him.

So he had found himself endeavoring to identify all manner of delights to oblige his bride. But Daphne was not like most women. Whereas society ladies preferred expensive jewels, furs, and clothes, his wife's tastes leaned toward the utilitarian, as evidenced by his latest purchase, which he knew would please her.

"You wished to see me?" Ah, there she stood, gowned in another mourning dress that failed to diminish her inner light, which flared every time she looked him.

"Come in, sweetheart." Sitting at Dirk's desk in the study, Dalton pushed back the chair and slapped his thighs. "Join me, here."

"Should I lock the door?" she inquired, with a winsome blush.

"Are you not the naughty minx?" He whistled in monotone. "But I prefer you that way. And while I love your idea, and we will not abandon it entirely, we are expecting our solicitor, and I would gift you a present before he arrives."

"What have you done now?" Though she attempted to appear vexed, she had not fooled him for a second, as she stepped about his legs and settled in his lap.

He handed her the wrapped item. "Open it."

"Dalton, you make me feel terribly guilty, as I have given you nothing but pressed flowers." She untied the ribbon.

"Trust me, you have given me plenty." He waggled his brows and patted her bottom, and she swatted him, in play. "And I must make some attempt to keep pace."

She peeled open the brown paper and squealed with

unmasked joy. "They are beautiful, and the pages are lined. Oh, thank you."

Any other woman would have raised holy hell, had their husband given them a matched set of leather-bound ledgers, albeit embossed with roses, for documenting household accounts, as a treat, but his sensible bride clutched the books to her chest, as priceless treasures, and kissed him. "Given you have always maintained the governor's holdings, including Courtenay Hall, I had wondered if you might want to manage ours, as my duties for the Brethren often call me to sea."

"You would have me record our expenditures and supervise our stores, beyond the usual duties of chatelaine?" She looked so hopeful, as she rocked her hips, that he could not tease her.

"That and more, if you are amenable." Of course, he doubted her not for a second.

"I should be uncontrollably excited to assist you." She flipped through the crisp parchment and toyed with the bright red silk bookmark. "If you will show me your methods, I would be content to continue your archives as you prefer."

"I would appreciate that, more than you realize." In that moment, she glowed. "And I would sail, safe in the knowledge that you are at the helm of my hearth and heart."

Then you can teach me." She leaned against his chest. "And I shall be your most ardent pupil."

"A fact you have already proven to my everlasting gratitude." That should garner a pleasant reaction. And not to disappoint him, Daphne rested her head to his shoulder and pressed her palm to his chest.

"I do love you, Dalton." She nibbled his neck. "And I am so glad I boarded your ship that night."

For a while, he simply held her. Attuned to her emotions, which had taken a desolate turn, he rubbed her shoulders. "It will be all right, Daphne. I will let no one harm you. And if all else fails, we will pay the extortion." A knock at the door intruded on their brief interlude, and he stood, carrying her with him. As Daphne rounded the desk to occupy one of the Hepplewhite chairs, he said, "Come."

"Mr. Mortimer is just arrived for Sir Dalton." Hughes bowed and ushered in the solicitor.

"Thank you, Hughes." Dalton extended his hand in greeting. "Good to see you, Finlay. May I present my wife, Daphne."

"Sir Dalton, congratulations on your nuptials." The short, squatty-bodied man dipped his chin. "And it is a pleasure to make your acquaintance, Mrs. Randolph."

"Please, permit me to make you free with my name, sir." She glanced at Dalton, then to the legal expert, and then back to Dalton. "Should I leave you?"

"No, as this appointment concerns you." Dalton reclined in the leather high back chair and crossed his legs. "Have you drawn up the papers I commissioned?"

"Indeed, sir." Mr. Mortimer opened his folio and set various documents atop the blotter. "Everything is just as you requested. It took some research, on my part, but I believe legal precedent supports your position. So we need only your signatures to certify the agreements."

"Will you explain to my wife what I have asked of you?" Dalton was about to make a major move on his part, and he wanted Daphne to know exactly what he expected for their future.

"Mrs. Randolph, these records extend to you the right to make financial decisions on your husband's behalf, in his absence." The solicitor marked the page. "This item represents your husband's last will and testament, providing for you a generous per annum, along with principal occupancy of Courtenay Hall, as well as any future London residences procured during the tenure of your marriage, until your death. As you well know, English law forbids women from owning property, so the deed to your family's estate shall remain in trust, until such time as any male children reach full maturation and can thus be endowed, given your eldest brother has expressed no interest in the ancestral home. Should the union produce no male children, then the real estate would be supervised by a qualified surviving member of Sir Dalton's family."

"You would do that for me?" Daphne asked, in a small voice.

Dalton picked up the pen, dipped it in the inkwell, and signed his name. "It is done, my angel."

"Well then, my business is concluded." Mr. Mortimer resituated the parchment in his folio. "These copies are for your records, sir. I shall file everything with the proper authorities, in the morning. If I can be of further assistance, please, do not hesitate to call on me."

"Thank you, Finlay." Again, they exchanged the customary male handshake, and Dalton escorted the solicitor to the door. He closed the oak panel and turned—right into Daphne's kiss.

"You fear the worst, when we journey to Portsea." She clung to him, and he cursed himself for frightening her. "Else why would you apply for a will?"

"My dear, your assumptions are incorrect." When she turned the key in the lock, she caught the attention of every inch of him, and a few lethal ones in particular. "In light of our wedding, I had to update my will to include provisions for your care, but I have no plans to die anytime soon.

However, I am a military man, subject to the whims of His Majesty. I can be called upon, without notice, and I would not leave you unprotected, so the will is for my peace of mind."

"And the financial arrangement?" She appeared skeptical, as she bit her lip. "What purpose does that serve?"

"That, my sharp bride, is a vote of confidence, and I thought the added responsibilities would please you." And he knew well her game, so he had pleased her. "Do you wish me to rescind the powers I have bestowed upon you? I suppose you could use the ledgers as a personal journal, if you like."

"Oh, no." She gasped, when he bent and swept her into his arms. "I want to help you, if you will have me."

"Then that settles it." He sat her on the blotter, nipped her cute little nose, flicked up her skirts, unfastened his breeches, and situated himself between her thighs. "Now, if you have no more questions, I should very much like to make love to you on my stodgy brother's desk."

Those were the last coherent words uttered for the next hour.

CHAPTER SEVENTEEN

*T*he journey to Portsea Island, the site of her ancestral home, had been interesting, to say the least, for Daphne. When her husband had insisted they take their own coach, despite the fact that the viscount's elegant equipage would have seated the entire party in lush comfort, she had been confused. Until they departed the city, proper, on the first leg of the two-day trip, and he lowered the shades and enacted another titillating tutelage for the next several miles. She would never look at their rig the same again.

"Well that was inspiring, my angel." At her side, Dalton restored his clothing and hooked his breeches.

"You are insatiable." And she would never complain, as she smoothed her skirts and re-secured her bodice.

"I am in love." With his arm about her shoulders, he kissed her hard and fast. "And you knew that when you married me."

"What—that you were in love or that you were insatiable?" She shrieked, when he tickled her. "Stop, as I can just imagine what our driver thinks we are doing in here."

"Both." He pulled her into his lap, cradled her head to his shoulder, and chuckled. "And I would wager he knows exactly what we are doing in here, as well he should, given we are newlyweds."

With a sigh, she relaxed in his embrace, as the passing Portsea landscape declared they neared the grand estate, and he hugged her tight. The tenor of his passion had intensified, as they counted down their date with destiny, and his underlying urgency had, in turn, fed her desire, which had spiraled beyond her ability to control it. Thus she sought comfort in his body at every opportunity, and, chivalrous knight that he was, he indulged her.

And sometime during the night, after a rigorous round of coitus, whereupon they had rattled the walls of their tiny room at a coach inn, it had dawned on Daphne that the unknown villain could destroy her, if he directed his attentions to her husband. Was that not what felled Rebecca?

The traitor struck Dirk to lure the spy into the open, whereupon she had been kidnapped. So far, Dalton's plans and added protections revolved around the presumption that the mysterious scoundrel would attack Daphne.

"We are almost home, sweetheart." As they passed through the main gate, he caressed her cheek. "Are you excited to see the renovations, despite the unfortunate circumstance of our visit?"

"Yes, and I have a surprise for you." She recalled her last minute changes to the plans, which converted the master suites into a single large sitting room and bedchamber combination. "And I hope you will be pleased."

"My dear, I like whatever you like." He kissed her crown of curls and sighed. "You will remain close to me. You are to abstain from your charitable visits and entertain no callers. And you will forgo your morning walks and confine your movements to the estate, within sight, at all times. If you receive any correspondence from the villain, you are to bring it to me before you open it, whereupon we shall meet with Dirk and Sir Ross. Promise you will obey my edicts, until we apprehend the criminal, darling."

"You have my solemn vow I will do as you command." Easing her arms about his waist, she shivered, though it was quite warm on that July afternoon. "But we will have to arrange a community party, to set things right, once our nasty business is done, else our neighbors will think me a snob."

"Angel, you may hold soirees to your heart's content, once we catch the blackguard." The coach navigated the drive and halted before the entrance, and Dalton held her in check.

Prior to her marriage, she never would have considered allowing anyone to see her in such a compromising position. But they were in Portsea, the charming island town she adored, and London society, and its ridiculous web of rules, meant nothing in the backwater, so she kept her place. When the footman opened the door, Dalton scooted from the squabs and handed her down.

Standing at attention, with the household staff arranged in a line, Hicks smiled. "Welcome home, Miss—er, Mrs. Randolph."

"Old habits are hard to break, my friend." And she still refused to believe that Hicks or Mrs. Jones had anything to do with the reprehensible incidents. "And how are you?"

"Quite well, ma'am." The butler lifted his chin. "And Mrs. Jones and I have brought the personnel to almost full capacity, and we are grateful for their assistance."

"We hope our hires meet with your approval, Mrs. Randolph." Mrs. Jones appeared tentative, in the face of such esteemed guests, so Daphne made the effort to hug the housekeeper, who smelled of her unique recipe for home-made soap. "Oh, it is good to have you home, ma'am."

"We should have tea, tomorrow, and catch up, as it has been too long." Before Dalton discovered their reworked room, she caught him by the wrist. "Right now, I would have a bath and wash away the road dust. If you could settle the viscount and viscountess, I would appreciate it. And I will show my husband to his accommodation."

"Of course, Mrs. Randolph." Hicks clicked his heels and hurried to direct the footmen.

"My lovely wife, what are you about?" Dalton narrowed his stare. "Did you overspend your budget?"

"I told you there were unanticipated cost overruns, and you indicated it was not a problem." She dragged him into the foyer, up the stairs, and down the hall. "And it is too late to complain now."

"Indeed it is, and my brother warned me about such extravagances, when it comes to wives and wallets." He groaned. "Wait a minute, what happened to the door to my apartment?"

"It has moved." She gave him a swift yank. "Permit me to give you a grand tour of your new and improved space." With heightened anticipation, and a little bit of nervous anxiety, Daphne pushed open the double oak panels and ushered her knight into their new sanctuary. "What do you think?"

"Good God, it is massive." He rotated slowly, taking in the refined elegance of his signature shade trimmed in mahogany. "I could chase you for hours and never catch you."

Velvet drapes framed the floor to ceiling windows of the sitting room, and matching damask overstuffed chairs and a sofa blended with the crème colored *chaise*. Sapphire wall coverings, in the flock-tradition, featured a taupe floral ogee motif, and she had limited the accessories to the bare necessities interspersed with nautical antiques, including some resplendent spyglasses and her framed creations, which she had composed specifically for their private abode.

"You would never have to catch me, my darling husband." She hugged him from behind. "Because I am yours for the taking."

"And I do so love that about you." He covered her hands with his. "So show me your lair of licentious iniquity."

"*Our* lair, my naughty knight." In the inner sanctum, she paused before the footboard of the massive four-poster. When Dalton strolled to the bedside table that would be his, given their usual preferences, drew from his coat pocket the small oval frame in which she had pressed his rosebud, and situated the keepsake in pride of place, she inhaled a shaky breath. "Are you pleased?"

"How could I not be, when you planned it." In that instant, she shed the last concerns regarding the hastily sketched remodel. "And constructing dressers in the expanded closets was a stroke of brilliance."

"But how could—you knew." And just like that, her sails deflated. "Who told you?"

"Sorry, angel." He gifted her the lopsided grin that never failed to melt her insides. "Mr. Benson let it slip, when I approved the closing disbursements. Your alterations were included in the final sketches, and Mr. Dumas was quite put out, given he had kept your confidence to the very end, and I did not want to spoil it for you." Dalton flicked his fingers, and she ran to him. "But it gave me hope, such as I had dared not covet, as we had yet to consummate our vows, so I said nothing."

"Well I know you have not seen everything, as I procured a few items once we returned to London." She led him to the wash area, tucked behind a half-wall. "Does it meet your requirements, sir?"

"Great heavens, that tub looks as if it could seat four people." He patted her bottom, as had become his habit, of late.

"Only two, actually." Resting her palm to his chest, she found solace in the steady beat of his heart. "Will you join me for a bath?"

"There is nothing I would prefer more." After claiming another kiss, which was far too brief for her, he spanked her derriere and said, "But first I should confer with Sir Ross and Dirk, to make sure there are no loose ends. Then I shall return and ravish you, so prepare to be conquered."

"You prepare, sir." Daphne stuck her tongue in her cheek and batted her lashes. "As I just might vanquish you."

"Angel, I look forward to it." With a wink, he swaggered from their apartments.

After the footmen delivered the trunks, Daphne supervised the unpacking. The last items had just been stored, when the maids began filling the huge tub. In search of something sheer to inspire her husband, not that he required stimulus, she opted to await his presence in his primary choice.

But the ugliness of blackmail intruded on her musings, and she strolled to the windows to admire the familiar landscape, which had always soothed her soul. She wasn't sure if weariness from the journey or the monumental task looming at the fore had ravaged her nerves, but she soon succumbed to a fit of tears.

Giving herself to the misery, she sobbed without restraint, in the privacy of her room, until the tension eating at her gut abated. So much had happened, so much had changed in so little time, and now some unforeseen rogue threatened everything.

"Daphne, are you in there?" Through the haze of despair, a cherished voice called to her.

With arms splayed wide in welcome, she charged into the sitting room and flung herself at her youngest brother. "*Richard.*"

"How I missed you, Daph." The gadling hugged her tight. "And why are you crying?"

"Oh, it is stress from our predicament." She rued involving her sibling in the horrid affair, but it could not be avoided. "But I am better, now that you are here. And how are you?"

"Fine, I suppose." Shuffling his feet, he shrugged. "It has been lonely here, without you and Robert. But I had a letter from him, and he sounds content, in service to Beresford. Yet he longs for Portsea and our simpler days."

"Me, too," she responded, with a sigh.

"Don't worry, Daph." Richard kissed her cheek. "Everything will be all right, as I will protect you."

"My, but you have grown in the months since I first departed Courtenay Hall." In play, she chucked his chin. "And I am so proud of you. Have you given any thought to Dalton's offer to finance a formal education? You always dreamed of attending university, and it would be a wonderful opportunity for you."

"Do you wish to be rid of me?" At his frown, she retreated a step. "Am I to be packed off, like Robert?"

"Of course, not." Her blood ran cold at the thought. "How could you suggest such a thing? And Robert begged for a commission, which you well know."

"You are right." Richard ambled toward the door. With

his hand on the knob, he peered over his shoulder. "I will speak with Sir Dalton about his proposal."

"We only want you to be happy." How she adored her sensitive brother, as he always bore the weight of the world on his coat sleeves.

Alone, Daphne hugged herself, returned to the bedchamber, and shut the doors behind her. Wafts of steam rose from the surface of the bath, and she kicked off her slippers. Wrenching left and then right, she untied her laces and stripped her gown and chemise. Then she removed her garters and hose. Naked, she crawled atop the huge four-poster and stretched across the luxurious counterpane of sapphire satin. Closing her eyes, she grinned, sank into the mattress, and wondered just what salacious tactic her husband would employ to rouse her, upon his return.

THREE DAYS LATER, Daphne strolled into her chamber to resituate her coiffure, because her one true knight destroyed her style during a rollicking lovemaking session in the hayloft of the old barn. Midway through the erotic escapade, Dirk and Sir Ross had entered the stables, to ensure their horses remained at the ready. As a result of the unexpected interlopers, Dalton and Daphne had achieved glorious completion only after countless minutes in heated, panting, groping, *intensely* silent endeavors.

It was with such flirty musings dancing in her brain that she discovered a now familiar missive propped against the mirror of her vanity, with her name inscribed on the envelope, and she cried out in horror. Without hesitation, she ran to the bellpull and gave it a yank. Pacing, she peered left and then right, as she feared the villain might jump from the shadows or a hiding place. In seconds, she checked the wash area, behind the half-wall, and their respective closets, and discovered them empty.

"How may I help you, Mrs. Randolph?" Daisy, the new lady's maid curtseyed.

"Tell Hicks I need to speak with my husband and Viscount Wainsbrough, here, in my quarters, at once."

"Yes, ma'am."

Trembling, she scanned the immediate vicinity and then ran into the sitting room. The polished apartment, decorated with love and hope for a charmed future, had become a refuge, wherein Daphne and Dalton often lingered, sans clothing, and discussed their shared dreams. Just then, Dalton charged through the double-door entry, with Dirk, Sir Ross, and Rebecca in tow.

"Daphne, what is it?" With a worried expression, her husband walked straight to her. "What happened?"

"I have had another note from the blackmailer." She pointed. "It sits atop my vanity."

"Bloody everlasting hell. The bastard was in our home?" Dalton set her aside and stormed into the inner chamber. "Sir Ross, will you do the honors?"

"Of course." The head of the Counterintelligence Corps produced a leather pouch from his coat pocket, from which he retrieved tweezers and picked up the correspondence. With great care, he opened the envelope and removed the folded parchment. "Damn, he is good. We have but two hours to plan our delivery, and he claims Daphne knows the locale."

"What does it say?" Dirk inquired.

"I am puzzled." Dalton scratched his chin. "He has reduced his demands by half, asking for only twenty-five-hundred pounds. What do you suppose is his purpose?"

"He may mistakenly believe it will be easier to spend the smaller amount, without rousing suspicion." Sir Ross snickered. "But that is his first blunder, as the notes are marked."

"It commands us to place the amount in a small bundle, near a large oak by a stone wall, along the road to Eastney." Dalton met her gaze. "It is the tree beneath which we took our ease, after concluding your charitable visits, that day in March."

"The very one." And so the criminal tarnished another cherished memory, with his nefarious schemes.

"Then Daphne and I will remain here, with Mrs. Jones and Richard." Rebecca framed Dirk's face. "Please, be careful, as I love you, and you are quite irreplaceable."

Likewise, Daphne hugged her husband. "You presume Hicks is involved, and I do not agree, but I would ask you to use caution, as I love you, too. And I need you."

"It will be all right, my angel." Dalton held her, as if for the last time, and her fear spiraled to vaunted heights. "One way or another, this business will end tonight. But keep watch for Hicks, as he must depart to collect his boon, unless he works in concert with another."

After an intense strategy session, Dalton, Dirk, and Sir Ross set out to catch the blackmailer, while Daphne, Rebecca, and Mrs. Jones gathered in the drawing room to await the outcome.

"Everything will work out, fine, Daphne." Despite her reassurance, Rebecca paced before the hearth. "Dalton has Dirk and Sir Ross, and I would wager the scoundrel has never faced such an impressive front."

"Well I am nervous, nonetheless, and nothing soothes my spirit like balancing the stillroom accounts." Daphne jumped to her feet. "If it will not offend you, I will retrieve my ledger from the study and complete the task in your company, else I may lose my mind and run amok."

Rolling her shoulders, she stepped into the hall and searched for Hicks, but her friend was not present, yet she assumed it a coincidence, as she did not doubt his loyalty. In the foyer, an audial summons at the main entrance brought her alert, as the men had departed almost fifteen minutes ago. Holding her breath against the chill of unease seeping to her marrow, Daphne opened the front door and peered outside. A gust of wind cooled by the sea, as the evening sun loomed on the horizon, buffeted her cheeks, and she was surprised to find no one. Glancing down the drive, she wondered if she had imagined the sharp rap of the knocker—until she spied another telltale envelope on the threshold.

In a flash, she bent, snatched the missive, shut the heavy oak panel, and secured the latch. Then she tore into the correspondence, read the message, and sobbed.

Mrs. Randolph,

If you have received this note in the company of your allies, do not permit them to read it. Should you value your brother's life, tell no one of the contents herein. I have Richard in my possession. Bring 2,500 pounds to the old barn on the back of your estate. You have ten minutes from the time this warning was remitted, else I will kill young Richard.

A wave of nausea swept over her, as she pondered her gentle sibling in the custody of a ruthless villain. Her initial instinct was to obey the evildoer's demands, but then she recalled Rebecca's story. Once her captor had revealed his identity, he had to kill her to conceal his crimes. Daphne's mind raced, and she made her decision, just as Hicks appeared.

"Mrs. Randolph, I thought I heard—"

"You did." Quick as a wink, she grabbed the butler by the wrist. "Accompany me to the drawing room, as we have no time to spare, and my brother's life hangs in the balance."

AS HE CHARGED the lane he recalled so well, with the tall grass swaying in the wind on either side of the verge, Dalton replayed every detail of the rushed plot. He veered left, then right, and then left, again, until they neared the water's edge, when they steered inland. Driven by determination to protect his wife, he pushed the stallion harder and faster, until the large oak came into view.

"Hold hard, men." Sir Ross drew rein on the hilltop overlooking the meadow. "We can gain an excellent survey of the terrain from this vantage, and we are early, so we should take the opportunity to reconnoiter. Tomorrow, the bastard will dance at Beilby's ball for his treachery."

"What would you inspect, given the lay?" Dirk steered his mount to a small overlook. "The countryside is flat, and there are no homes or out buildings."

"You are correct." Using his spyglass, Dalton scrutinized every shrub and fence line for any sign of a suitable hide-away. "Given we have the high ground, the blackmailer has no advantage." And then a chill of dread settled in his chest, and he tried but failed to brush off the dark sense of fore-boding. "Something is wrong."

"Listen." With his head inclined, Sir Ross pulled a pistol from his waistband. "Someone comes through the field at our flank."

Dalton turned his horse, just as Hicks spurred a bay to jump a low-lying stone wall. "Well, well, look who is here."

When the butler glimpsed them, he waved frantically, with an envelope clutched in his fist. "Sir Dalton, you must come home, quickly. Mrs. Randolph received another letter, and it brings ill tidings."

After unfolding the well-known stationary, Dalton swallowed hard. With every sentence he read, he plummeted into a new and more tormenting form of hell, as he realized he had been duped. But what struck him, as a wicked punch to the gut, was Daphne's plea, in her graceful script, which he recognized from her ledger entries, written at the bottom of the parchment.

Ride hard, my love. I need you.

"Sir, we must go—now." Hicks reined his horse. "We can take a trail through the pastureland, as it is much shorter. Please, I was born and raised on Portsea, I know it like the back of my hand, and we have not a minute to lose."

In obeisance of his wife's request, Dalton spurred the flanks of his stallion and raced along the path, with Hicks navigating the narrow track. As they swerved to evade the haphazard loose stock, they kicked up a dust storm in their wake. His pulse pounded in his ears, in rhythm with the galloping hoofbeats, and a tidal wave of apprehension swamped him. Marking the passage of time with the setting sun, he prayed he was not too late.

When they neared a dense thicket, Dalton cursed, as the brush impeded their advance. Then the trees thinned, and the butler extended his arm and slowed to a canter. It was then Dalton realized the barn sat in a clearing, on the other side of the grove.

"We should dismount now, as I would not clue the villain to our presence." Sir Ross passed the reins to Hicks. "Stay here."

Together, Dalton, Dirk, and Sir Ross moved toward the edge of the brake. At the corner of the dilapidated structure, a lone figure crouched behind the remains of the old ruined phaeton.

"By all that is holy, I swear I am going to heat her posterior." Dirk bared his teeth and then tiptoed to Rebecca. In seconds, he covered her mouth and lifted her from her feet. After carrying her into the coppice, he put her down. In a low voice, he said, "My God, woman, but you are with child. What in bloody hell do you think you are about?"

"Shh." The former spy placed a finger to her lips. "You know, very well, I could not let Daphne confront the villain, alone. But fortune smiles upon Dalton, as the scoundrels arrived late, and your bride has kept them talking, just as I advised. There are two assailants, both wearing hoods, and the larger one is armed. I watched them approach from the trail on the far side of the yard. They circled the barn before entering, and there is no sign of Richard."

"Solid intelligence, as always." Sir Ross winked.

"All right. You have done your duty." Dirk yanked the pistol from her grasp. "Now remain with Hicks, and I will deal with you tonight."

"The path leads to the beach, and I would assert the villains are locals. So what is the plan?" Dalton pictured his wife, negotiating to save Richard, with her precious neck in the noose, and his spirits plunged to heretofore-inconceivable depths of agony. "As I would save Daphne."

"We must work fast, as a team, and I will brook no unplanned heroics, else we risk serious injury—or worse. Take the money, stroll into the barn with imperturbable sangfroid, and draw their attention from Daphne." Sir Ross glanced at Dirk. "You and I will wait for a clear shot to fell the criminals, as I do not expect reason to suffice, and the blackguards must be stopped."

"I can enter via the side." Dalton sifted through his memory and envisioned a detailed sketch of the interior, which he had gleaned from ribald romps with Daphne in the hayloft. "The large cottage doors have no latch to secure them, and you need only give the panels a good push to gain easy access."

And so they moved, as men on a mission, weaving through the trees, until they ventured into the clearing. As scripted, Dalton perched to the east and loitered, until Sir Ross and Dirk reached their prescribed spots. Inside, Daphne's panicked voice leveled a mortal blow, and he ached for her.

"Mr. Allen, I should have known you would be the source of this despicable offense, as you have shown, in your past dealings with me, that you have no conscience." She scoffed. "And Richard, remove that ridiculous hood, this instant, as I would know you anywhere, and I would have an explanation for your involvement in this hideous plot."

"I was just trying to get enough money to free you from Sir Dalton," Richard stated, and Dalton wanted to throttle the lad. "I warned you not to marry him. He made you sad, and I saw you crying."

"I wept because this abhorrent affair has hung as a black cloud over the man I love." Peering between the worn boards, Dalton spied his wife, as she hugged a bundle he surmised contained the requested money. To the casual observer, she appeared none the worse for wear. But to him, the lines of strain about the corners of her eyes and mouth, and the rigidity of her stature, along with her white knuckles, belied her well-composed serenity. "In essence, *you* hurt me, not my husband."

"Well, I do not care a whit for you or your fancy man. I want my money." Mr. Allen doffed his disguise. "And I would have you know your brother joined my band of thieves, in your absence, so you are no one, governor's daughter. Your father was a gambler and a wencher, and young Richard is a swindler." Then the bastard pointed a pistol in Daphne's direction. "And you will get what's coming to you."

"Hold hard." Dalton leaped into action and launched into the barn. With palms splayed, and the rucksack thrown over his shoulder, he said, "I come in peace, and I am unarmed. Let my wife and her brother go free, and you may take the entire ransom. We have no quarrel with you."

"I will take what I want, along with the money." The blackguard sneered with unequivocal intent. "Perhaps I will keep the lady, too, for my enjoyment. But I will not leave you or this sniveling runt to report me to the constable and raise the alarm."

"But that was not our agreement." With a watery gaze, Richard's mouth fell agape. "You said you would help me save my sister. You said I could have half to support my family, if I cooperated. And Daphne was not to be harmed."

With an expression of urgency, Dalton cast Daphne a side-glance, and she inched closer.

"And in your greed, you believed me, bantling." In a display of unchecked brutality, Mr. Allen struck Richard with the butt of the weapon, and Daphne availed herself of the opportunity to shift ever nearer. But Mr. Allen spotted her new position and took aim in her direction. "As you were, or I will kill you, now."

As his mind raced for a solution, Dalton said, "Allen, let us make a deal that suits us both—"

"Shut up. No one cares about your connections, *Londoner*." When the evildoer caught Dalton in his sights, Richard shoved hard on the bastard, Daphne screamed and flung herself at Dalton, and gunfire rent the air.

Time suspended for a handful of minutes, as Allen collapsed, with two large wounds that had ripped open his chest. Dirk and Sir Ross charged the fray, and Richard stood upright, dusting himself off. As he hugged his wife, Dalton realized he was uninjured, and he uttered a silent prayer of thanks—until he lifted Daphne's chin, as she was uncharacteristically quiet, to claim a quick kiss and noted the terror in her blue gaze.

"Angel, what is wrong?" Then her knees buckled, he adjusted his hold, and he discovered the bloodstain spreading at the shoulder of her gown. "*Daphne*. Oh, no. She is wounded."

CHAPTER EIGHTEEN

*W*ith Daphne cradled in his arms, Dalton carried her to Courtenay Hall. Entering via the terrace, he cut through the morning room and met Rebecca and Mrs. Jones in the foyer. And all the while, he kept telling himself she would not die, because he would not allow it, and he was the lucky one. But did it stand to reason that such good fortune automatically extended to his wife?

"Bring towels, hot water, brandy, and extra soap to the master suite." Then he ascended the stairs, two at a time.

"I should fetch a doctor." Sir Ross flung open the double doors. "Is there a reputable medical professional in town?"

"Ride to Portsmouth." He eased his wife to the mattress. "Find the best military physician, and bring him here."

"Permit me to accompany Sir Ross." Hicks glanced at Daphne and wiped a stray tear. "She is as a daughter to me, sir. Given my knowledge of the landscape, I can get us there and back, much faster."

"Thank you." Then Dalton grabbed the butler's wrist. "Please, I beg you, hurry."

"And I will summon the constable and manage the scene in the barn." With a scowl, Dirk leveled his stare on Richard. "Come with me, as we must align our stories to keep your miserable arse out of prison, as I assume your benevolent sister would prefer."

"But what about Daph?" The scamp rushed to the fore. "It is all my fault, but I wanted to make her happy."

Baring his teeth, Dalton lowered his chin. "Come near her again, and I will—"

"You will do nothing, as he is my brother." With her jaw clenched, Daphne shifted and winced. "Who among us is perfect? He is young and foolish, and he made a mistake, my love. And I forgive him, as he is not the one who shot me."

"But Richard conspired with Allen and placed you in peril." Seething with unchecked anger, Dalton wanted blood in recompense for Daphne's injury. "Even now, you have a lead ball in your shoulder, which must be removed." To Richard, Dalton said, "Can you not fathom the magnitude of what your actions wrought upon her?"

"Dalton, I need you." In that single declarative sentence, his bride spiked his guns, but he suspected she knew that. "Let Richard go with Dirk, as I will hurt far worse than I do now, if my brother is tried and incarcerated."

"My angel, what can I do for you?" In that instant, he bent his head and pressed his lips to the sensitive flesh behind her ear. "Be strong for me, sweetheart. As I need you, too."

With towels stacked beneath her shoulder, Daphne rested on her belly, with her face turned aside, and Dalton perched at the edge of the bed and pressed a cloth to her wound, to staunch the bleeding. After about an hour, the seepage abated, and he sighed in relief, when he lifted the rag and discovered no pulsating crimson spray. That was their first break. They would need several more for Daphne to survive.

And so commenced the long wait.

It was just before midnight, when the whinny of horses brought him alert, and he discovered Daphne dozing.

"Rebecca, would you see if it is Hicks?" Dalton asked, even as he assured himself that help had arrived.

Minutes later, Hicks and a bespectacled gentleman, wielding a telltale black bag, rushed into the chamber.

"This is Dr. Langdon, of the HMS *Temeraire*." The manservant stood at attention. "And I present Sir Dalton Randolph, of London."

"Sir Dalton, it is good to make your acquaintance, present circumstances excepted." The grey-haired doctor smiled. "And how fares the patient? Hicks related the details surrounding the wound, and I would like to remove the ball, posthaste. But I would prepare your wife and my instruments, before we begin."

"Tell me what you require, and I and my household are at your service, sir." As the physician retrieved and arranged the tools of his trade, Dalton monitored Daphne's condition. "It appears the bleeding has stopped, and my wife sleeps comfortably."

"Bring me an additional basin and pour the entire bottle of alcohol therein. And I need plenty of light, so I would avail myself of your candelabra from the hall." Dr. Langdon doffed his hat, coat, and rolled up his shirtsleeves. "If you remain to assist me, you must submerge your hands in the antiseptic, else you risk transferring infection to Mrs. Randolph, which could kill her."

"Right away, sir." Mrs. Jones half-curtseyed.

"Wake her." Dr. Langdon thrust a bottle into Dalton's

grasp. "Dispense about a quarter of the contents, now. And I need hot water, as what is in this ewer is tepid. Also, we will need two extra persons to hold down Mrs. Randolph, while I probe for the shot, as it will be unpleasant, to say the least."

"You may rely on me." At the footboard, Sir Ross nodded once.

"And I will assist you." Hicks gulped. "As must needs."

"Darling, wake up." With infinite care, Dalton shook her. "Drink this, sweetheart."

"No." Wrinkling her nose, Daphne came alert. "If that is laudanum, I will not take it."

"It is for the pain and to aid her recovery, as she will need uninterrupted rest." As he wiped various instruments, Dr. Langdon frowned. "If she will not consume it willingly, then you must force it down her throat. Believe me, you will be doing her a kindness, Sir Dalton."

Regardless of the situation, and her grievous condition, Dalton could not manhandle his wife. But then he recalled the governor's demise and understood her fears, and he opted for a different tack.

Dropping low, he met her, face to face. "Angel, do you love me?"

"You know I do." She bit her lip. "I would give my life for you."

And she almost had, which was not lost on him. "Then do this, for me."

Her answering whimper tore at his heart. "But papa—"

"You are not your father, and I will be here with you." Caressing her cheek, he kissed her. "Please, my angel."

"All right." Then she sipped from the bottle, which he held for her, and she squinted and choked. "Oh, it tastes dreadful."

"Is that enough?" Dalton held up the container, and Dr. Langdon narrowed his stare.

"Give her another good swallow." The physician adjusted his glasses. "Mark the time as half past midnight, and we shall commence the procedure at the top of the hour." Then he passed a stubby wood dowel to Dalton and said, "Put this between her teeth, when we begin, as she will need it."

As the mantel clock signaled the approach of an ominous deadline, Dalton monitored Daphne's state, as she rambled incoherent nonsense interspersed with the occasional giggle and the mention of his name. When the resonant tone sounded, the doctor dipped his chin, and everyone sprang into action.

With Mrs. Jones holding a single taper, Dr. Langdon cut away the top of Daphne's dress. "It appears a piece of material from the gown and the chemise went in with the ball, so I must fish out everything, else the wound will fester, and she will die." With his finger, the physician probed the injury, and Daphne moaned and then kicked. "Hold her still, as I have located the shot, and it is wedged near the joint and the blade. Hand me the spreaders, Mrs. Jones."

"Aye, sir." Dalton noted the housekeeper's tears, as she fetched the requested utensil.

Blood pooled from the site, and Dalton winced, as the physician worked. But when Daphne screamed and wrenched hard, Hicks and Sir Ross bore down on her legs, while Dalton clutched her wrists behind her back.

"Worry not, Sir Dalton. It is the laudanum talking. She will remember nothing, in the morning." Then Dr. Langdon glanced at Mrs. Jones. "Locking forceps."

When the doctor dug deep into Daphne's flesh, she spat out the dowel and shrieked in unveiled agony, and Dalton suffered with her. When he could stand no more of her wails, he shifted and spoke into her ear.

"Can you hear me, angel? Focus on my voice, as I am with you." When she quieted, he kissed her fleshy lobe and declared, for all to hear, "I love you, Daphne. I love you." Again and again, he repeated the refrain, until she calmed.

"I have the ball, as well as the textiles, Sir Dalton." The physician rinsed the blood from his hands. "Your wife appears to have fainted, blissfully so, given I must remove some damaged tissue, in order to avoid possible necrosis, and then clean and stitch the wound. But she will heal nicely, I predict."

"Dr. Langdon, I am in your debt." Likewise, Dalton owed his angel, an evermore-appropriate moniker in light of the day's events, a sum he could never repay, given she had sacrificed herself in exchange for his life. Yet, at some point during her ordeal, he realized he did not want to be saved if it cost him his wife, as he could not fathom a world without her in it.

THE MANTEL CLOCK chimed the hour, and Daphne stirred and counted the tenor dongs. Resting on her belly, an unusual practice for her, she reached across the bed for her husband, as it was past due for him to wake her for his favorite activity. When she found him clothed and resting atop the counterpane, she frowned and squeezed his fingers.

Dalton sniffed and then jerked awake. "Daphne, darling, you are with me still."

"Of course." She smiled, shifted to roll over, and searing pain had her moaning. "Oh, dear. I feel as if a runaway coach has struck me. Why am I so sore?"

"Mrs. Randolph, I am Dr. Langdon." A polished gentleman, vaguely familiar, bowed. "Do you think you can
manage, if we sit you upright?"

"I believe so." With her husband's unfailing support, she
changed positions and gasped when her dress sagged.
"What happened to my gown?"

Glimpsing the dried blood that marred the material,
Daphne clutched the bodice to her chest and sobbed, as a
cascade of fragmented memories assailed her. The threatening note. Richard's betrayal. Mr. Allen bearing down
with a pistol pointed at Dalton. The echoing shots. The
acrid stench of gunpowder. The intense ache from her
injury. But it was the last reminiscence, a series of words,
simple on their own, but taken together as a whole a
promise of everlasting devotion, which quelled her fears.

I love you, Daphne. I love you.

"*Oh*, I am going to be unwell." As she leaned against
Dalton, the doctor brought her a basin.

"Take deep breaths, Mrs. Randolph. You are safe and on
the mend, but you suffer a severe case of nerves, which is
understandable, so try to relax." With a kind expression, Dr.
Langdon pressed the back of his hand to her forehead and
her cheeks. "No fever, which is an excellent sign." To
Dalton, the doctor said, "Fetch her a nightgown, and I will
clean the stitches, apply a styptic, and dress her wound."

At his suggestion, Daphne gulped. Propped forward,
she bit her tongue, as Dalton disappeared into her closet. A
few minutes later, he emerged, only to repair to his dressing
room. When he returned, holding one of his lawn shirts, he
winked, and she grinned.

"This might serve our purposes better, as you intend to
put her arm in a sling, to allow her shoulder to heal." As he
draped the garment over her head, Dalton cast her a

conspiratorial glance, conveying a wealth of meaning she comprehended too well.

Given her husband's predilections, her nightwear, if she could call it that, consisted of the sheerest materials, which functioned as more an afterthought than functional clothing. Although she felt poorly, she did not want to send the physician into an apoplectic fit.

After Dr. Langdon completed his work, he donned his coat and hat. "I shall check your progress, tomorrow, around noon." He retrieved his black bag and, to Dalton, stated, "If there is any change in her condition, send for me, at once. Otherwise, I expect it to take a full two months for Mrs. Randolph's complete recovery, but I shall monitor her closely, every day, for a sennight."

"May I bathe?" How she longed for a hot soak with her husband.

"Yes." The doctor pointed for emphasis. "But do not submerge the wound or wet the bandages."

A half hour later, despite her pleas, she could not coax her suddenly shy husband into the water, but he washed her as if she were a porcelain doll. And once he had tucked her beneath the covers, he fed her a light repast.

When Mrs. Jones collected the dishes, she shed a few tears. "My dear, it does my heart good to see you looking better. Hicks and I thought we had lost you, and we could not bear it. And Mr. Anderson, the constable, is just arrived from Portsmouth. He wants to interview you, about the events."

"That will be fine, Mrs. Jones." Dalton wrapped a shawl about Daphne's shoulders. "But first I would have a word with you and Hicks."

"Yes, sir." The housekeeper curtseyed.

"Is something wrong?" Daphne studied her brooding

husband. "You have been awfully quiet since Dr. Langdon departed."

"When the constable questions you, give him honest replies, save your brother's involvement with Allen." It had not escaped her notice that he evaded her query. "Do not temper your responses, and all will be fine."

"You wished to see me, sir?" Hicks strolled into the bedchamber, with Mrs. Jones at his side.

"Indeed, as I must apologize to you, both." Dalton stood and approached what Daphne considered the combined backbone of Courtenay Hall. "In my desperation to identify the villain, I suspected your involvement in the nefarious caper. Owing to our brief acquaintance, I hid the truth of Sir Ross's persona, and I am not proud of my behavior. In my wife's defense, she never once doubted your constancy, and she objected to my accusations. To my everlasting shame, she was correct in her assertions, and you are true and loyal friends. I humbly beg your forgiveness."

Hicks and Mrs. Jones stared at each other and blinked.

Then Mrs. Jones clutched a fist to her chest. "Sir Dalton, we have cared for the Harcourts as we would our own children, if we had any. It is to your credit that you confess your notions, however misplaced, and I bear no grudge."

"Neither do I." The butler, so long Daphne's protector, shook Dalton's proffered hand. "As I have served this family since before Mrs. Randolph was born, I must say it is nice to see happiness fill this grand estate, after so much misery, so we will consider the matter closed and dwell no more on it. Now, should I send in Mr. Anderson?"

The constable had once represented Daphne's worst nightmare, given her raids on passing ships, but those days were no more, and he had no interest in the singular practices that had brought her to her husband. Now, he posited an end to a dark chapter in her life, one she was more than ready to leave behind.

"Remember what I told you, angel." Dalton met her gaze and sat beside her, after she patted the empty space on the bed."

"Stay with me." She scooted close and rested her head to his shoulder. "I am afraid."

Just then, the constable traversed the sitting room and paused in the entry to the interior chamber. "May I come in?"

"Of course, Mr. Anderson." Dalton waved a greeting. "I have agreed to the interview, but under duress, as my wife is injured, and I would not risk her health for the sake of your report."

"I understand, Sir Dalton, and I have only a few questions, as Richard has been very forthcoming." The constable flipped through the pages of a small notebook and pulled a pencil from his coat pocket. "When did you first receive the threatening letters?"

"In London, just prior to my wedding." She cleared her throat.

"And why did you not notify the proper authorities?" Mr. Anderson narrowed his stare. "Did you inform anyone of the situation?"

"I told no one." Nervous, she swallowed hard. "Given I thought it was someone's idea of a horrible prank, I did not wish to alarm my husband."

"And what secret did Mr. Allen intend to reveal?" The constable inclined his head. "What manner of disclosure was at the center of the blackmail?"

As she had promised Dalton, she dissembled in that respect. But Mr. Allen, ironically enough, had provided her answer, that night in the study, and it coincided beautifully with the interrogation. "Mr. Allen threatened to divulge unflattering information about Governor Harcourt. It seems my father borrowed a great deal of money from Mr. Allen, and the blackguard threatened to disparage my family's reputation unless I paid him to remain silent."

Little by little, she recounted the details of the past month, providing as many particulars as possible, and the constable took copious notes. But the truth came easy, as she had lived the incidents, and she concealed nothing else excepting Richard's part in the drama. It was, perhaps, for that reason Mr. Anderson never debated her responses. So when he put away his pencil, Daphne enjoyed a modicum of relief.

"Indeed, this has been a most distressing case, Mrs. Randolph." The constable shifted his weight. "There will be an inquest, to record the facts, but I anticipate no difficulties, as the evidence and witness accounts match your statement. And Allen has a lengthy record of nefarious deeds. You will be notified of the date, but you are not required to attend, especially in light of your injury. I appreciate your cooperation and wish you a speedy recovery."

"Thank you, for conducting a complete and thorough investigation, Mr. Anderson." Dalton escorted the constable to the sitting room door. "If you need anything else, we are at your service."

When her husband returned, he eased beside her, lifted her to his lap, and kissed her. "My angel, it is, at long last, over."

~

A FORTNIGHT HAD PASSED, when Daphne fidgeted in her bedchamber, as Hicks unwrapped her most recent purchase. The previous week, a magistrate in Portsmouth conducted an inquest to review the facts surrounding Mr. Allen's crimes and death. Dalton had attended the inquiry but had not been called upon to testify, and the entire matter had been closed.

Yet an invisible but very real barrier loomed between Daphne and her erstwhile fervent husband, and she intended to breach his imaginary walls, after consulting with Rebecca. If not for the former spy, Daphne would have lamented the apparent loss of her once passionate knight. But Rebecca explained that Dirk had suffered the same unwelcome symptom, owing to the depth of his devotion, as she had recovered from Varringdale's torture. In short, her husband refused to make love to her. And to Daphne's frustration, Dalton suffered the same malady.

"Should I leave it here, Mrs. Randolph?" Hicks stood upright and bundled the brown paper into a ball. "Or would you prefer I move it against the wall, as someone might trip and fall."

"Oh, no." The orientation suited her purpose, so she shook her head. "Is dinner ready?"

"It should be delivered, any second." The butler bowed. "Shall I summon Mrs. Jones?"

"No, you need not." The housekeeper snorted. "As I am right here, you old hawk."

"Then I will leave you ladies." With a smile, Hicks arched a brow. "Am I still to send Sir Dalton precisely at half past six?"

"Yes." Enclosed in her lair, Daphne kicked off her slippers and turned, so Mrs. Jones could untie the laces of her dress. Since Dr. Langdon had removed the stitches and the sling, she had only a bandage to draw attention to her wound. And while the injury still hurt, an ache of a different sort had become unbearable, and she decided to act. "Hurry, Mrs. Jones. Dalton will be here in ten minutes, and I want to take his breath away."

"I doubt that is seriously in question, Mrs. Randolph." Mrs. Jones snickered. "I'd wager my bonnet, as I think it remains safe. Now which nightgown would you wear, though I wonder why you bother?"

"The sapphire, as I wore it on my wedding night." And she thought it past due to redeem it. "And I want to take down my hair."

"Oh, and I reassigned Daisy." The housekeeper removed the pins and brushed Daphne's locks. "When I explained that you were comfortable with me, as I have acted as your lady's maid since you were a girl, Daisy understood. Daresay she is happy to have an occupation."

"Thank you." Daphne stood and scrutinized her reflection in the long mirror. The diaphanous material hid nothing, and that was exactly what she wanted. "You are family to me, and I could not part with you."

"And I was loathe to relinquish my responsibilities." Mrs. Jones picked up the slippers and the other garments and conveyed them to the closet. Then she checked the sitting room, discovered the trolley loaded with covered dishes, and rolled the cart into the bedchamber. "Now then, everything is in place, and I wish you a lovely evening with Sir Dalton."

Alone in the quiet solitude of her haven, Daphne twiddled her thumbs. As she surveyed her surroundings, she evaluated the efficacy of various poses and positions, which might show her figure at its best. In a last second change of plan, she unbuttoned the robe and dropped it to the floor and stood before the candelabra on the small table for two, which Hicks had situated, and hoped the candles provided fortuitous illumination—just as Dalton entered their quarters.

"Daphne, is everything all right?" When his gaze settled on her, unmistakable stillness invested his large frame, and telltale sparks flickered in his amber eyes.

"Hello." She rotated, so he could look his fill. "Are you hungry?"

To her surprise, Dalton stood stock-still and mute, and she sensed the indecision waging war in his brain, given his rigid posture. So she strolled to her reticent spouse, kissed his cheek, and unhooked his breeches. When she slipped her hand inside, she found him raring to go, just as she had anticipated.

"Ah, you are hungry." In a replay of an earlier scene, she worked his length, and on the third tug, as usual, her chivalrous knight gritted his teeth, emitted a feral groan, and sprayed his seed in an impressive cannonade. In that moment, the irrational worry she had denied ever existed seemed to melt, and she sighed, as his response affirmed he still desired her. "Oh, thank heavens. I had thought, perhaps, you no longer wanted me."

"What?" Dalton flinched and grabbed her wrist. "You think me an indifferent husband?"

"We share a bed." She shrugged. "But you refuse to make love to me, and I am not happy about it."

He opened his mouth and then closed it. "I am angry with you."

"I beg your pardon?" Daphne blinked, as she never would have fathomed the cause of his detachment. "What have I done to displease you?"

"You have to ask?" He snorted. "You put yourself between me and a lunatic bent on evil and took a lead shot for me. I want to spank you for being so careless with your person, when I hold you so dear."

"All right." With ruthless determination, she marched to the four-poster, lifted her nightgown to bare her bottom, and bent over the side of the mattress. "Do your worst."

Studying the delicate scrollwork sewn into the counterpane, she swallowed hard, when he settled his palm to her flesh. Bracing for impact, she bit her lip, until he massaged her derriere.

"You are incredibly beautiful, my angel." The sadness in his voice spoke volumes, and her heart yearned for him. "I love you so much it terrifies me, and I know not how to cope."

"Oh, Dalton." She gasped, when he lifted her in his arms, carried her to the overstuffed chair by the windows, sat, and nestled her in his lap. Framing his face, she kissed him. "I love you, too. And I could not conceive of my life without you, especially here on Portsea, as this is where we met, and everything about my childhood home reminds me of you. That is why I could not let Mr. Allen hurt you. Without you, I am lost."

For a while, they simply touched each other, learning their respective peaks and curves anew, and saying with their hands what could not be conveyed in words. When Daphne lifted her chin, Dalton met her halfway, covering her lips with his, and they ignited.

Desire blossomed, slow at first, but it gathered strength, as a zephyr wind, which carried them into the conflagration. Together, they shed the stress of the past months, finding comfort in mutual pleasure, until they parted. Dalton nipped her nose and chuckled, and she giggled, in response.

Resting his forehead to hers, he said, "If you ever do anything like that again, I will—"

"Nothing like that will ever happen, again, as I will not allow it." She scored her fingernails to the nape of his neck. "Now may we enjoy our evening?"

"It would be my honor." Then he averted his gaze and frowned. "What is a two-seater bench doing in the middle of the room?"

"Oh—that?" Daphne untied his cravat and tossed aside the yard-length of linen. "I bought it on Rebecca's recommendation."

"What for?" Furrowing his brow, Dalton huffed a breath. "As we have no need of it."

"I beg to disagree." Daphne whispered in his ear the primary function of the item in question, explaining Dirk's preferred use.

Choking violently, his eyes widened. "You can't be serious."

"But I am, and I demand you indulge me." She unbuttoned his waistcoat and shirt and splayed her palms to his impressive chest. "Else I may conk you on the noggin with my hairbrush and have my wicked way with you, sir."

For a few minutes, he simply stared at her. Then his demeanor changed, and her naughty knight emerged from his cocoon. "All right, my angel." With Daphne in his grasp, Dalton stood. "Hold tight, as you are about to take a ride on the wild side."

EPILOGUE

*D*ecember roared onto Portsea Island with a blizzard, and Dalton had opted to forgo a return to the city, as he fretted for Daphne's health, which had become downright tenuous. To his frustration, his wife showed no inclination to slow her busy schedule, which included her customary charitable visits and mediation of community issues for the newly appointed governor of Portsea Island, her cousin Harold.

To further compound the situation, she had invited the entire family to spend Christmas at Courtenay Hall, and the Brethren of the Coast were set to arrive in a sennight. As he sat at his desk in the study, he audited her ledger entries and was nonplussed to discover no errors, given he had made two trips to the Continent to transport injured soldiers home and had not checked her numbers in three months.

"Good afternoon, darling." He glanced up to discover her lingering in the doorway, holding a blanket, and he smiled.

"Hello, my angel." Dropping the pen to the blotter, he

pushed back the chair and then stood. "Ready for your nap?"

"Indeed." As was her way, she marched to their usual spot—the overstuffed chair near the windows, which afforded a spectacular view of the harbor.

After untying his cravat, he flung it to the daybed, unfastened the top button of his shirt, and sat. True to form, Daphne stepped about his legs, eased to his lap, unfolded the blanket, and draped it with care. As she snuggled close, he tucked the cover beneath her chin and kissed her forehead.

"How do you feel?" Resting his cheek to her crown of curls, he sighed. "What did Dr. Langdon say? Could he prescribe a tonic?"

"No." Skimming her hand beneath the fine lawn, she pressed her palm to his chest. "But not to worry, as it will work itself out. And I had a letter from Blake."

"Is he returned from the voyage?" In light of Dalton's reluctance to leave Daphne, given her fragile constitution, Blake had volunteered to assume the latest mission. "I owe him a debt."

"So it would seem." She drew imaginary circles on his flesh. "He accepted our invitation and is bringing guests."

"Oh?" Sifting through the skirts of her blue gown, he finally located her bare calf and stroked her supple skin. "Who?"

"Two young ladies, one of whom has caught his special attention." Daphne snickered. "At least, that is what Caroline's missive said."

"Bloody hell." Dalton laughed. "Never thought I would see the day the great Blake Elliott fell victim to the fairer sex. Well I can't wait to meet her, as she must be a paragon. And it will be no trouble, as we have plenty of rooms."

"Speaking of rooms, I would send a note to Mr. Benson, as I require a change to our home." She parted his shirt and trailed feathery kisses between his nipples.

"I beg your pardon?" He dropped his head on the back of the chair and stared at the ceiling. "What more would you have, as we just renovated the entire house?"

"But we have a very important person coming to stay with us, and I would have everything perfect." She teased him with a playful nibble.

"Who is this very important person, and why would they find none of our accommodations satisfactory?" He inched his hand higher and squeezed her supple thigh. "And when do they arrive?"

"I know not, as we have yet to be introduced," she replied in a flirty lilt. "And they will not arrive for another seven months, according to Dr. Langdon."

Whatever he had intended to say, words failed him, as the full import of her statement dawned, and Dalton peered at his wife. "My angel, you are with child?"

"Happy Christmas, a tad early." With an arm wound about his neck, she hugged him. "Are you as thrilled as I am?"

"Oh, sweetheart." So many emotions surged in his veins he could identify none of them. "I am beside myself with joy. I gather that is the source of your fatigue, of late?"

"Yes." Once again, she reclined and closed her eyes. "And I should take my nap, as Dr. Langdon prescribes it."

He tucked the blanket about her feet. "We should arrange a suitable ceremony, when the family gathers, so we might—"

"Please, let us keep it to ourselves, as our secret, just for a little while." Daphne nuzzled him and giggled. "For fun, we could toss your coin and guess the sex."

"But I no longer have it in my possession." He recalled the starry November night, when he docked in Portsea after his last mission. Since his marriage, whenever his bride awaited his return at Courtenay Hall, he dropped anchor at the location nearest her. Compelled by a sensation he could neither comprehend nor explain, he had flung the gold brothel token into Portsmouth Harbor, before riding hell-bent for leather into her arms.

"That is too bad." Elegant in repose, she yawned, and soon her slow and steady breath signaled she slept.

As always, Dalton guarded her slumber, but that afternoon he studied his wife with renewed fascination. Guinea-gold curls framed her face, blessed with classical features and accented with an internal glow that now made perfect sense, and he gave her a gentle squeeze. A new life grew inside her, the fruit of their love derived from their shared passion, and it was a humbling prospect.

Yet, had she chosen a different ship to board, all those months ago, his existence would have been something else, entirely. The center of his universe, she was his saving grace, his world, and he owed her everything. With care, so as not to disturb her slumber, he bent his head and kissed her, and she gifted him a feminine smile. He would gladly spend the rest of his days endeavoring to keep that smile on her lips. And then it dawned on him—Daphne was his talisman. If he was her one true knight, she was the source of his good fortune. Indeed, he was the lucky one.

ABOUT BARBARA DEVLIN

A proud Latina, USA Today bestselling author Barbara Devlin was born a storyteller, but it was a weeklong vacation to Bethany Beach, Delaware that forever changed her life. The little house her parents rented had a collection of books by Kathleen Woodiwiss, which exposed Barbara to the world of romance, and *Shanna* remains a personal favorite.

Barbara writes heartfelt historical romances that feature not so perfect heroes who may know how to seduce a woman but know nothing of marriage. And she prefers feisty but smart heroines who sometimes save the hero before they find their happily ever after.

Barbara is a disabled-in-the-line-of-duty retired police officer, and she earned an MA in English and continued a course of study for a Doctorate in Literature and Rhetoric. She happily considered herself an exceedingly eccentric English professor, until success in Indie publishing lured her into writing, full-time, featuring her fictional knighthood, the Brethren of the Coast.

Connect with Barbara Devlin at BarbaraDevlin.com, where you can sign up for her newsletter, The Knightly News.

ALSO BY BARBARA DEVLIN

BRETHREN OF THE COAST

Loving Lieutenant Douglas

Enter the Brethren

My Lady, the Spy

The Most Unlikely Lady

One-Knight Stand

Captain of Her Heart

The Lucky One

Love with an Improper Stranger

To Catch a Fallen Spy

Hold Me, Thrill Me, Kiss Me

The Duke Wears Nada

A Very Brethren Christmas

Owner of a Lonely Heart

BRETHREN ORIGINS

Arucard

Demetrius

Aristide

Morgan

Geoffrey

PIRATES OF THE COAST

The Black Morass

The Iron Corsair

The Buccaneer

The Stablemaster's Daughter

The Marooner

Once Upon a Christmas Knight

The Reaper

WORLD OF DE WOLFE PACK

Lone Wolfe

The Big Bad De Wolfe

Tall, Dark & De Wolfe

MAGICK TRILOGY

Magick, Straight Up

A Taste of Magick

Magick in the Air

PIRATES OF BRITANNIA

The Blood Reaver

THE MAD MATCHMAKING MEN OF WATERLOO

The Accidental Duke

The Accidental Groom